Kornukopia

KORNUKOPIA

by David Annandale

Kornukopia
copyright © David Annandale 2004

Published by Ravenstone
an imprint of Turnstone Press
607-100 Arthur Street
Artspace Building
Winnipeg, MB
R3B 1H3 Canada
www.TurnstonePress.com

All rights reserved. No part of this book may be reproduced or transmitted in any form or by any means—graphic, electronic or mechanical—without the prior written permission of the publisher. Any request to photocopy any part of this book shall be directed in writing to Access Copyright (formerly Cancopy the Canadian Copyright Licensing Agency), Toronto.

Turnstone Press gratefully acknowledges the assistance of the Canada Council for the Arts, the Manitoba Arts Council and the Government of Canada through the Book Publishing Industry Development Program and the Government of Manitoba through the Department of Culture, Heritage and Tourism, Arts Branch, for our publishing activities.

Cover design: Doowah Design
Interior design: Sharon Caseburg
Printed and bound in Canada by
AGMV Marquis for Turnstone Press.

Library and Archives Canada Cataloguing in Publication

Annandale, David, 1967-
 Kornukopia / by David Annandale.

ISBN 0-88801-303-5

I. Title.

PS8551.N527K67 2004   C813'.6   C2004-905986-6

Once again, this is for my family.

KORNUKOPIA

Prologue

The war machine stood beside her lover's bed and watched him sleep. Outside the hospital, the universe unfolded. Not as it should, or even as it could, but as it would. The war machine heard the universe's call, but she resisted. For a few moments, anyway. A few instants, amber-frozen so she could look back on them later, if she had to. Hold them like rough jewels. She could allow herself that. She looked at her lover, memorizing his smooth features. He didn't stand out in the crowd, and the war machine knew some would dismiss his brown-hair-brown-eyed generic symmetry as boring. She looked at his face, and felt the hurt-throb of want. Jen Blaylock reached out to touch Mike Flanagan's cheek. Flanagan twitched away and woke up. The war machine pulled her hand back.

"Jen?" Flanagan rubbed his eyes clear. He stared at her. "You're dressed?"

Blaylock nodded. "Checking out today."

Flanagan stared harder. "Are you well enough?"

"Well enough." She touched the puckered scab on her left cheek where wood had spiked through. Her tongue tasted roughness on the inside. No big deal. Hair starting to grow back, burns healing, broken rib looked after, yeah, she was well enough to leave. She would finish recuperating elsewhere, on her own, away from questions. Away from Joe Chapel.

It wasn't like she hadn't been expecting questions. She and Flanagan were interesting people, after all. The only survivors of a forest fire and guerilla war that took out the leaders of the G8? Damned interesting. Lock-them-up-forever interesting if she wasn't careful. So she was careful. During the airlift from Ember Lake to the Health Sciences Centre in Winnipeg, she had worked on her story. Flanagan didn't need to worry. The truth, with only a couple of omissions, would work for him. Mid-level Integrated Security executive forced to help big boss Arthur Pembroke blackmail the heads of state? Sorry-ass employee whose own sister and nephew had been whacked by InSec? Collateral victim dragged along by Pembroke to the big showdown? Oh yeah, the truth would work for him. His tale would be interesting enough to satisfy while still exonerating him. Blaylock, though, had brought the militia into the woods, had started the war that had started the fire, had swum through the gore of her enemies. She needed something other than the truth.

Old lies and absolute violence will set you free. The solution, simple in its irony, hit her well before they reached Winnipeg. Her old cover identity, Jen Baylor, was still intact. Other than Flanagan, no one who had known both Baylor the Freelance Business Writer and Blaylock the Angel of Death was still alive. Which meant Baylor could continue to live and prosper. Baylor wrote mainly annual reports and other corporate copy, but she had also done some news stories for the *Report on Business* and the

Wall Street Journal. Not a lot, just enough to keep credentials current. So Baylor had good reasons to be at the Ember Lake lodge. InSec had been major business-scandal fodder recently. Baylor, hungry for a story and smelling one, had followed Pembroke too closely, been caught. Wrong place, wrong time. Simple. Easy to keep straight, even while being questioned in the burn unit. Easy to make good. Easy to pass.

The story passed. The questions came, and she gave good answers. The Inquisitors from every nationality came and left, came and left, and they all looked satisfied. Only one Frowny Face in the bunch, but that was enough to tell her to duck out of the line of fire.

Joe Chapel. Smooth mid-forties, *GQ*-perfect hair a gray so steel and authoritative Blaylock was sure he dyed it. Jaw by Testosterone, eyes by Glock. His suit had beyond-military creases, and hung on a body that suggested a hardness won by fieldwork, not office politics. He was polite when he came to speak to her. Solicitous, even. But when he introduced himself, and gave his name but not his professional affiliation, Blaylock sniffed acronym. Who, though? American, definitely. CIA? Maybe. Be careful? Absolutely.

She answered his questions, took him through the same story she'd given everyone else. Joe Chapel, polite: listening, requesting clarifications. No hardball cross-examination. Blaylock didn't like that. Direct aggression would have told her what the game was. Joe Chapel, solicitous: he came when she was still in her hospital bed, still on the IV, and he brought her a glass of water. How nice. He placed it on the bedside tray for her. How nice. Then, in the middle of asking her a question, his right hand accidentally (how nice) knocked the glass over. Already on alert, Blaylock's instincts clamped down on her reflexes. She did not snap a hand out and catch the glass. She let the water spill, let the sheets get wet. She saw Chapel watching her, and she knew she had done the right thing.

The rub: had he noticed her watching him watch her? How well did they now know each other? It wasn't a relationship Blaylock wanted to encourage. When Chapel left, he looked satisfied. Sort of. But there was a question mark in those eyes (by Glock). There was no point sticking around and letting that question develop. Out of sight, out of mind, yes? Yes. Time to go.

Besides, there was that call of the universe to answer.

Flanagan, face still almost as pale as his leg cast, asked, "Where will you go?"

"Thought I'd lie low for a while."

Flanagan's lips twitched in amused disbelief. "You're so euphemistic."

Blaylock shrugged, deadpan. But she wanted to smile. He was joking with her, and that was a good sign, wasn't it?

"And what do I do?" Flanagan asked, fear and despair and uncertainty in his tone. Little boy lost.

"What do you want to do?"

"I don't know."

"You have options. Are you still in the war?"

Flanagan looked at her. Said nothing.

Blaylock swallowed, kept talking. "You can go home. You can find new work. You can go back to InSec—" Flanagan winced, opened his mouth to interrupt, but Blaylock continued, "—and do nothing. Or you can fight on."

"How?"

"By keeping your eyes open. By being a well-placed ally."

He seemed to think about this. "A mole."

"More like a termite."

"Right." Flanagan turned his head to face the ceiling. "Will I see you again?" he asked.

No eye contact when he asked that question. Why couldn't he meet her gaze? Would she see the same shock and fear she had seen on his face by the charred ruins of the lodge? She forced the issue. "Do you want to?"

The silence stretched long. "Yes," finally. Then he turned his head back to her, and his look and a single extra syllable were the qualifier. "I . . ."

I think so, Blaylock finished for him. *I don't know.* One of those classic options. Pick your poison. "You need some space," she said, and surprised herself by not sounding bitter.

"No. That's not what I—"

"It's okay, Mike. You do. I'll see you when I see you." And to show that she really wasn't bitter, that this really was for the best, she leaned down and kissed him gently on the lips. "Remember my number in New York," she whispered.

The universe unfolded, but not as it should.

Flanagan felt Blaylock's lips against his, watched her face as she straightened up. That face and its eagle-sharp lines, but a cheek that was now raven-kissed. The faint diagonal rage of her old scar that ran from hairline to eye to cheekbone. The black hair and the darker eyes, the eyes that frightened him most of all. She looked back at him for a moment, then left. There had been no pain visible on her face. Of course there hadn't.

The second she vanished, Flanagan felt an ache that shamed his fear. What are you doing? he thought. Call her back. Do it. Open your mouth and say it. One word: "Jen." He didn't. Maybe she was right. Maybe he needed the space to realize the mistake he was making. Maybe. But the image of the woman who had saved his life still struggled with the sight of the demon who had sent the crews of eight superfreighters to the bottom of the Atlantic. I love you. You scare the shit out of me. Moral clarity. Gotta love it. So Flanagan stared at the empty doorway, stared at Blaylock's absence, and felt all the guilt of a traitor.

The universe unfolded, but not even as it could.

The leaders of the G8 dead. Some shot, others burned. Add these to the list of the dead: the CEO of InSec, an international collection of known mercenaries, the US President's Secret Service bodyguards, and a group of armed unknowns. Dental records eventually coughed up their identities, and oh look, they're all from Montana. The RCMP and the FBI did not even murmur the word "militia." They didn't need to. The media, hungry for its next September 11, opened wide its maw and *screamed*.

The universe unfolded, but as it *would*.

Leon West, head of InSec's Russian division, stared at the front page of the *New York Times*. The paper was weeks old, and howling all the colors of global chaos. West wasn't reading about fire and blood in northern

Ontario, however. He was looking at a smaller, below-the-fold piece on a spectacular multi-ship collision in the North Atlantic. "I don't know what happened," he said. His hands felt fat and numb. The ropes around his wrists had cut off his circulation.

Stepan Sherbina took the paper away from West's face. "This wasn't, I take it, part of Arthur Pembroke's master plan." His English was purged of all trace of Russian accent. He sounded as if his blood were the bluest New England had to offer. When West shook his head, Sherbina went on. "Neither was being killed, I don't suppose." He smiled.

West didn't smile back. He couldn't. If he tried, he was sure his fear would shoot puke through his teeth. He was tied to a steel folding chair. He was sitting in a windowless room. The walls and floor, painted a deep institutional gray, sheened waxy in the flicker of the fluorescents. The only other furniture was a desk at the far end of the room. Another man sat at it, taking notes on a laptop. Sherbina had introduced him as Yevgeny Nevzlin. He was huge, a mass of muscle and fat bulging like squeezed dough out of a business suit. His face was pockmarked nasty. And he didn't scare West half as much as Sherbina. The Mob king was tall, ice-model handsome. Über-Aryan *übermensch* with a Russian birth certificate. His eyes were glittering blue death. Whenever they turned his way, West felt his bowels loosen.

"Do let's be clear," Sherbina said. "I'm not upset. A few million AK-47s and some bonus surface-to-air missiles are lost, but I was paid. If that's what Pembroke wanted for his merchandise . . ." Sherbina shrugged with his hands. "But you tell me no. So what was Pembroke doing?"

"He was going to use them for leverage," West answered. Tell him everything, he thought. Sing until he begs you to stop. They haven't tortured you yet. Keep them happy. "He wanted some provisions of his own in the Multilateral Agreement on Investment, and he wanted the MAI passed."

Sherbina digested this in silence. Shutters went down over the blue eyes. West sensed calculations. Finally, "That is the germ of a very good idea." He walked over to West and placed his thumb and forefinger over West's nose, over the bump that marked where Karl Noonan, Pembroke's right-hand thug, had smashed cartilage. "Do you think we should work together?" He squeezed. West nodded, whimpered. Sherbina went on. "I would like to think so. But here's what troubles me. You surrendered your former employer's information without so much as a struggle. I realize he isn't likely to cause trouble for you, being dead and all, but it's the principle of the thing. So, you're working for me now, correct?"

"Yuh ... yuh ... yuh ..." West stammered through the staples-to-sinus pain.

"Good. Think of this as incentive to be more circumspect in the future." Sherbina smiled. He squeezed. West made high gurgling noises. His nose snapped.

1

Blaylock moved down the Sparks Street mall. She was in Ottawa, as Baylor, to cover the ruckus. She was dressed like a war-zone reporter. At the back of her mind, as she pushed through the crowd, she was hoping that she could become Blaylock, and finally answer the universe's call.

She'd been underground for a year. The wait had been frustrating, but not useless. Training was perpetual. Skills were honed, new ones acquired. She added languages to her already fluent French. This was all just marking time. She'd never thought her war would be suspended for so long. But the battles had to be well chosen, and she needed the means. Her war chest had been depleted in the struggle against Pembroke: no more money, the arsenal expended and lost at the Ember Lake lodge. Only a few caches left, scattered about Canada and the States. When she'd stepped out of the Health Sciences Centre, she'd been conscious of having come full circle. She was back home in Winnipeg, and she had to retrench, regroup, and rearm all over again. So Jen Baylor had gone to work, writing up a storm, building a reputation, financing what she could of Jen Blaylock's weapons and intelligence. The world had rocked and shrieked, injustice had stalked, the innocent had been slaughtered, but there were no openings, no target-of-opportunity wheels whose spokes she could shatter. At least, not without a bit more strength. She was wolf, not martyr. No point being stupid.

Flanagan hadn't been in touch with her. Funny how a year could evaporate before she had turned around, and still be an emotional marathon. She'd checked her New York number once a month, and there had never been anything. Rationally, she was glad. The media had glommed onto Flanagan as the iconic Ember Lake survivor. Blaylock had made sure to bore and annoy by spouting economic theory at every interview, and it hadn't been long before Jen Baylor faded from view, her visibility increased only in the number of articles she had published. But it was only in the last few months that Flanagan's name no longer showed up, even as a passing mention, with knee-jerk regularity in the news. So he was being smart by keeping quiet. Good. But still. *I miss him.*

Whatever. Shut up. Focus.

She was still not used to the novelty of looking for war. Pembroke had been personal. Taking him down had been about blood, about her family blown up because they were an inconvenience. Now, though, battle was not personal. It was vocation. Now she was looking for the right monsters with which to wrestle. Now, in September, under the soggy perpetuity of Ottawa rain, she was still looking, still homing in on the likely trouble spots, instincts a-twitch for the right situation, the right angle, the right leverage. Ottawa today was another possible source of inspiration. The G20 finance ministers had gathered, there were protests in the street, and there was magic in the air.

There was nothing unique about the finance ministers' meeting itself. The event had been on the books for over a year, and the wonks had plenty to talk about. Since the Ember Lake fire, the world economy had been a toilet-paper roll caught in the whirlpool flush of the markets. The meeting should have been routine. But there were two wild cards, and they had brought Blaylock running. One was the rumor. Down Internet message boards uncounted had come the whisper: WTO, WTO, WTO. The World Trade Organization and its Brahmins wanted an end-game. Finish the negotiations, carve the body's rules in stone. The momentum, lost in Seattle, regained in Doha, knocked down again in the flame-out of the revived MAI, was back. The ministers would make sure of that.

The second wild card was the street theater. The anti-globalization movement's fortunes had been as bipolar as the WTO's. Fragile organization had been dealt a body blow by September 11, and anything but war protests had fizzled for years. Then the MAI and its promise of unfettered corporate rule attempted a comeback, sponsored by InSec, and the movement had found second wind. The G8 slaughter, unlike the New York attacks, had fanned the flames. The street was back in action, angrier than ever.

And just as naive, Blaylock thought, as she walked through a megaton's worth of misdirected energy. Sparks Street usually had all the life of an after-hours office building, but this afternoon, drizzle or not, it was packed and charged, wicked with rainbow fire. Opponents of every evil from genetically modified foods to reduced seniors' pensions had gathered together. Blaylock saw a group of students assembling giant crêpe-paper fish puppets. The salmon would be voiceless no longer. Blaylock smirked, but even in her sarcasm, her step began to pick up the world-music beat. The crowd was boisterous, high on purpose and hope. *If you only knew,* Blaylock wanted to tell them. *If you only knew how zero a difference you're making.* She glanced at the storefronts, and corrected herself. Here a difference was being made, all right. Most of the windows were covered with metal grating or plywood. Few of the stores were open. Nervous shopkeepers haunted the doorways, ready to bolt. *The natives are terrified,* Blaylock thought. *Long live the revolution.* She saw one merchant possessed by a demon of optimism. His store sold Canadian souvenir kitsch and cheapjack soapstone sculpture. He was wide open. He even had a sign: PROTEST SPECIAL! 25% OFF EVERYTHING! Blaylock laughed.

The mall ended at Confederation Square. Blaylock stood with her back to the statue of a bear. The animal was rearing up, frozen in black metal, its claws spearing a fish. Ahead was the war memorial. Beyond that, the protest march at high-do. Rideau, MacKenzie, Sussex, and Colonel By had all been closed to traffic. Steel gates and crowd-control vehicles blocked all access to the Conference Centre. The protesters bottlenecked in their thousands in the square. Ripples moved through the crowd, currents of energy looking for release. Scraps of chants floated Blaylock's way on the currents.

"Hey hey, ho ho, the corporate plan has got to go, hey hey, ho ho."

Blaylock sighed, pulled out her notebook, and began to jot down some observations. She watched the crowd, watched the currents, waiting for the signal for everything to go to smash. And there it came: a big current, a massive surge forward against the barricades. The surf voice of thousands of people became a breaker's roar. Over their heads came the smoke arcs of the tear gas. Clouds burst up as the canisters landed. The roar grew louder, but now it was the white noise of chaos, and the currents turned frantic. Then came the backwash. Blaylock stepped closer to the bear and let the flash flood stream by on either side of her. Old news, she thought. Reruns. She could call each step of the protest dance, nail each beat down to the second. So why am I here? she asked herself. Because maybe one of these times I'll see the right variation. And because I have to be somewhere. She put the notebook away. The next phase of the game was due to begin.

She spotted the first balaclava about fifty yards off. The second was five yards behind him and to the left. Blaylock scanned the crowd, spotted more and more of the masked faces closing in. They were running with the crowd, but not in fear. They were running, not from the tear gas, but *for* Sparks Street. The Black Bloc was ready to party. A few had spray paint. More had crowbars. They ran by Blaylock and set to work. Shutters were slamming down on the fronts of the stores that had been open, but not fast enough. New music now, the high exhilaration of breaking glass. Plywood came down and was used to smash more windows. If the barriers were too strong, the paint came out. Blaylock lost the amusement in her contempt.

The souvenir shop's front imploded. Blaylock saw two balaclavas storm inside. Someone screamed, and it was the sound of the universe calling, for real and for true. Blaylock answered. She stepped out from the bear and into the flow of the crowd, let the current carry her to the store. She jumped through the shattered window and stepped over the fallen display shelving. She checked for security cameras, saw that they'd already been smashed. The shopkeeper was on the ground. He had a hand over his mouth. Blood dripped through his fingers, soaked his aging hippie beard. The two masked men stood over him. One, a couple of steps back from the merchant, had his arms crossed and his legs apart just so. Calling the shots, the full-on alpha. He said, "Don't think he's learned his lesson yet, Ralphie."

Ralphie kicked the man in the face. "Sellout."

Blaylock booted a soapstone walrus. It skittered over the floor and clunked against Ralphie's boot. He and Alpha turned around. Blaylock said, "Could you be any more pathetic? Just asking."

"Better leave now," Alpha told her.

"What, and miss you smash the oppressors?"

The two masks looked at each other. She wasn't computing. Alpha tried again. "Only one warning, sister."

Ralphie hefted a crowbar.

Blaylock snorted. Ralphie lunged. He swung the crowbar. Blaylock leaned back. The crowbar swished past, and she grabbed Ralphie's wrist. She twisted and pulled down. Ralphie grunted, stumbling. Blaylock slammed her shoulder against his elbow, and Ralphie was on the ground. She stomped a boot on his shoulder, popping his arm out of its socket. Ralphie screamed and writhed. Alpha came at Blaylock and threw a punch. Blaylock caught his wrist, too, pulled his arm to full extension, and brought the palm of her left hand up against his elbow. Bone snapped. Alpha sank to his knees, clutching his arm.

Blaylock yanked the balaclavas off. The cream of the Black Bloc looked less impressive in the light. Ralphie was trying to grow a biker mustache, but the facial hair was too spotty. Alpha was retro-punk with his spiked purple hair. "Love the look," Blaylock told him. "Very unique. Never been done." Alpha whined and spat. Blaylock pulled the crowbar out from under Ralphie and handed it to the shopkeeper. "You want to keep them here for the police?" she asked.

"Should I?"

Blaylock shrugged. "Your choice. If you do, take the credit." She dropped one of the balaclavas to the floor and pocketed the other. She headed for the doorway to the shop, then paused to watch the rest of the dance.

The bulk of the crowd had moved up Sparks, and was still running. Some protesters sat down in the street, linked arms, and waited for the hurt to arrive. The police, a solid black wall of crowd control, closed in. The air was sharp with the tang of tear gas, but no more was being fired now that the rout was happening. Bang bang bang of clubs against shields, tromp of boots, a formation Caesar would have blessed, and here was the armored darkness of the forces of order. The sitting protestors were hit by pepper spray. Blaylock saw an officer stop over one woman, spray her, then use his gloves to grind the pepper into her eyes. She screamed. Blaylock held her impulse in check, recognizing the futility in the urge to rescue. The clubs went wild. Anyone on the street, protester or bystander, who didn't move fast enough went down in bruises, blood, and broken teeth. Blaylock glanced over her shoulder at the shopkeeper. The man was surrounded by terrors, afraid of the Black Bloc, afraid of the police, afraid of her. She gave him an encouraging smile. He didn't respond.

The police moved on. Blaylock counted to thirty, then left the shop. She walked up the mall, following the sounds of the disintegrating protest. Wreckage all around. The puppets were shredded and bleeding paper. The displays and school-kid collages were flattened garbage. People crouched in doorways or lay moaning in the street.

Someone had taken a lungful of tear gas and was on her hands and knees, retching on the paving stones. The street had the look of broken aftermath, but Blaylock's instincts were still keyed up. She scanned, begging for trouble, begging for the call.

At the corner of Sparks and Bank Street, volunteers had set up a canteen tent. Blaylock had strolled by it earlier, and seen people filing in and filing out, clutching bagged lunches. Most of the customers had been protesters, but more than a few had been homeless. No lineup now. Police emerged, hauling men and women in full passive resistance. Blaylock came closer. One officer's nose was bleeding. Blaylock's eyes narrowed. The uniform turned back to the entrance and pulled a flap back. "You coming?" Blaylock heard him call.

"In a minute," from inside.

The cops moved on. Blaylock gave them space, then slipped into the tent. All the tables and chairs were overturned. Sandwiches were scattered like soggy confetti. An officer stood at the far end with his back to Blaylock. He had put his shield down, but not his baton. He was bending down. "Stand up."

"You're going to hit me again," said a muffled female voice.

Blaylock moved forward, quiet. She saw a woman at the cop's feet. She was face down, curled in a ball, arms wrapped around her stomach. Her long, dirty-blond hair hung over her face and spread out on the ground. The cop said, "You know I will if you don't stand." He raised the baton.

Answer the call. Blaylock pulled Alpha's balaclava out of her pocket and slipped it on. She took out her pen, uncapped it. The pen was heavy, metal, sharp. She held it in her fist, and it became a spike. She ghosted up behind the cop, then moved in two snaps. Snap one wrapped her left arm around his head and hauled back with a whiplash yank. Snap two jabbed the pen hard against his Adam's apple. The cop choked. She kept the pressure up, a cough away from penetration. "Serve and protect, asshole," she whispered. He tried to reach back with the baton. It swished by her ear. She kicked his right knee, heard the second dislocation pop of the day. The cop crashed down. Blaylock sat on him. She unbuckled his helmet, threw it away, and pulled his head back by his chin. She moved the pen from his throat to his nose. She inserted it in a nostril. "Want me to shove?" she asked.

"Hnnh," said the cop. He was young, younger than the anarchists at the souvenir shop. Stripped of his Darth Vader mode, he was cracking, terrified.

Blaylock removed his belt one-handed. Her pen didn't move. "We're going to leave," she said. "You're going to count to a hundred. So am I. I see you step outside before I finish, I shoot you." She poked with the pen for emphasis. "Go on," she told the woman without turning her head. She heard her stand up and move toward the exit. Blaylock glanced to her right and saw the woman leave the tent. "Be good now," she said, and patted the cop's head. She jerked the pen away, angle bad so it would hurt. She pulled the Glock .22 from the belt and stood up. She grabbed the baton, smashed the radio with it, then ran from the tent.

"Rammer?" said a voice.

Blaylock froze. The past reached out and parched her mouth. There was no way for her to bluff, tripped and tumbled by a nickname she hadn't heard since the army. She turned her head. The woman had waited for her outside the tent. Blaylock stared at her face. For a moment the long hair threw her off. Then, "Kelly?" A name she hadn't spoken since Bosnia.

"I thought I recognized your voice," said Kelly Grimson.

"Oh, Christ." Do this fast. She ejected the Glock's clip, threw it as far as she could. She wiped the gun and dropped it. Better the cop retrieve it than a street creature. "Come *on*," she said, grabbed Grimson's arm, and hauled her away from the tent. They ran down Bank Street. Blaylock pulled the balaclava off and stuffed it back in a pocket. They turned left on Queen, stormed down another block, crossed O'Connor. Blaylock pulled Grimson into the World Exchange Plaza, and shopping mall anonymity dropped its veil over them. They leaned against a wall, catching their breath.

"That was exciting," Grimson deadpanned.

Blaylock looked at her. "Kelly, why didn't you fight? You could have taken that guy."

Grimson shook her head. "Not like you. I was never up to the Rammer. Anyway," she rubbed her stomach, "I'm being careful."

Pregnant. Okay, too much at once, and there was still unfinished business. "You're okay, though?"

"Yes. And thanks, Jen."

"Good. You're welcome. Right." She still felt thrown, confused by a too-big surprise. "Okay, I have to go."

"*What?*"

"Mop-up." She took a step.

"Meet you back here?"

"Uh . . . I don't know . . . I don't know how long this will take."

"The hell is wrong with you?"

"Nothing, I just have to—"

"—meet me tomorrow, then."

The smart answer: no. Do not reconnect with old friends. Do not link up with people who mustn't know what you do. Especially people who know your real name. She opened her mouth, and the other answer came out, the answer shaped by a year of isolation, by the inability to withstand the temptation of seeing a *friend*. "Okay."

Blaylock crouched on the Plaza's roof, peered over the parapet at Sparks Street. She could see both the souvenir shop and the food tent. No action at either. So no one had called the police yet. She wanted to know how long the response took and how many showed up, especially at the tent. A show of force and she'd have to go back underground again. She hoped she hadn't screwed up. She didn't think so. Her battle instincts were humming with satisfaction. Guiltless sex.

She watched for a quarter of an hour. The cop must have left. The fact that no crime scene elements were springing up suggested he was going to keep the incident to himself. Another five minutes. Then a commotion from the souvenir shop. Alpha and Ralphie stumbled out, the owner brandishing the crowbar and shouting. He yelled at them as they walked up Sparks, yelled until they turned onto Bank, then went back in his shop. Bored waiting for the police, Blaylock guessed. His phone must have been out.

Blaylock thought for a moment, then left the rooftop. The hunch: find Alpha and Ralphie. She jogged along Bank. After three blocks she spotted Alpha's hair spikes, and she slowed down. She followed a hundred yards back. The good-time anarchists turned into a bar near the corner of Flora. Blaylock slowed as she approached the entrance, evaluating. The bar's interior was too dark to gauge from outside. She shrugged. Live a little, she thought, and stepped inside. She moved away from the entrance, out of the silhouetting light, then paused, waiting for her eyes to adjust. No ByWard Market exercise in cozy Irishness, this. Terry towel tablecloths, dollar-a-glass watery draft and no pitchers. The cancer-tang of smoke, Ottawa bylaws be damned. The atmosphere was biker-tough, yet mind-your-own-business private. A couple of hard faces glanced up from tables loaded with glasses, took her in, then looked away, disinterested. She looked for Alpha and Ralphie, and there was the hair. They were sitting at a booth in the rear of the bar, their backs to the door. Seated facing them was the cop from the food tent.

Blaylock blinked, felt the tensile strength of battle excitement. She forced herself not to grin. There was an empty booth two down from the boys. Blaylock hit the bar, ordered a glass of faded piss, sat down at the booth. The cop's eyes flicked her way, and she felt the tingle of risk. But he hadn't seen her face in the tent. Risk was managed. She nursed the beer, tuned out the bar noise, listened. It took her a moment before she could isolate their voices.

"... need a hospital, man," Ralphie was whining.

"Me too and shut up." That was Alpha. "After we're paid."

"Better be here soon," the cop muttered.

Who? Blaylock had time to wonder, and here came the man. Green suit, green shoes, green tie, green shirt, green attaché case, but damn if the stride didn't make him dangerous instead of silly. Long black hair greased back into a ponytail, amber-tinted Lennon glasses, clean-shaven, jaw narrow and porcelain-fragile. Ding ding ding, went the bell in Blaylock's head. Where have I seen you before?

She heard Greenman sit down, heard the clunk of his briefcase on the table. "Ladies." *Chik-chak* of locks snapping open. Crackle of envelopes. "Don't spend it all in one place."

"Should pay us goddamn danger pay," said the cop.

"Yeah," Ralphie chimed in. "Didn't say nothing about psycho-bitches."

"Sorry you girls were hurt. We'll keep you in at recess next time."

"You weren't there." Ralphie, still whining.

"Shut up," said Alpha, and Blaylock toasted him.

Slam, *chik-chak,* sounds of Greenman standing up. "Don't cry. You're still walking and you have your money. If you hadn't done the job, you wouldn't be walking. Tell you that for nothing." Blaylock watched as he breezed past. That face, that face, who the hell are you? She stood up and followed him out of the bar.

Greenman walked around the corner. He pulled keys out of his pocket, bleeped off a car alarm. A Jaguar was parked three vehicles up. Its trunk drifted open. Blaylock caught up as Greenman tossed the attaché case into the trunk. She shoved his back. He stumbled forward, and she slammed the trunk down on the back of his head. She caught him as he slumped forward. She looked up and gave a sheepish grin to a couple on the sidewalk who had stopped to stare. "Oh boy," she told them. "Oh boy. He's going to be soooo mad at me when he wakes up."

The couple looked doubtful. "Do you need help?" the man asked.

"That would be great. If you could give me a hand putting him in the car . . ." The man stepped forward. The woman opened the passenger door. Blaylock and the man wrestled Greenman into the seat. Blaylock did up his safety belt and kissed his forehead. "Poor dear," she said. "I'm so sorry, honey." She looked back at the couple. "Thanks so much."

"You're sure you're okay?" the woman asked.

Blaylock nodded, smiled, kept smiling and stroking Greenman's forehead until the couple moved on. Then she slipped Greenman's wallet out of his jacket pocket. The wallet was green leather. Of course it was. Blaylock flipped it open and looked at the driver's licence. Edward Brownsworth. Ding ding ding *ka-ching*, face and name fell into place. Brownsworth had been a fixture in the national papers for about six months a few years ago, during one of the media-circus Hell's Angels trials that Ontario put itself through periodically. The RCMP had tried, and failed, to nail Brownsworth as the man the Angels spoke to when they did business with the Canadian branch of the Coscarelli crime family.

Blaylock stuffed Brownsworth's wallet back in his vest pocket. She walked away from the car, thinking. The Mob financing bent cops and jerk-off anarchists to stir up shit at anti-globalization protests, now did that make sense? Yes, or it wouldn't be happening. So? She thought some more. Mental wheels spun. Questions multiplied and hooked into possibilities. The wheels lined up jackpot cherries. Blaylock grinned.

2

"Holy shit, man, you rocked the world."

Images of Jonathan Alloway rocking the world. On the front line of the protest, spitting distance from the concrete-and-chainlink wall blocking access to Rideau. The Conference Centre in sight, smug and safe inside its stormtrooper cordon. Alloway pissed as he'd never been, righteous fury turning to inspiration, turning to high-octane fuel for Global Response. Alloway seizing the moment. Take the Global Response name, make it more than a big-fish collective in the Winnipeg pond. Make it a national force. Make it everybody. (Rocking the world.) Alloway bounding up to the fence, scrambling up to high visibility, perching against odds on the peak. Alloway not here to tear down the wall, because he had a bullhorn. Alloway raising the horn to his lips, catching that pause in the crowd's noise, that perfect, once-in-a-lifetime, now-or-never-again moment of silence, that vacuum waiting to be filled.

(Rock.)

And so he spoke. He was a good speaker, he knew that. He'd never failed to be the big noise at activism evenings back in the 'Peg. He knew how to put gospel force into phrasing, and he knew how to shape the sound bite with real teeth. And today, the words flowed out into that perfect silence, and he had the crowd. Everyone in earshot paused and fed him attention. He gorged, and his exhortations transcended. He connected with the sublime. He transformed energy into words and words into energy. He gave the performance of a lifetime. He built up to the punch, to the finale that would make him immortal, that would (he knew this, he did) summon revolution, when he became aware of a red flash in the corner of his eye. He paused, turned his head. He saw a cop aiming a rifle his way. Laser light dazzled him. Something hard (rock?) hit his forehead. His head jerked back, smacked by an invisible haymaker. He yelled, and took a lungful of the pepper cloud released by the pellet. More of the pepper went into his eyes, and the world shrank to fire and tears. He pitched over backwards and fell off the fence. He hit the ground like lead and broken sticks. He screamed and coughed, felt molten claws in his throat. He heard the crowd roar and surge forward, and through his agony he realized he was going to be trampled, that the perfect moment had also been his last.

Hands yanked him up. "Got you, man." Darryl Avery looking out for his ass yet again. Alloway, gagging, rubbed his eyes, but the tears didn't stop and the pain only grew worse. He struggled to keep his feet as the crowd's wave broke against him and the fence rocked back and forth. Then he heard the sounds that promised still worse, the *foomp foomp* of the tear gas grenades being launched. Avery said, "Oh shit." A few seconds later there were more screams, and after that there was no more breathing at all.

No images now, only the spectrum of pain. Chemical pain in his lungs and eyes, battering-ram bruises over his body. Then somebody shouting in his ear, but Alloway couldn't hear, so he shook his head. That brought more pain, hard and insistent with a four-four rhythm against his shoulders and head. He fell down again, heard Avery screaming, too. Someone yanked his arms behind his back. Plastic constricted his wrists.

Fragments: floating in and out of blackout, being hauled and stumbling, being shoved into the back of a van. Falling from his seat during the drive, pitching face-first into his own vomit. Finally clawing his way back to the world, to seeing again, as he was ushered into his home away from home. By the time they'd made him shower off the tear gas and change into prison sweats, he was able to string coherent thoughts together. Forms were shoved at him, demanding signature. A number of the other prisoners were refusing to sign, keeping their names to themselves. Alloway had no trouble giving his name. As he signed, he thought about news of his arrest making it back home. He pictured the shit that would be kicked up around his parents at the golf club. He was told to wipe that smile off his face.

It was gone now.

"Rocked, man, I'm tellin' you. Totally. Fantastic. Totally fantastic."

Avery was waxing enthusiastic again, deploying his favorite word and pronouncing it "fuhn-TAS-tic." Terrific. Alloway's back throbbed. His head throbbed. His eyes throbbed. His butt was numb, but it throbbed, too. "Thanks, Darryl. But I just want to sleep now."

"Sure, sure, cool. Ready for battle tomorrow, eh?"

Whatever. Alloway didn't answer. He'd never been in prison before. He didn't know what to do. He was sitting with his back against the cell door. The bars bit hard into his back, rubbing against the abrasions he'd picked up during the arrest. The floor was cold, but there wasn't room on a bunk. There were four bunks, but twelve men in the cell. Two each in the beds, two sleeping on the floor. Alloway and Avery had been the last to arrive. Barely room for them to sit. Avery wasn't bothered. He was grooving on the adventure, crack-high on his political flowering. Alloway looked at him. Avery had lost his bandanna, and his shoulder-length red curls were a matted mess. His face, in the faint illumination of the prison hallway, was smeared with filth, but plump cheeks, too-small nose, and too-big eyes still had the cherub glow of a Mary Poppins chimney sweep. Avery was still in the fight, all right.

Alloway shut his eyes. Come on, he told himself. You knew this would happen, and not just when you climbed the fence. You knew you were going to wind up in a cell before you even hit Ottawa. So why are you feeling sorry for yourself? Darryl's right, you know. You did pretty well up there. That was some sexy speech.

Accomplishing what? he asked himself. And Kelly, he thought. Kelly's going to be having kittens. She doesn't know where I am. He folded his arms, tried to push the worry away.

"*Up!*"

Alloway jerked. Had he been asleep? Even five minutes? He struggled to his feet. Three men stood at the cell door. One of them was slamming a baton against the bars, *clang-bash* wake-up call. The door opened. The men walked in, shoving Alloway and Avery back. They stumbled against the other prisoners.

"*Tags!*" a guard yelled.

Alloway held up the name tag that hung around his

neck. He blinked, blinded as a flashlight shone in his eyes, at the tag, back in his eyes. Then he was pushed aside and it was Avery's turn. The guards worked their way through the prisoners. The inspection was rough. The voices never stopped yelling. The cell door clanged shut behind the guards like an exclamation point.

Avery slumped back down on the floor. Alloway remained standing. He glared at the hallway, willed the guards to come back so they could stoke his anger some more. One of the other prisoners groaned. "The hell time is it?"

"Who knows," another answered. All their watches had been confiscated.

"Why do they have to do that?" the first asked.

Alloway said, "Because they can."

"Hey," said one of the top-bunk occupants, "you're the guy who made that speech."

"Too right," Avery said. "My man Jonathan. Global Response, people. Global Response."

"That was some amazing stuff, dude," said a shape on the floor.

"For all the good it did," Alloway muttered.

"No way, dude, we heard you. We heard you."

Avery reached out and tapped Alloway's knee. "What'd I tell you?"

Alloway stared at the bars. "Not good enough. We're in here. The world out there isn't changing."

The commute to and from the Geneva battlegrounds took an hour and a half each way. That meant three hours a day out of Irina Zelkova's life, three hours of being trapped in her car, doing nothing except her little contribution to global warming. She fumed over the trip on the way in. Driving back didn't bother her as much. By then, head sore from banging it against bureaucratic walls, stomach clenched from a rich and rotten diet of multinational stews, she was ready for escape. Geneva dropped behind her as she drove home, and with it the combat receded for the night.

Home was in the mountains. The style was Swiss chalet, but the scale was jet set. The mansion had a small valley to itself, and snuggled against the mountainside. Its size and luxury were Zelkova's comfort and her guilt. Comfort and guilt because of the memory of two Moscow apartments. The first was the one-bedroom where she'd lived with her parents. Father was a low-level functionary, mother was a doctor, and their combined salaries could afford nothing better. The second apartment was smaller yet, and was another landscape in gray concrete. That one was hers, a home scrabbled together as she worked on her history degree. Toilet in the kitchenette, bedroom also the main room, tiny beyond words, and still her parents had come to live with her there after the economic collapse had wiped out what meaning their money had had. Both apartments were receding into the past, but the contrast with the mansion was a reminder. Do not take this for granted. And do not forget where you came from.

Zelkova pulled up the gravel drive and parked her Alfa Romeo 156 by the porch. The lights inside were on. When she opened the front door, she smelled dinner, and closed her eyes for a moment. She wasn't feeling the guilt now. Only the luxury. Only the thanks for having a full staff.

Inna came running to greet her. She was eight, and already so multilingual Zelkova doubted she had a true mother tongue. My daughter, she thought, Citizen of the World. She crouched to hug her.

"Guess what?" Inna whispered. She was speaking Russian today.

"What?"

"Papa's home."

"Is he?" And they giggled at each other.

Inna held a finger up to her lips. "Shhh." She took Zelkova's hand and led her, tiptoeing, to the living room. Here windows looked down the valley on one side, up at the mountains on the other. The curtains were drawn now, keeping in the warmth of the fireplace. Inna pointed. Zelkova obeyed, and crept up behind the couch facing the hearth, reached around her husband's head, and covered his eyes. His startled jump was high theater.

"Oh no!" Stepan Sherbina exclaimed. "Who has me now?" He reached up, grabbed Zelkova's arms, and hauled her over the couch. Zelkova shrieked, somersaulting, and landed in Sherbina's lap. Inna squealed, delighted. Her father smiled at her. "Dinner smells like it's ready," he said. "Go wash up and meet us at the table, okay?"

Inna took off.

Zelkova wrapped her arms around Sherbina's neck. "You're back early," she said. She snuggled into his body's strength.

"Wrapped things up faster than I expected. And besides," he added, switching to English, "the charms of Moscow are faint indeed when my lady wife awaits."

She tugged his hair. "Cut that out." She didn't like the sneer that lurked beneath the surface when he spoke English. He sounded warmer, less posed, in Russian.

"Sorry." He kissed her cheek. "So how did it go today?"

She groaned, leaned her head against his shoulder. "Another ream of fair trade initiatives up in smoke. I know you couldn't care less, but—"

"I do, you know." He rubbed her back. "I don't like seeing the bastards wearing you down."

She tapped his nose. "Even though you're one of them?"

"When have I ever failed to support you?"

"Never." He had always helped her fight against everything he worked for, provided all the money she needed to try to shut down, among other things, the source of that money. The paradox of their relationship sometimes made her laugh. More frequently, it kept her awake.

Sherbina asked, "How much of the Ottawa conference coverage have you been catching?"

"What I can."

"You were mentioned in the press."

"In *The Guardian,* as usual, I suppose. Preaching to the converted."

Sherbina smiled. "Hardly." He picked up the folded newspaper beside him. "*The Wall Street Journal,*" he said. "Editorial page. 'Irina Zelkova'," he read, "'the Queen of the NGOs, is well on her way to becoming a presence as irritating as she is ubiquitous. The prospect of a Naomi Klein with unlimited funds no doubt cheers the anti-globalization mythmakers. We can only hope that the patent hypocrisy of her position, as beneficiary of one of the new Russia's most successful multinationals, will be as apparent to anyone who stops to think as it is clearly invisible to her.' You are officially an annoyance."

Zelkova giggled. "I see the nickname is catching on."

"Exactly. And I think you should build on the exposure. I have to go to the States next week. Come with me. Do the North American rock tour."

"Be careful. How much support do you really want to give your nemesis?"

Sherbina touched her chin. "You know what is said about keeping your enemies close."

Mind rev rev revving, then bang into gear. Three a.m. and no more sleep tonight. Get up. Do work. Sherbina's eyes clicked open. He was lying on his side, face to face with his wife. He inhaled, breathing in her scent, granting himself a moment of calm. He watched the REM of her eyes behind their lids. His gaze traced a curl of her dark brown hair that fell down the center of her forehead. Her lips, thin and delicate, were parted. He almost kissed her. Instead, he bowed to the inevitable and slid out of the bed, careful not to wake Zelkova. He shrugged into a dressing gown, then pulled the covers back up to Zelkova's chin. He felt the familiar gut-twinge that came with obscene luck.

They had met in 1991. Sherbina, knowing writing on the wall when he saw it, had just walked away from the KGB. He had hung on to his underworld contacts, though, and he had his new business connections. He had his ducks all lined up to launch Kornukopia as a public entity and private empire, right down to the internationalist faux-Russian English of the name. Part of the groundwork was PR, establishing the profile of a company whose above-the-surface trade alone would consist in oil, chemicals, metals, fertilizers, and weapons. So he attended a charity function for the destitute of the new capitalism. A young woman was emceeing the event. One look at her and he felt physical pain. That was a novelty. So was the fact that when he approached her, she turned him down. Double whammy, and this was not how life worked for Stepan Sherbina. Everything had always come easily to him. His father was high-end *nomenklatura*. His mother was the daughter of one of the top *vory v zakone*. The thieves-in-law, crime Svengalis, had followed the organizational principles of the 1917 Revolution, and had thrived.

The union of Petr and Anna Sherbina had brought together the best that government and crime had to offer, and they had bequeathed this gift to young Stepan. They encouraged his sense of entitlement. He had reveled in his privilege, and then lived up to it. Marks in school were easy, athletics easier still. The KGB spotted a star early, snapped him up, and sent him to Yale. Spetznaz training followed, finishing school for the well-rounded gentleman. And through the years, sex had been the easiest thing of all. He had the looks, he had the charm, he had the eye. The girls came running. He collected them, sampling and moving on. And then bang, the poverty activist. He was head over heels for the first time in his life, and Zelkova said "no." It was as if she'd blasted him back in time, forcing him to experience the pain of adolescent awkwardness and rejection that he'd skipped over. He pursued. She rejected. His wealth and looks were the same useless currency as the ruble. He persisted. He hung around. He helped with her projects. And he finally won. It had been his hardest fought battle, and the victory he felt he least deserved.

Sherbina walked down the hall, one hand brushing lightly against the varnished wood. He peeked into Inna's room, then went downstairs to his office. He sat in the leather chair behind the desk and fired up the computer. While he waited for the boot to finish, he thumbed a remote, turning on the television mounted above the door in a diagonal line from the computer monitor. When he was really multitasking, he could scan the Internet and channel surf at the same time. He jumped around the news channels until he found footage of the Ottawa protests. He watched, listened, studied. Evaluated. He noted the images repeated most frequently. He turned to the computer. He had a search engine set up that took him to the protest sites with the most hits. He spent an hour reading. When he finished, he turned off the television, sat back in the chair, and smiled. Operations should always be running this smoothly.

Kelly Grimson said, "You're scanning."

Damn it, she was, too. Blaylock forced her eyes back to Grimson's face, made them stay there. She and Grimson were having lunch at The Open Window, a vegetarian restaurant in Ottawa's trendy Glebe district, on a block that was an alternating series of antique shops, used bookstores, and copper-priced kitchen boutiques. The Open Window offered a buffet where you paid by the weight of your plate. It did not offer targets of opportunity. It was not a potential combat zone. "Sorry," Blaylock said.

Grimson laughed. "Still the Rammer. You can take the girl out of the army, but you can't—"

"Oh yes, you can. Look at you, Hippiechick. You're wearing *Birkenstocks,* for Chrissake."

"They're comfortable."

Blaylock rolled her eyes. "Completely beside the point. I mean, the long hair thing, the fashions by Value Village, the... the..." She pointed at Grimson's stomach.

"And this." Grimson held up her hand, waggled fingers, flashing wedding band.

"Yeah, that, too."

Grimson sipped her peppermint tea. "Poor Jen. All these scary changes. Be honest, though, are you really that surprised?"

Blaylock let the smile creep onto her face slowly. No. If she thought about it, she wasn't surprised. Grimson dragging that acoustic guitar around Bosnia and singing the Best of the Weavers should have been a clue. The guitar had finally settled Grimson's nickname as "Strummer." Only Blaylock called her "Hippiechick"—the other troops instinctively recoiled from the anathema the name pronounced. For Blaylock and Grimson, though, the name was fun. They already had their cynic vs. idealist schtick well developed by the time of the Balkans. It dovetailed with their mock class warfare. They'd both grown up in Winnipeg, but hadn't met until, budding RadOps, they were doing their trade training in Kingston. They were bad girls there, Blaylock's child of privilege from River Heights raising hell with Grimson's North End daughter of the working class. Sometimes they switched roles and played at caricatures of each other's backgrounds, Grimson going ultrasnob while Blaylock went sublumpen.

It was in Kingston that Blaylock's nickname emerged. She and Grimson were at the Junior Ranks. A drunken private put the moves on Grimson, didn't take no for an answer. Also drunk (blasted out of her mind, in fact), Blaylock taunted the man, twice her size, into a fight. The thunder-pain of his fist in her face shocked her into an exhilaration of anger. She laughed, hard and loud, then ducked her head down and charged, maddened bull. She rammed. He flew back hard enough to crack the Plexiglas of the jukebox. The soldier slumped, winded, and Blaylock was all over him. By the time she was dragged off, the infirmary had been alerted, and the word was out: don't mess with the Rammer. Grimson didn't stop laughing for three days.

Their schtick changed with the Gulf War. It developed an edge they directed at a world that paid fellating lip service to ideals. Then InSec killed Blaylock's family. Then there was Bosnia. Grimson still sang. She and Blaylock still joked, but the fun was sour now, bitter. Blaylock went rogue and pulled out of the army. She hadn't seen Grimson since. Blaylock asked, "When did you leave the forces?"

"'98. It was time to sign up again or ..." She shrugged.

"You wanted to redirect your energies."

Grimson nodded, not rising to the sarcasm. "I can make more of a difference this way. And don't roll your eyes at me, young lady."

"I take it your hubby is of a like mind."

Grimson smiled, fond. "Jonathan's more of a dreamer."

"What's he up to?"

"Getting out of jail. He was grabbed during the protest yesterday." Her smile faded. "The bastards held him overnight."

"Jesus, you must have been frantic."

Grimson nodded. "I had no idea where he was. I didn't even know he was missing until after you left yesterday. They didn't let him call me until today. And of course all the charges, whatever they were, are being dropped." She brightened. "Anyway, he's out now." She glanced at her watch. "They're supposed to meet us here."

"'They'?"

"His friend Darryl, too."

The reunion was becoming crowded. Time to take steps. Blaylock was reluctant, but she'd known she was going to have to do this since Grimson had recognized her. "I need you to look at something," she said, and pulled her press card out of her jeans pocket. She handed the ID to Grimson.

"Your name's misspelled," Grimson said.

"No, it isn't." She waited for Grimson to look at her before she went on. "My name's Baylor. I write freelance. You've never heard different. You with me, Kelly?"

"Yes. My God, Jen, what have you been up to?"

Blaylock took a breath. "I went after the man who killed my parents and my sister. I slit his throat." She grunted. "Didn't bother to tell him who I was or why I was killing him."

Grimson brought a hand to her mouth. "Who—?" she began.

"How much do you really want to know?"

"Okay, okay," shaking her head.

Blaylock looked up. Two men were approaching their table. "This them?"

Grimson turned around in her seat, then leaped up and threw her arms around the first man. Jonathan Alloway looked like a match for Grimson, all right, especially now that her Hippiechick persona was the dominant one. They were both dressed in recycled Bohemian, both had fine features, both had long blond hair. Some differences, though. Grimson had freckles, and let her hair hang free. Alloway's face was alabaster pure, and he had a ponytail. Enviro-Christ, Blaylock thought, taking in his goatee and his enormously open eyes. There were more crow's feet around Grimson's eyes, and the idealism in them couldn't drown out the hard knowledge of the Gulf and the Balkans. Behind the couple, Darryl Avery loomed. He was fat, but huge enough to look strong. His beard, straight and untamed, was a red so bright it verged on orange. He was the love child of standing stone and leprechaun.

They sat down. The talk turned to war stories of yesterday's crusade. Blaylock smiled, remained polite, let the power and the glory and Avery's braying laugh wash over her for almost thirty minutes. She watched Grimson in her environment, saw her happy, and tempered her disdain. Remember why you do what you do, she told herself. It's so they won't have to.

"Kelly tells me you helped her out of a jam," Alloway said.

Blaylock shrugged. "Nothing she couldn't have done."

"Still. Thank you. You know, Global Response could really benefit from someone like—"

"Sorry. Not much of a joiner, you know?" She stood up to go.

"We're going to see you again, yes?" Grimson said. It was a command. "Come stay with us in Winnipeg."

"You all set up in the Granola Belt?" The Wolseley district didn't just have streets with names like Chestnut and Walnut. It also had a massive overrepresentation of the counterculture.

"Actually we're in a new co-housing project."

"It's called Greenham Common," Avery put in.

Blaylock laughed. "Okay. Too much information."

"If you change your mind, the door's always open," Alloway told her. "We're where the action is. You think you saw a show yesterday, just wait till Davos."

Blaylock looked at him. "You're all going to Switzerland?" That would be one expensive field trip.

"World Economic Forum, man." Avery bounced in his seat. The chair creaked. "The nexus of eeeeeevil."

"Where are you heading?" Grimson asked.

"Chasing down a story in New York," Blaylock answered. Her heart gave a deep beat of ugly anticipation.

3

Head down, nose clean, eyes wide: Michael Flanagan's existence for the last year. His reward: promotion. His reward: festering conscience. He was head of shipping. He knew where all the guns were going. He made sure they arrived there. He had some pretty clear ideas about where the bodies were buried. He barely slept. Blaylock's words by the ruins of the Ember Lake lodge had become a bitter mantra. *You think this is going to make a huge difference? Not much it won't. A bit maybe, but not much.* Too right. InSec chugged along, the grand unified machine of the arms trade absorbing the death of its founder without so much as a hiccup. Flanagan hadn't thought that would be possible. Arthur Pembroke *was* InSec. He and his lieutenants were dead. InSec was decapitated. How could it continue to march? When Flanagan had first set foot back in the InSec building, he'd expected to find tumbleweeds blowing through the lobby, leaves in the central fountain, cobwebs over the cubicles. But no. The machine rolled on, smooth as ever.

But not as free. There was that change. Stern men in suits walked the halls those first few months, and they were not employees. They had the clout of agencies behind them, and they were calling the shots. They did not see InSec as a machine. They saw it as a dog that had slipped its leash and gone on a mauling rampage. Only InSec's power, its indispensability, prevented it from being put down. The board of directors, freed of Pembroke's choke hold, cowered, waiting for the guillotine of retribution to roll their way. Ps and Qs were universally minded. Outside InSec's walls, the media watched. InSec's name had entered the public imagination as the worst-case fusion of Enron and al-Qaida. Flanagan was on his third unlisted number.

He came back to work, though. He couldn't walk away from the war, even if he didn't know how to fight. Blaylock had said to be the termite. Fine. But what to eat? And then there were the other agendas that had uses for him. The day of his promotion, three weeks after his return, Joe Chapel stopped by his new office, full of congratulations. Joe Chapel, who had terrified him at the hospital, and was no less frightening now, even though he wasn't acting threatening. Especially because he wasn't acting threatening.

"I'm glad this position was filled by someone like you," Chapel said. Affable, smiling. But standing, arms crossed, making no move to sit down.

Flanagan placed the box of papers he had been carrying on the desk. He fingered a cardboard flap. "Meaning?" he asked, already wondering how much Chapel had had to do with the promotion.

"Someone who knows right from wrong." Chapel waited a beat. "Who knows the sort of thing that can go on here." Beat. "Who knows what to keep an eye out for."

Oh. "I see," Flanagan said. Wonderful.

Chapel handed him a card. It was blank except for a phone number. "Day or night," he said, and left.

Flanagan didn't call. InSec was behaving itself. Sort of. Nothing happened to interest the likes of Chapel, not while the stern men in suits were underfoot. But he kept his eyes open. Nose clean. Head down. And there was another phone number to think about, too.

The men in suits gradually drifted away. Two months ago, Flanagan caught an order that sent up red flags: a large shipment of M-16s and RPGs to Sierra Leone. The destination was not Freetown. Flanagan checked a map, saw how close to the Liberian border the weapons were supposed to go. He thought about blood diamonds. He thought about rebels. He thought a bit longer, then set himself up an account with a Finnish anonymous e-mail server. He processed the order, did his bit to make InSec richer, than sent an e-mail to the relevant authorities. The shipment was seized in transit. Flanagan bought a bottle of champagne that night and toasted himself. You did a good thing, he thought. All by your lonesome. (But when he thought that, the apartment suddenly felt big and empty.)

Eyes open even wider from that point on. Not for Chapel. Maybe for Blaylock. Certainly for himself. Watching for another opportunity. He didn't see one. What he saw instead happened in three stages. Stage One was hard to notice. He didn't even pick up on it except retroactively. As the stern men in suits faded from the scene, other strangers began to take their place. A lot of them had Russian accents. By October, InSec's lower Manhattan footprint felt like an outpost of Brighton Beach. As well, ever larger proportions of the orders were being filled in partnership with something called Kornukopia.

Stage Two happened last week. Flanagan was in the lobby, waiting for the elevator. Its doors opened, and he jumped out of the way of the man who stormed out, yelling. The man was Pat Forbes, whose every pore shouted Texan. Trying to keep up was Nick Brentlinger, an undertaker with three-thousand-dollar suits. They were both on the board of directors. Flanagan had never been aware of the board in the Pembroke days. Back then, its authority had been hypothetical, a ceremonial sop tossed to vassals by the Sun King. Now it was a force, but one of chaos and power struggle. Brentlinger was trying to make Forbes cool it. Forbes kept it hot. "By Jesus, I won't have it! I will not have that man come to mah country and tell me what's what about *mah* company. I won't!" Flanagan stepped into the elevator. He watched Forbes flail his arms until the doors shut out the view.

Stage Three was today, and the media were squealing with pleasure. Forbes had been found floating face-down in the Hudson. One, Two, Three. Connect the dots. Flanagan sensed big and bad muscles flexing, perhaps big and bad enough to justify the destruction that summoning a war demon would surely cause. Flanagan gave himself the day to work up his nerve. On his way home to his Battery Park City apartment, he decided to leave a message. He stopped at a pay phone, dialed the number he'd avoided for a year.

"Hello?" Blaylock answered.

Flanagan yelped. The demon was already in town.

They sat in Flanagan's apartment. He was on the couch, perched on the edge of the middle cushion. His hands were clasped. He was trying not to twist them. Blaylock was in the armchair, facing him. She was leaning back. She rested one foot on one knee, beat a metronome rhythm with the raised leg. Flanagan asked, "What do you think?" All he could think about was that he didn't know how he felt about seeing her again.

Blaylock tapped a finger on the chair's arm. "Does sound like a takeover." She sighed. "Guess I'm more naive than I thought. I'd hoped the hydra would take a bit longer before growing its heads back."

"What should we do?" The "we" surfaced without thought. He caught it only after he'd spoken.

"Nothing just now. We need to know more first. I need money and weapons before I can be serious. And I'm in the middle of something else right now. I need to know if it's going to lead anywhere before I do anything else."

"So I just watch for now?"

Blaylock nodded. Then she stood up, crossed the living room to Flanagan, and crouched in front of him. "It's been a long time, Mike," she said. She placed a hand on his knee.

He touched her hand, stroked her fingers with small, feather movements. "I'm sorry," he said.

"That wasn't an accusation."

He nodded. "I'm still sorry. It's not like I wasn't thinking about you."

"I've missed you."

"I've missed you, too. I was just afraid."

"Of me?"

"I don't know."

Blaylock rose from her crouch. Her eyes were soft, but the movement still had the steel grace of panther and cobra. She leaned into Flanagan, forcing him back against the couch. She slipped her fingers into his shirt, unbuttoning. She kissed his forehead. He felt her lips as warmth without pressure. He took a deep, shuddering breath, teetered on the edge of surrender, then murmured, "Wait."

Blaylock stopped. She pulled her hand out of his shirt, but let it rest against his chest. She lowered her head so her lips were brushing against his ear. "What is it?" she whispered.

He put his arms around her. "I want to be with you."

"But . . . ?"

"All we have is blood and fire."

She was silent for a long moment before answering. "That's all I have to offer."

"I don't want to believe that. And Jen," he stroked her cheek, "I can't go down that path again."

Flanagan felt Blaylock swallow hard. She pulled away and sat beside him. "So where are we at?"

He touched her shoulder. "I want to be with you. I want to help you. There are just certain lengths—"

"You mean certain depths to which you won't sink. It's all right, Mike," she carried on when he opened his mouth to protest. "You're not supposed to. That's the whole idea." She grabbed his hand. "Do your best to keep me human, eh?" She said this with a straight face, and Flanagan couldn't tell if she was joking or not.

Joe Chapel's desk faced away from the window. There was no point in teasing himself with a non-view. The windows of the CIA's old building at Langley were small, and the only things to see from the sixth-floor office of the deputy director of counterterrorism were the envy-inspiring windows of the new building. Chapel looked up sharply from the report he was reading, stared at his open doorway. Ten seconds later Jim Korda, the Director of Central Intelligence, appeared. Korda grinned when he saw Chapel looking at him. "No sneaking up on you. Prescient as ever."

"No," Chapel answered, "just field instincts." He tossed the report onto his desk. "What's up?"

Korda settled his bulk into a chair. His bald head was red and sweating from the exertion of a corridor walk. "You are." Typical Korda. His response sounded like good news, but was open to interpretation. Chapel knew a lot of people who had begun to celebrate only to be eviscerated with the next sentence. He didn't play Korda's game. He said nothing, forcing Korda's hand. The Director finally continued. "I've been asked to sound you out about becoming DD of Operations."

"I'd accept, of course," Chapel said. Covert action, special operations, counterintelligence, counterterrorism, counternarcotics—the whole direct action ball of wax fell under Operations. Chapel felt he was doing some good in counterterrorism. He knew he could do more good higher up the intelligence pyramid. The day suddenly seemed very bright and strong. Then he noticed Korda's phrasing. "You've been asked, you say."

Korda nodded. "You haven't exactly brought the Pembroke file to closure"—jab—"but you've managed to put out a lot of fires." Was that a pun? Another jab maybe?

"Just looking out for the country's interest."

"Sure. Anyway, high places have noticed your efforts." Definite jab, this time at Chapel's indirect family links to ex-Vice-President, now alpha dog, Sam Reed. Chapel kept his snort in check. Korda was in the most fragile of glass houses when it came to appointments. He'd been Walter Campbell's appointee to the headship of the Agency, and Chapel didn't think having been a one-term governor of New Hampshire and CEO of a middling investment firm was much by way of qualification. He shouldn't have been surprised, though. Campbell had been a politician from birth, and Korda was the same. Goddamn birds of a feather. Reed was a different story. He'd done intelligence work in Vietnam. Though Chapel had pushed his people hard for results on the Pembroke fiasco, secretly he wanted to shake the hand of whoever had broken Walter Campbell's neck. America had been delivered into much surer care.

Korda levered himself out of the chair. "Your watch is a hell of a lot bigger now. Keep good track."

"I will." Chapel allowed himself the tiniest emphasis on the "I." Korda shot him a look. Chapel smiled, pleasant. Korda grunted and left. Chapel eyed him as he receded down the corridor. He saw the man on whose watch the leaders of the G8 had been incinerated. He saw a man whose head was on a chopping block.

Good.

Three goals: information, resources, damage. A three-stage plan: shake the tree, gather its fruit, whip out the chainsaw. Did I ask you to keep me human, Mike? Good luck.

Time to do the ugly. Blaylock stood in the shadows, beyond the street light's reach, under the haven of trees. She watched the gate to the Riverdale mansion that Danny "Little Forks" Petraglia called home.

In their recent climb to the top of the New York families, the Coscarellis had generated enough headlines for three insta-books. Doing the research was not hard. Blaylock knew the important players in the 250-strong outfit before she hit the city. She put the Queens home of Don

Salvatore Coscarelli under surveillance and confirmed the faces. All she had to do was pick a target. Petraglia had the most drug charges of the capos, and he lived the largest, his ostentation bordering on insubordination. Coscarelli put up with him, though, so his tributes must be consistent and impressive. He was perfect. All Blaylock needed was access. So she was here tonight. It was Petraglia's birthday. He was throwing a party.

Every window in the mansion was lit, shining warm through the trees on the grounds. Three distinct sound systems were in competition. Blaylock could hear snippets of Frank Sinatra twining with Eminem and Tears for Fears. There were two guards at the gate. Blaylock was packing, but she didn't to want make that big an entrance. She didn't mind waiting. Petraglia was a drug dealer stupid enough to live like one. Opportunity would come.

It came around 0100. Two groups of women approached the gate from opposite directions. Group One looked fresh from a limo. Girlfriends, Blaylock assumed. Group Two was made up of professionals. Blaylock crossed the street and joined the crowd as they met and milled. "Come on, Frankie," one woman called as a guard moved to unlock the gate. Blaylock smiled at Frankie as she walked by. He smiled back.

"Who you with?" a woman asked as they made their way up the short drive.

Blaylock pulled a name out of her ass. "Danny asked me to come for Jimmy," she said.

The woman laughed. "Jimmy's going for the casual look now?" Blaylock was the only one not showing leg, ass, and stilettos. "If that ain't Jimmy all over." She laughed again, click-clicked up the front porch. "I'm Julia."

"Jen. Go rock 'em hard."

"You know it, girl."

Blaylock noted two other guards on the porch, saw a flashlight moving through the grounds. Then she stepped inside. The party was go-go excess. Blaylock had to push through a triple-digit crowd in the entryway alone. The laughter was overexcited, pushing hysteria. Pupils were dilated idiocies. No one asked her any questions, and she moved into the mansion, searching. The living room was Sinatra's domain, though the floor throbbed with the hip-hop pumping up from the basement. A wide-screen plasma TV was showing *The Boondock Saints*, the gunfire competing with the stereo's crooning. The furniture and decor were the fusion chaos that came with unlimited purchasing power and zero taste. Art deco slammed up against First Empire and La-z-Boy x-treme. Pollock and Vargas fought for wall space. For Petraglia, the '80s had never died, and every flat surface held mirrors, razors, and coke. And at every coke setting, there were silver spoons and forks. Blaylock snorted. Nickname humor. Too hilarious. But the party crowd, high and charged electric, got the joke and got it good. Blaylock watched people sit down, snort, notice the forks, and piss themselves.

The fun was beyond special, and she moved on, shark. She crossed the kitchen, and someone shoved some canapes at her. She grabbed one, munched fish and cheese, hit the main hall, kept looking. You have one, she thought. I know you do. You've seen too many movies not to. At the end of the corridor she saw oak double doors. Crowded as the hallway was, the doors were being granted a five-foot buffer zone. No one leaned against them. There you are, Blaylock thought.

"Jen! Hey, Jen!" It was Julia, leaning over the grand staircase's balustrade. "I found Jimmy for ya!"

Shit. "Tell him I'll be there in a minute!" She mimed applying lipstick.

Grinning, Julia pressed an index finger against one side of her nose, took a caricatured snort. She hooted and trotted back up the stairs.

Blaylock pushed her way through the crowd until she had almost reached the doors. She hung back, smiled at the young and the stoned, at the older and drunker, and waited, rolling the dice on the big gamble.

She rolled a natural seven. The doors opened and Petraglia stepped out, the man of the hour in multigrand designer silk, tie still knotted tight all these hours into the celebration. He was backslapping with two other men. Their suits had the silk thing, too, but of a lower order. Faithful soldiers, paying their tribute. The crew was doing right by Little Forks, and that was pay dirt for Blaylock. The boys left the doors to the den open as they threw themselves back into the party fray. Blaylock watched. No one went through the doorway. The room didn't appear forbidden, just uninteresting: no drugs or booze. Petraglia pushed past Blaylock. When he left the hallway, she stepped into his office. She did it casually, drawing no attention, then moved left, out of sight from the corridor.

The den was another regurgitated pop-culture fantasy. Monolithic, marble-topped desk. Wall-length bookcases with leather editions of unread books. Even a brandy snifter on the desk, for Chrissake. A large portrait of Petraglia in bad Gainsborough hung behind the desk. Blaylock didn't have to look to know there would be a wall safe behind the painting. She looked for a place to wait. The curtains, thick and high, were drawn over the windows on the left-hand side of the room. Perfect, and she liked the quaintness of the idea. She checked behind the drapes at the end closest to the desk. There was a good two feet of wall before the window began. She'd be invisible from outside. She took her position, shrouded in full dark by the curtains. She pulled a SIG-Sauer P-228 out of the back waistband of her jeans, its suppressor out of an interior pocket of her leather jacket. She took a balaclava from another pocket, slipped it on. From somewhere above, A-ha was begging to be taken on.

Fifteen minutes. And then Julia's voice. "Jen?" Blaylock grimaced in frustration. *No witnesses*, she thought. *I can't afford witnesses.* If Julia thought she was here, a mask wouldn't do any good. *Go away*, she thought. *Just go, leave.* Julia didn't. Blaylock heard her move through the room. "You in here?" Spoken an arm's reach away. If she looked behind the curtains, what then? Blaylock ran the options, and they were all bad.

"You lost something?" A man's voice.

"Hey, Danny. Just looking for Jimmy's friend."

"Well, I don't see her," Petraglia said.

"Yeah . . ." Translation: *yeah, but*. Julia sounding stubborn and still close. Blaylock's throat dried. *No no no no.* "I thought I saw her—"

"She ain't here. Beat it, Julia. We got business."

"Tell me something new," Julia grumped, but her voice faded. Blaylock sagged with relief.

"Get the doors, Al."

Blaylock followed the sounds. She heard the doors close. She counted three voices plus Petraglia. She heard something being placed on the desk. She heard Petraglia moving something. Pulling back the painting? Yes. There was the jingle of keys, the snick of a lock turning, the clunk of a heavy metal latch being opened. Blaylock visualized her position relative to the desk, where Petraglia would be, where attention would be focused. She waited. Petraglia took a couple of steps. Sound of a long zipper being opened.

Petraglia: "You boys are spoiling me."

Go. Blaylock slid out from behind the curtains, pistol up, both hands steadying. Petraglia had his back to her. The three men facing the desk stared. She took the second of surprise to plant her feet apart, find her center, take the aim. She squeezed the trigger. No such thing as a true silencer, but the dulled report vanished into the roar of the party. The supersonic crack of the bullet was louder, but she could live with the risk. The man nearest her, seated, was gaping wide and stupid. The gape remained even as a dark hole appeared in his forehead. The back of his head burst and sprayed hard. Brain splashed the man who stood behind him. The wise guy flinched. Blaylock took his mistake and shot him in the throat. He fell, silent. She moved the gun right. The third man was reacting, rising from his chair. He was fast. Blaylock thought *headshot* but caught him mid-leap in the gut. He slammed down on the desk. Petraglia recoiled, made a friend of blind luck. He stumbled into Blaylock, his flailing arm smacking her wrists the moment she fired. The surprise of the blow hit with the kickback of the pistol. She dropped the weapon. The bullet went wide, hit the curtains, smashed window glass. Blaylock fell on her back. Petraglia landed on her. His reactions were lightning. He straddled her, grabbed her throat, and squeezed. His face was purple with rage. Blaylock wrapped her legs around his body and held tight. Petraglia looked surprised, but kept squeezing. Blaylock ignored her system's panic at the oxygen shutdown and reached up. She grabbed Petraglia's head with both hands and wrenched it left. There was a crack, Petraglia slumped down, and Blaylock could breathe again. She shoved the body away, contemptuous. She'd been throttled by better.

The man on the desk was still moving. His blood had slicked the marble a deep, reflective crimson, and was making rain-patter noises on the carpet. He was dying, but might have a few hours yet. Blaylock retrieved her handgun and shot him in the head. She glanced at the window. She would be having more company very soon. She picked up the gym bag that sat on the desk. Its bottom was soaked red. She looked in the safe. Bagged drugs, stacks of bills. She tossed the drugs to the floor, scooped the money into the bag. She filled it to bursting, and there were still three bundles of hundreds that simply would not fit. She stuffed them in her pockets.

Tick tick tick. Let's go. She removed the suppressor from her P-228. One last search of the den. No more money, but a palm-size .22 in the desk. Useless. She opened up the wardrobe on the wall opposite the windows and found a shotgun and box of double-ought cartridges. She loaded the shotgun, and it was time to complete the terror. She checked Petraglia's pockets and took his Zippo. She turned the lights off in the study and peeked between the curtains. No flashlights running this way. So hard to find competent help. She held the Zippo's flame to the curtains. The fibers went up quickly, expensive but dangerous. Blaylock backed up to the center of the room and fired the shotgun at the ceiling. The report was deafening, and in its wake Blaylock heard a shock wave of silence spread through the party. The den became bright as the curtains turned into a wall of flame. The bookcases caught fire. Blaylock stood in front of the doors, reloaded shotgun at her feet, SIG-Sauer out, and aimed. The silence beyond turned into the babble of worry. The birthday mood was deflating. Now footsteps running down the hall. A shout: "Boss!" Blaylock began to apply pressure to the trigger. The doors were yanked open. Blaylock fired. Frankie flipped backward, tapped head spraying. The kill was quick, loud, messy, and public. On cue, the party went panic and the stampede out began.

The windows blew in. Blaylock dropped, eyes away from the spraying glass. The first man in tripped on the sill, tangled in the curtains, and brought them all down. He screamed, writhing in a burning straightjacket. Two other men followed him in, jumping over the body. Blaylock twisted, grabbed the shotgun. One of the goons had time to squeeze off a shot. Wood exploded beside Blaylock's cheek. She let loose with both barrels. A hail of .33 caliber pellets shredded the men, knocked their bodies back outside.

Blaylock scrambled to her feet, grabbing SIG and gym bag. She ran from the room and into the screaming crowd. Those who saw her gave her terrified berth. Most, single-minded on escaping explosions and fire, didn't notice. At the entrance, the other door guard, gun drawn, was trying to swim against the current. Blaylock flowed towards him. He saw her when they were a yard apart. She shot him point-blank. The bullet thunked into the doorway as it exited his back.

Screams followed her into the grounds. She moved off the drive, into the isolation of shadows. She hit the eight-foot wall that surrounded Petraglia's property, followed it until she found an oak whose branches reached over the top. She pulled off the balaclava and watched the mansion. She didn't leave until the fire was strong and fierce and looking like an old friend.

4

Knocking on the bedroom door. Persistent, peremptory as a prison-guard command. Salvatore Coscarelli struggled up from sleep. Gina, grumbling, shoved his shoulder. "I know, I know," he muttered. He bleared at the clock radio. Just after five. And the pounding went on. Bang bang bang, no deference at all. Fast, too, bangbangbang, the speed of panic. "All right!" he shouted. "What is it?" The door opened. Dickie "Big Inches" Polacco and Matt Guidabondi, underboss and consigliere, stood in the doorway. "What?" Coscarelli repeated. When they told him, he said, "Dunn. Bring him here."

The car was an aging Honda Civic. Blaylock had picked it up, cash, when she arrived in New York. The car made noises when she drove, but none of them sounded lethal. It did the job. It was ordinary, it was inconspicuous, it was good for surveillance. She was parked across the street and a block down from Coscarelli's two-story home. She'd come straight here from Petraglia's. She wanted to see what the reaction was. And she needed to calm down. The thrill-high of combat was fading, and the guilt was coming back. The guilt that had failed her.

The guilt that she needed to feel *before*, not after, she did the wrong thing. The bad moment with Julia was the problem. What would she have done if Julia had pulled back the curtain? The problem, the cancer in her chest, was that she didn't *know*. She knew what she should have done. If Julia had seen her, and recognized her, then that was just too bad. It was part of the risk of war, and Blaylock, blackened by murder, would be the one to take the cost, not Julia. Blaylock saw precious few noncombatants, but those people did exist, and she *must not touch them*. What the hell had she been thinking? She didn't know. Had she, even if only for the tiniest moment, considered taking Julia out? She wasn't sure. Her gut roiled.

All the lights in the house went on around dawn. At six, an '85 Lincoln, loud and dirty, pulled up. Blaylock raised binoculars. Two gorillas emerged, and escorted a third man to the house. Blaylock watched the man carefully, memorizing his features. Tall, slim, early fifties, large glasses two years out of style, pinched face, permafrown. Who are you? Blaylock wondered. Bad shit for the Coscarellis goes down, and you are the first person to show up. Who are you?

Lawrence Dunn stood in Salvatore Coscarelli's living room. The don sat in an armchair. The chair had been reupholstered, but so long ago that surgery was required again. The seat and back sagged, soft and deep, and Coscarelli's small frame disappeared into a plush cave. Dunn thought of a troll in his lair.

"Thank you for making time to see me, Mr. Dunn," Coscarelli began, as if choice had been involved. "Coffee?" His voice was level, monotone, cold. The word somehow was a threat, not an offer. When Dunn shook his head, Coscarelli asked, "How's your family?"

You vicious old bastard. "They're fine, thank you." You evil, wrinkled lizard. You cold-hearted, cold-blooded, slime-dripping piece of—

"That's good. That's good. A family's an important thing. You with me, Mr. Dunn? Good. My family's important, too. We look out for our families. That's the kind of men we are."

Where are you going? Dunn wondered. "Have I done something wrong?" he asked.

Coscarelli shook his head. "Somebody else did. Somebody else hurt my family. You'll hear about it. But this is what I want you to hear from me. This somebody is going to be hurt back. I take care of my family. I say this, and you listen. And our thing, this thing we have, you and me, it doesn't change."

"I understand." Something big had gone down, and Coscarelli didn't want him running.

Coscarelli smiled. "Just so you're not worried."

Just so I'm not hoping, you mean. Just so I don't think I can be free of you.

"You take care of my family," Coscarelli croaked, "and I take care of yours."

Blaylock followed the car. The two gorillas were sitting in front, the frightened man in the back. She stayed several car lengths back. Sometimes this meant hanging back on the wrong side of a red light, letting them gain as much as a block's lead. But the traffic was so much sludge, and she had no trouble keeping the Lincoln in sight. They led her to Riverside Drive, and pulled up in front of the

450s. Dropping the cargo home? Blaylock wondered. If so, more interesting still. The quiet street, the restrained elegance of the tree-lined walk to Grant's Tomb, the stone respectability of the buildings and their art deco mosaics, all this spoke of taste and money. And then there was the proximity to Columbia. The Mob didn't compute here. *I need to know who you are*, Blaylock thought. She found a parking spot a third of the way down the block. She left her car and walked back towards the Lincoln. The gorillas were speaking to their passenger. He was nodding. They finished with him when Blaylock was twenty feet away. The man stepped out of the car. He walked into the recessed entranceway to 452. Blaylock followed, her stride casual, brisk, and homeward-bound. She caught up just as the man unlocked the door. He jumped, eyes blinking like strobe lights, as she brushed past him.

"Thank you," she said, and gave him her best smile. She bounded up the stairs ahead of him, didn't give him time to wonder who she was. She heard his steps stop at the first landing. She stopped climbing and peered over the railing, saw which apartment he was letting himself into. She waited until he was inside, then walked softly down, checked the number on his door. Back outside then, to look at the intercom, to match a number with a name: Dunn. *Gotcha*, she thought. She walked away from the building, back onto the sidewalk. The gorillas were still in their Lincoln. Blaylock exchanged looks with them.

Linda rushed to the door as Dunn let himself in. Her face was garrote-taut. "Are you all right?"

"I'm fine." *In a pig's eye.* "The kids?" He wouldn't put

it past Coscarelli to toss in a little bonus terror for emphasis. So far, Angie and Jake had been left alone. They didn't even know their dad was doing a forced dance for the Mob. But could he see Coscarelli goons cruising by CUNY to kick up the fear? Yes, he could.

"I called Angie on her cell." Linda's laugh was a hair away from being a sob. "She couldn't figure out why Mom was calling for no reason at all."

Dunn sighed. "At least they're okay."

"What did he want?"

He shook his head. "It was just a friendly reminder of who's calling the shots. I don't know what the emergency was. I've been behaving myself."

"You haven't heard, then?"

He looked at her, wondering what loop his wife and Coscarelli were both in. She took his arm and led him to the living room. They sat down on the red felt couch, an overstuffed antique that was only half as uncomfortable as it looked. Linda picked up the remote, thumbed the mute off. The news was on. The words MOB WAR pulsed red and excited at the bottom left of the screen. The picture showed smoking wreckage, roaming police, and shapes under sheets. It took a moment for the commentary to break through Dunn's confused fog, but when it did, he heard the words *home of Daniel Petraglia*. "Oh no," he whispered. "That's why he wanted to speak to me. He's keeping his claws in, no matter what."

"'No matter what'?"

"If the Coscarellis go down, so do we."

Linda twisted the remote in her hands. Her nails had been gnawed ragged. "God*damn* it. Why are you so important to them?"

"I don't know." He knew how he'd fallen, though. He

knew that very well. Stupid. He was so stupid. He was an educated man. He was well read. He knew what hubris was. Thirty years ago, as an undergraduate, hadn't he written a fine paper on *Oedipus Rex*? He surely had. But literature didn't apply to real people. Especially not to him. Most especially not because he had chosen the pragmatic path of the dismal science, and had become an economist. The lessons of Greek drama didn't kick in until too late, with the will-to-suicide self-loathing of hindsight. Two years ago he was at a conference in Las Vegas. He hit the casinos for the first time, and liked them. They tickled his pride. An economist should be able to figure out a system. His profession required him to deal with the irrational voodoo of the market, after all, and point the way to safe talismans.

He didn't find his system. He found debt instead. He kept going, though, the drug worse than intravenous. Roulette, slots, VLTs, horses, sports, the symptoms multiplied. The only skill he developed was maintaining appearances. He kept the disease secret. So Linda wouldn't notice sudden big holes in their joint account, he started to borrow. A lot. From untraceable sources. The game played out, the roulette wheel spun, and did Dunn ever, for an honest moment, believe that the ball wouldn't drop into the zero, that the House wouldn't cash in? No. But he lied to himself a lot, too. The House cashed in ten months ago. Dunn saw the last of his chips swept away, saw the meaning of the debt click over from dangerous to deadly, and told Linda the truth. By then, it was too late. By then, he was only hours away from his first meeting with Salvatore Coscarelli.

The meeting was both emphatic and confusing. The Coscarellis had been watching him, Dunn was told. They liked him. They had plans for him. And if he didn't want his debt payment to mean more pain and death than his soul could endure, then he would submit to the plans. *You listening to us, Larry?* So he was good. And life, which hadn't been bad, suddenly turned amazing. His media profile soared. He was appointed Visiting Scholar at Columbia. The fear was his cancer-friend, but the demands he expected never materialized. He thought the Mob would want him to curtail his opinion pieces, or at least change their slant. They didn't. Go for it, they said. Give it to the bastards, they said. Hell, they said, stick it to us. It was as if the world's most heavily armed support group was forcing him to stick to the straight and narrow. The set-up made no sense. And now this.

"Do they want you to stay put?" Linda asked.

Dunn grunted. "The last thing he told me was to do a good job in Washington."

His plane was leaving at five. Dunn started packing. He was slow, distracted by the Petraglia frenzy on the tube. A little after two, he noticed Linda was standing at the window, face stricken. "What is it?" he asked.

"They didn't leave."

He joined her, looked down. The Lincoln was still parked outside the building.

"What do they want?" Linda pleaded.

"Maybe they're going to escort me to the airport."

"That's great. My husband gets full limo service from the Mafia. I guess you've really arrived."

"Don't..."

"Damn you for doing this to our lives." She stalked away from him.

At three it was time to go. The car was still there. Dunn picked up his briefcase and duffel bag. He looked at Linda. She wasn't angry now. "What if they're waiting for you to leave? And for the kids to come home?"

"They aren't. Why would they?"

"Why wouldn't they? Nothing these people do with us makes any sense."

Too right. He swallowed, and his throat hurt. "They're here for me. You'll see."

"And if they're not?"

"Come down with me. We'll ask them."

"What am I supposed to do if things go bad? Run?"

"Better than being trapped up here."

They went downstairs. Linda lagged two steps behind. Dunn tried to look confident. The car's driver's side window was rolled down. Dunn approached. "You're waiting for—" he began. He stopped. He dropped his bags. The two goons were slumped back in their seats. They had small holes in their foreheads. The back seat was a swamp of red and bone fragments.

Dunn was known to Google. There were even pictures, confirming identity. Blaylock scanned the titles of his articles, and realized why his name had sounded familiar. "You ever hear of Lawrence Dunn?" she called out.

From the kitchen, Flanagan answered, "Doesn't he write for *The Nation* a lot?"

"That's him. *Mother Jones* and TV, too. You have any idea why a left-wing, anti-globalization economist would be big-time important to the Mob?"

No answer. Instead, a grunt of disgust. "This money has blood on it."

"So?" Blaylock said, turning from the computer. She left the bedroom and joined Flanagan. He had the gym bag she'd taken from Petraglia open on the tile floor and was counting the bills. He put a stained stack to one side. Blaylock touched the bag with a toe. "I don't think InSec's going to mind," she said.

"Are you going to be bringing in a lot of cash like this?"

"No. Not practical. But will that be enough for what I want?"

Flanagan stood up from his crouch, glanced at the shopping list on the counter. "Oh yeah. This is plenty."

"Is the LR account still active?" LR INC. had been the company name she'd used when she was purchasing weapons for her militia, hoisting InSec with its own top-of-the-line petards. She'd been a pretty good customer.

"Yeah. You made yourself look so much like Colombian paramilitaries that nobody ever sniffed your way, as far as I know."

"Good. So you'll get me the stuff?" When he nodded, she asked, "Are you okay with this?"

"I'll let you know."

Chapel hated parties. Pains in the ass to organize, bigger pains yet to attend. Two-faced pleasantries, hail-fellow backslaps, have-you-heard gossip trivialities. Real intelligence being lost in a flood of useless white-noise data. He wasn't good at networking. Never had been. Oh, he knew enough not to call an asshole by its name when confronted with the stink. But he couldn't kiss. His civility turned into absolute-zero brittleness. He didn't fool anybody. That had rarely been a problem, though. In the field, he had called shots, and he had taken them. The two-steps he left to those who were good at them. It was often the only thing they were good at. No avoiding this party, though. This was an upper stratosphere event, and part of the price to pay for the gift of being DD Operations. Sam Reed had asked him to attend. You don't say no to the President. Anyway, Chapel had never known Reed's reasons to be trivial.

The shindig was being held in a Georgetown mansion, a palace so big it boasted a full-size ballroom with all the Gilded Age trimmings. At one end of the room, a drum-tight big band was set up on a raised stage. The musicians swung through classic Goodman, Ellington, and Basie, and they were good; half the guests were dancing instead of networking. The evening called itself a fundraiser, and at first Chapel had assumed the funds were for Reed's party. It took him a while to notice the names on the donation boxes. Greenpeace? Amnesty International? The Christic Institute? The Fair Trade Council? If he hadn't seen the look of disgust on one man's face as he slipped a check into the FTC's war chest, Chapel would have thought he was in the wrong place. He sipped his Scotch and scanned the crowd. He recognized most of the faces, and not one of them belonged at an event with this sort of political slant. He moved through the room, happy in his anonymity. No one tried to corner him in a conversation. He knew them, but they didn't know him. He didn't register *player* for the status warriors, so he wasn't useful. They could useful to him, though, and he pulled in snippets of conversation, a basking shark gathering plankton. The consensus: swell party, shitty causes.

Around eleven he finally saw Reed. The President entered the ballroom in the company of another man. Reed saw Chapel and gestured him over. Chapel made his way to their corner, trying to place the other man, wondering why his face was sending up warning flags of deep, deep red. The recognition click happened just as he reached them.

"Joe," Reed said. "Glad you're here." Reed's voice and his face were at odds with each other. The voice was promise—smooth, seduction-deep, and fortress-firm. If radio had still ruled, Reed would never have played second fiddle to Walter Campbell's TV slickness. But his face was an obstacle. It was narrow, it had started sagging early, it had been pockmarked permanently by acne, and far too much of it showed under hair that looked like a receding oil slick. Reed had taken his hits in Vietnam, and his left eye was glass. The camera did not love him, and the feeling was mutual. "I'd like you to meet our host," the President continued, gesturing to the other man.

"Stepan Sherbina," Chapel said. He shook hands, but he wasn't happy about it. At least this explained all the bleeding-heart causes. Sherbina's wife's pet projects. The FTC was almost completely bankrolled by her.

"Impressive." Sherbina was smiling, amused.

"If he didn't know, he wouldn't be doing his job," said Reed.

"Good to know that we're all professionals here."

Chapel frowned, turned to Reed. "Mr. President," he began, "I know this is all leading somewhere, but..."

Sherbina stepped in. "The President and I thought you and I should meet. To avoid misunderstandings later." His eyes looked behind Chapel. "Will you excuse me a moment?"

Chapel waited for Sherbina to be out of earshot. That gave him a chance to hold his temper in check. He felt insubordination bubbling up, and he would not have it.

Not in Joe Chapel. "Mr. President, do you know who that man is? He's head of the largest Russian crime syndicate going, and—"

Reed cut him off. "He's also head of Kornukopia, which is Russia's largest corporation. They're both businesses, Joe."

"They're the same business."

"He's a man with a vision. One which we should support, because I think it will benefit America."

"A Russian."

"Arthur Pembroke was an American. Look where that led Walter."

Chapel held up his hands. "I mean no disrespect, but the logic—"

And Sherbina was back. He had Irina Zelkova with him, and a man Chapel barely recognized as Lawrence Dunn. The drawn, haggard face looked a whole war away from the authoritative headshot that topped his columns. Sherbina did the introductions. "Keep your eye on this man," he said, pointing to Dunn. "I hear astonishing and terrific things about him."

"I'll agree with the first part," Chapel spat, his frustration breaking through. When Dunn looked confused, Chapel spelled it out. "You do realize that more than a few intelligent people view you as a traitor? That I wouldn't be out of line seeing a huge security risk in your standing so close to the President?"

"I'm sorry," Dunn said. His tone was civil, but ready for a fight. "I don't under—"

"You don't? And I thought you were smart. You sure sounded pretty smart after the G8 fire. You had plenty of opinions after that, and none of them involved tears."

Silence for a moment. The other three were scrambling

to catch up with the collapse of the niceties and failing. The band started playing "Tonight We Love." Dunn traded in civility for contempt. "I never condoned what happened." He spoke with exaggerated, withering patience.

"You never condemned it, either. But you did say a lot about how we brought it on ourselves. And you haven't been much of a help lately. All this anti-globalization bullshit. Haven't you noticed there's an economic and political crisis going on? Christ, you self-hating liberals make me sick."

"Disagreeing with the prevailing wisdom doesn't make me any less of an American."

"Oh, spare me. There's a time and a place, you know, a time and a place." Chapel turned and stormed off. All right, he'd come to the party, he was thigh-deep in shit and sinking, and if he didn't leave now he'd drown.

Reed caught up to him as he was stepping out the front door. "Just a minute, Joe."

Chapel sighed. "I'm sorry, Mr. President."

"Don't be. You know I agree with you." Reed shrugged, grimaced. "But like you said, there's a time and a place. And I have to watch mine always. So good for you. But listen. When I was comparing Pembroke to Sherbina earlier, I was just trying to point out the difference. Pembroke was insane. Sherbina is not. He isn't going to do anything that would jeopardize the proper functioning of international markets. In fact, I think he's going to be a help to the global economy. A big help."

"How?"

"Come with me." Reed started down the porch steps. The Secret Service agents, poised on the steps, on the drive, in the grounds, moved. The President's limo pulled up before Reed set foot on gravel. Reed turned to one of the agents as he climbed into the car's spacious rear. "Find Ms Taber, will you?" he asked. The agent nodded and disappeared back into the mansion. Reed asked the driver to wait beside the car for a minute. He sat back and offered Chapel the seat opposite. When Chapel shut the door, Reed began to talk. He explained Sherbina's usefulness. He outlined a program of radical risk and enormous potential. He took Chapel's breath away. When he had finished, Reed asked, "Well?"

Chapel admired the courage. He feared the risk. "If even a single thing goes wrong, the optics would be ..." Words failed. The disaster would be that big.

"I know." Reed didn't sound worried. His glass eye looked like it wanted to wink.

An agent tapped on the window. Reed smiled and opened the door to let a woman in. "Joe Chapel," Reed said, "Charlotte Taber."

Chapel shook hands with the Undersecretary of State for Public Diplomacy. She was also CEO of Taber & Hackbarth, a PR firm big enough to rate its own building in midtown Manhattan. Taber was in her early fifties, and swathed in a diaphanous scarf and silked animal prints. Her perfume was just a bit too strong for the interior of the limo. Her hair was a Margaret Thatcher mushroom cloud. She should have been ridiculous. She wasn't. She wore her camp like a trademark. She was the consciousness of irony and image made flesh. Reed had appointed her shortly after the Ember Lake fire. Her orchestration of domestic ad campaigns and international public appearances by administration figures had done a lot to smother the flames of the crisis. She had fused messages of strength at home with restraint and sensitivity abroad.

Her goal was to transform a terror attack that had taken place in a foreign nation and wiped out the leaders of *all* the major industrial powers into a specifically American tragedy. She'd come very close to achieving that goal. "I'm pleased to meet you," Chapel told her. "You do good work." Taber answered with a smile that was demure, but backed up with the knowledge of her clout.

Reed said, "You're my team. You help make the good things happen, and Charlotte will deal with the contingencies. The bad things will be good, and the good things will be great."

"Fine," Chapel agreed. The project was a strong one. But. "I still don't trust Sherbina."

"That's why I want *you* to work with him." Reed leaned forward. "Guard our interests, Joe. Guard them well." His lids lowered, concealing his eyes as he gave Chapel carte blanche. "Do what you need to do."

5

November. Night. The first real bone-chill of the year hitting New York. The rain came down, and it bit hard. Blaylock stood at the window of her Clinton safe house, a room paid for long-term in a crumbling SRO. She watched the rain, and waited to make the right choice. Behind her, the equipment paid for with Petraglia's money also waited. It was game if she was. She bit her lip.

Blood and fire.

She'd been at Flanagan's earlier in the evening. They had dinner. He was dressed up. He cooked a nice pork tenderloin, even put candles on the table. They tried to talk about something other than the blood and fire. They tried on the role of the ordinary couple. They tried to close the gap. But between them, the river of blood and fire flowed. The conversation kept dying. Blaylock would panic, flailing around for a new subject, another stab at talking and laughing, but her mind kept going blank, and the whole evening was nothing more than a collection of so many motions gone through.

Blood and fire. All I have to offer. So she offered him her gifts: a Colt .38 for the basics, and a shotgun. The shotgun was a Saiga 12-gauge. "What am I supposed to do with these?" Flanagan asked.

"I don't want you unprotected."

"I don't know how to use a gun!"

She showed him how to load, unload. He didn't want to touch the weapons. She made him hold the shotgun. "This is idiot-proof," she said. "It's self-loading. Even you could fire five rounds without thinking. Aiming isn't an issue. For close range, you just need to point it in the general direction of the target." She handed him boxes of different ammo. Flanagan said nothing, and hid the guns away as soon as she finished the lesson.

Keep me human, Mike.

And so he tried. He asked, "Jen, what the hell is this war about? When you were after Pembroke, I knew. And that was my war, too. But now . . . I mean, this has to be about more than whacking wise guys. Isn't it?"

"I think it is."

"You think."

"There are all these threads linking the Mob to the whole globalization issue. I can't quite untangle them yet."

"And wiping out the Coscarelli crime family is going to fix that?"

"There's a plan to all this."

Flanagan looked skeptical. "It's coincidental, then, that this plan seems to involve killing as many people as possible?"

Was it? She had turned cold, telling him that she did what was necessary and refusing to say more. Now she looked out the window, at the unquestioned and relentless rain, and wondered if she should have told him what she really believed. *I do this so you won't have to. Somebody has to become a monster to wrestle with the other monsters, and win. I'm becoming dirty for you.*

And then she thought, Really? Do you really buy that Christ-with-a-Gun scenario? Do you so love the world that you will kill for its sins? Come on. There was another possibility. It was a statistic that curled at the back of her mind. There was that two percent of soldiers for whom aggression and killing were natural. The two percent who knew empathy, but not remorse. The two percent for whom combat was even more than a vocation, more than a calling. The two percent who did fifty percent of the killing on the field. She knew she was a member of that club. The problem was, she was also rogue, her safety catch broken and lost. The soldier was trained to kill, to overcome the resistance to that act, but trained to kill *on command*. Never at any other time. She had taken herself out of the chain of command years ago. So what did that make her?

There was that other segment of the population, wasn't there? The segment that felt no empathy at all. You one of them, Jen? You that dangerous?

No.

No. The guilt was still there, wasn't it? The guilt that she had clung to, life preserver, in the aftermath of the Ember Lake slaughter. It was that guilt that had stepped in and twisted her guts with fear for Julia's safety. The guilt was still there, so the judgment was still there. She was no Pembroke.

Feeling better? Yes. She and Flanagan would bridge their gap, or they wouldn't, but at least he was still helping her, and she had work to do. She turned from the window and faced her equipment. She'd shaken the Coscarelli tree, but had gathered precious little fruit. Time to stop kidding around. Yesterday, she'd given two more small shakes. Now she was going to use the chainsaw.

The rain was just this side of freezing when Guidabondi pulled up to the Jersey City warehouse. Crap weather, crap time of night, crap job, crap mood. Everything crap these days, and here he was, weathervane in a shitstorm, spinning three-sixty and then some at the whim of Salvatore Coscarelli's panic. The man said run here, and he did. The man said run there, and he did that, too. Dickie Polacco was being run just as ragged. Coscarelli wanted top muscle and eyes everywhere. Couldn't be done. They needed to centralize. Concentrate their defenses for the duration of the war. Circle the wagons. At least Coscarelli was finally listening to reason.

Not that Guidabondi blamed Coscarelli for freaking. He was as wired-ass worried as the boss. They'd had a couple of weeks with no hits, and then bang, two yesterday. A soldier in Washington Heights, throat slit in his car. Then another, catching a double-tap to the head as he was standing outside his Bedford-Stuy walk-up. Both of the men were low end, but they were still made, still full-fledged Coscarelli family members. Guidabondi could almost put the kills down to coincidence, but the connection was there. Hell, each of these guys had had his picture in the papers. They were *known* Coscarellis. That was supposed to count for something. Maybe it did, but not for the right things anymore. The worst part of the war was not knowing who the enemy was. Guidabondi and Coscarelli had worked the phones and called the favors, but none of the other families admitted to so much as a grudge. The peace was still holding, as far as they were concerned. To Guidabondi, some of them sounded scared, as if they were expecting to be next on the chopping block. So what the hell, what the hell, *what the hell?* Pop pop pop and no demands? No warnings? What kind of war is that?

Coscarelli was convinced it was the Russians being greedy, wanting Dunn for themselves. Guidabondi didn't buy it. Why would they go about grabbing Dunn in so roundabout and random a way? No. Something else and someone else.

He was parked barely twenty feet from the entrance to the warehouse, but the rain nailed him good and proper even over that distance. Ice claws snagged in under his coat collar, dragged chills out of his spine. He fumbled with the key to the fire exit to the right of the loading door. The wind hit him with a gust. He winced, then had the key in.

In the corner of his eye, a shadow, a deeper dark, moving. He turned his head. Nothing. He looked down the street. Typical three a.m. industrial park desolation. Warehouses a go-go on both sides, cars and trucks parked and dreaming. The hiss of the rain muffled the occasional big-metal bang that drifted in from the other warehouses. Guidabondi couldn't see any figures sitting in the parked vehicles, but visibility was a joke. He waited another minute, grew uncomfortable. Too many shadows.

Go inside. He turned the key, pushed the door open. His neck hairs prickled and he rushed in, shoulders hunched against a blow, against the terminal pain of a bullet. He threw himself around the doorway, back to the wall, out of the street's line of sight. The fire door, teasing him, closed slowly, letting shadows in. The floor of the warehouse was dark, lights out. There was a faint glow bleeding from the upper-level office on the other side of the building. Shadows everywhere, and right beside him. Guidabondi's imagination gave them life and knives. He fumbled on the wall, found the switch, flipped it. Boom: light, and the big empty of the loading docks. But still shadows, creeping in from stacked palettes ahead of him, and a hiding place behind every crate, around every stack. The warehouse was half full, the merchandise ranging from hijacked electronics to small arms to the full drug spectrum, one-stop shopping. To Guidabondi's right was the furnace room. Beside it, stairs led to a metal catwalk that ran the perimeter of the warehouse. The office perched above the furnace room, fifteen feet up, its waist-to-ceiling windows on two walls giving a full view of the space. Guidabondi trotted for the stairs.

Jerry McKersie was in the office. His computer screen was jumping with spreadsheets. Bobby "D-Cup" Busnelli was sprawled on a worn couch, gut spilling over belt, feet on coffee table. He was flipping through an old issue of *Screw*. His Colt was on a cushion beside him.

From the doorway, Guidabondi demanded, "Why the hell were the lights off?"

McKersie turned in his chair. The accountant looked grumpy, pissed at being up during the limbo hours. His tie was loose, and his suit had been up and at it for too long a day. He said, "The shipment's not due for another two hours. Why waste—"

Guidabondi cut him off. "The shipment's coming in an hour. We're screwing with timing to throw off any ambush." He turned to Busnelli. "And you, numbnuts, you're supposed to be security. Jerk off on your own time."

Busnelli's eyes widened. Guidabondi felt his collar yanked back. He stumbled. Someone whirled him around. A shadow slammed a metallic blur against his cheekbone. His vision shattered into fractal pain. He was shoved hard to his left. The railing of the catwalk hit his waist, and he went over. He saw the floor rush up. His mind wondered why he didn't have time to scream. He hit with his arms stretched out. Crunching.

The fat boy on the couch was doing an all-thumbs thing with his gun. Blaylock nine-millimetered him in the head. She turned her SIG to the target gifted her by patience, research, and surveillance. Jerry McKersie, the man with the passwords. He had his hands up. High. He looked scared, but his eyes were sharp. He was still thinking. Not what she wanted. With her free hand, she unzipped her jacket, pulled out a black cloth bundle. She unrolled it on the coffee table. Laid out now and glinting silver: scalpel, clamps, syringe, bone saw. She waited for McKersie to look into her eyes. She let him see what was there. The crotch of his pants stained dark. Blaylock said, "Understand?" and McKersie nodded.

The process took a good half-hour. Blaylock, eye on the clock, held the gun on McKersie and kept him honest, but he wasn't stalling. Coscarelli had a lot of accounts. "Okay," McKersie said when he had the digital vaults cracked wide open.

"Transfer to here," Blaylock said, and gave him the number of a Cayman Islands account. She would move the funds herself later.

"How much?"

"All of it."

McKersie's fingers froze over the keyboard. Enormity was making him think again. "They'll . . ."

Blaylock picked up the scalpel. She held the flat of the blade against the back of his neck. Let him feel the smooth cold. "They'll what? Do worse than me?"

"If you kill me, you don't get—"

She turned the scalpel, tickled his flesh with the edge. "You're right. But you know, the fact that I can't let you die should be scaring you." She pricked, drew a trickle of blood. "Last chance. Do it now, or I won't ask you again for an hour." She began to twist the blade.

McKersie believed. He made the transfer. Blaylock's war chest went mass destruction. Then the windows blew in.

Blaylock hit the floor, glass and bullets whistling lover-close. Something whined and ripped the sleeve of her jacket as she went down. McKersie jumped up from behind his smoking monitor and yelled, *"Wait!"* Bullets took off the top of his head. Blaylock rolled to the exterior wall, sat up. She felt the combat thrill build even as the operation went diarrhetic on her. No way this was the shipment's escort. She'd given herself a massive margin. Somebody must have called in troops. And me not even dressed, she thought. Her surprise package wasn't close to ready. Her position was boxed. She only had twelve shots in the P-228 left, and one spare clip. Full-auto bursts were seeking her out. She grinned.

The enemy was firing from the ground floor, so the angle of the shots was steep. There was a reload pause. Blaylock glanced out the office door. No one coming up yet. She thought of the only exits, now blocked by gunmen. She eyed the hundred-mile length of the catwalk, the towers of crates. Adrenaline was holy fire. She ran from the office, steam locomotive down the catwalk. She had a three-second lead before the artillery opened up again. Metal sparked and sang ricochets. She fired behind and down without looking. She was a third of the way down the length of the warehouse. Bullets hit in a concentrated burst just ahead, then moved her way. Someone had her measure and she was going to run right into the walking fire. She looked left, saw the chance she wanted. She turned hard and jumped, sailed over the railing, landed on the top crate. A second of silence as the shooters changed their aim. She dropped down behind the crate, falling into the shadows of the aisles. She had some moments of invisibility now, but the space around the exit was wide open. Sooner or later, she would have to break cover.

"Kill the bitch!" she heard. *"Get in there and fucking kill her!"* The stupid move she was hoping for. She ran to the rear of the warehouse, cut across, still moving left, and started back down the next-to-last aisle. The stacks were uneven, and there wasn't a clear line of sight to the exit. Good. She moved quietly, listening for footsteps coming her way. She heard shouts and the occasional shot coming from other aisles. She flowed with the shadows until she saw the end of cover coming up. She was looking at a fifty-foot run over a killing floor to the open loading door. Three men were standing guard, cradling Uzis. A fourth, she recognized as Dickie Polacco. He was crouched beside Guidabondi, that son of a bitch still alive and resting against the warehouse wall. His left arm had weird angles. His right hand still held a cellphone.

Running behind her. Blaylock whirled and fired. It took her three shots to find her aim and drop the man. She threw herself to the ground at the same time, ducking the fire from behind. The crates over her head blew apart. Microchips rained down. Staying flat, Blaylock turned herself around. Chaos in the air, a maelstrom of wood and lead and excelsior. The firing was wide, wild, sweeping. She sniffed panic in the enemy. She took her time, aimed, two-handed. "Discipline, dipshits," she muttered. Three shots, three kills. Polacco ran. Guidabondi screamed at him. Blaylock broke cover.

She flew across the loading bay. Guidabondi looked at her and screamed again, and for a second the warehouse had only two sounds, his shrieks and the hollow *clops* of her footsteps. Halfway to the door. She jerked right. A bullet hummed by on her left. She jerked again. Two thirds there. Bullets on both sides now. She ran straight, loving speed, and then there was rain on her face and darkness all around. Her Civic was parked a block down. The farther she ran, the more the bullets were random, stray threats she didn't take seriously. She jumped into her car, reached down for the metal case that sat on the floor in front of the passenger seat. Headlights flashed on by the warehouse. Shit. Out of time. She gave up on the case, started the engine, and pulled out, tires shrieking in the agony of her one-eighty. She gunned the accelerator. In the rear-view mirror, she saw two SUVs give chase.

6

"Shut up!" Polacco screamed at Guidabondi. "Shut up shut up *shut up!* She's gone!" He looked at the men standing by the SUVs, headlights aimed at the Civic. He yelled some more: "Get her! Go, you dumb whores, go!" Two teams, two men each, piled into the Explorers and took off. Kill her, Polacco thought. Kill her good, and then kill her again. He lowered the loading door, then stood still, taking in the carnage. "Holy sweet mother," he muttered. He'd arrived with ten men, more than enough, he'd thought, to take care of the single attacker Guidabondi had called in. Four were dead. Then there was Busnelli, lying in the office like a gutted whale. And McKersie, shit-for-brains standing up in the line of fire. Christ, what a mess. They were only four in the warehouse now: him, Guidabondi, two trigger-men. Implications hit. They were short-handed, sitting ducks. Maybe the broad was a diversion? He looked at the bodies. *Diversion?* "You," he pointed at Vic Belardo. "Call this in. Get everybody here."

"Everybod—"

"Goddamn right, everybody. This is goddamn World War Three. Goddamn do it!" He turned away, shaking his head. "Sal was right. Goddamn Russians. Shoulda known we couldn't trust 'em."

Guidabondi was calming down, starting to think again. "We don't know this was the Russians." He was rocking back and forth, right hand hovering over, but not touching, his shattered arm. His face looked like he'd headbutted a Mack truck.

"Who the hell else? The Danes?" Polacco swept his arm, taking in the field of battle. "Who do you think is crazy enough to do shit like this?" He lowered his voice. "This isn't just a takeover of Dunn. They're trying to wipe us out."

"Makes no sense," Guidabondi said. "Makes no sense. This isn't business. It's madness."

"So what? It's still happening. Screw 'em. This shit stops now. They want a show of force, I'll goddamn show 'em force."

They started shooting at the first turn. Blaylock had a two-block lead. She took a right, and for a second she was on a nice diagonal for the shooters in the passenger seat. Hitting a moving target is hard enough. When you're moving, too, the luck factor goes exponential. The shooters opened up full-auto, bystanders be damned. The bullets slammed into the Civic. Luck laughed and played a harsh game. The passenger windows took hits, blew in with a sharp bang. The bullets passed through. Blaylock felt the hair on the top of her head move in the slipstream of the near miss. Something blurred in front of her eyes. Glass slapped against the side of her face, stinging and cutting. Then the rear side windows were hit, and then the shooters lost their angle.

Wind and rain whipped in through the shattered windows. One side of her face was warm with blood. Blaylock took a sudden left, gaining distance with the Civic's greater maneuverability. The streets were close to deserted at four in the morning. Blaylock held the accelerator down, never thought of the brake. She did better than eighty through the urban sprawl. The SUVs kept pace. Every bit of distance she gained on a turn, she more than lost on the straightaways. They were going to catch her. She needed the metal case. She needed just a few seconds without oncoming or side traffic to think about. She needed a clear road. Instead, she had traffic. She came up behind a trundling delivery van. She shifted lanes, overtaking in fury, and there were headlights in her face, big and bright and oh-shit close. No brakes, full accelerator, and she hauled right, inches from the front of the van. It swerved and banged against the sidewalk. The other car was a blur as it went past, its horn outraged Doppler. Blaylock swore, fierce. Then she saw the signposts for the Pulaski Skyway. Jackpot.

She hit the Pulaski where it began. She came up the US 1 & 9 ramp. There was no acceleration lane to merge with NJ 139. She blew past the stop sign, too fast to register the mistake. She cut off a tractor trailer. His bumper touched hers. At this speed, that was enough to slew the rear of the car out of control. The steering wheel jumped from her hands. The car spun. The air roared with the truck's brakes. The night turned into a smear of light and dark, a flipflipflip snapshot collection of concrete and looming metal. Blaylock grabbed the wheel back, fought it. She saw the breadth of the trailer come at her, God's baseball bat. She tromped the accelerator, turned the wheel hard into the spin. The trailer clipped her, shoved her against the low concrete divider. Metal screamed. Her right headlight went out as the hood buckled. But the car straightened. She pulled away. She looked in the mirror, saw the truck come to a shrieking halt, a diagonal across both lanes. Tickticktick of seconds, piling up in her favor.

She looked ahead. The road was clear. She had her time. She reached down, yanked at the case. It resisted, catching on the seat and glove compartment. "Come on, you stupid son of a bitch." She jerked. The case came free. She put it on the seat beside her, fumbled with the catches, and drove one-handed as she pushed the accelerator down all the way. Check the mirror. Still nothing. Blaylock released the catches, flipped open the case's lid. A bridge took her over a rail line. She kept half an eye on the mirror. She crossed a second rail line, and here they came, reflected glares of side-by-side murder. The SUVs raced each other, gaining hard, their dinosaur strength unleashed on the straight lines of the Skyway.

Muzzle flashes, *pingcrackwhizz*. Frozen ripples and stars appeared in the windshield. Her view distorted and she winced as the bullets, repelled by the nylon-reinforced glass, banged through the car's interior. A round grazed her right earlobe. It burned. Her rear-view mirror shattered, its shards savage. She glanced at her side mirror in time to see it shot away. Another burst. Her dashboard spat plastic at her.

The Hackensack River bridge came up, a watery blur. There were no high beams heading her way, no cars that she was about to overtake. Now, she thought. She moved to the center, straddling the lanes, inviting a pincer attack. She reached into the case, pulled out an incendiary grenade. She removed the pin with her teeth, then placed the grenade in her left hand. Driving max speed, feeling every bump in the pavement as an invitation to a rollover, steering with the back of her hand while she held the grenade's handle down: she loved it. She grabbed a second grenade, pulled its pin. Death in each hand now. She twisted around to check rear. The SUVs had split, were grazing divider and bridge curb. There was just enough space between them for the Explorers to come up on either side of her. They closed. She watched for less then a second, war machine gauging distance.

Her situational awareness was explosive, and there was more. She felt every element, every variable, had the moves to supernova the sun if she wanted. And more, everything everything *everything* combining into a now-or-never moment. Blaylock felt the orgasm euphoria of art.

She released the grenade handles. (One Mississippi.) She slammed on the brakes. (Two Mississippi.) The SUVs closed with eye-blink speed. (Three Mississippi.) She let go of the steering wheel and threw the grenades out the windows (four Mississippi), and when she struck, she yelled, "*Hah*," an inarticulate joyburst yanked from her by the beauty of art and war. She dropped behind the Explorers as the grenades bounced on their hoods. (Five—) The grenades exploded. Day bloomed. Thermate mixture became molten iron. The Explorers drove into 4000 degrees Fahrenheit and went bronco wild, collided, flipped. One smashed itself over the divider. It slid, crumpled roof first, down the northbound lanes, slow-motion meteor. The other somersaulted against the bridge girders, shedding metal and flame. It rammed itself between steel and stuck, suspended and slaughtered over the Hackensack River. Blaylock shielded her eyes. She picked glass from her face as she watched the burn.

The surprise truck was still where she'd left it, a block down and around the corner from the Coscarelli warehouse. It had belonged to the Bedford-Stuy soldier, and was what had clinched him as a target. Blaylock stepped out of the Civic. She was bone-soaked. Her clothes clung to her like a clammy fist. Her fingers were numb, but she made them work. They had to, or the surprise would kill her. She pulled the tarp off the truck's box, jumped on board, and finished the wiring. She couldn't feel her movements, but she could see them. She took each step slowly, making sure her gestures followed what her eyes commanded. The job took her half an hour. While she worked, she listened to trucks rumble past the intersection, the shipment coming in. The unloading must have gone panic-fast. The trucks were gone and the street was quiet again by the time Blaylock was happy with the wiring. When she was done, she opened the door to the cab, climbed in. On the seat beside her were a cinder block, a new C7 to replace the old assault rifle she'd had to abandon at Ember Lake, and a yard-long metal tube. She started the truck up.

The approach to the warehouse was crowded with cars. They lined both sides of the street. Two were parked in the middle, creating an obstacle course. Blaylock drove slowly. She watched the roof of the warehouse. She was past the first car when the shooting started. She threw open the door and jumped out. She ran across the street, firing at the roof but not aiming, more concerned with drawing fire away from the truck. Bullets chipped at the street, following her. Someone opened up with something big. She was just reaching the curb when a rifled slug slammed into a fire hydrant three feet from her. The hydrant burst. Water geysered, rammed Blaylock in the chest, and knocked her flat. A river pushed her down the street. A bullet hit the curb in front of her face, spraying concrete chips in her eyes. Blind, slipping in the water flow, she lunged forward, collided with a car door. She grunted, rolled beneath the car, rubbed her eyes clear. She crawled backwards out from under the car, then crouched behind the trunk. She raised her head just enough to see the warehouse roof, to see exactly where the flashes were coming from. Then she brought up the C7, used the scope, and raked the roof.

Polacco looked up. "Gone quiet," he said.

Guidabondi was lying on the couch in the office. He was gray pale with shock. "Think that's it?"

"We should be so lucky." Polacco half-hoped not. He had gathered the Coscarelli might. The warehouse was rafter-packed with firepower. The boys were keyed up. So was he. If he was going to fight a war, he wanted his chance to hit hard. He punched his walkie-talkie. "Joey? What's the word?" Static came back. He clattered down the stairs from the office. "Vic!" he called. "Go check on Joey."

Belardo opened his mouth to answer. He disappeared when the loading door exploded.

Blaylock dropped the LAW. The light anti-tank weapon was overkill on a warehouse entrance, but the job was thorough. She had moved the truck past the second blocking car, and now she ran to the back of the box, lowered the tailgate, and unreeled the land-line spool until she had a good lead of wire. The risks now: would the line survive her improvisation, would the surprise last long enough for her to connect the detonator? The fun of war. Back to the cabin now, put the truck in gear, aim the wheel, and shove the cinder block onto the accelerator. She ran for the spool, snatching it up before the truck stole all the slack as it charged the warehouse.

Polacco picked himself up, coughing. His ears were ringing. He could see men shouting and running, but couldn't hear them. He saw two fire out the door, then dive out of the way as a pickup truck burst in. It plowed through men, Polacco's army suddenly looking too densely packed. The loading bay was still cluttered with crates and forklifts. The truck slewed into a stack and stopped, its motor whining. There was no driver. Polacco ran to the truck, dimly noticing a wire running out from the back. He hopped onto the tailgate. The box was packed with metal rectangles. Each was a bit larger than his hand, and slightly convex. The faces read FRONT TOWARD ENEMY.

Blaylock detonated the Claymores. She heard the roar as each one let loose with 700 BBs in a fan-shaped embrace of multiplied death. The kill range of a single anti-personnel mine was fifty yards, and the danger reached three times that far. The interior of the warehouse turned into a shredding machine. The echoes of the blast faded, replaced by the *pingpingpingpingping* of ricocheting BBs. Blaylock heard some short, severed screams. They stopped. The sound of the rain came back, dominant, clearing the air of war. Blaylock put a fresh clip in her C7, and went to look for survivors.

7

Salvatore Coscarelli stared at the phone. He thought about calling again. All night he'd been checking in with Polacco every fifteen minutes. Now, dawn, it was half an hour since Polacco had last answered. Since anybody at the warehouse had answered. The phone sat on an end table beside the armchair. It stared back at Coscarelli and dared him to call. He rubbed his hands together, felt sweat. He glanced at his two bodyguards. One was seated by the window, eyes on the street. The other was standing in the doorway to the entrance hall. He met Coscarelli's gaze, then looked away. Both men were death pale. The living room stank of fear.

Coscarelli felt a hand on his shoulder. Gina had come into the room and was standing beside the chair. Coscarelli patted her hand. "What's going to happen?" Gina whispered.

Coscarelli started to say, "Nothing." He started to say there was nothing to worry about. He started to lie. The habit was old, instinctual. But the lie was too big this time, and he was too frightened. He did say, "Don't be scared."

"Do we have to leave?" She knew, then, as well as he did, that war had come and destroyed them. There was iron in her tone, though. This was their home. It had been all their married life. She would not leave. She would fight back.

"No," Coscarelli answered. "I mean, you don't." At least the rules were still being respected, as far as he could tell. Civilians were still off limits. (And yet, he worried about the fire at Petraglia's. No civilian deaths there, but was that by design or just stupid luck?)

"You're going away?"

He needed neutral territory. "I gotta call a truce. And a meeting." That Russian bastard wasn't having the prizes handed to him that easily. He was cheating, and Coscarelli still had recourse to the umpires.

Blaylock found files in the BMW she took from outside the warehouse. She flipped through the papers. They were transaction records for the night's shipment. The car had belonged to Guidabondi, looked like. Whatever. It was a good replacement for her battle-shattered Civic. She turned onto Coscarelli's street and saw him and two bodyguards pile into a car. She followed them, annoyed. She'd wanted to collar Coscarelli, scare some knowledge out of him, not start yet another surveillance game. But the hand was dealt, and she played it out. The cards took her to JFK. She shadowed Coscarelli and his goons into the airport, watched from the crowd as he bought a ticket. The transaction took a few minutes. "Come on," she muttered. She wanted this over with. She was still dripping water. She wanted to change and she wanted to sleep. When he stepped away from the counter, she let him go. She went up to the ticket agent, muscling in front of the next customer. "Excuse me, sir," she said, silencing his objections with a look. She turned to the agent and flashed her press badge, too fast for it to be read. "FBI," she said. "I need to know the destination of the last ticket you sold."

Flanagan strolled through the Trinity churchyard. He was on his lunch hour. The rain had let up late morning, and the sun had broken through, giving the day one of the last kicks of warmth as winter closed in. Flanagan wasn't eating. He was remembering. This had been his regular lunch spot with Rebecca Harland, dead best friend, courtesy InSec. He came down here at least once each week. The gesture felt like an apology. He hadn't saved her. He hadn't saved her family. Or his own. He could save her memory, though. He turned his head, looking back toward the InSec building. He wondered if he should make a phone call. When he looked forward again, Blaylock was standing beside the church wall. He didn't say anything until he was two feet from her. There was a tracery of fresh cuts all over her cheeks and forehead. To Flanagan, after what he'd seen on the news this morning, the wounds looked like the mark of Cain. He folded his arms, turned his body language icy. "Was it you who turned Jersey City into Beirut last night?" *Like I need to ask*, he thought.

Blaylock shrugged. "No one died who wasn't supposed to."

Flanagan took a step back, shocked. He looked hard into her eyes. Iron gave nothing away. "Great," Flanagan said. "Color me reassured. And just how is your investigation going?"

She didn't blink at his sarcasm. "I'm leaving town on a lead."

"Oh? Who are you going to nuke this time?"

She still didn't rise to the bait. "No one," she said, as if the question had been serious. "I think this mission will be largely surveillance. Have another shopping list, though." She held out a small notebook.

Flanagan flipped through it. He felt his eyes widen. "Christ," he murmured. Her order was huge, and broken down by continent, subdivided by country and city. The result would be a guerilla's wet dream. She would have a major arms cache waiting for her almost anywhere she went.

"This is easier than trying to smuggle the goods across borders," she said. "Thought I'd let InSec do that for me."

Flanagan kept turning pages. "You like your C7s," he said, feeling stupid, feeling numb, feeling scared.

"Sweetheart in every port. Can InSec keep my toys warehoused until I call for them?"

Flanagan nodded, then looked up from the notebook. He half-expected to see smoke rising from the ground around Blaylock's feet, thunderheads gathering above her. "You can pay for all this?"

"Don't worry." Her smile was twisted. "I'm not asking you to fudge the books. Wouldn't want you to break the law or anything."

"That's not what I'm worried about. You're turning InSec into a subsidiary of Blaylock, Incorporated."

Her smile became genuine. "I know. Sweet, eh?"

"No. No. No, it isn't sweet. None of this is. Why are you so happy to do business with InSec now?"

"I'm not. I'm using them."

"I guess everything's under control, then. InSec is officially defanged."

"You're there. You're watching."

Flanagan rolled his eyes. "I don't believe this. You and

Joe Chapel should sing a duet. Yeah, I'm there. And I see things happening. And I tell you about it. And you agree, 'Yes, Mike, looks like the Russians are moving in.' And then what? Nothing."

"What do you want me to do?" she snapped. "Go around killing every Russian I see?"

"Why not? You're already doing that with Italians."

That stopped her. Her lips went thin, tight. She raised an index finger, shook it at him once—no. She started to walk away.

"Jen," Flanagan said. He followed her. He said her name again, but she lengthened her stride. He jogged to catch up. "Can't you see what you're doing? Can't you see that it's wrong?"

She had almost reached the gate to the street. Now she whirled on him. "Of course it is, you idiot! That's the point! Don't you get it? I'm the second wrong." She smiled again, and Flanagan recoiled. The smile was wide, narrow, sharp, a snarl. "Every so often the collision makes a right."

Silence hovered between them, taut with shock and lightning. Flanagan avoided Blaylock's eyes. He was scared of their depths. "You really believe that," he whispered.

"Don't you?" she purred, quieter yet, seductive as razors.

He didn't answer. He couldn't. He raised his eyes, though, and looked at her face, at its fire and its cold and the tensile shadow of its scars, and in his chest there was a yank and a crack. "You'll have your weapons," he said.

"Thank you." Soft now, kind. Did he hear regret, too, as if she were sorry she had won this battle?

"So you're leaving again," he said, feeling loss close in on him once again. He couldn't bear the absence of the terror that she was. "For how long?"

"As long as it takes."

"I see."

"Mike, about the Russians. You're right. I shouldn't be letting that slide. But I've started something I have to finish. You said Joe Chapel wanted you to watch things, too. Call him."

"Are you sure?"

"No. But I guarantee that'll screw something up. Might as well keep things interesting."

Dean Garnett looked like the happiest man on Earth. He always did. His eyes were extremely wide, his gaze one of permanent pleasant surprise. The eyes, the vertical brush-wire blond hair, and the sunburst of the goatee disarmed. Completely. Chapel admired him. See Garnett, and you wanted to make sure he was never hurt. See his left hand, and cue the violins. His ring finger was missing, shot off in Iraq during the fiasco of September '96. The CIA-sponsored coup attempt had gone south in a welter of dead generals, and Garnett had been one of the last operatives out, climbing aboard the extracting helo with blood pumping out of his hand, Republican Guard troops laying down serious-business fire. He was a good man. Chapel had been right behind him. He and Garnett had operated well in the field together. Now Chapel was one of the gods, and Garnett had the InSec file.

"So nothing new," Chapel said. They were seated at a window table in the Langley cafeteria.

Garnett shrugged. "Nothing significant, anyway. You've heard otherwise? Tell me no."

"Had a call from that Ember Lake survivor. He says the whole place is going seriously Russian."

Garnett forked up some potato salad. "The board of

directors is pretty much the same. There were a couple of deaths a few weeks back, but you know how a place like that works. Pembroke was God. Bound to be some power struggles when the vacuum happened. I'm surprised there wasn't more blood spilled." Garnett peered at Chapel, grinned. "Is the man happy? Tell me yes."

"Why so many Russians?"

"What do you want, Joe? Who has tons of surplus weaponry lying around? And when you get down to it, without Pembroke, InSec's no more American than the Internet."

"How's the corporate behavior?"

"Pure as the driven snow. Something up you want to let me in on?"

Chapel looked out at the courtyard, thinking. He didn't think a Kornukopia takeover of InSec had a direct bearing on the project Reed had told him about. The move was probably just Sherbina snatching an easy prize. "No," Chapel told Garnett. "Nothing specific." The unease was still there, though. Kornukopia's ubiquity rankled. "InSec even sneezes the wrong way, I want to know."

Garnett nodded. "By the way, Carol wanted me to ask you if dinner next weekend works for you. Tell me yes."

"I'll check." He already knew the answer. Reed's project was going to swallow him whole and leave nothing for his friends. He saw Garnett's eyes narrow as much as they ever did. "What is it?" Chapel asked.

"Incoming."

Chapel looked over his shoulder. Jim Korda homed in on their table. "Ladies," Korda said. "I wonder if you can help me. This being an *intelligence* agency, you might have heard about the events in New Jersey last night. I've been canvassing the directorates to see if anyone has anything *intelligent* to say about this since, like I said, we're in the *intelligence* business. Crazy idea, I realize, but that's me."

"We weren't involved, if that's what you're wondering," Chapel answered.

"I wasn't. I don't think even Operations is dumb enough to pull a stunt like that domestically. I was hoping you might tell me something I could tell the President. You know, stop him from worrying. The New York area catches the jitters when things go bang, after all."

Chapel stood up. So did Garnett. "That's enough," Chapel said. He said it quietly, with a smile, in case anyone was watching.

Korda was smiling, too. "Big words. You going to back them up? I don't think so. Not here. What would that do to morale, having the top boys tearing throats in the cafeteria?" His eyes were deep with contempt. "You won't let that happen. You love the Company too much for that."

Chapel leaned back against the table. He gripped the edge, did his best to look casual. He spoke at whisper volume. "And what about you?"

Korda's expression didn't flicker. "Boy Scout response. I know what you think of me. I don't care. Dig this. I'm not going to let the Agency be my political grave."

Chapel looked at Garnett, who was staring at the tabletop, no help at all. Chapel turned back to Korda. "I don't know why you're telling me this. I don't—"

"Play the games, yeah yeah, I know. Goddamn good-soldier bullshit. You're strapped to a rocket because your niece married Sam Reed's nephew, and you pull this high and holy meritocratic crap. Well, you know what? I do play the games. I'm good at them. Believe it. I read the signs. So I don't care how cozy you are with the President. You two are not levering me out. Not without damage."

Chapel realized he was squeezing the table. He saw Korda's eyes flicker, take in his white knuckles.

"I know," Korda said, and his smile was his sunniest yet. "There are names for people like me."

Flanagan stood by the police barrier. He didn't feel conspicuous. There were plenty of other voyeurs. He looked down the street toward the warehouse. He took in the scars of Blaylock's passage. He dosed himself with reality. He felt its grip tighten around his chest, purging the taint of the television networks. Theirs was a shrieking delight. Their ecstacy was a neon parade of news logos, each one more urgent than the other, streamlined joy conjured by the myth of Mob Armageddon. Here there was no rapid-fire editing or electronica soundtrack. Instead, he heard the background mutter of the city. A jet left a contrail, the sound of its passing on tape delay. Flanagan felt November breathing with soft insistence on his neck. He shivered, Blaylock's phantom kiss on his spine.

The police were still working on the battleground. There was no calling the street anything else. The road still glinted with broken glass from the windows of cars. Wreckage everywhere. Stump of a fire hydrant, vehicles slumped down and battered in death, gaping damage in the front of the warehouse. Even from this distance, Flanagan could make out twisted shadows inside the building, hinting at deeper wounds. He shifted his gaze from one echo of war to the next, took in the whole scene, then went through the pattern again, specific to general, general to specific. He brought up memories of Ember Lake, of slaughter and of flame.

Blaylock's words: *No one died who wasn't supposed to.*

What do I feel?

Doubt. Fear. Horror.

All we have is blood and fire. Yes. So he looked at what blood and fire had wrought. He looked at the aftermath of power deployed. He felt a tug. She *did* this, he thought. She did this. Beneath the doubt, fear, and horror, he felt excitement. Yes. An undertow hauling him, *willing or not, here we go*, to the seduction of Blaylock and the war she was. Yes.

Yes.

8

Ciudad del Este was a shithole. Blaylock liked it. The city *knew* it was a shithole. That was its saving grace. That was its vibe. Alfredo Stroessner founded it in 1957 and called it Ciudad Presidente Stroessner. That was sleaze and balls Blaylock could almost admire. There were a couple of hundred thousand people there now, and the city had shrugged off the dictator's name, but the violence and corruption made sure the city was still in his image.

Blaylock had made a tactical decision once she knew where Coscarelli was headed. She could have tried to book a seat on the same flight, followed him all the way down to Paraguay. But then she'd be limited to line-of-sight surveillance. She might miss an information motherlode. Ciudad del Este was a great place to hide. But it was also the United Nations of crime. So she rolled the dice. She went back to her safe house and retrieved the surveillance equipment left over from her InSec campaign. By the time she reached Ciudad del Este, Coscarelli had a twenty-four-hour head start.

The city was a metastasizing cancer on the banks of the Alto Parana river. The tumor festered in the shape of prefab concrete. It scoured greenspace in a purge of gray and dirty brown. Scrub grass, corruption-yellow, clung like scabs to the hills surrounding the blight. The cancer was ravenous. Feeding it and spreading its cells was the Friendship Bridge, a two-lane traffic jam that connected Ciudad del Este to Foz do Iguaçu, across the river in Brazil. Back and forth, on the bridge and under it, back and forth from Argentina and Brazil, from the plague of unofficial airstrips in the tri-border area, back and forth went the food and the strength of the cancer. Three million tons of cocaine alone coursed through the system each month. The cancer rewarded its host. Its black economy was half again as big as Paraguay's GDP.

The cancer's servants gathered in multicultural harmony. Mafia, *Maffiya*, Triad, and Yakuza. Shot-callers from Colombia and Nigeria. Hezbollah. The whole sick crew, meeting and greeting, wheeling and dealing on the common ground. Blaylock had known of Ciudad del Este for years. It was impossible to spend as much time underground as she had and not hear of Shangri-La. Blaylock thought about the concentration of crime, the player-per-square-foot ratio. She thought of the organization damage one rogue with firepower could do here. She smiled. I could live here.

She moved through the streets, through the bleeding abscess of capitalism. Everything for sale, everyone selling. Shoeshines, fruit, knock-off fashions, fell-off-the-back-of-the-truck electronics, bargain basement hit jobs (surcharge if the target is Caucasian)—the city as absolute market. The voice of the city was the hell-babble of an entire population hawking the goods. The air of the city was diesel and urine. Blaylock breathed through her mouth for the first half hour. Then she grew used to the stench. An hour later, she liked it. The smell was honest in its filth. There was no dissembling. Ciudad del Este was as dirty as she was, as blasted by sin. Feeling at home, she pushed through the crowds, sidestepping garbage. She asked questions, distributed dollars. Shopkeepers, stall owners, beggars, bartenders. She canvassed. Her Spanish was rough, and she had no Guaraní at all. She managed, though. English was the language of cash. She was looking for an Italian, she said. An older man. Very respectable. Very important. She chased down twenty false leads in the first two hours. But she spread the money, and she spread the questions. Bit by bit, she encountered flashes of recognition. By evening, she was smelling Coscarelli. She continued spending. She made herself visible. She made herself ostentatious. At nightfall, the information came looking for her.

The streets were just as busy after dark. The shops stayed open, screaming neon of perpetual closing-out sales. Blaylock saw more predators out now, more chains and visible blades. At a street corner, she approached a group of three prostitutes. A truck blatted by as she started to speak. The air tasted blue. Blaylock began her Italian Señor speech. One of the prostitutes saw something behind Blaylock and started to back away, nervous. Blaylock turned around. She smiled at the cop.

He didn't smile back. He was a couple of inches shorter than she was, and shaped like a brick. His face was expressionless, and so anonymous it was as if he had no features at all. Here, Blaylock thought, is a man who can blend. He eyed her, evaluating. The prostitutes scampered off in a hurry. "You the one looking for Italian?" he asked. His *you* sounded like *Hugh*.

Blaylock nodded. She held up twenties in a wide fan. The cop looked at them, grabbed half, then strode off. Blaylock followed into a switchback maze of back alleys.

She almost told the cop not to bother with the routine. She couldn't be lost if there was nowhere else she was trying to reach. Half an hour of this shit and they wound up at a fire door in a grime-black concrete wall. The lane was so narrow you could shoot a man and he'd stay standing. The cop pulled out a ring of keys and unlocked the door. He held it open for Blaylock. She looked at the dark corridor. How stupid does he think I am? she wondered. Stupid enough, anyway. She stepped forward. The cop held up a hand, patted her down. He took her knife and her SIG. Then he gestured. *After you.* She winked at him, and walked into the darkness. The trap of the building closed around her. The cop was two steps behind.

The corridor opened into a back room. Blaylock could hear the sounds of a large kitchen coming through the door in the left side of the far wall. A bar took up the rest of the wall. The shelves were stocked for permanent high-end binges. All the bottles were full—no shortages allowed. The counter shone rich oak. On the counter, three Tiffany lamps were the room's illumination. A man stood behind the counter. He didn't look like a bartender. He was gene-doped muscle in sunglasses. He was cradling a shotgun. In front of the bar was a single table, covered in a white cloth. Another man sat at the table, facing Blaylock. He was round, happy-looking. He had a glass of red wine and a bottle before him, and was smoking a cigar. The rest of the room was bare concrete. There was a drain in the center of the floor. Over it, chains hung from the ceiling. The concrete had dark stains. The man with the cigar gestured to the steel chair on the other side of the table. Blaylock sat down. The cop stood behind her.

"Drink?" the man asked in English.

"Whatever's on tap."

Shotgun brought a mug of draft, then went back to his post and his gun.

Deep drag on the cigar. Contemplative cloud. "I am Eduardo Chávez."

"Congratulations. How's that working out?"

Chávez's eyes narrowed. He asked, "And you are?"

"Busy." Blaylock sensed the cop shifting uneasily. She made a point of looking at her watch. "So, you going to tell me where I can find Sal Coscarelli, or what?"

Chávez covered surprise with a sip of his wine. He didn't cover well. He looked at Blaylock, shifted his eyes to her left, in the direction of chains and drain. She refused to follow his gaze, kept her face expectant. Finally, Chávez said, "I should tell you, why?"

"To do him a favor."

Another sip. Blaylock hoped a game of poker would break out. She'd take this guy to the cleaners. "You doan' know me. Okay. You doan' do business here. But you do business here, then you know me. You want a meeting here, I make sure you doan' get disturbed." He contemplated his cigar. He raised it to his mouth, hesitated, and gave Blaylock a long, serious look. "Reputation," he said, and drew smoke deep. His exhale was one that honored the cigar. "What favor?" he asked.

She was flying on improv. Chávez and his precious reputation gave her something to build on, and he'd confirmed her guess. Coscarelli wasn't here just for the refuge. "I'm here to warn him," she lied. "Something's going to go down at the meeting," she added, speaking truth. She drank some of the beer. It was good.

Chávez drummed fingers, thinking. "He know you?"

"He should." Blaylock smiled.

Chávez shook his head, shook his finger. "No answer. No, no, and no. You jerking me off, bitch."

"How is it for you?" She pumped her fist up and down a phantom shaft.

No wine sip this time. Chávez just stared. He looked over his shoulder at Shotgun, whose face wasn't computing. Chávez turned back to Blaylock, opened and closed his mouth a few times. Then, "I could kill you."

"Yeah."

"What? You crazy? Not afraid of death?"

"He and I have an understanding." She wondered what she was doing. She wondered why she was enjoying herself. She wondered if Chávez might be right.

He did his slow burn. He finished his wine. Shotgun came, poured, retreated again. Chávez's mustache twitched. Blaylock wasn't sure if that was laughter, or if it meant he had worked something out. "Okay," he said. "Okay." He pulled a cellphone out of a vest pocket and hit a speed dial. "We give him your message."

Shit, Blaylock thought. No good. She'd just rolled snake eyes. Walk away or own the loss?

Chávez spoke in Spanish to someone on the other end. Blaylock missed what he said, but she made out the number "221." Then Chávez switched to English. "Somebody here to see you," he said, and told Blaylock's story. He paused, listening. "What's your name?" he asked Blaylock.

Own the loss. Stir the shit. "Dunn," she said.

Chávez repeated the name. Blaylock heard a tinny voice go ballistic. Chávez held the phone away from his ear, but he was listening, hard. Blaylock picked up her beer mug. She checked Shotgun. His head was lowered. He was watching Chávez, not her. She threw the beer up over her shoulder. Splash, grunt, sounds of the startled cop taking steps back. Blaylock was on her feet. She launched the mug at Shotgun. It smashed on the bridge of his nose. He dropped his gun and fell. Blaylock hooked her arm through the back of the chair. She turned on the spot, swinging the chair into huge momentum. She slammed steel into the cop's jaw, shaking his brain hard. He collapsed, unconscious. Chávez was motionless, still holding the phone, eyes wide. Blaylock ignored him, leaped on top of the counter, saw the shotgun rise to meet her. She threw herself backward, hit the floor with a bruising smack, and the gun went off high and wide. Her lungs were flattened. She made herself move, made herself not try to breathe until she could. She rolled flush against the counter as the second barrel boomed, smashing concrete on the floor between her and Chávez. Chávez shrieked and jumped from his chair, knocking it over. Chest screaming, Blaylock lunged upward and grabbed the shaft of the shotgun. The man let go. She didn't expect that, and she fell on her face, empty gun in her hands. She twisted around onto her back, and Shotgun was over the counter. Her lungs pulled, and the air came in, scraping claws, gravel, and glass. Shotgun came at her, a wall of muscle. Blaylock kicked up and crushed his throat. Shotgun dropped, no air forever now. Blaylock stood up. She grabbed the wine bottle by the neck. Chávez was fighting with the cop's holster. Blaylock broke the bottle over his head.

While she waited for the pain of breathing to ease, she looked at the chains. She made herself think about what they meant. She thought about long hours of hanging and cutting. Did you want this? she asked herself. No. Then why were you pushing them? Why were you practically slipping the manacles on yourself? To confuse them. Worked, too.

No. You were lucky. You stupid, cocky idiot.

She picked up the cellphone, hit redial.

"Hotel Parana," said the voice on the other end.

The Parana turned out to be three blocks from the fleabag Blaylock had checked into. She retrieved her bags, then reconnoitered Coscarelli's home away from home. The Parana, no surprise, was two-faced. The front entrance was high luxury and inviting. The building was set back from the street. A circular entrance drive surrounded a central fountain that was shaded by some of the only trees Blaylock had seen in the city. The rear of the hotel was a multistory parkade, further isolating the main building. Nothing to be done about the sides, though. They looked out onto lanes that were well on their way to becoming permanent refuse dumps. Garbage cans and dumpsters were overflowing horns of plenty. They were disappearing, buried beneath the riot of refuse. Mountains of cardboard, food, rotting furniture, broken glass: a still life in putrescence. No one was ever going to collect the heaps, but the hotel continued to defecate. There was so much trash piling up within and without that the fire exit doors on both sides were jammed open with the spillover of excess cans. Blaylock's eyes watered as she walked past. Ciudad del Este's tourniquet smell tightened several notches. Rats weren't renting anymore. They were setting up condos. They were too busy and confident even to look at her.

Blaylock returned to the front entrance. As she stepped inside, she looked at the gilt and bronze and glass and the illusion was wafer-thin, wealth and comfort denying the quicksand of rot that was sucking at the foundations. She liked this city more all the time. At the front desk, she produced a roll of hundreds, and felt herself made welcome. "It's nice to be back," she told the clerk.

"We're delighted to see you again," the woman replied, sincere as plastic but her face straight and her English clipped.

"Is my usual room available?"

"I'm sure it is," said the clerk, with just a trace of panic in her voice now. Blaylock saw her eyes go distant as her mind ransacked an internal Rolodex for Blaylock's non-existent face and room preferences.

Blaylock let her off the hook. "321," she said.

"Ah." The clerk, happy now, rattled away at the keyboard. "Here you go," she handed Blaylock the access card and beamed, too relieved now to register anything other than having avoided a customer's potential wrath.

Blaylock let herself into the room. She could hear the muffled sound of a raised voice coming up through the floor. *Move, girl, you're missing the meeting.* She opened the window and looked down. The view was the black canyon of an alley. The garbage smell wafted up to her. She unpacked her C7, slapped in a clip, and placed it on the floor beneath the window, close to hand. She tucked her SIG into her belt, and sorted through her surveillance equipment. She discarded the amplified shotgun microphone. The floor was too thick for clear sound. The bugs were useless now, too. The situation had moved beyond plant-and-listen possibilities. She chose a mini-mic on a twenty-five-foot cable and a fiberscope. The fiberscope's cable was only ten feet, but that was enough. She took the equipment to the window, plugged the mini-mike into a cassette recorder, and slipped on headphones. She braided the mini-mike's cable around the fiberscope's, creating a single AV unit, then lowered the cable down the face of the building toward the window of 221.

The voices resolved into tinny clarity. She looked through the fiberscope's eyepiece. The room was a fish-eyed distortion, but she could make out faces. The bed had been removed from the room. In its place were armchairs, facing each other in a wide circle. Coscarelli was ramping around center stage. The other men lounged in the chairs. They watched the show, letting Coscarelli vent steam. Blaylock matched the faces to newspaper photos. Answering the roll call were the heads of all the New York families.

"Dunn!" Coscarelli yelled. "Can you goddamn believe it? That Russian bastard sends some broad to play mind games with me and she calls herself Dunn!"

"Sal, you don't know it's Sherbina."

"Who the hell else, Lou? Who the hell else?"

Lou blew smoke through his nose, shrugged.

Blaylock heard the sound of a door opening beyond the view of the 'scope. Coscarelli turned to look. "About time," he said to the man who strode into the room. This the Russian? Blaylock wondered.

"Apologies." He didn't sound Russian. There was a trill. "Apologies again." He produced a cellphone, looked at the screen for a second. "Will you gentlemen excuse me?" He ducked out of the room.

"You see?" Coscarelli demanded of his audience. "He makes us wait, and then wait again. He's yankin' our chains."

Okay, Blaylock decided. The guy was this Sherbina that Coscarelli was handing her credit to.

"Don't like the way he speaks," Lou conceded. "Fancy faggy English."

"Rubbing our noses in it," Coscarelli said. "High and mighty."

"Who is?" Sherbina was back.

"You are, cocksucker." Coscarelli jabbed a finger at him. "We had a deal." Dramatic pause. "You got no honor." Sentence passed.

Sherbina didn't say anything right away. He cocked his head at Coscarelli. When he made that gesture, a quiet move of amusement and curiosity, Blaylock could almost hear the crackle of power. Her instincts shrieked max alarm. Sherbina spoke quietly. "Have we flown all this way to hear this?"

"Damn straight. Listen, asshole, you screw with New York, you're finished."

Sherbina didn't look away from Coscarelli. "Is that so, gentlemen?"

The others shifted, uncomfortable.

"Don Coscarelli," Sherbina said. "I came here out of respect for you, and in the spirit of cooperation of our joint venture."

"Bullshit."

A deep sigh. "In return, I receive calumny."

"Cal— What?"

"Not to mention incompetence. I have no idea what venture of yours has gone so sour, but it's clear solving the problem is beyond you. So is an assured control of Lawrence Dunn."

"You see?" Coscarelli looked around for support. "You see?" To Sherbina: "We're not out of this yet. I say the word, and Dunn is toast. Without him, your big show at Davos is—" Coscarelli's head jerked back with a loud snap. His limbs spasmed, and he fell. Sherbina's strike had been so fast Blaylock barely saw it. The uppercut broke Coscarelli's neck.

Blaylock saw trouble writ large. She thought, Davos?

The room was death-quiet. The Mobfathers sat still, behaving. The most fit were former brawlers in late middle-age seed. None of them looked capable of Spetznaz moves. Sherbina straightened his cuffs. "Respected colleagues," he said, his tone respectful enough to be a lie, "I trust the message has been received."

Blaylock focused on the men's faces. Message received, all right. Sherbina's kill was tantamount to a throat slitting in the UN Security Council chamber. He'd stained the neutral ground, and he wanted the act noticed. He was strong enough to do this, and his goal was important enough to do this.

"Good. Now, will your men help take care of the spy upstairs? Or do the locals have to do everything?" He looked straight at the fiberscope and winked.

Blaylock thought, Oh shit. Blaylock thought, His cellphone. It was a bug detector. She had time only for those two thoughts. She started to reach for her C7. There was a loud *bang* behind her. She whirled. Her door flew in off its hinges. She stood. She saw men and guns. Her options evaporated. She leaped backwards, out the window. The muzzles flashed. Fire and pain slashed through the air above her as she fell.

Three stories down. She dropped back-first. She tucked her head in, let the rushing air lift her arms and legs up. The building flashed by. There were jaws opening beneath her. Impact was the surprise of God's fist, all sensation smashed black. Her body folded as she plowed, meteor, into the garbage piles, her Hail Mary gamble. Pain was anvils landing on every bone. Her breath punched out *rrrrraaahhhh*. A moment of full dark. Then the world came stabbing back, an unforgiving mosaic of steel-trap teeth and an iron vise around her torso. She hauled the air back *hhhhaaaaahhhh* and rolled to her knees. She snarled, a sound of deep war and gargling glass, and pushed herself deeper into the trash until she was buried. Exploded garbage bags poured slimed paper and viscous food over her. Rats squealed. She tried to move her right arm, found she could, though the agony was blinding. She twisted her shriek into another snarl. Rage was the only way to fight off the dark. She found the SIG, faithful friend still at her side. She pulled it out, stretched her arm forward though a world of incandescent nails. She poked the muzzle through the trash, saw through a tunnel. Her vision was gray, but she could make out the fire door. She saw the men, three of them, as they shoved the door open, struggling against a barrier of tumbled garbage cans. The men were framed by the doorway, constrained. Blaylock opened fire on the fish in the barrel.

9

The plane had been in the air, heading north, for an hour. The cabin was turning into a mess, papers spreading out in ripples from Sherbina and Yevgeny Nevzlin. They were seated in leather swivel chairs at opposite ends of the cabin. Sherbina had progress reports and appended psych evaluations spread out on the table in front of him. He was trying to read them. He couldn't. He kept waiting for the phone to ring. He kept wondering what detail he had missed. He had walked away from the Hotel Parana listening to a gunfire serenade. All in order. So why no call? Why hadn't he been told who the spy was? Something was out of order.

The penny finally dropped. "One gun," he said, startled.

Nevzlin looked up. "Pardon?"

"I only heard one gun firing. The second time. Just when I was leaving. Individual shots, no response."

"Maybe they were being restrained."

Sherbina shook his head. "Not that crowd."

"So you think..."

"They were taking fire, not giving it." He sighed. You throw a bone to the home team. You give them something a dog couldn't screw up: a surprise attack on a hotel room with no back door. And this is what happens.

"Idiots are too afraid to call. Yevgeny, call the police chief. I want a casualty list."

Nevzlin phoned, barked some orders, and then listened. Sherbina saw the big man's face become pinched. He looked worried when he hung up. "They're all dead," he said.

Sherbina had guessed that much. "What about the room?"

"Clean. Eduardo Chávez is dead, too."

Sherbina took this in. "What," he wanted to know, "the *hell* was Coscarelli up to?" Something on the side, with someone strong and, lately, pissed. But who? The illogic of the war bothered him. A Coscarelli pogrom had been triggered, and no one knew why. The plague had followed the don down to Paraguay. At least Lawrence Dunn was still untouched. The big question: now that the Coscarellis were extinct, did the war end? Sherbina did not want someone else's shitstorm gumming up his own machinery. "I want to know who was after the Coscarellis," he told Nevzlin. "Put the word out. New York, Ciudad del Este, everywhere. Make it clear I'm not just curious. Make it clear I might be *angry*." Nevzlin nodded.

Sherbina turned back to the reports. He'd taken action, and could concentrate now. He liked what he saw. The balancing act was delicate, but holding. The tipping point was coming up, though. The Black Bloc was ramping up its activities, and the backlash was building. He sorted through the papers until he found the schedule for Zelkova's speaking tour. He began to plot out the activation timetable.

"It's almost time," Nevzlin said.

Sherbina turned on the cabin's television.

Sam Reed at Brown University. The President taking questions from the student body. The venue perfect for the message. Right demographic, likely to ask the trigger question. The vibe a patriot's light year from Berkeley. Dog and pony show in full media glare. Reed and the camera, dueling again. Reed knew his weakness, knew he made Nixon look like the king of suave. He used the weakness, made it his weapon. He gave the camera his hatred. His eyes were unblinking coals. His look meant business. It said, *Listen to me.* People did, and when they did, they heard his voice. His other weapon. The voice hummed low, a distant B-52. The voice was quiet, but it hooked. It hauled the listener in. It spoke with authority that could easily be moved to anger. It was a voice that gathered momentum slowly, but at full flight, at full volume, it didn't present arguments, but was a rock slide. Reed used the weapon strategically. He didn't thunder. He didn't rant. He gave his opponents plenty of rope, and yanked the noose hard only when he was sure of a neck-snap.

He waited for the trigger question. It would show up. It always did. Put yourself in front of a large crowd of students, be patient, and the perfect question will arrive. Guaranteed. Reed bided his time, idly batting the softball questions. There were no real challenges. The aura of office and celebrity still kept him untouchable in the right precincts. This was one of them.

The trigger question was twenty minutes in coming. The media flacks were looking bored. Even they recognized the question, though, and perked up at its entrance. "Mr. President," a student began. His clothes were expensive. His haircut was very short. He had *main chance* written all over him. "You've explained to us what the goals of your economic policy are. But there are many people, many young people my age, who oppose these policies. They think these initiatives will cause harm. What do you say to them?" The student smiled, sat back down.

Reed smiled back at him. *What do you say to them?* How nicely worded. Them, not us. The question had sounded very prepared: scripted, then memorized. Reed wondered if the boy knew damn well what a trigger question was, and had made it a personal goal to ask it. Good for you, son, Reed thought. You'll go far. "That is an important question," he said. He brought the weapon to bear. He calibrated it. "I'm very glad you asked it. There is something that needs to be said." In fact, it had already been said, the night before. It had been fine-tuned, polished until the gloss put out eyes. It was sitting, printed out, on Reed's lectern, waiting for its moment. Reed barely glanced at his notes. There was nothing wrong with his memorization skills, either. "America is a democracy. That is our greatness. And no small element of a democracy is the freedom that is enshrined in our First Amendment, the freedom of speech. Without an open exchange of conflicting views, liberty will wither and die. Well, not on my watch." Punch that last sentence up, then drop the volume for the dramatic repetition. "Not on my watch." There, give the media a refrain. Now pause, look down. Frown. Eyes back up, audience in his sights. Determined set of jaw. "I have watched the anti-globalization demonstrations. I have listened to the arguments. But I have also paid attention to something more important yet. The actions. And what I am seeing is not free speech. Do you know what I am seeing?" Rhetorical pause. "Let me tell you. I see every effort being expended to shut down civilized exchange. I see representatives, *the elected representatives of the people,* being silenced. Let there be no mistake, that is the same as silencing the people." Let the voice build now, let the thunderblast of anger through. "I see law-abiding citizens having their lives disrupted. I see people being prevented from conducting their business. I see people, everyday people, who are being prevented from earning a living. And I see violence. I see shops and lives being destroyed." Mournful pause. Let this all sink in. Reset the weapon for another build. "I know the stories. I know the excuses. 'These are voices that need to be heard.' But who elected them? Some might say, 'This is the misguided energy of youth. It will pass.'" Rapid crescendo, now. Shock them with your fury. "Well, that's not good enough. Where are the values, the *real* values, that make us what we are? Where are the traditions of duty, honor, and service?" Deliver the lesson. "Those are true and important concepts. Duty. Honor. Service. They cannot be yoked to chaos. Don't believe the lies." Pause again, then climax. "Real people are being harmed. The real economy is being harmed. America's interests are being harmed. *America* is being harmed. There is a name for this disruption. No, that's too weak a word. There is a name for this *destruction*. What do you call it when you make people afraid for their livelihoods, for their property, even for their lives? What do you call it when you make people afraid? I know what I call it. I call it terrorism. And it will not stand." Quiet finish, firm and resolute. "Not on my watch. Not on my watch."

Blanket coverage. The message hits home. Audience reaction, straw poll:

Sherbina and Nevzlin looked at each other. Nevzlin lost his straight face first and brayed laughter.

Irina Zelkova caught the speech as she drove into Geneva. "Not on my watch," she mimicked. She refrained from spitting.

Kelly Grimson caught the condensed version on *The National* that night. She paid no attention to the other items. She sat in her living room, alone, and felt very small beside an immense hostility.

Jonathan Alloway was in the crowded common room, watching the news with Darryl Avery. Alloway screamed at the TV screen for a full two minutes.

Charlotte Taber made calls, throwing the spin machine into high gear. Life was good.

Blaylock filed the information away.

Chapel phoned Reed that night. Congratulations were in order. "That was incredible," Chapel said.

Reed laughed. "You liked it?"

"I've been waiting years for that kind of moral clarity from the top. Mr. President, you are speaking to one proud American. Who's your speechwriter?"

"New guy. Leon West."

"He's a keeper."

Linda asked, "What do you think he's going to do?"

Lawrence Dunn shook his head. "I don't know." He scrubbed at a pot, handed it to Linda to dry.

"He sounded like he meant business." When Dunn nodded, Linda added, "And Washington's still on speaking terms with you?"

"I can't figure it. They're doing everything but sending flowers and chocolates." He let the water out of the sink.

Linda hung the copper pot from the rack above the kitchen island. The pots were arranged from left to right in ascending order of size. "I would have thought they'd be packing you off to Guantánamo or something."

"Don't joke about it."

She touched his shoulder. "My God, you're so tense."

"Shouldn't I be?"

"Aren't things better? When was the last time you heard from Coscarelli? I don't think those people are interested in you anymore. They have other problems. If any of them are still alive."

Dunn leaned against the sink, eyes on the blank night outside the window. His hands dripped. "Sure. Life's that easy."

"Can't it be?"

He turned his head to look into Linda's eyes. He saw hope there, a candle bright as it was fragile. A breath, and the shine would become fear. "I want it to be. Jesus, you can't imagine."

"Yes, I can."

He nodded. Yes, he supposed she could.

The phone rang. Dunn answered. The voice that flowed out was cool, polite, sure of itself. Sherbina. "Mr. Dunn," he began, "I do want to apologize on behalf of my erstwhile colleague Salvatore Coscarelli. His bad judgment and ham-fisted business approach must have cost you more than a couple of sleepless nights."

Oh, no. "That's okay," Dunn muttered.

"I thought I should make this courtesy call to let you know that I'll be personally looking after your file now, and there should be no further such hiccups." Translation:

Your ass is mine, pal. "On another note, did you happen to catch your President's speech?"

"I did."

"What did you think?"

"Uh ..."

"Your honest opinion, Mr. Dunn. Your honest opinion."

"I thought it was a dangerous speech."

"I couldn't agree with you more. I assume you'll be putting your opinion in print?"

"Uhm ..." *What's the right answer here? Which one won't kill your family?*

"I really think you should."

"Fine." He undermined his obedience with a freezing monotone.

"Passion, Lawrence. May I call you Lawrence? Where's your passion? If this isn't a moment for defenders of lawful and necessary dissent to speak up, then what is? These are the times that try a man's mettle. Stand up and be counted. Don't let the bastards get away with it. If you don't speak up now, who knows whom they'll be coming for next?"

"Yes." His voice was dead. Sherbina was throwing his own beliefs back at him, forcing him to live by his principles, and he wanted to vomit. He knew he was being played, and Sherbina wasn't even going to tell him what the game was.

"I don't want you worrying about any fallout, now. Remember, we're right behind you. All the way." Sherbina broke the connection.

Dunn looked up. Linda was watching him. "Well?" she asked.

"The Russians own me now."

"The Russians." Linda shook her head. "Damn you, Larry," she said. She sounded very, very tired. "Goddamn you." She left the kitchen, shut the bedroom door behind her.

Dunn stood still. He saw his life divide into two hells. One half was a forever of yanked strings. The other half was the fracture and death by rot of everything he loved. He stood there, and he discovered a new thing. He discovered that despair, concentrated, is an active, violent force. He made a noise that was moan and yell and denial, and the noise was so loud his throat hurt for three days. He slammed his hand against the dangling pots, smashed them and the rack to the ground. Copper crashed, the toll of chaos. Dunn took deep breaths, gazed at the wreckage.

Then it hit him. He grunted, sensing the first, tiny, will-'o-the-wisp gesture of resistance he could make. He grabbed his wallet and fumbled through it until he found the card Irina Zelkova had given him in Washington. He sat up well past midnight, waiting for morning in Switzerland. Then he called her. She sounded pleased to hear from him. They exchanged pleasantries. Zelkova made noises about Sam *Not on My Watch* Reed. She said, "You're going to let him have it, I hope."

Dunn said, "Absolutely." Then he gambled, playing against the house once again. "When you're on your North American tour, we might think about doing some collaborative work, too, now that we'll be seeing more of each other."

"I'm sorry?"

You just drew blackjack, boy. Don't you love that old thrill? "I mean, now that I'm working for your husband."

"You are?" Voice as surprised as it was suddenly hard.

Chapel, bored with surfing, turned the TV off. He sipped his beer. He was lying on the couch in the living room of his Foggy Bottom row house. With the TV dark, the only light was from the street lamp. It shone amber, its glow turning the interior of the house gray near the windows, ink and pitch further in. Chapel didn't bother turning lamps on. There wasn't much to see, after all. No prints on the walls. No eye-candy furniture. Home was a place Chapel slept, caught up on work, and sometimes ate. When he had a moment, he flopped on his couch and watched the tube. He was giving himself the evening off, a full three hours before he went to bed and then took off for NYC in the morning. He raised his beer, toasting Reed and his speech.

Three words. Duty. Honor. Service. He had heard the President speak the Chapel mantra. He basked, knew he was basking, went ahead and indulged. He'd grown up with those words. The words had been there in his father's household. The general had made sure the son knew their value. The words had followed him to West Point. They had followed him to the CIA, and there they had sustained him. There had been the dark moments. There had been the black bag jobs, the dances in the shadows, the moments where he had killed his country's enemies in ways that, were it not for orders, he would have spat on as beneath the worst coward. But he had held on to the words. They reminded him of what he was working towards. They reminded him of who he was. Of the three commandments. Always live up to the mantra. Always live the mantra. Always be the mantra.

The answering machine on the coffee table was blinking, had been since he arrived home. He could guess what the message was. He surrendered, sat up, and hit

PLAY. "Hi Joe, this is Lynne. Coffee next week? Give me a—" ERASE.

Chapel sighed. He liked Lynne. Smart woman. Attractive. Worked in the Directorate of Science and Technology, and so was off limits. Chapel knew Garnett would hit him for that stricture. Most of the couples Chapel was friendly with were Company products. It was easier if you were both in the game, after all. Fewer secrets between you, or at least greater understanding about the secrets that were kept. Garnett's wife Ann was from Science & Tech. She'd engineered the meeting with Lynne at a dinner party last week. Thanks, Ann. Nice try. But no. Chapel thought about relationships going wrong within the Agency, and thought *can of worms*. Same worms, different can if he dated outside talent. Better off not looking.

He hadn't dated since Carol left. Hadn't bought anything new for the house, either. Only lack of time, or laziness maybe, had prevented him from selling the place. The trendy neighborhood had been her idea. The studied elegance of the home during their marriage had been hers, too. When she left, she took her stuff, and with her had gone the need to step one inch beyond the utilitarian. He had purged her memory from the place, a full pogrom against reminders of his intelligence failure. She needed to explore her sexuality, she had said. She had used terms like *heterosexist matrix*. The euphemisms, he could live with. It was when she had uttered the words *coming out* that he had shut down. He refused to believe. His job was to know things. His life was vital and accurate information. If she were telling the truth, he would have seen signs. They'd been married eight years. He would have known. This, he believed. The real explanation, the one he put together for himself, was that he had been away from home too much. She'd become bored. He hadn't been there to prevent ... Well, he hadn't been there. So there, lesson learned. Fool me once, fine, but no second mistake.

He'd learned another thing from the fiasco, too. He didn't miss being in a relationship. He now knew the true worth of his work. It wasn't a job. It was a responsibility. There were no distractions, nothing to get in the way of duty, of honor, of service.

This, he believed.

"Where are you?" Grimson asked.

Blaylock propped herself up against the bank of pay phones. "The airport."

"You're in town? That's fabulous!"

Yeah, yeah, yeah. "Need to see you, Kel." Fatigue was clamping down with a general anesthetic. At least it kept the pain dull.

"Come on over! Do you need a place to stay?"

Blaylock sagged.

"Hit the bastard, you stupid shit!"

Winnipeg. November. Hockey season. Cheer on the kids.

"Hit him! No no no no no *no!* Don't you skate away from— Go! Go go go go go! Hit him! Hit him! *Hiiiiiiit hiiiiiim!* Goddamn it!" The ref broke up the fight. Barry Reynolds slammed his fist against the Plexiglas. Son Danny skated to the penalty box. Reynolds sat down, disgusted. *Danny gets it to Christ right for the first time, lets the other guy have it, I mean for shit's sake listens to* the old man for a change, can you believe it, and the fight is shut down by some candy-ass who doesn't want twelve-year-olds to have some fun and play some real *hockey* for a change, I mean, Jesus. He shifted, uncomfortable, ass too big for the width of the bench. When were they going to get some decent seating in this community arena, I mean, Jesus. Couldn't even have a smoke. Hell of a way to spend Saturday night. Game was pansy piss. Shit.

His cellphone rang. "What?" Reynolds answered, definitely not in the mood for whatever. The voice on the other end spoke. Reynolds straightened. He said, "Yes." He ran a hand over his skull's five o'clock shadow. He swallowed, nervous and excited. He said, "Absolutely." He turned to Bobbie, who was looking at him funny. He pointed at her purse. "Pen and paper," he hissed. The voice spoke some more. Reynolds kept saying *yes*. He took notes. He did not interrupt. When the voice was finished, Reynolds asked, "When?"

10

"Oh my God."

Blaylock finished pulling her shirt down and turned around. Grimson had come into the room with some towels for her. "Good morning to you, too."

"Your back." Grimson held the towels as if to shield them from the sight.

"Yeah." She'd just been checking things out in the mirror. Her back was a Technicolor nightmare of brown and yellow and blue. She knew what those colors felt like, too. Yellow was a throb of iron jabbing. Brown squeezed. Blue was a memory fist. They all tasted like hard breath. But she'd just had fourteen hours' sleep, and the colors had lost some of their bite.

"What the hell happened?"

"I fell down." She didn't elaborate. She waited for Grimson to respond.

Grimson glanced at Blaylock's bag. "You armed?"

"No." She itched, naked without firepower. Having multinational caches made crossing borders easy, but also created these limbo times when she was missing claws.

"No weapons while you're here, Jen."

"Fine." Not fine. "Last time I saw you," she said, "you guys were planning to go to Davos in February." She had tried to bring this up last night, when Grimson met her at the airport. Grimson, seeing her exhaustion, had made her wait.

"We still are."

"I wish you wouldn't."

"Why?"

Blaylock hesitated. She almost gave Grimson a need-to-know fragment. Instead, she respected her intelligence. She respected the friendship. She gave Grimson the truth, in all its blood. By the time she was finished, Grimson was sitting on the bed, and now she was clutching the towels for comfort. She looked up, and Blaylock saw in her eyes the same withdrawing and fear she was becoming used to seeing in Flanagan's. Grimson's expression was worse, though. It was shocked through with the force of fresh knowledge. Flanagan, at least, had seen the bodies pile up gradually. He'd been part of the war. He was, she thought, adapting.

Grimson stared at Blaylock for a long time before speaking. "All that Mob war stuff that was in the news," she said. "That was you." When Blaylock nodded, Grimson insisted, "Just you?"

Blaylock nodded again. "Were you listening to me about Davos?" she asked, impatient.

"Yes. Yes, I was." Grimson's words were slow, quiet. Her tone and her pallor belonged on a post-artillery battlefield. "You didn't say exactly what is going to happen there."

"That's because I don't know."

"You don't even know if they were talking about the World Economic Forum."

"Safe bet, though. What, organized crime would be that interested in skiing?"

Grimson conceded the point. "You're going?" she asked.

"Yes."

Grimson was silent again for a bit. When she spoke again, some of the shock had left her voice, and some of the strength Blaylock knew was back. She stood up, folded her arms. "Tell me why you're going there, knowing what you do."

"I'm going *because* of what I know."

"To stop whatever this is?"

"If I can."

"But if you're telling me all this, it's because you think the situation is going to be dangerous. Why put yourself in harm's way?"

"I have to."

"Exactly." More strength now. Blaylock saw the soldier re-emerging from underneath neo-Bohemian clothing. "I'm trying to stop a bad thing from happening, too. I can't sit on the sidelines. I can't not go."

Blaylock couldn't help herself. She glanced at Grimson's swelling belly.

Grimson caught the look. "Don't you goddamn dare," she said. "Who do you think I'm fighting this war for, anyway?"

"Will you at least speak to the others? Let them know there's a risk?"

"You know I will. How much can I tell them?"

Blaylock felt her cover leaking away. "As little as possible."

"I'm going to have to give Jonathan more than 'it's dangerous.' He's going to want to know why. I'll have to tell him about Ciudad del Este, at the very least."

"Can we trust him?"

Flint gaze. "He's my husband."

Well done, girl. Hitting them out of the park today. "Sorry. I didn't—I mean ... I ..."

Grimson laughed. "You're blushing! When did you last do that?"

Blaylock twisted her lips. "Not since I discovered I could have gone out with James Easterman in Grade 11." She hadn't come by that little bit of info until the end of Grade 12.

Grimson touched her arm. "Are you going to go to Davos with us?"

"I was thinking about it."

"Our protection?" When Blaylock didn't answer, Grimson squeezed her arm. "I'm glad. Old times again, eh?"

Well ... "I'm not beating any drums, Kel. No finger paint. No marching. That's not why I'm going."

Shadow over Grimson's face, the cold touch of Blaylock's blood-truth. "I know." Solemn. Then the shadow passed. Hope and mischief replaced it. "You'll stay here, right?"

"Sure. Thanks."

"Don't thank me." Twinkle twinkle. "February's not for a while yet. Plenty of time to convert you."

"Riiiiight."

"Well, come on. You might as well see the rest of the cult compound." She hustled Blaylock out of the guest bedroom. "Grand tour, girlfriend. Welcome to Greenham Common."

Joe Chapel leaned against the window in Flanagan's office, let Flanagan walk him through the InSec hierarchy. "These guys are the board of directors," Flanagan said, calling up the names on his monitor. "Technically, anyway."

"How much do you see of them?"

"Not that much. Never did. And they were strictly figureheads when Pembroke was running things."

"And now?"

"It's like I told you. They used to be invisible. Now they're showing up all over the place, poking their heads in offices, throwing staff parties. You can't take the elevator without bumping into one of them. It's as if the only thing they do all day is wander around the building, being seen."

"What are you telling me?"

"That they're protesting too much."

"What about the Russians?"

"A lot more of them, but they're also very low key. I first noticed the change because so many of the orders were being routed for approval through the Moscow office."

"Does the name Stepan Sherbina mean anything to you?"

"Should it?"

"Never mind. Go on."

"One of our louder directors got himself dead, and then . . ." Flanagan turned away from his computer. Chapel watched him search for words. "It's hard to describe. It's one of those nuance things. Until Forbes was killed, when Russians were here, they were always 'visiting delegates' or some such thing. Honored guests, you know? Since then, they're just here. Sometimes one, sometimes a group, but they're always around."

"Like they own the place," Chapel summarized.

Flanagan shrugged. "These are just observations."

"I understand."

"Okay. Then there's the other weird thing. A couple of

weeks ago, our Russian division chief shows up. He's been in Moscow for years, and all of a sudden he's back and running around like a mad thing. Giving a lot of orders, too. He's gone again now, but I don't think he's back in Moscow. Somebody else is handling things at that end now."

"You think this guy's been disappeared, too?"

"No idea."

"What's his name?"

Flanagan called another picture up on the computer. "Leon West," he said.

Joe Chapel's blood, flash-frozen.

Blaylock thought, Conspicuous redemption. Blaylock thought, I am in hell. Greenham Common was co-housing in full flight. It soared. It thrived. It made Blaylock's skin crawl. By the end of her first twenty-four hours, she was fantasizing about being back in Ciudad del Este. By the end of her first week, not slitting Jonathan Alloway's throat had become a full-time job. As the new year closed in, Blaylock felt a tick developing in her cheek. But she stayed. She let the weeks pile up. Davos came closer. Blaylock eyed Grimson's belly, and felt cold.

Greenham Common was a complex of two dozen townhouses and apartments built around a central courtyard. There were entrances to the lower floor homes and their little gardens from the street, but otherwise access was off the courtyard. The idea was community. You couldn't avoid running into your neighbors. There were two ways to the courtyard. One was through the main entrance to the complex, on the Young Street side. On the opposite side, a narrow passage between the underground parkade and the housing came in off Langside.

The north side of the complex, facing onto Sargent Avenue, was the common house, where the dream of co-housing was made flesh. There was a dining room, big enough to haul in the entire community twice a week. Each household took a shift in the kitchen to prepare the big meals. There was a meeting room, where Blaylock had expected to see Sandinista banners and posters of Che Guevara, but it was sober and Power Point-friendly. There was a lounge with a TV big enough for football parties, and connected through an open archway was a kids' playroom. There was an office with three networked computers. There was a laundry room. Everything to make the common house into the beating heart of the co-housing.

Grimson and Alloway had a second-floor, two-bedroom apartment that looked out onto Young. Darryl Avery lived in a one-bedroom diagonally across the courtyard. His unit shared a rear wall with a townhouse, but his side windows had a view of Langside. Blaylock had trouble computing the view thing. The windows were big, huge apertures of invitation. They were the wide eyes of a teary Margaret Keane waif. In this neighborhood, they were begging to cry. Langside was Gangside, and Young was no more innocent. Greenham Common was a lie. It believed it was a utopian dream of urban renewal. Instead, it was a sasquatch footprint of first-strike gentrification. After the first communal dinner she attended, Blaylock asked Grimson, "You have to pass for WASP to live here?"

Grimson looked uncomfortable. "It just worked out that way."

"You guys blend right in around this neighborhood."

"Give us time. We're only beginning."

Marxists with Maids. Blaylock kept the thought to

herself. Not that she had a leg to stand on. Her family had been of that number. Grimson was trying to do more, Blaylock knew. She was walking the walk. Greenham Common wasn't the be-all. It was just the kind of home that fit with Grimson's principles. Curious to see how consistent the faithful were, Blaylock had a gander at the garage. Not a single SUV.

She put her foot wrong at the end of her second week there. Thursday nights, a crowd gathered in the common room to watch a movie. Blaylock, as guest, was invited to select the film. She went out, hesitated over the *Mystery Science Theater 3000* reunion treatment of *The Passion of the Christ*, wound up renting her favorite: *Patton*. The audience watched in a silence of cold and stone. When George C. Scott said, "Compared to war, all other forms of human endeavor shrink to insignificance," all heads turned to stare at Blaylock.

Two of the heads were amused. Judy Liang and Chuck Bilodeau. Other than Grimson, they were, for Blaylock, the saving graces of Greenham Common. Liang was a tiny, compressed ball of energy topped by curly black hair. Bilodeau was a tall drink of clean-shaven sobriety. They wrote opposing columns for *Winnipeg Eye*, a what's-happening weekly. Liang's beat was militant left. Bilodeau's was a right that flirted with libertarianism. In print, they constructed straw men of each other's beliefs and torched them bright. At the Common, they were a comedy team. One routine had them mock-frothing, clawing for each other's throats, caricaturing their own positions and unable to keep their faces straight. The other gag was older. They'd been friends since high school, when Bilodeau, bucking all the draconian rules of that cesspit of social Darwinism, had come out of the closet. Their game, as arch as it was affectionate, was queen and fag hag to the *n*th degree. When they went into that act, and they were *on*, Blaylock worried about Judy's husband, Mark. She didn't think anyone could laugh that hard and long without rupturing something.

During one of the community dinners, Blaylock buttonholed Bilodeau. She had to know. "Explain it to me," she said. "You here. This place's philosophy and yours..."

Bilodeau smiled. "I like people." And because the smile was so broad, and the sentiment so clear-eyed and genuine, Blaylock felt the surprise gut-pinch of shame.

Then there was Alloway. Figure this guy out. Hell, figure the whole marriage out. Blaylock knew she was in trouble the first day at the Common. Grimson had finished showing her around, and they were in the apartment, kicking back in the living room. The furniture was pure garage sale: sprung springs, worn fabric, patterns a heartburn reminder of the seventies. Blaylock sat down in a blue felt armchair and almost fell over backwards when it turned out to be a rocker. She glared at Grimson, steadying herself. Grimson laughed. "Mortgage is a killer, what can I say? This is all we can afford for now." Grimson was a mechanic. Alloway did freelance Web design. The money came in, but they were living large for their means.

On the wall facing the living room window, Blaylock saw a series of dry-mounted posters. They announced protests and talks. There were a lot of raised fists, spray-paint lettering, and exclamation marks. Alloway's name was on all of them.

"Yeah, yeah, I know," Grimson said. "You don't have to tell me." She grabbed a file folder from the top of a bookcase. "Check these out."

Blaylock flipped through the clippings. They were all

anti-globalization movement coverage. Alloway started out as a blob in crowd photographs, circled with yellow highlighter. Then he began to be mentioned by name. In the most recent pieces, he was front and center in the pictures, and being quoted all over the place. Blaylock had been out of the Canadian protest loop while she was in the States and Paraguay. Alloway had turned into a big fish. "You're married to a superstar."

"Not yet. The turning point was Ottawa, though. He really made a splash there."

"Good for him."

"Don't give me that tone. Yes, he does love the sound of his own voice. Yes, the publicity is major ego-fuel. But ..."

"There's a reason why you love him."

"His voice is worth listening to. I'm involved in this struggle because of him."

"You already had these tendencies when we were in the forces."

Grimson sat cross-legged on the carpet. "Tendencies aren't the same as direction."

"Kel, if I find out you left the army because of him—"

"Relax. I was looking for something. Then I saw him give a talk at Mondragon." The coffee shop and bookstore held court in the Exchange district. The warehouses that had seen the 1919 general strike now clustered protectively around the last but determined gasp of public Winnipeg radicalism.

"And you were converted." Blaylock found the narrative arc depressing.

Grimson shook her head. "Already was. I saw something I could take an active role in." Her face had the glow Blaylock remembered from the early idealism in the army. Before Bosnia. "Jonathan speaks well. I mean, he'll knock your socks off. That's what started Darryl's hero-worship."

"I'd figured they were childhood pals."

Grimson shook her head. "Darryl joined up about a year before we ran into you. Anyway, good speeches and all, the Global Response thing was still a bit ..." She waggled her hand. "Needed some discipline."

"Oh, Christ. Behind every great man ..."

Grimson leaned forward and swatted Blaylock's knee. "Cut it out. And behave."

Blaylock behaved. It was hard. Alloway had put her off when she'd met him in Ottawa. Grimson's fairy tale of romance and activism didn't help. When he showed up at the apartment, Blaylock went max effort on civility, but she couldn't see him with Grimson's eyes. Just couldn't. She didn't want him to know anything about her, but she surrendered, let Grimson give him the army background, and enough about Ciudad del Este to make the Davos tip sound good. Result: he was even more excited about going. Figured. And dig this weird thing. Though the best Blaylock could muster was the polite smile and the cool interest (and that was harder than a death march), Alloway treated her like the Second Coming. The hell?

Blaylock behaved. She gave the couple quality time alone. She took a long walk through the neighborhood every night. At least an hour, savoring the December bite of the air. She enjoyed the walks. She liked winter. It hurt good. The air was a scalpel, slicing clean. Her nose was anesthetized by wind chill. The cold, dropping below -20, summoned sounds that snapped, hard and brittle: *kr-krunch* of boots on snow, harsh *crack* of trees, deeper *bang* of house walls. Winnipeg in winter, pure as iron.

One night, her walk stretched to two hours. She wandered over the Maryland bridge and into River Heights. She took the path she knew would hurt, down Academy, turning left onto Harrow, and then right onto Harvard. It was old-home night. She stood beneath the snow-covered elms, and stared at the address where she had grown up. There was a new house there now. Any trace of the explosion had vanished years ago. The fir her father had planted the year she was born still stood, towering now above the roof of the house. She listened to the night. The silence felt like nostalgia. Christmas lights flickered in the windows, wreaths hung on doors, but this wasn't a block of ostentatious displays. This was old Winnipeg at its most Christmas-card perfect. Nostalgia became melancholy. She was surrounded by good memories, but there was the barrier of the terrible night that blocked her now and forever from reconnecting with the world where someone named Jennifer had built snowmen, sung carols, and never killed.

Being here brought back her mother's last, deep worry. *I'm not sure what upsets me more: that you feel some people need killing, or that you believe you're one of those chosen to do the killing.* The echo was old now, and had lost its teeth. There had been too many deaths. "I'm sorry, Mum," she whispered. "But I'm damned good at it." The echo fell into silence.

She walked back to Greenham Common. There, the apartment was bathed in wavering candleglow. Alloway and Grimson were seated in the living room, disheveled, their faces almost as flushed as her own. Alloway coughed and excused himself. Blaylock rolled her eyes.

"Sorry." Grimson only the teeniest bit sheepish.

Blaylock hung up her parka. "I guess this was a good one."

Now Grimson sounded contrite. "I don't mean to rub your face in it."

Blaylock snorted. "No worries." She perched on the arm of the sofa.

"How long has it been for you?" Contrition had given way to the concern of the well-fed.

"A year-plus."

"Do you miss it?"

"No." The answer was quick, automatic. Blaylock startled herself. She thought for a moment, and realized she hadn't lied. She missed Flanagan. Or she missed the promise, the potential of what might have been, what might be, but was still floating in unrealized ether. She missed the confidence of reaching out and knowing there would be contact. She missed all this. She acknowledged the absences, then shut them up again.

Grimson cinched her robe tighter. Her fingers clutched the terry cloth once, twice, three times. "I'm going to say something, and I'm saying it to help, not to make you mad, okay?"

"No worries," Blaylock said again. A tea-light candelabra stood on a small, white end table beside the couch. Blaylock moved her index finger back and forth through a flame.

"You know when I teased you about scanning when we met for coffee in Ottawa? You did it again here."

"Really?"

"When I gave you the tour. You were checking for exits, weak flanks, I don't know what else. Jen, do you ever turn it off?"

"No." Quick and automatic and honest again.

"Not even in bed?"

Blaylock didn't answer. She remembered making love

to Flanagan the night he had killed for the first time. Her memories of their sex were tinged hazy with battlefield smoke.

"You know what I think?" Grimson said. "I think you're sublimating sex into war."

Blaylock thought about the experience of battle, and how the word that came to mind to describe it was *absolute*. "No," she said, with the hardest honesty yet. She met Grimson's gaze and held it. "Sex is sublimated war."

11

Just before Christmas, Blaylock realized she'd picked up a stalker. The stalker's name was Jenny, and she was six. There was no tripping of Blaylock's threat antennae, and she didn't notice her shadow at first. She registered the girl's presence, but took some time to pick up on the pattern. Jenny watching from the window of the lower floor townhouse when Blaylock left Grimson's apartment. Jenny watching when Blaylock came home. Jenny nearby everywhere Blaylock went in the Common. Jenny with the big, big eyes and the uncombable red hair. Blaylock clued in during a communal dinner. It wasn't tricky. Jenny wolfed down her food and stood just behind Blaylock's chair for the rest of the meal. Blaylock felt the eyes, finally understood. She twisted around in her seat, smiled, and asked the girl her name. The answer was a whisper out of a huge well of timidity. "I'm a Jennifer, too," Blaylock said.

Jenny nodded. This was not news. Blaylock sensed the name coincidence was the root cause of the fascination. "Mommy says you're a soldier."

"I used to be." She'd let a censored version of the truth out for public consumption.

"You don't fight any more?" Disappointed.

"I still fight."

"Oh." Eyes fixed on Blaylock's face. "What happened to your cheek?"

"A tree bit me."

Eyes very, very wide.

Big mistake, being glib. Blaylock learned her lesson Christmas Eve. She was returning from her night walk. Grimson and Alloway had been looking moons at each other, and Blaylock had fled before the Christmas spirit had her choking up eggnog. She'd made it another long walk, another two hours. Jenny's mother, Faye McNicoll, opened her front door and called out. "Jen! Hi! Could I speak with you for a minute?"

Now her antennae picked up danger. Vaguely curious, but ready to be pissed, Blaylock walked over. McNicoll, still shrugging into her parka, pulled the front door closed behind her. Blaylock's nose twitched at the hint of pot pourri incense that wafted out of the apartment. McNicoll was holding a sheet of paper. "I really think you need to see this," she said. It was a child's drawing. Thick Crayola lines showed a woman in a tree. The tree had big yellow eyes, and a bigger red mouth. The woman had a red splotch on her face. Blaylock chuckled. McNicoll stiffened. "I don't think driving a wedge between my daughter and nature is a laughing matter."

"Oh, come off it. Is she crying? Is she having nightmares?"

"No," McNicoll admitted. "But I don't want her to."

Blaylock had a vision of Jenny in a foam-rubber cocoon. She said nothing.

"I'm sorry," McNicoll said, climbing down. She smiled at Blaylock, and the smile was so emphatic in its welcome and self-comfort that Blaylock felt her hackles rise. "I don't mean to be hostile. That's not my mode."

Mode? Blaylock thought. "No problem," she said. "I won't tell Jenny any horror stories," she added, hoping the promise would end the conversation.

"I've been meaning to have a chat with you for a while," McNicoll went on, and Blaylock thought, Oh no. "Please don't take this the wrong way, but your aura seems so dark."

"I'll have a word with it."

"Oh, don't joke. Please don't. I'm serious. I'd really like to help."

"I don't need—"

"You do. You may not think so, but you do. I really don't want to offend you ..."

"Don't worry," Blaylock said, resigned.

"Thank you. I was going to say that you seem so disconnected from the Goddess."

Blaylock kept her face straight, and she did not close her eyes. "I suppose I am." Deadpan.

"There are exercises, you know. I'd be happy to show you. We could plug your energy right back into the Earth Current. You'd be amazed at the difference this would make. I don't mean to brag, but I am a good teacher in this area. I've had positive results before. One good meditation on the stars, and I bet we could put you into a State of Breath without even breaking a sweat."

Terrific. "Very kind. I'll think about it." Blaylock took a step towards the stairs leading to Grimson's apartment.

"Promise that you will."

"Sure." There, done. Thought about and dismissed.

"Thank you." McNicoll's eyes shone as she said goodnight and went back inside.

Blaylock blew air, her breath a crystal fog, and she stomped up the stairs. The effort of civility had rotted her mood. "New Age sewage ditz-brain *moron*," she muttered as she let herself in. She smelled the detergent tang of grass, began to wish she had walked for three hours.

Grimson looked up. She was lying on the couch. The only lights were on the potted fir tree in the far right corner. The television was on, set to an infomercial station. Grimson wasn't watching. She was waiting for me, Blaylock thought. Everybody's worried about my bloody welfare tonight. "Merry Christmas to you, too," Grimson said.

"Har." Blaylock pulled off her coat. "Where's Jonathan?"

"Sleeping. Who got your dander up?"

Blaylock kicked off her boots and slumped into the armchair. "That walking argument for eugenics downstairs."

"That's unkind."

"Damn straight. You want more?"

"Why are you so mad?"

"Some things get me. Spiritual wanking is one of them."

Grimson killed the flickering glow of the TV. Her hair picked up red tints from the tree lights. "You don't even know her! All this venom on the basis of how many seconds of conversation?"

"If I come to know her any better, I might have to kill her." She bounced her knee up and down, tapping anger.

"You know, I almost believe you."

"I'm kidding."

"Sure. And what would you do if I told you I've joined Faye in her worship now and then?"

Blaylock's knee stopped moving. She stared at Grimson, looking for the joke, trying to hear the irony, getting no joy. "Hippiechick," she said, "you disappoint me." She felt very tired.

"Why? Would you feel better if I was toddling off to All Saints Anglican every Sunday?"

"I wouldn't give a shit if you were singing the choir fantastic at Calvary Temple. You still disappoint me."

"Why?"

"Because you were in Bosnia. You know the world. You know reality, or at least you should. No excuses, girlfriend. None."

"There is room for the spiritual in the world."

"Not in mine."

Grimson swung her legs off the couch and sat up. "You worry me, Rammer," she said, her voice soft. "You're much too hard."

"You going to stage an intervention every time I come back from a stroll?" Grimson didn't answer, but Blaylock read the hurt on her face. Blaylock didn't stop. She was still angry. "Meanwhile, you let me know as soon as a healing circle changes the world."

"And you're changing the world for the better by hurting people?"

"Never said I was."

"Don't bullshit me. You believe in something. I know you do. So what is it? What do you believe in?"

The silence stretched tense. The building shifted in the cold: bang. A window rattled. Blaylock said, "Go to bed, Hippiechick."

"Whatcha reading?" Darryl Avery asked. His voice was loud, a chest echo bouncing off the windows of the Millennium Library's indoor terrace. Avery's volume knob was jammed at supermax. He took off his Walkman, pulled out the chair next to Alloway, and settled his bulk at the table. Alloway turned the book so Avery could see the cover. Che Guevara's eyes glittered with purpose. "*Guerilla Warfare?*"

Avery said. "Jeez, man." Alloway watched Avery's face take in the pages of foolscap on the table, the deep clusters of notes. "Man," Avery said again. "You're totally serious."

"It's the situation that's serious."

"Hey, you know it. But, uh . . ." He couldn't seem to keep his eyes off the book. "I didn't know . . . I mean—"

"You mean you thought I've been talking through my ass the last few weeks," Alloway snapped, irritated. "If even you won't take me at my word, who will?"

"No no no, man. Hey, it's just me bein' scared."

"Darryl, we've been talking about more direct action since Ottawa."

"Yeah, but some of that stuff was pot dreams, you know?" When Alloway sighed, Avery added quickly, "For me, I mean. That's me. That's why it won't ever be me taking that totally fantastic next step first."

Alloway put the book down. "We're not taking that step yet. I don't know how useful this thing is going to be anyway."

"No tips?"

"Oh sure, but it's all theory and strategy that's not really applicable. We're not going to be in the jungle. And there's no *Anarchist's Cookbook* stuff, either."

"Oh, well." Avery looked relieved. "You sure we should be going this route, man?"

"I don't think it's a question of should. I don't think we have any choice. You know I'm right."

Avery didn't nod. He fingered one of the sheets of foolscap. "You been a lot heavier about all this since Jen came to stay with you guys." He cleared his throat, didn't meet Alloway's eyes.

"Meaning what?"

Avery shrugged. "Nothing. Just noticing."

"Notice all you want. It's a coincidence," Alloway lied. "We were heading in this direction. She just happened to show up at the right time. Call it fate." If he didn't think about it too hard, he could almost believe what he was saying. He *had* been frustrated after Ottawa, *had* been looking for a meaningful way to fight back. But he and Avery hadn't really done anything more concrete than create baroque revenge fantasies. He'd felt shame. And then the media had become a lot more interested in what he had to say. He'd become a Voice. Just over a month ago, he'd actually been attacked, *by name*, in a *National Post* editorial. Sure, just in passing, and in a list of names that began and ended with Naomi Klein, but still. He and Grimson had thrown a big party to celebrate. He'd become distracted, enjoying the attention too much, not noticing that he wasn't making a damn bit of difference. The World Economic Forum was coming up, and was it all just going to be more of the same? What good would that do? Much more uselessness, and he wouldn't be attacked, just mocked.

Then Blaylock came. She was still using the name Baylor, but Grimson took him aside, told him the truth. Told him her name, told him what she'd done in Paraguay, and told him to keep his trap shut, for Chrissake, *or else*. He promised, and kept the promise. Pretty much the worst thing he could think of was to have Grimson disappointed in him. Never going to happen, and so the loop ended with him. Wall of iron, tower of silence. Darryl, you would just *shit* if you knew what I knew, but this is a need-to-know situation, and you don't, buddy. Alloway knew he was seeing the iceberg tip of Blaylock. If Paraguay had happened, then sure as dogma there was a lot more that went down. And who was Blaylock? He knew she and his wife had been army buddies, but who was she now? Was she working for anyone? Not for the multinationals, or the States, he would put money on that. She was spooky, money down on that, too. When he got up this morning, he found her sitting, thunder-shadow, in the living room. Some survival instinct had said, *Don't bother her. Just don't.* Because this is what he knew for good and true: someone hard and dangerous was staying in his home. That excited him. Inspired him. He could do serious damage, too. He would prove it.

Avery asked, "You really planning something for Davos?"

"What was it you told me after Ottawa? You said next time the pigs come after us, we give them a taste of their own medicine. Hit back hard so they know we mean business as much as they do."

"Yeah, but I was just flapping my yap."

"Doesn't change the fact that you were right." Plus there was Blaylock's warning. Something bad was going to happen at Davos. Letting Avery and the other members of Global Response know about a risk without saying how he came by the information had been tricky. But he'd promised Grimson. So he said the info came from Internet rumor. Everybody believed that. Everybody also believed the warning was so much cybershit. Fine by him. Nobody backing out.

"Hit them back. . . . Yeah." Avery's face glazed with concentration and thought. Then he slapped the tabletop. "*Yeah!*" He grinned. "Fantastic. We hit 'em back."

"See. You did take that step first. You pointed the way."

Avery beamed.

"If only I could figure out *how* we'll hit back, though," Alloway added, frowning at the book. Should he ask

Blaylock? He wasn't sure she'd tell him. He didn't want to seem like the clumsy puppy, either. There was also the other problem. "Whole thing's going to be moot if we can't even reach Davos," he muttered. Over the years, the Swiss had turned security around the WEF into a high and fine art. Only a small number of authorized protestors would be allowed into the town. The army would be out in force, probably outnumbering the ranks of civil society. And Alloway doubted Global Response could hike it in by stealth.

Sure. Good excuses all. But giggling at the back of his mind, sticking it to his self-worth, came the question, *Would you dare?* Came the doubt, *No.*

Avery slapped his forehead. "Oh hey, man, hit me stupid. I totally forgot why I came. Kelly told me I could probably find you here. Global Response took one hell of a fantastic phone call today."

"Yeah?"

"Irina Zelkova wants to meet you when she's here."

Alloway's mouth dried. Possibilities bloomed, sudden roses in the desert.

Barry Reynolds went shopping. He went to Home Hardware. He went to Canadian Tire. He went to Costco. He went to Shoppers Drug Mart. On his list: matches, potassium chlorate, sugar, soap, kerosene, charcoal, sulfur, wax, sawdust. The only thing he couldn't buy was potassium nitrate. No problemo: one of the guys ran a farm.

Then it was workshop time.

Hot *damn*.

12

January 13. The Messiah in town.
"Jen, you absolutely have to hear her speak."
"Yeah, I'd like to."
Startled pause. "You would? Just like that?"
"Just like that."

The Hotel Fort Garry. Vintage railroad hotel, New World comfort dresssed up as an Old World chateau. Top-floor suite. Room service. The Messiah at breakfast.

Zelkova had almost finished her scrambled eggs when she heard the suite door unlock. She turned her head, opened her mouth to say, "Not yet," thinking she'd forgotten to put out the DO NOT DISTURB. Then, mouth still hanging, her breath caught in surprise as Sherbina stepped in. He dropped a carryall and spread his arms, cat-grinning.

"Remember me?"

Barely. Weeks of travel on mutually exclusive agendas. Zelkova: across the room in one bound and into her husband's arms. "What the *hell* are you doing here?"

"Freed up some time. I have a few irons in the fire in Canada, so I thought I'd take care of them now, join you for this leg." He kissed her. "All right with you?"

She showed him how all right it was. Afterwards, sheets sweat-tangled, she rubbed eyes bleary from passion and saw the bedside clock. It glared digital red, told her that she only had twenty-five minutes to get her clothes, her papers, herself, and her daughter, still sleeping in the adjoining room, over to the University of Winnipeg. No time. But time anyway, time for the question that she had not wanted to ask over the phone. She rested her chin on Sherbina's chest, played with a long hair that curled around his nipple, focused on the hair and not on his face, and asked, "Have you heard from Lawrence Dunn recently?" When, of course, there was no answer, she raised her head and did watch his face. "Because I have."

Sherbina pursed his lips. "Oops."

"Oops? *Oops?*" She shook her head. "I knew it. Are you trying to shut him down? Because if you are ..."

"No. I swear, Irina. If anything, I'm giving him an even higher profile."

"I thought he'd been on CNN a lot lately. Still, he didn't sound happy when he called me."

"He should be. If you talk to him again, tell him to relax. I'm not going to hurt him, I swear on my father's grave."

"When your father finally dies, he is *not* going to be buried in consecrated ground, I can tell you that. You should know better than to try that one on me. What are you up to?"

Sherbina grinned. He raised his palms, Mr. Innocence. "I thought I'd do a nice thing for you. I thought I'd throw the opposition a bone. Make the game interesting."

"I don't believe you." She climbed off the bed and gathered her clothes. No time for a shower now. No time even to glance at the notes for her talk. Another thought struck her as she dressed. "Is Dunn still coming to Davos?"

"As far as I know. I told you, I'm not going to do anything to silence him." He stood up, too. "Why don't I take Inna to a movie while you're busy?"

She gave him a sharp look. "Very nice and don't change the subject. What are you planning?"

"Irina..."

"I want to know."

He sighed. "You know it doesn't work when our worlds collide."

"That's right. But I don't think I'm the one who's bringing them together."

"Touché." He shrugged into his pants.

"I want some of my people at Davos, too," she stated.

He met her gaze. They stared each other down. "I'm not in charge of Swiss security."

"That's a cop-out."

"Okay, okay. But they'd better behave themselves. I have a lot riding on Davos."

A strange notion surfaced. "You want to go legitimate?"

"I want to bring the legitimate in line."

Eckhardt-Grammaté Hall at the U of Winnipeg. Steep raked seating, a bum in every seat, and above each bum a rapt face. The Messiah speaking.

Blaylock was impressed. Zelkova was good. She had notes, but she barely glanced at them. Her English was excellent, her accent pushing her W and V sounds to the front of her mouth and charging her inflections with passion. Her speech wasn't just come-the-revolution fantasies and paranoid dreams. She'd been in the trenches in Geneva, and it showed. She had tasted bureaucracy in all its marble inertia, and it showed. The battle had scarred her, tempered her, and it showed. Oh, the energy was there. But so was the cynicism. So were the facts. She mustered statistics like massed artillery. Best of all, Blaylock thought, was the anger. Zelkova raged. She raged with intelligence. She had had her illusions burned away, and wasn't happy about it. Blaylock watched, judged, liked what she saw.

The speech went well, Zelkova thought. Of course it did. Preaching to the choir. She'd done her research, knew that being anti-globalization at the U of W was like singing *God Bless America* at a Republican Party convention. That was fine. She was giving another talk, meaning identical but tenor very different, to the Winnipeg Chamber of Commerce in the afternoon. She was entitled to a light warm-up before facing the tough crowd. She had almost stumbled, though. Just once. She believed in eye contact, worked hard at it, used an eye-lock with someone in the crowd to punch up each assertion. Five minutes into her presentation, she had met the eyes of a woman sitting at the back of the hall. Zelkova hit a wall of ice and glass, of lasers and the unforgiving. Her words tangled and piled up, froze. Zelkova looked away, cleared her throat, moved on. She didn't stumble again, but kept half an eye on the woman, wondering what sort of Scud would be sent her way come question time. She needn't have worried. The woman didn't participate. She sat quiet and dark all the way through the session. She applauded at the end, though, and Zelkova stupidly felt like that was the biggest victory of the tour.

Seated in the front row was Jonathan Alloway, somehow looking different from his media appearances. She couldn't put her finger on the change while she was speaking. Afterwards, once the students had filed out and there were only the few people left she had arranged to meet, Alloway stepped forward to introduce himself, and Zelkova realized what was different. He had the same look on his face as the students who had come to shake her hand after the speech. His face didn't say *warrior*. It said *acolyte*. Zelkova's heart sank.

Blaylock waited until only the Global Response gang was still in the hall, clustered around Zelkova, then she made her way down. Alloway was going on and on, *honor* this and *excited* that, fanboy worship. Embarrassing. Zelkova had a stricken look on her face. Grimson, Avery, and a couple of other hangers-on waited to squeeze a word in. Faye McNicoll was there, eyes aglow. Chuck Bilodeau and Judy Liang were crouched, ready to pounce with warring questions. Alloway turned his head as Blaylock approached. Without breaking his flow, he said, "And this is—"

"Jen Baylor," Blaylock cut him off, not trusting him, in his excitement, to keep the alias straight.

Zelkova shook her hand. Her gaze was searching. "Do I know your name? I seem to feel I should."

Blaylock felt Zelkova trying to take her measure, probing for friend or foe. She shrugged. "I doubt it. I write freelance. Maybe in the business pages. Can't say I have a high profile."

Zelkova was looking puzzled. "Business?" she said, and looked from Blaylock to the rainbow-blast fashions of Global Response.

"She's our worm in the apple," Alloway said, smug as a swagger.

Blaylock shrugged again, bristling at the appropriation.

She thought, Shut up, shut up, *shut up*. She'd be lucky to have a cover left by lunch. Zelkova was smiling now. "We should talk," she said.

They did that evening. Blaylock met her in the Fort Garry's Palm Room. The lounge's domed ceiling was ballroom-high. The gold scrollwork on the white walls and ceiling, set off against the green curtains, bespoke austere luxury. Intimacy was restored by the warm reds of the carpet and seats. A jazz trio was set up in front of the windows, and was playing low-key standards. Zelkova was at a table near the entrance, far enough from the band that the music wouldn't be intrusive. Blaylock sat down, ordered a coffee. "Everything I say here is off the record," Zelkova said.

"Fine."

Zelkova cocked her head. "That was easy. You do not want a story?"

"I'm on vacation."

"Hmm. What exactly is your connection with Global Response?"

"Kelly Grimson's an old friend. She's putting me up for a while."

"I see. And was Jonathan correct about your role in the business community?"

"You're asking where I stand." When Zelkova nodded, Blaylock said, "I'm a cynic, not a cheerleader." She gave Zelkova her sunniest smile. "So did you have a good lunch with the gang?"

Zelkova took a deep breath, as if she was about to sigh. She stopped herself. "Their enthusiasm is commendable," she said.

Blaylock snorted. "Diplomatic."

"I was impressed by your friend."

"Smart girl," Blaylock agreed. "A good person. Backbone of their little movement, I would say." She decided to probe, see where things would lead. "She's wasting her time."

Zelkova studied her. Blaylock kept her face neutral. "You do not share their optimism, I take it."

"Jonathan Alloway is the best kind of bullshit artist. He's so convinced that what is coming out of his ass is pure gold that he has the others smelting it into bricks and loving it."

Zelkova choked on her tea. "You are off the record, too, I suppose." She didn't wait for an answer. "But they have their co-housing project." The argument sounded to Blaylock like another probe, sent her way. "They showed me around. Isn't that a concrete accomplishment?"

Blaylock rolled her eyes. "More like stucco. I don't see a touchy-feely condo rolling back the forces of slavering capitalism, but hey, that's just me." She took the probe and launched it back. "Do you?"

Zelkova didn't answer at first. She stared into the middle distance. Blaylock waited for her to make a decision. "After I finish my speaking tour, I will be participating in the World Economic Forum." Davos again. Blaylock worked to keep from looking too interested. Zelkova smiled, and it was a smile Blaylock recognized as one she used herself: a delight at the perversity of the universe's unfolding. "My husband and I do not agree about the directions the WEF should take."

Her husband? And *wham*, the epiphany was a kick to the back of her head. Blaylock's mouth dried as that slow, stupid brain of hers finally took the names, lined them up, saw the combination. Irina Zelkova, supernova activist, thorn in global capital's side, spender of Kornukopia's money, wife of CEO Stepan Sherbina. Sherbina at Ciudad del Este. The big show at Davos. One tumbler after another falling into place, the steel door on Pandora's box ready to swing open. And still she didn't have enough pieces, still the picture made no sense. She nodded for Zelkova to go on, hoping that she hadn't gone pale.

"He is going to have lots of friends at the forum." Zelkova poured herself some more tea. She seemed more concerned with finding words than watching Blaylock. "I will have some, but I am always looking for more. After seeing his press interviews, I had hoped Jonathan might be..." She fumbled for the words.

"Useful?" Blaylock prompted.

"You sound like my husband. That is not what I wanted to say, but..."

"I understand. But now you've met him, and he's just another street shouter."

"The street has a role to play, too, though."

"Not in Davos, if the last few years are anything to go by."

"True, but there are ways of opening up the streets again. A bit, perhaps. I think Global Response could make their presence known."

"And you'll help them do that." Wishing that she wouldn't.

Zelkova nodded. "But I do not know if I can help them into the WEF itself."

Blaylock laughed. "Fat lot of good they'd do. Anyway, why would you need to? You're there, mounting the NGO charge."

"I was thinking more of the media."

"Are you proposing something?"

"You dismissed what Jonathan said about you, but

what if you really were the worm in the apple? I looked up some of your articles on the Internet after lunch. You are..." Zelkova gestured, hunting for the words again.

"Untainted by an anti-business bias?" Blaylock suggested. "More likely to be taken seriously, however briefly?"

"You would reach a wide audience. That I can guarantee." The player in Zelkova's eyes emerged, and for a moment Blaylock had no trouble seeing the union of left-wing activist and robber baron. "Admission to the forum is very expensive," Zelkova continued, "but I would be happy to pay your way."

Blaylock tried to keep a straight face. She thought of the ocean of blood money she already had at her disposal. She thought about the Nancy Drew covert op Zelkova was proposing, one that would drop her poison straight into the heart of the action in Davos. She lost the battle and laughed until she was blind with tears.

Sam Reed wanted him in Davos for the big show. Chapel didn't know the details of the show. Nor, apparently, did the President. Reed knew the expected results, and that was enough for him. Not for Chapel. Serving his President was his duty and his honor, and he was worrying.

He was worrying about Leon West. Reed was gambling. This was a big roll, an all-or-nothing, break-the-bank or break-the-kneecaps bet. What had kept Chapel awake and sweating nights since his last visit to Flanagan was the thought that the dice might be loaded. By Sherbina. So Chapel was in the dark of West's apartment, waiting for the man to come home. It had been a while since Chapel had done fieldwork, but the old moves had come back fast, easy as breathing. The action felt good. It had the honesty of force. It took Chapel away from ulcer speculation. Chapel was a head-to-toe shadow, black clothes, black mask. He used a pocket Maglite to find his way around, kept the beam away from the windows. West's home was another question mark. On Central Park West at 82nd, it had belonged to Karl Noonan, ex of Special Ops, then InSec enforcer, lately DNAed as dead three or four times over at Ember Lake. Why had West moved in here? Chapel took a guess at assigned housing. Assume a Kornukopia takeover of InSec. Assume Sherbina at the center, not a sparrow falling to earth without his knowing. Giving West this home might be evidence of humor, black and bladed. I'm starting to know you, Chapel thought.

He paused in the kitchen and shone his light on the fridge. Magnets all over, covering most of the surface with a child's drawings. Horses, lots of horses. One of a family with square bodies, circle heads, crucifix arms and legs. The art signed SANDI in kidscrawl. The paper was curling, old. Chapel had checked: West was divorced, alimony his only contact with his daughter for five years. Beneath the drawings, a travel itinerary. Chapel glanced at it, saw that West was off to Switzerland. Another familiar face at Davos. Not a real surprise, but what hat would West be wearing there? The side of the fridge stopped Chapel. A rash of magnetic letters had been arranged to spell FUCK over and over, at least a dozen times, in a silent scream.

Chapel heard a key in the lock. He pocketed the light, moved in a silent glide through the apartment to stand next to the door. It opened, and West stepped in. He reached for the light switch. Chapel grabbed his wrist, twisted, threw West face-first against the wall. He slammed the door and locked it while West collapsed to the floor, whimpering. He curled into a ball and covered his face with his hands. "Not the nose," West pleaded. "Not the nose."

Chapel crouched over him, yanked West's hands away. He pulled the light back out and shone it in West's eyes. He noticed now the bad set on the bridge of West's nose. West had the damage of a boxer without the physique. "You don't know me," Chapel said, "but you're going to pretend I'm your sweet mother and you're going to tell me whatever I want to know, am I right?"

West's eyes widened with the purest terror Chapel had ever seen. "This is a test," West whispered.

That broke Chapel's stride for a minute. More question marks. He continued. "I know you work for InSec. I know you ran the Russian division. There are Russians all over InSec now, so I think that means you work for Stepan Sherbina, too." West's eyes bugged out. Roger that, Chapel thought. "And I know you're writing speeches for the President. Here's what I want you to tell me. Which one are you really working for?" West shook his head, no no no, and started to cry. "Come on," Chapel said, and he reached for West's nose.

"You don't need to do this!" West shrieked. "I'm loyal! *I'm loyal!*"

Chapel hesitated, startled by West's desperate terror. "Loyal to whom?" he pressed.

"*Both,*" West hissed. "*Both.*" The venom was as pure as the terror had been. The word was a curse, a lashing out, a spear-tip of hatred.

"You can't be," Chapel told him.

West scuttled back, spitting cat, jittery crab. "*I'm loyal,*" the rattlesnake scream again, and then another noise, part sob, part laugh. West scrambled to his feet and ran to the bedroom. The door slammed. *"Fuck all of you and your tests!"*

Chapel was still crouched, still startled. Then he stood, and walked to the bedroom. He opened the door, too weirded to be careful, and jerked back at the *bang*. He felt a wet sponge slap his face. He dropped, rolled away, and pulled out his pistol. Silence. He waited. Then he figured it out, stood, and walked into the bedroom, turning on the light. West's corpse was fetal on the floor, mouth sucking the muzzle of a pistol, fingers clamped in comfort around the trigger. Chapel grunted, wiped convulsively at his face. His hands came away sticky with West's mind.

Evening. Jenny was standing at the main entrance to Greenham Common as Blaylock approached. "I'm on guard," the girl said.

"Really. What are you guarding?"

Jenny giggled. "I'm watching for you." She turned solemn. "I have a message. They're having a meeting. They're waiting for you."

"Message received and acknowledged," Blaylock said, and Jenny beamed. She walked beside Blaylock into the complex. She reached up, and her mitten took Blaylock's glove. Blaylock froze. Her fingers went numb, her arm locked into rigor mortis. She looked down with something like fear into Jenny's face. Jenny was the first child she'd been around since Flanagan's nephew, Eddie. Eddie, incinerated by Karl Noonan. Before Eddie, there had been the little bodies of Bosnia. This gesture did not belong in the world Blaylock had chosen. She felt awkward, the natural response burnt and gone years ago. She didn't pull her hand away, but she didn't squeeze back. The war machine couldn't move. It was all she could do to croak, "Hey."

"I'm going to be like you when I grow up," Jenny said.

Blaylock swallowed, felt a huge stone go down her throat. It hurt like hell. She made herself move. She crouched, brought her face level with Jenny's. "That's..." She had to start again. "That's sweet. But you mustn't say that. Your mom wouldn't like it."

"It's a secret," Jenny whispered.

The gesture came, but she had to think each phase of the movement through consciously. She reached out with her right hand, turned it sideways, touched Jenny's cheek with the tips of her fingers. "No," she said. "You might not understand, but I am what I am so you won't ever have to be. The worst thing you could do is be like me." She pushed herself through the rest of the gesture. She kissed Jenny on the forehead. Then she fled.

13

The meeting room was full. Not every one of Greenham Common's seventy residents was a member of Global Response, but the sympathies were unanimous. Everyone wanted in on the planning. The place was hot, and Blaylock wished she'd left her coat at Grimson's apartment before coming here. She squeezed in, leaned against the wall, and watched the stagnation of consensus. The process cheered her. Maybe they wouldn't be able to get it together. Maybe the Davos mission would be another Alloway pipe dream. Something for him and Avery to stick in their bong. Blaylock liked the odds, except for the wild card in Grimson. After all, Greenham Common had been built.

"It's the money," Grimson said, and Blaylock forced herself not to grin. "Flying there, staying there, the whole bit. We're looking at a few grand each, *minimum*."

"Bastards pricing themselves into safety," Alloway glowered. The mood in the room was turning to sludge and gloom. Blaylock loved it.

Then Avery said, "There's always Mumsy and Dadsy."

Alloway reddened, but didn't contradict. Blaylock started worrying again. His mother had been a Conservative in the provincial legislature since the mountains cooled. His father owned a dry-cleaning chain. They had a house on Wellington Crescent, the big blue Boardwalk square on Winnipeg's Monopoly board. Their son spat on everything they stood for, but they kept pulling him out of financial holes, subsidizing his adventures in activism, and then sending him apoplectic by talking about his *phase* and his *hobbies*. Fur coats and pressed suits had helped raise Greenham Common from its foundations.

Grimson rubbed her forehead, deep shame clouding her features. "We can't do that again."

"We will if we have to," Alloway muttered. "We're going."

Wes Tibbit looked at Blaylock. "Are you going?" When she nodded, he asked, "Can you help?" Tibbit was ivory blond. His eyelashes were so white they were invisible, and they turned his eyes into permanent Os of vulnerability. His normal facial expression was a puppy hoping for a treat, but expecting a kick. When he pleaded, he was the puppy squared.

Faye McNicoll said, "Gaia will reward you."

Blaylock almost slapped her. "You, too?" she snapped. "Off with your daughter? Going to drag Jenny into a militarized zone?"

"She'll be with her grandmother," McNicoll replied, serene. "Anyway, I'm doing this for Jenny."

"For all the children." Sheila Kowalczyk corrected.

Blaylock saw innocence offering itself up to slaughter. Coming here had been useless. Her reality was no match for idealism daydreaming itself into oblivion. She looked at Judy Liang and Chuck Bilodeau. They were quiet, neither banging the drum nor sounding the toll for the idea. Blaylock read their silence. She said, "Not you two, as well."

"Big event," Judy said.

"She's right," Bilodeau agreed. "It's our beat. We should be there."

"I'll call Dad tomorrow," Alloway said. Grimson shrank in on herself.

Blaylock looked at the hunched shoulders of her friend. "Kelly," she said, "is it that important?"

"Yes," said Grimson, one soldier to another. "And yes, we know the risks."

So there. Blaylock's warning dismissed. She wanted to tell them that they did *not* know the risks, that that was the whole point of her warning. They couldn't protect themselves when her intelligence was so vague. What do you do? Throw everyone on Orange Alert and stock up on duct tape? Best she could do would be to watch over the little ducklings, try to keep harm away from them. For all she knew, Sherbina's big show was all diplomatic arm twisting. (Sure.) She sighed. "Fine, you idiots. I'll pay your way."

That raised eyebrows. The room stared at her. "*How?*" Alloway gasped.

"Mumsy and Dadsy left me some bucks when they died." She spat the lie. She meant the line more as an insult than as a sop to her cover, but the jab was water off the ducklings' backs. The sludge mood turned around *flash*, and now the meeting room was Woodstock and Haight Ashbury, summer of love and rave-culture high. The consensus, madness-charged, was self-congratulation and fight-the-power. Plans of neon enthusiasm multiplied. The voices climbed to hysteria shouts. The Spirit that was going to hit Davos wasn't 1968, but 1789. Blaylock tasted bile.

No refuge except back on the street, so that's where she headed, storming out of the Langside entrance, glad now she hadn't shed her coat. She heard "Jen!" from behind. Grudgingly, she slowed her pace, let Grimson catch up.

"Thank you," Grimson said.

"Thank me if all of you make it back alive."

"You know, this high and mighty paternalism is really, really old."

"So is rose-colored glaucoma."

They reached Sargent and turned left. They marched on, voices rising.

Chuck Bilodeau left the common house. He saw Grimson running after Baylor. He started to follow, too, then thought better of it once he reached the street. He watched the pair gesticulate as they passed under a street light. He was thinking questions. *Who are you? Where are you coming from?* He wasn't buying the freelance writer story, unless all the freelancing was from the center of war zones. And her attitude was confusing. Scratch her polite surface, as had just been done, and up welled nothing but venom for the Common and any whiff of idealism. But when they'd first met, her reaction to his columns had been just as corrosive a sneer.

"Hey, Chuck." Wes Tibbit appeared at his side. "You really coming, too?"

Bilodeau nodded, his attention drawn now to the garage door. It was open. No one was pulling in or out, and the door remained open. That was wrong. "Be right back," he told Tibbit. He thought he smelled smoke.

Then he heard breaking glass.

Barry Reynolds looked upon the good work. He stood with his arms folded, high on force and command. He and his men were power, they were strength, they were going to smash with excess and rage, they were going to be so *very very goddamn RICH*. DD Frazer danced and giggled as he threw the bottles, his voice turning screeching cat at every smash and leap of flame. Mick Pitt was methodical, opening gas tanks and choosing his vehicles for maximum spread. There were lots of flames already. Reynolds heard footsteps behind him. About time somebody noticed the bonfire was on.

Bilodeau saw the fires, saw the men, saw their clothes, saw red. Men in boots and leather and hate. He knew their kind. Bald heads or biker beards, chains or spikes, curb-stomper or face-breaker, they were a teeth-clenched, tendon-popping fist, and he hated them. He felt the sour anger birthed by too many memories of his university days, memories of being chased home along Assiniboine Avenue. He felt a newer rage at seeing his new home under attack. He took another step forward, murder in his heart. The leader, a big man with a shaved head and a pencil-thin goatee, was standing at the base of the ramp. He turned to face Bilodeau, grinning hard. Bilodeau stopped, thought smart. They were armed, he wasn't. They were three, he was one. He retreated, thinking reinforcements, thinking police. "Hey!" came the call as he ran back up the ramp. "Where *you* goin'?" The question, the taunt, was too familiar. It was part of a ritual.

The rest of the ritual played out. They were faster. They caught up with him just short of the entrance. The leader tripped him. Bilodeau slammed face-first into concrete. Pain and blood blew out of his nose and jaw. He was blind with the agony, but he still twisted around and struck back. Experience had taught him to fight dirty. He kicked up, hoping for balls. He connected with something soft, and somebody yelped high. Good. But then they were all over him before he could even crawl, boots hitting like bricks against face and ribs and groin and kidneys.

Someone yelled, "Stop!"

The blows paused. Bilodeau's vision cleared. Tibbit was at the entrance, his eyes gone rabbit with horror. One of the thugs, the one with the giggles, had a bottle in hand. He threw it at Tibbit. Trailing a flaming rag like a comet tail, the bottle arced. It hit the cement at Tibbit's feet and shattered. Liquid flame fountained, coating Tibbit in a blinding fist. He screamed, his register the pain above High C. Bilodeau smelled kerosene, saw the thick, slippery grasp the fire had on Tibbit, realized napalm. The giggling skinhead whooped, "Ho-ooooooly *shit*!" His voice was almost as high as the shrieks. Tibbit stumbled, flailed, collapsed into the street. The third goon looked a bit green.

The leader gave Bilodeau another kick. "Pick him up," he said. "Bring him." He fetched the case with the rest of the cocktails. "Let's give these faggots a show."

As they hauled Bilodeau out, the parkade shook with the first of the big explosions.

Grimson froze, cut off in mid-sentence by a muffled *boom*. "What was that?" she whispered. They were a block down Sargent from Langside.

Blaylock had already whirled to face the direction of the noise. Her knees were bent slightly. Her stance was grounded, combat-ready. Her knife was in her hand.

Grimson said, "I told you no weapons."

Blaylock said, "It's just a knife," but her mind wasn't on

Grimson's objections. There was another deep *whump*. The night pulsed with a glow.

"Oh, no," Grimson whispered, realizing what the source of the light and sound might be.

Blaylock ran.

Violence summoned the residents of Greenham Common into the courtyard. Violence was hatred and blows, the smash of glass, the flicker of flame. "Town hall meeting, hippie shits!" the leader of the apes yelled. They threw Bilodeau down. The scrawny ape danced on his face and giggled. Bilodeau struggled, but barely, consciousness slipping away. Horror sucked the crowd in. Flames pushed them closer as the stocky ape with a buzz cut launched homemade bombs against the facades of the apartments. The flames, slippery as sex, dug in, thrived, joined each other, multiplied. The ape threw, and threw, and threw. He was a machine. He took less than thirty seconds to toss his last bomb. Not all his explosives were bottles. Some were cans. The fire that burst from them was very, very bright, a silver sun. The crowd shivered and howled with cold and fear.

Judy Liang hung back at the rear. She was separated from Mark, who was caught in the crush ahead. She heard the blows, knew what was happening to Bilodeau, swallowed her shrieks of rage, and hit 911 on her cellphone. There was too much noise from the flames and the screams and the yells, and she couldn't hear the ring, couldn't hear if there was an answer or not. "Police," she said. "Please send police, ambulance, fire fighters." She gave the address, repeated the message, not knowing if anyone was even there at the other end. Then there was a commotion at her end of the crowd.

The waves parted, and Sheila Kowalczyk blasted through, running for the Young Street entrance. She was screaming and crying. She bowled Judy over and sent the phone flying. Kowalczyk stumbled, kept moving.

"Better stop," came the call. Judy had a clear view of the center of the courtyard. The leader of the trio held a gun. Kowalczyk didn't stop. The man fired. The first few shots missed, chipping plaster and spraying snow. The man kept firing, and Kowalczyk jerked and fell. She lay in the snow, pooling it red. The skinny thug *whoo-hoo-hooed* with hysterical joy. The third man, uncomfortable, turned away.

The fire and light were intensity, and it was intensity that Blaylock recognized as she reached the burning Common, intensity she had known and loved: thermite. This was no simple arson. This took organization and planning. Blaylock checked over her shoulder. Grimson was two blocks behind, too pregnant for a fast run. Good. Stay out of this, Blaylock thought. Flames gouted from the parkade door as she ran past. She hugged the wall as she came around the Langside entrance and took in the scene.

Judy kneeled over Kowalczyk's corpse. Mark had fought his way free and joined her. They shared sick hopelessness, and Judy looked back toward the center of the courtyard, at the leader of the assault. She saw a man in the midst of the best moment of his life. He had the gun trained on Avery, who didn't look ready to rush him. Alloway was a frozen, trembling stick beside his friend.

"Think they've learned their lesson, DD?" said the leader.

High giggle. "Doubt it, Barry."

"Mick?"

The third man turned back to face Barry. He shook his head. "Whatever."

"Know why we're here?" Barry announced. "To show you your place and keep you there. What place is that, DD?"

"In the shit, man, in the shit. Learn 'em, learn 'em."

Barry gestured. DD turned to the crowd and snatched Jenny. McNicoll screamed and ran forward, reaching for her daughter. Barry pistol-whipped her down.

Judy saw a blur.

Blaylock came in on demon wings when giggling DD took Jenny. A black wind, she came up behind Barry, and she felt the man shrink as her force of claws and darkness engulfed him. She drove her knife into the side of his neck, edge facing out. She jerked her arm forward. Flesh and muscle parted as the knife burst free. The man's head rocked back, half-severed. His blood sprayed wide, art of war against the canvas of snow. His death drenched DD. His death drenched Jenny. Mick stood with his jaw slack. Blaylock caught the pistol as it fell from the slumping corpse's hand and shot Mick in the head. DD wasn't giggling anymore. He was gabbling disbelief and denial. Blaylock gave him the full force of her contempt and turned the butt of the gun on him. She gave him three sharp blows to the temple. Two of them when he was on the ground. One after he had stopped breathing. She almost hit him again, but by then Grimson had caught up.

Jenny stared at Blaylock and screamed and screamed and screamed.

14

"I know this guy."

Sirens in the distance. The police and fire crews on their way to the party. Around Blaylock, a crowd of shell-shocked survivors, huddling close to the warmth of their burning home, staring at her as if she were Satan's wrath incarnate. Time for her to go. But there was Darryl Avery, staring at the corpse with the wide-open neck, and saying those words. "Holy shit, I know this guy. His name's Barry Reynolds. Jesus. He's a legend. You want a picket busted by scabs, he's your man. Practically has a full-time career doin' that."

"Hired gun."

Avery nodded.

Sirens coming. Blaylock checked Reynolds' pockets. She found a Dodge key chain. "Help me with the bodies," she ordered. "*Now*." Her tone made the residents move. She had them jumping. Bilodeau, barely able to stand, was the first to grab an arm, his anger giving him strength as he joined her over Reynolds. Three to a side, they lifted the corpses over their heads, and carried them, body count at the mosh pit, out onto Langside. Blaylock spotted the pickup truck. It had death's-head mud flaps. They loaded the bodies into the box. "I was never here," Blaylock said.

"These guys attacked, and then they left. Understood?" Nods. "Especially you." She pointed at Bilodeau and Judy. "Curtail those journalistic instincts." More nods. "I'll be in touch," she said. She hopped into the cab and drove off, still well ahead of the sirens. She headed for the river.

At least he wasn't puking anymore. Alloway sat on the bench in the police station and waited for Grimson to finish giving her statement. His hands and feet felt heavy, lead. His head was too big, and his brain rattled and swam inside. All his movements were wrong. Mind and body were talking over a bad transatlantic line. Shock, he thought. This is shock I'm experiencing. The numbness was the only thing keeping the grief from killing him. The anger was the only thing keeping the shock from putting him to sleep.

"What're we gonna do now, man?" Avery, sitting beside him, asked, sad and lost.

"Stay with my parents for a few days. They have room." Grimson was going to love the dawn-to-dusk of his mother hovering around the pregnant belly. "We'll look for something more permanent after Davos."

"You think the police will like us leaving town?"

"I don't care what they like," Alloway muttered. He wasn't asking permission. He would just go. That deep-marrow anger again. He kept thinking about what Blaylock had said. If those bastards had been following orders, then someone had deliberately targeted Global Response. "Do you have any enemies?" the police had asked. He could have given them a list, all right. He didn't. Instead, he took the silver lining that Global Response had actually become a worthy threat, and vowed war, good and proper.

Mixing with the anger, shame. They had been hit hard, and had he fought back? Had he done anything to defend his home and his people? Or had he screamed and cowered and left it all to Blaylock? Never again. And if they thought they could make Global Response back down, it was his duty to show them dangerously wrong. He pictured Blaylock in action, pictured enemies as threshed wheat. Knew what he had to do. He turned his head to look at Avery, judged what would be necessary to take his hugeness from harmless to biker. Not too difficult. A bit of coaching, and he could hit that Hell's Angels-connected shop on Main and be convincing. "Darryl," he said. "Have a mission for you."

Zelkova was still sleeping. Sherbina played quietly with Inna in the next room. They were arranging the toy horses she always traveled with. He had a transistor radio on the bed beside him, set to the CBC morning show with the volume low. He turned the sound up a bit for the 7:30 local news. The Greenham Common attack was the lead story. There were plenty of survivors. Good. A total slaughter would have been counterproductive. He was surprised how few casualties there were, though. He hadn't thought neo-hippies had that much fight in them. He heard Zelkova stirring and killed the radio. "Let's go say good morning to Mama," he said to Inna.

He kept the radio off while they had breakfast. No news intrusion into domestic bliss until after Zelkova was on her next flight. He left Winnipeg for Geneva that afternoon. The skewed body count bothered him. Then a phone call did two things. It told him the attackers had been killed. And it gave him a name: *Jennifer Baylor.*

Suburbia. For Joe Chapel, the unlived life. He walked up the driveway to Dean Garnett's house, stepping over toboggans. He looked at the snow toys on the lawn. Garnett had two daughters, but there was enough bright plastic crap here for a daycare. The clutter was the chaos Chapel excluded from his life, and the chaos it was his life's work to protect.

Ann answered the door. She smiled. "Short notice, Joe, but I think we can squeeze you in for dinner."

"Sorry, blowing through. Nice try, though. Dean in?"

"Downstairs, horsing around with the girls. I'll get him. Want to sit down?"

Chapel shook his head. "Need to steal him for a walk."

"Gotcha."

Summoned, Garnett shrugged into his coat and followed Chapel out onto the street. "What's up?"

"I just read your latest InSec sitrep."

"Yeah, that Leon West thing. Things are suddenly a lot more interesting. He looks like a suicide, but—"

"He is," Chapel interrupted. "I was there." He filled Garnett in.

"Jesus," Garnett muttered. "What bug was up his ass?"

"There's something big in play," Chapel answered.

"How much can you tell me?"

"Nothing."

"That big? Tell me yes."

"Yeah. If things go down well, our interests and Kornukopia's will both be served."

"But?"

"But West thought I was testing him. I'm guessing he thought I was sent by Sherbina. But he wasn't sure. He was terrified of giving the wrong answer, especially when I forced him to choose his loyalty."

Garnett stepped over a puddle. "You think he was playing both ends against the middle?"

Chapel shook his head. "I think Sherbina owned him to the bones. He had West so tight he broke. West didn't have a good answer for me. If I wasn't with Sherbina, then he was screwed if he didn't say he was loyal to the President. If I *was* with Sherbina, he was screwed either way, because I might have been testing him to see if he would talk."

"And what do you think Sherbina was doing with him?"

Chapel saw darkness up ahead. He thought he had a better understanding now of why Reed had brought him in on the project. "Think about it. A Kornukopia slave putting words in the President's mouth? Sherbina's trying to take over the game." He turned around, heading back towards Garnett's house. "I want you to put more resources onto InSec while I'm gone. How are your assets there?"

"Okay. Nothing spectacular."

"Have you spoken to Mike Flanagan?"

"Should I?"

Chapel frowned. Had he really kept Flanagan that much to himself? "He's a strong source. He has zero loyalty to InSec after what they did to him. He knows what to look for, too. Work with him."

Another order came in from Blaylock. Flanagan read through it. She was beefing up her Swiss arsenal. At the bottom of the message, she had appended two numbers. One looked like a phone number. He checked the country code. Yes, Switzerland. He wasn't sure about the other, three-digit figure. Flanagan deleted the e-mail and went for lunch. He picked a restaurant on Pearl he hadn't been to before, ate, then used the pay phone at the entrance. He punched in the number, and the voice that picked up after the first ring said, "Hotel du Salut."

Oh, Flanagan thought. "Room 423, please," he said, and was put through.

"Mike?" Blaylock answered. Her voice was heavy with fatigue.

"Yes. Where are you?"

"Geneva now. Davos next."

The thought of Blaylock and world leaders in close proximity made Flanagan uneasy. "Going to tell me why?" he asked.

"Business." Not, clearly, what she wanted to talk to him about. "Mike, you're not keeping me human." She didn't even sound flip.

"How can I when you're not here?"

"I'm kidding."

"I don't believe you."

She was silent for a minute. Flanagan listened to her breathing. Finally, she said, "I feel so tired sometimes."

"Of fighting?" He meant *killing*.

"No." She understood. "Of being the monster."

Now he was silent, now he understood. The cost of being the monster was not the action, but the reaction. The terror of the ones the monster saved. She'd had that look from him. She must have seen it again recently. "I went to see where the Coscarellis died," he told her. "I..." He struggled with the truth, spat it out. "I liked it."

On the other side of the Atlantic, a sudden intake of breath.

15

Monday, January 28. Countdown. Four days to the World Economic Forum. One day to the meeting with Zelkova. Big moment for Kornukopia this very day. Blaylock had spent the last two weeks learning Geneva, watching the name *Kornukopia* become bigger and bigger news. She read the papers, shook her head at Sherbina's gall. The man had wrecking balls between his legs. He was shameless, she thought. He was performing spotlit, center stage. She still didn't know what the Davos show was. The Geneva one, though, that was open to the public. She bought her tickets.

"See it?" Sam Reed asked.

Chapel hadn't slept on the flight over. He was jet-lagged, it was late morning, and he was depressed by the knowledge that he had to keep himself awake for another ten hours if he wanted to reset his body clock. Now he and the President were sitting in a limo, heading into Geneva. The ride was smooth, the seats comfortable, and Chapel was popping mints every two minutes to ward off sleep. But as they drew near Kornukopia One, he didn't need the mints anymore. He was alert. He'd been waiting for this. He narrowed his eyes as he had his first good view of the complex. He tasted acid distrust.

Contrasts, Blaylock thought. InSec didn't believe in the public face. It hadn't under Pembroke, and it still didn't, new management be damned. It believed in hiding in plain sight. So it had its skyscraper, but that just made you one of the crowd in Manhattan. InSec was strictly business. It didn't host charity fundraisers. It didn't sponsor the arts. Dealing arms and ensuring their limitless proliferation were ends sufficient unto themselves. Contrasts. When Kornukopia opened a building, it threw a party. It wanted the world to know. It wanted the world to come. Blaylock didn't see GRAND OPENING banners, clouds of balloons, or flights of doves as she approached the Kornukopia grounds, but only, she thought, because those gestures lacked scale, and so were forbidden. A concert, though? Now we're talking. There was a full-page ad in *Le Temps* trumpeting Kornukopia's largess to Geneva and the program for the day. The climax was a night performance by Henri Andrevon, a Swiss love-child hybrid of Jean-Michel Jarre synths and lasers with John Tesh keyboard sentiment. During the day, come one come all for the big tour. Bring the family. Bring the earplugs. See the end-of-afternoon demonstration. Spectacular spectacular.

Sherbina's baby covered several acres along the west shore of Lake Geneva. Sherbina had bought up the private properties stretching between the public parks to the south and the embassies to the north, then shipped in tons of earth to expand the narrow strip into the lake. The result was visible from every lake promenade, another jewel in Geneva's crown. From a distance, the impression was landscaped greenery with spire. Closer up, the signs of fortress rose. Stone walls and gates along the Rue de Lausanne had formerly hidden the estates and private beaches. Sherbina's complex had replaced the homes, and now a steep berm hid everything but the telecommunications mast. From a distance, the mast was the world's largest tulip, delicate and vertical as a Japanese print, the bulb at the top closed but ripe with potential. The berm was rugged rock, twenty feet high, studiously natural in its look, vicious leg-breaker for anyone climbing. The look won out, though. The berm was its own camouflage. Blaylock loved the message reversal. The berm wasn't protecting the complex from prying eyes. It was protecting the eyes of the sensitive from the unwanted sight of postmodernity. The only break in the berm was the access road. Blaylock joined the lineup, waited her turn to pass through into the kingdom. Security today was one big smile. The guards might as well have been Disney World attendants. They waved everyone through, the gates were open, and the barrier was raised. Blaylock still noticed the road-wide metal detector that she walked through. She was clean. Nothing to make anyone nervous today.

The road sloped up as it passed through the berm. When Blaylock emerged onto the grounds proper, she was only six feet from the top of the wall. She had expected to see chain-link fence adding another line of defense. Instead, discreet poles sat every twenty feet along the peak of the berm. Each pole was capped by a small sphere. Blaylock focused on the nearest pole, saw the sphere rotate as another visitor passed onto the grounds. Cameras, she realized, cameras with motion sensors. Good one. The other sides of the grounds weren't near a road, and, as far as Blaylock could tell, the berm protected this flank only. She squinted, and in the distance made out chain-link, making itself subtle, blending in with trees. At regular intervals, a tall pole. More cameras, right where she'd want a sentry tower to be. Lakeside, she could make out more of the same unobtrusive but panoptic security. Well done, she thought.

The gardens were eighteenth-century English, perfect trims and rigorous symmetry all the more striking in the bloomless severity of winter. Blaylock admired the lines, was impressed by the way they pulled her eyes toward the complex. The grounds were art radiating out from the epicenter of the buildings, a perfect folding fan. Perfect, too, for sightlines. Blaylock pictured herself sentinel, pictured an intruder, pictured the rigor of the gardens taking her bullets home. The beauty put a lump in her throat. This was the architecture of the sublime.

A golf-cart train was loading up with visitors. Choo-choo for the tour. Blaylock boarded. Once it was full, the train started down the road toward the Kornukopia buildings. The road was wide enough for another group of carts to pass them, heading back to the entrance, but its S-curves were sharp. More security. Try to barrel straight through to the buildings, and you'll run off the road and into the low stone walls of the gardens. Blaylock registered each new barrier, nodded her appreciation, and watched the complex approach.

The sky was cloudless, and the sun turned the buildings to a dazzle of white, twinning them with the snow of Mont Blanc visible across the lake. The mast still looked fragile. Free-standing steel and concrete, it rose six hundred feet, a six-story tripod base tapering from triangle to cylinder before hitting the Mylar-and-Kevlar sheath of the tulip bulb. The mast seemed to float, haiku-delicate and rapier-elegant, over the incandescent white of the domes beneath. These were low geodesics, four storys high, purity in white tile and random triangular windows. There were six altogether. One, smaller than the others, sprouted from the ground beneath the mast. The other five, bubbles of strength, surrounded the mast. They overlapped and grew out of each other. Foam, Blaylock thought. Blisters. Tumors.

The train pulled to a stop in a parking lot in front of the first and largest of the domes. To the right, the access road continued around the dome. To the left, there were only gardens. Blaylock wondered where the road ended. She descended from the train. Guides approached the visitors and sectioned tour groups off by language. Blaylock joined the English group. They waited while another train arrived and unloaded its cargo. Blaylock stared. One of the visitors was Joe Chapel. He walked forward to join her group, spotted her, and stumbled, poleaxed by surprise. Blaylock grinned, running with the black irony. "Fancy meeting you here," she said.

"Fancy that," said Chapel.

They faced each other, scans on full, defenses at high, expressions extreme neutral. Blaylock thought, Are we really fooling anyone? "What brings you here?" she asked. Her tone was harmless curiosity writ large.

"Business," he said. "What about you?" he asked.

"Chasing down a story." She made her tone say, *What else?*

A slight pause. Chapel trying to decide what sort of dance this was. "I haven't seen much by you lately."

Was that an attack? Was he expecting her to collapse in tears of guilt? Or was it just a probe? She gave him nothing. "Which shows how much of a fan you are. You can't kid me. You just haven't been looking."

Chapel's smile said, *Good one.* Blaylock smiled back, sunny, innocent, sure their game had real teeth. Chapel had been wary of her after Ember Lake. Whatever his campaign here was, she could tell her presence was a disturbing stick in the spokes.

The tour guide interrupted the dance. "Ladies and gentlemen, welcome to Kornukopia One, and the future of workplace security. My name is Jerome, and if you'll follow me, I will be happy to open up the world of Kornukopia One to you." Jerome was in his early twenties, gay-porn handsome and airline plastic. His teeth were as white as the domes, and as draft-table perfect as the creases of his uniform. The suit was navy blue, the tie fluorescent pink.

Blaylock and Chapel exchanged glances. "Hug me, I'm harmless," Blaylock quipped as they followed Jerome to the entrance of the dome.

"You're up on more than Kornukopia's public face," Chapel said.

Still probing. "Doesn't take much. Even *Maxim* sees through that."

The reception area inside the dome was a huge rectangle. A bank of elevators at the far end was blocked by a security desk. The reception desk at this end, unoccupied, flowed out of the floor, marble from marble. On the right was a gift shop. The display windows were filled with scale models of the complex, ranging in size from paperweight to multi-thousand-piece 3D puzzles. The space was two storys high. Stalactite chandeliers hung from the ceiling, delicate as they were long. The area was so open, so airy, Blaylock thought she was going to float.

"Welcome to the Administration Center," Jerome

said. His voice was moisturizing cream as he philosophized about esthetics, about the need for a work environment that instilled *pride*. "This," he said, turning and sweeping arms, "is where the Kornukopia experience begins every day. This is also," wink to the tour group, "where your Kornukopia experience can end this evening, if you will join us for cocktails in conjunction with the concert."

"Think he can product-place the company's name a bit more?" Blaylock asked Chapel out of the corner of her mouth.

"What name is that again?" His snort was unguarded, genuine humor.

Jerome still at it. "As you can see, Kornukopia does not believe that security means compromises on beauty and comfort. But security, as you will see—" He made show of looking at his watch, giving his wrist a diva flip. He held up a finger. "—shortly, is priority one." Another wink, this one clearly for the women in the crowd. Ladies, doesn't the merchandise make you weak all over?

"I might have to kill him," Chapel said.

"I'll hold him down."

Blaylock thought they were going to see more of the building. She expected a sales job on the office facilities. But Jerome led them back outside again. She saw Chapel craning his neck, disappointed, trying to catch a glimpse of anything, anything at all, that wasn't reception. Give it up, she thought. They aren't pushing rentals here. Next question: so what are they pushing? What's the point of the dog and pony show? Security, security, security, that's all the Ken doll wants to talk about. And that was all he did talk about. The theme became the single tune, the relentless chord, of the rest of the tour. Jerome took them clockwise around the domes. After Administration came Support, Recreation, Conference, and finally Security. There were no tours inside any of the buildings. When one woman asked what the dome under the mast was, Jerome beamed at her. He'd been given his segue. "That is the physical plant," he said, and there was real love in his voice. "We live in an interdependent world, but sometimes security demands self-sufficiency. You will notice," he swept his arm around, "that there are no power lines. Kornukopia One is not connected to the power grid." A switch flipped and he was sober, not huckster. "No matter what happens, Kornukopia One will have power." The switch flicked back. "We are also at the cutting edge of environmentally friendly energy sources. Kornukopia taps into the inexhaustible supply of Lake Geneva's water. Our solar panels, securely built into the covering of every dome, supply the electricity that converts the water into hydrogen and oxygen. Kornukopia One is powered entirely by hydrogen fuel cells. We are safe, and we are clean." Show the teeth, look inspired, take a beat, and he was back to principles and generalities. No details on anything except the power. Blaylock caught the angle. The physical plant's security was non-threatening and audience-friendly. Playing perverse, she tried a couple of times to force him onto the aggressive side of security. Come on, she thought, at least point out the cameras. They're obvious. They're no secret. Let the good people know they're being watched. Jerome wouldn't bite. Instead, he explained how vital security was, how crucial it was in a world that had become terribly insecure.

"That's a tautology," Blaylock told him.

Jerome blinked and spoke about the gardens. Plenty of detail there, but the plant and tree and landscape artist specifics were mere interlude, and then he was back on security, security, security. Blaylock began to see him as more than an animatronic mannequin. She felt the undertow of his spiel. His performance wasn't monotony, it was Philip Glass minimalism, hypnotic, hooking, drawing you in with the promise of climax. Several of the other visitors had very wide eyes. They were being pulled into the gospel. They were becoming jumpy, unnerved by the implications of free-floating insecurity, of without-warning apocalypse held at bay only by Kornukopia One. They needed reassurance now. They needed to be shown the might of Kornukopia One. They needed the climax. It was waiting for them when they completed the circuit, and arrived at the point where the Security and Administration domes merged.

A cordon had been erected, keeping the tour groups a few hundred yards away from the dome. There were a lot of people behind the line, the accumulated tours of the entire day. Time for the demonstration. Time for the relief. Between the cordon and the domes, Blaylock saw a group of Swiss soldiers and Kornukopia security. The soldiers were standing to one side, looking unhappy. Blaylock didn't blame them. One of the security guards carried a rocket launcher.

Chapel was laughing, shaking his head. "No," he said. "I will not believe. That thing is going to shoot T-shirts into the crowd. Good money says so."

"Ladies," Jerome said. "Gentlemen." Down the length of the cordon, the other guides spoke, too. The Kornukopia Kwire, Blaylock thought. "There are forces in this world that no one can control. There are events that no one can prevent. We have seen them, and we will again. But we can prepare. Terror need not be our master.

We should, we *can*, go to work without fear of madmen with causes, and anarchists with bombs. Ladies. Gentlemen. I give you the security of Kornukopia One." Jerome smiled. He winked again. He and the other guides raised their hands to their ears, role models. The crowd, keyed to the max, obeyed. The guard raised the launcher. The soldiers stepped back. The guard fired. Harsh engine blast, streak of light straight for a ground-floor window, then explosion, the boom echoing off the complex, the retina-burn rosebloom of fire. Screams in the crowd. Fade of the echo, fade of the rosebloom. Smoke in the air slowly dissipating, the parting curtain. Ta-daa. The dome was untouched.

One by one, the guides took their groups forward to examine the miracle. When it was their turn, Jerome had Blaylock and the others run their hands over the window. Blaylock felt ripples, but no damage. "Going to let us in on the trick?" she asked Jerome.

"There is no trick," he said, purring cream and unction, "only security." He shifted into sales pitch. "This is just a hint of how safe Kornukopia One is. This is just one example of how every detail of this complex works towards a security synergy." Blaylock managed not to roll her eyes. "Forgive me if I become technical for a moment," Jerome went on. "These windows are a series of layers of tempered glass; Lexan, which is a composite of bulletproof glass and acrylic; and fast-melt acrylic. This acrylic immediately turns to liquid at the point of impact, creating a wave form that spreads the force of the impact to the entire frame of the structure."

"Wouldn't that damage the whole building?" a man asked.

Jerome smiled, shook his head at the cute questions

kids ask. "Not at all. Spread over such a large area, the force is diluted to nothing." He turned solemn. "Kornukopia has learned from the hard experience of others."

Tasteful, Blaylock thought. She glanced at Chapel, saw steam coming out of his ears.

The Andrevon concert kicked off at dusk, a couple of hours later. Andrevon and his banks of instruments were set up on the roof of the physical plant dome. He was all but invisible beneath the straddle of the communications mast. There were no bleachers set up. They weren't needed. The audience filled the gardens, and Kornukopia One became the show. The music was deep swells and sighing swirls of electronic melodrama. Lasers strobed a color riot. Film loops of silent movie stars and starving Ethiopians were projected into giant, distorted sprawls over the domes. Fireworks punctuated the emotional climaxes of the music, subtle as a kick in the eye. The audience lapped it up. Blaylock couldn't blame them. The spectacle was so unashamed, wore its bleeding and tacky heart so proudly on its sleeve, that it moved beyond cheese and built up a raw and honest power.

Chapel was still hovering nearby. "Buy you a drink?" he asked, cocking his head toward Administration and its reception gala.

You flirting or digging? Blaylock wondered. Either way, she was bored with the dance. "No thanks," she said, and moved off, putting cone-shaped hedges between them. She wandered the gravel paths of the gardens, weaving between knots of spectators. There were lots of families. There were even more couples. Blaylock's consciousness of them grew as daylight gave way to the music-pulsed flashes of the night. Light and sound washed over her, waves and currents. The sensorium assault was near total.

The effect was phantasmagoria and deprivation tank. Surrounded by thousands, she felt complete privacy. Others did, too. The couples sank into individual universes, cradled by digital illusions that mimicked the outside world only to deny it access. Blaylock thought about Flanagan. She missed him. She wanted him here. She knew she was being manipulated by the show, but it wasn't conjuring lies. It was rubbing her skin with sandpaper, forcing the suppressed to the light. Lately, the ache didn't need much rubbing to surface. Since the Greenham Common fire, the ache took any excuse to blister. Jenny had screamed and spike-driven home the price Blaylock was paying for her embrace of war.

The call from Flanagan when she'd first arrived in Switzerland. She had made damn sure he'd phone her, hadn't she? Appending the hotel number to the order. Cute. Strategically unnecessary, borderline stupid. And the sound of his voice had sharpened, not soothed, the ache. What had she expected? Didn't matter. It was what she had needed, and she knew the need was an indulgent capitulation to weakness, but damn it, war could spare her those few moments, couldn't it? Touching, said her reason, said war. Very touching. Now where do you think you're going with this? What do you think you're doing to Mike?

Ah. The lessons of Ember Lodge, of slaughters past, that she still wouldn't let sink in. *Keep me human.* What tender bullshit. How selfish to the bone. She wanted Flanagan there when she needed him. Did he ever need her? Did she ever think of that? If he did, he was out of luck. She was the great absence, descending on him only for logistical support. She was the unilateralist of intimacy. And now there was more: the pleasure he took from the site of the Coscarelli slaughter. How nice that that was bringing the two closer. How nice that maybe he wouldn't be as frightened of her anymore. How nice.

What are you doing to him?

What do you really want?

She rounded a corner of topiary. The path passed under a mock-ruin stone arch. Chapel stood beneath it, arms crossed, blocking her way. "We have to stop meeting like this," Blaylock said.

Chapel held up a cellphone. "Just made a couple of calls," he said. He put the phone in his jacket pocket. "I was feeling badly that I hadn't read any of your stories recently, you know?" The lie was obvious, meant to be so. "I thought I should see what you've been up to lately. I hear you were in Winnipeg recently. Where there was another big fire. What was this? Just a little trip home? Anonymously?"

Masks off. War coursed through her veins. Blaylock felt better instantly. She smiled, glowing. "Oh, I don't know. I think I left a signature."

"Is that what you call those dead men?"

Blaylock kept smiling. Chapel took a step forward. He was keeping himself backlit by the sound and fury of the concert. His approach was silhouette intimidation. Blaylock's grin grew wider. She hoped he saw the laser reflections in her eyes. She hoped he learned something. Chapel said, "What are you doing here?"

"My business. Not yours."

"Who are you working for?"

Blaylock laughed.

"You can become my business," Chapel warned. "I can shut you down."

Blaylock closed the gap between them, put her face

into his space and kept it there. "Do it," Blaylock said, gaze seizing Chapel's and locking it down. "Try it. We'll have fun. You're Agency. That makes you a combatant. Fair game." The night flashed, heat lightning in winter.

16

Blaylock sat on the steps beneath the monument to Albert Thomas, first director of the International Labor Organization. Heroic, but very un-Soviet Realism, workers stood on top of a block of stone. They faced, across the Rue de Lausanne, the headquarters of the World Trade Organization. Blaylock didn't think Geneva went in for irony, but she took what she could find. She leaned back, felt the small glow of heat where the late afternoon sun hit her face. The sun had real warmth today, Swiss winter passing for Canadian spring. Blaylock kept her eyes on the building's exit. The WTO headquarters was nondescript grayness. Four utterly unadorned floors were topped by a red tile roof, the monotony broken only by a squat, vaguely prison-like tower on the left-hand side. To Blaylock's rear, a few hundred yards uphill on the Avenue de la Paix, the International Meteorological Organization had for itself an exercise in gigantic green steel and dark glass ultramodernism. But the WTO, where real might dwelled, looked like an appropriated manufacturing plant. For Blaylock, the biggest surprise was the complex's lack of security. There wasn't even a guard booth at the street entrance to the courtyard. As an experiment, twenty minutes ago she had ambled through the gate and into the building's grounds. Some chickens wandering the small lawns beneath the trees had noticed her. No one else had.

Now she saw Irina Zelkova emerge. Blaylock stood up and waited. "Thank you for meeting me here," Zelkova said as she reached the monument.

"You're having me for dinner. Least I could do." She hooked a thumb at the headquarters. "How did it go?"

Zelkova sighed. She had deep pouches under her eyes. "Sometimes, I am very tired of tilting at windmills."

"Have you ever considered burning them down?"

Zelkova said nothing. They walked in silence up the Avenue de la Paix, where Zelkova had left her car.

"Well?" Blaylock prompted.

"I was wondering how to answer. I was wondering if you were trying to trick me into saying something controversial."

Blaylock chuckled. "Don't worry. I'm here as your media vassal, remember?"

Zelkova paused before unlocking the car. She thought for a moment, gave Blaylock a hard look. "You are very difficult to read," she said.

"Why's that?" Blaylock asked, open and sweet, as she climbed into the passenger seat.

Zelkova was shaking her head. "*That* is why. When you speak that way. Your sarcasm." She started the car and pulled into the traffic.

"Since when does sarcasm make a person difficult to read?"

"When the person is *always* sarcastic. Sometimes I think you mean what you say, but sometimes, I do not think you mean anything at all. Ever."

Blaylock considered this. "Interesting," she said.

"And that does not bother you?"

Blaylock shrugged. "Should it?" She batted her eyes.

Zelkova sighed again. "If you carry on, I will change my mind about your strategic utility and leave you by the side of the road. I have had enough of smashing my head against walls for one day."

"I thought it was windmills." Zelkova didn't laugh. She drove, stonefaced. Blaylock apologized. "Sorry." She pulled a notebook out of her pocket, going through the motions. She doubted Jennifer Baylor would ever file another story. "Tell me why things went badly."

"They always go badly at the WTO. I was intervening on behalf of African countries. They need an extension on the agreement allowing them to manufacture generic versions of essential drugs during times of national emergency. The companies said that life is always an emergency in Africa, and since the conditions have not improved during the term of the agreement, there is no point in continuing the experiment." Her lips tightened pale, and Blaylock saw her anger turn her driving into a bundle of hard, jagged gestures. "That is what they called the agreement. An experiment. All those lives, economic guinea pigs." Her shoulders went up, rigid and furious. "The Dispute Settlement Board ruled in favor of the drug companies."

"And there's no recourse for appeal?"

"There is the Appellate Body. It is worse. There are seven members, each serving a four-year term. Three members sit on a board every time there is an appeal."

"And they're the final word?"

"Yes."

"You have to admire a world body that powerful that is also so unaccountable. It's a remarkable human achievement."

"You are wrong," Zelkova said. "The people there *are*

accountable. *That* is the problem. They are accountable to an agreement. They are accountable to rules. They are accountable to pieces of papers and signatures that are accountable to no one."

"So they're just following orders." Blaylock smirked. "Bretton Woods equals Wannsee."

Zelkova's mouth twisted. She looked disgusted, with Blaylock's taste or with the WTO, Blaylock wasn't sure. She cleared her throat, and when she spoke, the coolness of her tone let Blaylock know she'd gone over the line. "Not quite," Zelkova said. "There is no intent to harm at the WTO. There is only . . ." She paused.

"Collateral damage?" Blaylock suggested.

Zelkova nodded. And willful ignorance, Blaylock added to herself. Slavish adherence to bureaucratic and market dogma. Blind allegiance to the corporate. She stared out the window as they drove out of Geneva. She watched the mountains lose definition in the dusk, become muscular, dark presences. She thought about the shape they gave Swiss life. The mountain was the first principle of existence here. It demanded obedience, demanded adaptation, made them one and the same. In Canada, too, the amoral fist of the land held illimitable dominion. She pictured the WTO in the same terms. As each round of negotiations passed, from Uruguay to Tokyo to Millennium, the organization gathered to itself not just the levers, but the very definitions of power. It spread into domains economic, environmental, social, judicial. The WTO was legislative, and it was executive, judge, and executioner, with international armed forces slaved to the purpose of making countries over in the WTO's image. The Universal Declaration of Human Rights was subject to perpetual override, a legalistic irrelevance to the almighty level playing field, the darkling plain of international trade. The WTO was becoming the human animal's first principle. It was the deity behind the curtain, the god whose commands could not be ignored, even if its existence was unknown. But Zelkova was right. The WTO had no one guiding intelligence. There was no spider at the center of the web.

She frowned, bothered by a speculation. She turned back to Zelkova. "Who sets the agenda at the WTO?" she asked.

"The Quad, and the Dispute Settlement Board enforces."

"Meaning?"

"The Quad is the US, the EU, Japan, and Canada. It is not officially the executive."

"But it is de facto."

"Yes. Great use is made of 'green room' meetings. These are 'informal' meetings, by invitation only. No minutes are kept."

"Let me guess. The big boys haul the little kids in and bully them into agreements." Blaylock took Zelkova's bitter smile as agreement. "And if someone doesn't like what comes out of the green room?"

"The Appellate Body is like the Supreme Court. All disputes come to a final end there."

And not an elected representative in sight, Blaylock thought. For all the difference that would make. "The Quad still sounds pretty diffuse."

Zelkova nodded. "That is why we still win sometimes. The Quad feels many influences. Usually corporate. Once in a while not. Why? What are you thinking?"

"Nothing. I just like working things out." She snorted. "You wouldn't want me running the show, I can tell you that."

"Why not?"

"Because the whole thing is still too chaotic. Too many chefs. If you're going to have a center, make sure it acts like one."

They arrived at Zelkova's home. Blaylock climbed out of the car, felt the adrenaline anticipation of battle. She was going to meet Sherbina. She was playing with explosives. She was having fun. Zelkova led her inside. From the living room, Blaylock heard the sounds of a child giggling on the silly edge of hysterical laughter. Racehorse Sherbina came pounding around the corner, his daughter perched on his shoulders. He kissed Zelkova, and in that second Blaylock felt a sick rush of nausea. This was a tight family. She knew this instantly and with certainty. The affection was so close to what she had known in her own that she felt the gut-clench of flashback. The nausea came from the realization that she had just been handed Sherbina's number. Horrified by the calculation she had made, she pushed the thought aside. Buried it. You will not, she told herself. *Ever*. Sherbina lowered Inna to the ground and turned to greet Blaylock. "Jennifer Baylor," Zelkova announced, and Blaylock saw Sherbina double-take. She didn't think he did that often. She sensed her risks shift to screaming red. The nausea faded and fun went ballistic. Sherbina shook her hand. Touch gloves, Blaylock thought, and come out fighting.

Round 1. Sherbina pouring drinks, Zelkova cross-legged with Inna on the rug by the fireplace, Blaylock on the couch. Sherbina, at the oak cabinet, spoke with his back to the room. "So you'll be traveling to Davos with us on our train."

"That's the plan."

"How does it feel to be Irina's pet press puppet?" He turned around with a wink. "If you don't mind the phrasing."

"Stepan," Irina sighed.

"Not at all," Blaylock said. Huge smile, *huge*. "It feels great. I take pride in only whoring myself out to the best." They might have been boxing, but she used a tai chi move: take the enemy's strike, extend it further than he planned, negate the blow.

Sherbina nodded his appreciation, served the drinks. He sat down at the other end of the couch from Blaylock. "I've read some of your pieces," he said.

Really? Blaylock thought. I doubt that. "Is that right?" They toasted each other. Blaylock sipped. The Scotch was old, refined fire filtered through smoke and peat.

"Don't believe him," Zelkova said. "He teases."

Sherbina looked pained. "Qui? Moi? I am impugned."

Inna asked, "What's 'impugned'?"

"It's what these two ladies are doing to me, darling. They are making me out to be a liar." He turned to Blaylock. "And if I told you how much I enjoyed your Northern Tiger article in the *Wall Street Journal* last fall? What then?"

What then? Then you land a solid blow, because nobody remembers newspaper articles that long, and nobody notices freelance bylines. You've been researching me, but you looked startled when you saw me. So what gives? She raised her glass to Sherbina, conceding the point.

Round 2. Dinner. They moved to the dining room. The help served a salmon terrine. The main course was veal Pojarski with demi-glace. Blaylock watched Inna scarf the exotica down, and not pause at the artichokes and peas. She drank milk, though, not the Willm Gewürztraminer white.

Sherbina said, "I take it, the *Journal* notwithstanding, that your views actually are in sympathy with my darling wife's."

"'Darling wife,'" Zelkova muttered. Inna giggled.

Blaylock said, "I've always viewed the stock market as the bastard child of astrology, fundamentalist religion, and organized crime."

Sherbina's smile, even huger than hers had been. "I couldn't agree more."

Blaylock bowed her head, acknowledging another blow landed.

Round 3. Dessert. Chocolate and hazelnut pavé. Denser than lead, heart-killer rich, taste worth the thousand deaths. Blaylock noticed Inna staring at her. The girl had been sneaking glances all evening. Now, losing shyness, she wouldn't take her eyes off Blaylock's face. Blaylock smiled at her, thought of Jenny and her carnivorous tree, thought of Jenny as she had last seen her. Blaylock felt her smile freeze.

Sherbina chuckled at his daughter's stare. "My daughter, being the offspring of two exceptional parents, is very observant. Tell me," he touched his cheek with his finger, then ran his finger over his left eye, mimicking the diagonal of Blaylock's old scar, "were you ever a war correspondent?"

You're not scoring a point that easily, Blaylock thought. Tag-team me with your kid? That's pathetic. "I was in the army," she said, uppercutting with the truth. "Peacekeeping in Bosnia." The scars came before and after, but so what?

Sherbina raised a finger, marking the point for Blaylok. She glanced at Zelkova, who was looking at the two of them with a worry that bordered on fear. Inna asked, "Are you still a soldier?"

The pavé caught in Blaylock's throat. Inna's tone, the admiration in her gaze, were a sudden hard echo. Not of Jenny this time, but of Celia. Little sister Celia, dead at fourteen from an InSec bomb. Celia, charcoal-bound with mother and father, Blaylock's family the center of a little half-acre of scorched earth. Blaylock had had her justice, had carved out her pound of flesh. Her family's cremation was no longer the goad to war, her mother's remembered disapproval no longer a phantom limb restraint. Goads were unnecessary, restraints unwanted. Her tragedy had receded to bedrock-scabbed absence, the perpetual fact of existence. Celia and her parents were history, the kill that had made her what she was. But Inna's question cracked the bedrock, let out a small flow of magmatic pain. The curiosity and the respect were the cloned image of Celia's the year Blaylock had enlisted. Celia, seeing her big sister in uniform for the first time, had asked, "Are you a soldier now?" The answer was obvious, but she wanted to hear it from the lips of her hero. Blaylock, puffed, had answered, "Yes," the single syllable an absolute fusion of pride and truth. Now, thrown against the ropes, she looked at Inna and tried to put the same truth into her answer: "No." She looked into Inna's eyes, felt communication arc down their mutual gaze. I'm not a soldier anymore, Blaylock thought. I'm war. And Inna looked frightened.

Sherbina leaned back in his chair, picked up his coffee, pretended to concentrate on it when he spoke. "Tell me. Have you ever been to Ciudad del Este?"

Wham. Body blow. Blaylock dropped to the mat. How did he know? Never mind, stand up, fight back. Turn his strike against him. "Yes," she answered. "Quite recently, in fact. The Coscarelli crime family was big news, and I managed to track Salvatore Coscarelli to Paraguay." She spread her hands. "I was hoping for a scoop." She shrugged. "I lost him there." She kept her gaze steady and on Sherbina's eyes for the full length of her lie.

"Commendably adventurous, though a little off your usual beat, wouldn't you say?"

"I was bored. Thought I'd branch out. Besides, it wasn't that much of a stretch. I already told you what I think of the stock market."

Sherbina put his coffee down. The bone china made a delicate click. Sherbina applauded silently. TKO.

Sherbina watched the lights of Zelkova's Alfa 156 recede. Inna stood beside him, holding his hand. She waved until the tail lights vanished. Sherbina ruffled her hair. "What did you think of Mama's friend?" he asked.

Inna thought this over. "Is she sad?" she asked, very serious and concerned.

Sherbina crouched, looked into his daughter's face. "What makes you say that?" If anything, the woman had struck him as someone who was in on the big cosmic joke, and liked the humor.

Inna shrugged. "I don't know." Her eyes were shades of deep solemn. She threw her arms around her father's neck. She began to cry.

"Hey," Sherbina whispered. "Hey, now." He hugged Inna, rocked side to side. "What's wrong?"

"Please don't die, Papa." Her arms clutched tighter. Her body was a tiny, fragile quivering of fears.

"There there, there there." He was thrown. "I'm not going to die." He lifted Inna's head from his shoulder. He cupped her face in his hands, leaned his forehead against hers. "What put that idea in your head?"

Sniffle. "I don't know."

"You know what I think? I think being very tired put the idea there." Inna started to shake her head, little child auto-denial, but Sherbina carried on. "When I'm overtired, I think all kinds of strange things, too." Inna wiped her nose, gave him a hopeful look. "Come on," he said, and picked her up. He carried her upstairs, put her in her PJs, and tucked her in. He crooned, he joked, he comforted. He sat beside her until she fell asleep.

He considered Baylor. When she'd walked in, some puzzle pieces, jagged as broken glass, had come together, and the *snick* of their edges had alarmed him. He'd almost forgotten what alarm felt like. What he had seen was a woman who matched the description of the one who had been asking questions about Salvatore Coscarelli all over Ciudad del Este. What he had heard was the name of the woman who took out Barry Reynolds and his team. He thought about motivated amateurs snuffed. He thought about the wipeout in Ciudad del Este. The dead there weren't amateurs. He wondered how dangerous Baylor was. He wondered if he should be worried. He realized he was smiling.

The car started following them when they hit the outskirts of Geneva. Blaylock noticed a faint glow reflecting from Zelkova's rear-view mirror. The glow remained steady, no one catching up to overtake. They reached the Old Town. The glow disappeared when Zelkova rounded corners, but it came back, consistent and closer.

"Is something wrong?" Zelkova asked.

"How many enemies did you make at the WTO today?"

"Many. That is my job. Why?"

"We're being tailed."

Zelkova's face turned to flint. "My husband will not be happy."

No, Blaylock didn't suppose he would. Unless Zelkova wasn't the target. "Has this happened to you before?"

Zelkova hesitated. "Once in a while." She chewed her lip. "I have never been in danger," she added.

Meaning you were being tracked by law enforcement, interested in hubby dear, Blaylock thought. Well, one way to find out who's interesting tonight. "Take the next left and drop me off," she said.

Zelkova turned onto the Rue St-Léger and pulled over. "I'll see you at the train, I hope," she said as Blaylock climbed out.

"I'll be there." Blaylock closed the door. Zelkova drove off. Blaylock stayed on the edge of the sidewalk, in the open and easy to spot, and watched the intersection. Headlights appeared. The car stopped. Blaylock nodded to herself and began to walk, putting space and people between her and the street. She glanced back. The car was moving again. It sped up and passed her. She saw a driver, but no passenger. She doubted the tail was a solo. His partner was on foot, somewhere behind her.

St-Léger wound uphill. The buildings in the Old Town were low, gray, private. Their facades were implacable in their unconcern. When the streets emptied, Blaylock would be on her own. She didn't mind. She moved up St-Léger until it reached place Bourg-de-Four, a split-level market square. Cafés dotted the circumference. She crossed the pavement, climbed the stairs to the uphill side, and walked into La Clémence. She sat down at a table close to the window, with a view of most of the square. She ordered a coffee and settled down to wait. She watched the foot traffic, eyeing any faces that passed by more than once. No hard data. She wasn't surprised. She'd probably been spotted entering the café, and her tail was playing the same waiting game, but with an edge. He knew who she was, and where she was.

She worked her way through coffees and hours. She considered looking for a back door, dismissed the idea. She wanted to engage. So she waited. The night grew old. The restaurants and bars began to close. The good burghers headed home. She loitered, annoying the staff. Just before they threw her out, she stood up and sauntered through the door. The square was close to deserted. She scanned. On the far side of the square, on the lower half, she saw a man standing by the door of the Café du Bourg-de-Four. The lights in the café flicked off, and a moment later the staff poured out. Blaylock's lips twitched. She thought, Last holdout, too, buddy? The man pulled out a cellphone. He spoke into it, moving casually up the stairs. Blaylock waited, but he moved past her. His clothes were dark, loose-fitting. They didn't stand out, they blended in with urban casual, but they were good for fast, unrestricted movement. The signs read *pro*. Got you, Blaylock thought. You're mine. She followed.

The man walked up the Rue de l'Hôtel de Ville. She kept a dozen yards back. She wished for a gun. Halfway up the street, the man jumped into the passenger side of a parked car. The car screeched a three-point turn away from the curb and roared Blaylock's way. She took a step back. Bullets *pinged* in from six o'clock, forcing her further into the street. She stumbled forward towards the car. It veered onto the sidewalk. It side-swiped a wrought-iron railing, trailed sparks as it scraped against building facades. Blaylock jumped straight up. The windshield clipped her boots as she came back down. She slammed face-first onto the car roof, bounced, and slid off the back. She hit the sidewalk hard, rattling bones. Blood poured from her lips and nose. The car reversed. She rolled to the side. She smelled exhaust and rubber as the tires whipped past her head. She heard gears grind. She rose to her knees, saw an uprooted parking sign lying in the middle of the street. She lunged for it, grabbed the pole with both hands, and hefted it. The car was coming at her again, angry metal, hard and fast. She sidestepped and swung the pole, cannonball dancing. The end of the pole smashed through the driver's window. Momentum spun Blaylock three-sixty. The car swerved right, slammed into a stone facade. Stalled.

Blaylock ran to the car. The man on the passenger side opened his door, but he was jammed up against the side of the building. The driver was wiping blood from his face with one hand, starting the car up with the other. The broken end of the pole was jagged. Blaylock lifted it high, spear, and rammed it through the window into the side of the driver's head. Bone crunched. The man's hands flapped butterfly at the steering wheel and stilled. The other man had pulled out a gun. Blaylock ducked against the door as he fired. Bullets whined off the wall on the other side of the street. Blaylock reached up, yanked the pole out of the car, and crouch-walked to the rear of the car. She scrambled onto the roof. The killer fired through the metal. Blaylock felt the air in front of her nose thrum heat as a bullet went past. She angled the pole and brought the point of the shaft down between the building facade and the car, broke the passenger window, raised the pole again, danced a step back and then forward as bullets pierced the roof. She thrust the spear down, felt it pierce something soft, heard a scream. The bullets stopped. Blaylock jumped down on the driver's side. She looked inside. She'd nailed the shooter in the thigh, and he was writhing, skewered. She reached in, felt inside the driver's jacket. No gun. Shit. She opened the car door. The bastard was wearing his seat belt, and he was big. He blocked her access to the passenger, who was rocking back and forth, fumbling with his pistol. He ejected a spent clip as Blaylock leaned in and undid the driver's belt. She pulled and he slumped her way, fell out of the car. The passenger had a new clip in his hands. He had steadied his breathing. Blaylock jumped into the car as he slammed the clip home. She hit him twice, hard, on the side of the neck, crushing his vagus nerves. Breathing and heartbeat stopped. He fish-flopped, fingers splayed and dropping his gun. He slumped.

Blaylock picked up the gun. Still the other shooter to deal with, somewhere out in the square, covering the exit from the street. She heard a motorcycle engine. She listened, heard it come closer, move away, repeat the pattern. She got out of the car, thought for a moment, and retrieved the pole. She hugged the facade and approached Bourg-de-Four, waited until the engine noise receded again, then popped into the square. She spotted the beast, a souped-up motocross. The biker was circling the square, was already on the return run on her level. He spotted Blaylock and fired. He was good: he steered one-handed as he fired. He was cocky: his shots didn't have a hope of accuracy at that speed and movement. Blaylock returned fire, teaching him caution but not fear, and ran. He aimed the motorcycle at her. With both of them moving, a vehicle hit was more likely than a bullet, and just as lethal. Blaylock leaped down the steps to the lower half of the square. He followed, shooting. She tripped as bullets chipped the ground in front of her feet. She fell, saw the bike heading for her head. She fired, and he veered off. She lunged up and doubled back. The killer gunned his engine and tore up the road, racing Blaylock to the upper level. She spoiled the race and stayed up on the middle step. The stairs were cut into a stone wall. If he wanted to run her down, he would have to do so here, not on the road. He took her wager and roared down hard. Blaylock threw herself to the side and flat on the stairs. The bike went by, airborne. As it passed, Blaylock shoved the metal shaft through the spokes of the front wheel. The somersault impact shook the ground. The biker's helmet didn't break. His neck did.

Blaylock stood, brushed herself off. She wiped the blood from her face with a sleeve. She looked around. The Old Town was quiet again, except for the death-ticks of the motorcycle. The buildings showed offense in their silence. She limped away from Bourg-de-Four, making for her hotel on the Rue Verdaine. She wondered who had ordered the hit. Chapel? Sherbina?

17

When Sherbina greeted her the next day at the train, he had a twinkle in his eye.

The train pulled out of the station. As it started, Blaylock heard rhythmic chuffing. She opened the window for a moment and poked her head out. She saw white puff from the locomotive's smokestack. She grinned, shook her head, closed the window. The engine was diesel, but looked like steam. Blaylock hadn't expected the illusion to go as far as phony smoke and ornamental sound. She sat down and looked across the cabin at Zelkova. "This train . . ." she said.

Zelkova nodded. "I know. It is my husband's, not mine."

"Toys for boys?"

Zelkova's smile was wry. "Very much so."

Sherbina stepped into the compartment. He looked from one woman to the other. "Have I missed something?" Zelkova and Blaylock rolled their eyes.

The train was two fantasies yoked together. With violence. The locomotive and the first two cars were Orient Express nostalgia, perfect late nineteenth-century replicas to the eye, but all mod cons lurking just below the surface. The other six cars were steel and might, troop-transport-plus in their metal shutters and reinforced shells. There was a large dome on the rear car, which Blaylock suspected opened into a turret. This fantasy was a train ready to invade Poland. Blaylock had watched Sherbina's men board. They were troops, no other word for them. "Stepan expecting a war?" she had asked Zelkova.

"Security."

"Let me guess. Kornukopia's got quite the reputation in that area, too, right?" Her opposition was impressive. Kornukopia's corporate philosophy wasn't specialization, but multiplication with excellence. The split personality of the train was a case in point. The strength was unforgiving, Kornukopia's security beyond reproach and beyond attack. The luxury was as absolute. The car where Blaylock sat with Zelkova, the second back from the locomotive, had two sections, lounge and dining compartment, both so spacious the only reminder she was on a train was the movement. The lounge was red carpets, Tiffany lamps, furniture that looked antique and uncomfortable but managed to be ergonomic and sinful at the same time. The dining compartment had stained-glass shutters. Pull them back for breakfast, let the sun flood in. Draw them in the evening, let them reflect first sunset, then candlelight. Nothing to disrupt the intimacy. Even the kitchen was banished to the first of the troop cars. The forward car held the sleeping compartments. The beds had queen mattresses. They didn't have posters, though. Instead, the car roofs had shutters that rolled back. Sleep beneath the stars and mountains. The compartments were family-friendly in size and facilities, but Inna was at home with the nanny.

Blaylock was sorry the trip was only a few hours long. Sorry beyond the indulgence of the luxury. She was having fun. She and Sherbina had their game, and it was a good one. She would beard the lion in his den, he would shelter the serpent in his Eden. Lion and serpent, strength and venom, circled each other, smiled at the dance, enjoyed the perversity of each other's company. She knew why Sherbina twinkled. He had her in full sight, contained. If he kept his enemy any closer, they'd be screwing. And that was fine. Blaylock had her own twinkle. Her luggage was calculated innocence. She had assumed Sherbina would search her suitcase, and she'd packed him something to find: fighting knife, SIG, a couple of clips. Anything less wouldn't have been convincing, and he might search harder. He might find what she had done the previous night. She had returned to the hotel, cleaned herself up, then gone out again. She'd hit the InSec warehouse, retrieved some of her cache. Next stop, the station. She'd located the Kornukopia train, attached her bag of toys beneath the fake coal tender. Her toys: C7, SIG, ammo, bricks of C4 explosive, timers, remotes, grenades. The modern career woman's travel kit. Twinkle twinkle.

Geneva. Two in the morning. Darryl Avery asked, "You sure you want to do this?"

Alloway stopped walking. "Why? You scared?"

"Just thinking about what happens if we get caught. Wouldn't be fantastic like in Ottawa. We'd be bending and spreading for the rest of our lives, dude."

"I'm not backing down. I'm not giving the bastards the satisfaction. We're going to hurt them, for real this time."

"What would Jen think about this?"

"She'd be happy that she's not the only one bringing the fight to the enemy. Now come on." He punched Avery in the shoulder, "Where do we go?"

Avery led the way. Alloway felt two hairs from ridiculous. They were at the Schtrumpfs. This was not the area he'd expected. Les Pâquis, Geneva's red-light central, maybe. But not this. Not this exercise in fairy-tale plasticine and storybook mushrooms. The public-housing estate was the architecture of tumorous imagination. Concrete and stone had given themselves over to a whimsy of protrusions. Alloway thought he might like the place during the day. He might have fun running with the out-of-control colors and mosaics. But now, night-gray, the Schtrumpfs had left fanciful and entered surreal. The bulges on the walls were not jokes, they were symptoms. And still Alloway felt like he should be paying admission. "I can't believe this is the address."

"Hey, don't blame me." Avery held up a scrap of paper. "Those guys said go here, so here we are. Maybe they were yanking my chain, but you know, they didn't look like they were big on practical jokes. Those were some scary people you made me see."

"Yeah, and I feel bad. But you're big, and you can pass. First Angel I spoke to would have whipped my sorry ass."

Avery grunted, consulted his map again under a street light. He found the address they wanted at the center of the estate. They stared at the list of names on the intercom. Avery's finger hovered over the button beside the name LAFONE. "Kinda late to be buzzing."

"This is the time they told you." Alloway reached past Avery and pushed the button.

Louis Lafone was waiting for them at the top of the third-floor landing. His look was even further from Hell's

Angels associate than Alloway's. He was tall, thin as malnutrition, had no chin but a prominent neck. His hair was albino-blond, cut short and still lank on his scalp. His skin was an undead, acne disaster. He held a finger to his lips and signaled for them to follow. He took them into his apartment, down a hallway to a bedroom that had been converted into an electronics workshop. He opened a metal trunk and pulled out a backpack. The backpack looked worn, well-traveled. A Canadian flag patch had been sewn onto the flap. Lafone crouched on the floor and opened the flap. Alloway leaned forward. Inside he saw what looked like a travel alarm clock connected by wires to a dark cylinder. The buttons on the clock looked standard. The clock was flashing 12:00. Alloway nodded, looked at Lafone. Slowly, each gesture obvious with no possibility of confusion, Lafone set the clock for 03:30. He pushed the button marked ALARM and a spot on the LCD began to pulse. He looked at Alloway to make sure he'd been understood. Alloway nodded again. Lafone hit RESET. The pulse stopped, and the display flashed 12:00 once more. "Got it," Alloway said.

Lafone's hand flashed, backhanded Alloway hard on the cheek. Alloway recoiled, eyes tearing. Lafone held his finger up. *Shhh*.

In their hotel room, Judy and Mark Liang were awake. They held each other. Mark said, "You think this is a mistake?"

"We're committed, now."

"You didn't answer my question."

Judy shut her eyes, snuggled against her husband's chest. "Answer mine. Are we doing the right thing?"

"Yes."

"And we know there's a risk?"

"Yes."

She squeezed his shoulders. "We know that the risk is that we might die." She heard Mark swallow. He clutched her tight, but didn't answer. "We already discussed this," she reminded him.

"Yes," he agreed, finally.

"Then say it. If we're in denial, then we are making a mistake."

"We might die," he whispered.

"But if we don't take a stand..." Judy began.

"... who will?" Mark finished.

In his room, Chuck Bilodeau had the lights on. Jet lag and nerves had his eyes wide and dry. He'd given up trying to read. He flicked through the TV channels, not seeing any of them. He was thinking of mistakes and risks, too, his mind slipping from one half-formed question and anxiety to another. At last, disgusted with himself, he turned the TV off and forced the issue. Why are you here? he asked himself. You don't agree with anything Global Response is doing. Why do you care? *Why* are you here?

The answers came with surprising ease, and when they did, he felt his body relax. Because they're my friends. Because I call myself a journalist. So I will bear witness.

Two ways only to reach Davos: road and rail. Grimson had looked into the possibility of chartering a bus for Global Response and other groups. She'd been laughed out of the office. Most of the protesters were flying into

Zurich, then taking the two-and-three-quarter-hour train trip from there. That made sense. But Alloway, ranting in vague terms about connections and allies, had insisted on logging more hours on the train by flying to Geneva first. Grimson had surrendered. Blaylock had given them more than enough money for the trip, and if going the long way around kept the peace, so be it.

Alloway and Avery looked exhausted as they boarded the train. "How late were you two out?" Grimson asked.

"We'll live," Alloway said. He was jumpy today, and surly. His right cheek was bright red.

"Were you in a fight last night?" Alloway shook his head and settled into his seat. Grimson and Avery put their bags in the overhead racks, but Alloway kept his backpack on the floor, clutched between his legs. Grimson looked at it, realized she hadn't seen it before. "What happened to your other pack?" she asked. Alloway went pale. He stared at Avery.

"Better tell her, man," Avery said.

Alloway's eyes bulged. He swallowed hard, Adam's apple bobbing yo-yo. "You do it," he croaked.

Avery turned to Grimson. "We were robbed," he explained.

Grimson rubbed her forehead. "Jesus, Jonathan. Trust you to find a way to get mugged in Switzerland."

"Hey, he fought back, Kelly. He was totally fantastic. But there were two guys, and I couldn't catch up, so . . ." Avery shrugged. "Anyway, we were hanging with some other protesters when it happened, and one of the guys had changed his mind and was going home, so he sold his pack to Jonathan." Avery spread his hands. "Problem solved." Big grin.

Problem solved. Terrific. But she let it go, worrying

about bigger problems down the line. Those problems showed up after Zurich, when they reached Landquart to change for the Davos line. Their train arrived, they boarded, and then they waited. The train sat, violating the rigor of Swiss timetables. After ten minutes, soldiers came on board and moved through the cars, checking passports. The train was packed with activists, and the soldiers took their time. Alloway turned to a shell of sweat and gray when his turn came. Grimson looked away, embarrassed. This wasn't like him. She hadn't thought he would fold the first time he came up against authorities that weren't known-quantity Canadian. She wondered if the end of Greenham Common had hit him harder than he'd let on. He'd been full of rage and fire in the days afterward, but perhaps that was the bluster of fear. Maybe he'd been broken. No. Not her Jonathan. The soldiers moved on. Alloway breathed again. Grimson squeezed his knee, gave him a smile.

The soldiers hauled three activists out of the car. Grimson saw another dozen gathered on the platform and held there until the train moved on. "They're doing it again," she said.

"I know," Alloway said. "Shit."

"We have the letter from Irina," Avery put in.

"That's no guarantee," Grimson said. "All that did was let us into the country." Which already made them among the elect. In the weeks leading up to the WEF, Switzerland had turned its borders into a slip-knot, choking out anyone who fit a very broad definition of undesirable. Some protesters had tried entering the country months in advance, but were crippled by expiring visas and stratospheric Swiss prices. Now the army was pulling the same trick as in previous years. Grimson fumed.

Everybody knew about the trick, but it was a good trick, and no one had found a way around it. The Swiss had come up with the trick after the 2002 forum. That year, the protesters had been prevented from even leaving Zurich. So they had stayed there and raised hell. The next year, the activists were allowed on the trains. Then, at every stop, their numbers were nickel-and-dimed. Little groups were taken off the trains and stranded. Division, reduction, irrelevancy, evaporation. The tactic was beautiful, foolproof. Grimson sighed, slumped back in her seat. "We're not going to make it there," she said.

Switzerland. Clockwork. The tick-tick of aligning gears went like this. Schiers was the first of the milk-run stops between Landquart and Davos. The station master sat in his ticket office, thumbing a paperback, bored. Two soldiers stood on the platform, waiting for the Landquart train so they could fill their quota of protesters. No one else was around, the locals staying the hell off this line until the circus was over and done. Between trains, the soldiers, like the station master, were bored. Out of their skulls. One of them felt his pockets, cursed. "Cigarette?" he asked the other, who shook his head. The first soldier walked into the building. The station master wasn't sitting at the ticket window. The soldier approached the window and peered in, searching the little office. No one there. On the back wall, a dark red splash smeared down train timetables. The soldier stared at the red, improbability blocking quick understanding. But when he heard a noise behind him, he knew right away that he was hearing a pistol being cocked, knew right away that he was going to die. He turned around anyway. He saw two men in Swiss military uniform. A third was dressed as a station master. He was pointing a silenced pistol at the soldier. The soldier saw the man pull the trigger. Before the darkness, he felt the bullet enter his forehead. The pain was very brief. It was also obscene.

The men dressed as soldiers remained inside, watching the entrance for passengers. The man with the pistol walked onto the platform. He came back a minute later, the other soldier's body slung over his shoulder. He and his partners moved the corpses into the office, shoved them under the counter so they would be invisible to ticket buyers. They covered up the blood on the wall with new timetables. The man in station master uniform sat down and picked up the paperback. The Schiers station would be business as usual for at least another twelve hours. The men in army uniform went out onto the platform to wait for the train. Fifteen minutes later, a couple of locals here now, necessity forcing them to face the circus, the train arrived. The passengers boarded. The soldiers did not board the train and remove protesters. They waved the train on. Then one of them radioed in to the dead men's commanding officer, and told a lie. Yevgeny Nevzlin, on quality control, monitored the transmission.

And so on. Like clockwork. Clickety-clack. All the way down the line.

Saturday morning, 0800 hours. Friday, the first day of the WEF, over and done and no blood in the streets. The cellphone rang. Blaylock let the connection happen, but didn't speak. Neither did her caller. She waited two seconds, then turned the phone off. She shrugged into her coat and left the Waldhotel Bellevue, where she nestled parasite-cozy with the gods of trade and politics. The hotel's luxury was sober, its architecture restrained Alpine. Its view, though, was commanding heights all the way. Davos was a two-mile strip of hotels and apartment buildings, hemmed in by the confines of its narrow valley. The Bellevue stood on the north slope of the valley, at the vertical edge of the town and halfway between the two train stations of Davos-Dorf and Davos-Platz. Blaylock could see all of Davos from the hotel's terrace. She marched downhill until she hit the Promenade, then walked west to the Davos-Platz station. Grimson was waiting beside a bank of pay phones. "So you made it," Blaylock said.

"Yeah. At first I didn't think we would. It was weird. Soldiers were hustling people off the train at Landquart. After that, they didn't bother." She grinned. "Somebody screwed up. This is going to be the biggest protest Davos has seen in years."

"You say that like it's a good thing."

Grimson's lips tightened. Blaylock could see the patience evaporating from her eyes. "You know, Jen, nobody granted you a monopoly on agency, and this whole Big Sister Knows Best thing is insulting."

A murder of reporters walked by. Blaylock put an arm around Grimson's shoulders. She smiled, looked sunny for the people. She put her face close to Grimson's, girlfriends in confidence, and kept her voice low. "Kelly, think. Your home is torched. Some of your friends are killed. I'd say those are already signs of a very serious game being played, wouldn't you? Now you tell me that the Swiss army fell asleep at the switch, leaving a gaping hole in the Davos security measures. This is something that has never happened. And we both know that something big is going to go down here, and that transnational organized crime is involved. Meanwhile, the mountains are crawling with armed soldiers. There are anti-aircraft positions on the ski slopes, for Chrissake." She looked Grimson in the eyes. "Don't. Be. Stupid." She emphasized each word with a punch on the shoulder. "Think really hard," she said, and nodded at Grimson's stomach. Grimson's coat concealed the six-month swelling. Blaylock couldn't get it out of her mind. "You can still leave."

"No."

Blaylock sighed. "Fine. Remember your training, at least."

"I haven't forgotten."

"And I want to know where you are."

"Yes, Mother."

"I'm not kidding. Any trouble, use your cell. I don't care who's monitoring." A thought struck her. "Where are you staying?" Davos' population was only 13,000. A few thousand protesters arriving on top of the 2000 business and government mandarins would stand out.

"We're all over." Grimson's tone was excited. She sounded like the commander of a successful Special Ops mission. Blaylock's worry became despair. Grimson hadn't forgotten her training. It was resurfacing in all the wrong ways. "A fair number even have authorization to be here, believe it or not. We're packed into the hostels. And you should see how many people are at the campsite."

"*Camping?* In February? How many have to die of exposure before you reach your quota of martyrs?" She doubted anybody was there in heated RVs.

"They're staying warm. Don't worry. Even the wanderers."

"The wanderers?"

Grimson nodded. "There isn't room for everybody.

And we're worried that the campsite is too concentrated a target. If the army wants to round everybody up quickly, that place is a gift. So people are sleeping in shifts. Those who aren't sleeping are just walking around. In town, in the mountains, everywhere. The protest's this evening. We only have to stay ahead of security for the day."

Blaylock swept her gaze over the street. High season plus WEF, and the resort was an anthill. The sidewalks were shoulder-to-shoulder packed. Blaylock tried to pick out activists from residents, tourists, and forum attendees. She couldn't. Winter wear was the great fashion leveler, and the anti-globalization movement was too rainbow. That grandmother might run a B&B, or she might be hoisting a placard later. There were a lot of young people around, and they were still the biggest chunk of the protesters, but every twenty-two-year-old she saw could just as easily be here skiing on Daddy's oil money. "It's goddamn *Invasion of the Body Snatchers*," she muttered. She felt security-force paranoia.

Grimson said, "Isn't it great?"

"Where's the march going?"

"As close to the Congress Center as they let us."

"The sessions will be over by this evening."

"I know."

"You guys are going to be yelling away during the banquet."

Grimson shrugged. "I kind of like the juxtaposition. The high and the mighty having their decadence disrupted by the revolting masses."

Blaylock laughed. "Yeah, nice image." She started to walk away. "You know what your deal is really going to be?" she called back. "After-dinner entertainment."

18

Davos' history was the shifting desires of wealth. Before skiing, the town's industry had been recovery. The resort had been sanatorium central, with twenty-nine institutions. Tuberculosis became passé, gave way to the lure of the ski runs. The hotel took over. Then came the WEF, born to Davos thanks to esthetic inaccessibility. The Congress Center, at the midpoint of the town, was a sprawling collision of disparate wings, half warm wood siding, half institutional concrete. It bridged the slope between the Promenade and the Talstrasse, the two parallel arteries that stretched the length of Davos. Without the forum, the Center would have been a middle-of-nowhere aberration, grotesque for a town this size. Thanks to the forum, it had a glove-fit perfection.

Blaylock reached the Center. She showed her pass, went through the fine-tooth security check. She was unarmed. This was becoming a habit. She strolled through the main lobby, and flipped through a program. There were over three hundred sessions during the forum's weekend. They were deeply Serious, deeply Worthy. There were quite a few self-consciously progressive panels, well-meaning hand-wringing over the developing world. One was titled *HIV-AIDS: Is Attention Being Paid?* Blaylock wondered if the presenters had delivered the same talk for the last ten years. She counted at least a dozen sessions that worried the bone of the Ember Lake fire. Most of them plotted out the ongoing economic meltdown. There was one, though, that asked, *Are Leaders Expendable?* The big keynote was at one. President Sam *Not on My Watch* Reed was promising to storm the barn.

Blaylock arrived at the lecture theater early, and it was already stuffed to standing room and beyond. Reed was a hot ticket these days. Threats of hellfire and crackdown could do that for a guy. Then there were the leaks. His staff had been busy, hints of big policy pronouncements falling like pigeon droppings. Everything from internment camps to war on France was suggested. Lots of selling going on, but Blaylock wasn't buying. Reed's talk was a good place to track the scent of a big show, though. Better yet, Reed wasn't just delivering a speech. He was also going to have a debate. With Lawrence Dunn. Welcome to superstardom, Mr. Dunn, Blaylock thought as she looked for a vantage point of the stage. She found a perch behind the last row of seats. When Reed walked onto the stage, he looked grave. He gripped the lectern, and looked at the audience for fifteen solid seconds before he said a word. The silence was so pregnant, Blaylock began to choke on a suppressed laughing fit. "We are at a critical juncture," Reed said, and Blaylock thought, Is that the best opening you can come up with? Reed began a catalog of the world's hell-in-a-handbasket condition. Blaylock's attention went AWOL. Her eyes wandered over the audience. She spotted Joe Chapel. He was sitting in the middle of the back row.

Blaylock shuffled her way left until she was standing behind Chapel's seat. She crouched and whispered into his ear. "Bang, he's dead." Chapel jumped, whirled his head around. She made a gun with thumb and index finger, blew smoke from the barrel. She winked. Chapel glared.

"These are our challenges," Reed said, and Blaylock listened again. She rested her chin on Chapel's shoulder, which went neurosis-rigid. Malice warmed her. She tickled the back of his neck with her fingernails. "We face them, not as individual nations, but as a world. So how do we, the world, respond? Not, I am afraid, through the United Nations. That body has failed all of us one too many times. Our nation, for one, will no longer be held hostage to its whims. True, the UN was founded with the noblest of dreams. So was the League of Nations. Dreams fade. So where do we turn? Is there a concrete, *practical* alternative to the UN?" Blaylock's fingers froze. "There is. Sometimes, when we set dreams aside, we find that reality has already provided us with what we need. There is no more effective means of bringing countries together in stability, mutual interest, and peace, than trade. And there is no more effective a body for bringing nations together in trade than the World Trade Organization. It is time for the WTO to realize the full potential of its name."

Bang, Blaylock thought. You're dead.

"Let's go," Grimson called.

"Be right out." Alloway was kneeling on the floor of hostel washroom. He opened the backpack, stared at his bomb. He wondered how big the bang would be. He'd wanted to ask Lafone, but had wanted more not to be hit again. The package was very heavy. It felt like lead. He practiced setting the clock again. He'd done this two-dozen times since leaving the Schtrumpfs. The thrill was sex-good. He didn't dare set the hour for real, yet. Not until he knew when the protest would be over. He reset the clock to the flashing 12:00. He shouldered the backpack and left the washroom.

"All pretty now?" Grimson asked.

"You bet." He kissed her. They held hands as they walked out of the hostel to take on the world.

The banquet was the big shit, and the aristocracy of late capitalism knew it. For a while, in the early years of the New Normal, the banquet had been put on ice. Modesty and shame were called for in the wake of Enron and market collapse. Now the market was gurgling in full toilet flush again, but the response was belligerence. The best defense was to circle the wagons and fire at will. The most heavily armed wagons were loud and proud, proclaiming themselves the role models. Kornukopia was loudest and proudest, headline grabbing as it preened its synergy and proliferation. The Russian miracle, coming to a town near you. So the banquet was back. Be there or be crushed.

Blaylock stepped into the banquet hall, feeling herself and not herself. The clothes were a lie, a Halloween costume. They bespoke a grace on which she had long since turned her back. But the costume was also a uniform, specialized camouflage for the battlefield of the hall. The look at the banquet was high formal. The men were a battalion of tuxedos. Many were half-past prime, embonpoint turning the banquet into penguins on parade. The women were in gowns, and divided into two castes. There were the trophy wives and target-of-opportunity mistresses, playing hard on the cleavage, front and back. Then there were the women who were here on their own power, still the minority breaking through the old boys' club, and they coded their worth into more fabric, less flesh. Blaylock scanned the sea of strapless and diamonds, and came up a with a quick rule of thumb: the higher the hair and the heels, the smaller the clout. Blaylock blended in. The camouflage was a fitted, sleeveless mock turtleneck, sparkling silver; a black satin skirt, fitted, too, but stretching enough to give her freedom of movement; and heels, though she refused to temper her stride. So armed, she hit the field.

She sat a table with Zelkova, whose gown was simple but her bearing regal. Lawrence Dunn was there, too, and knew Zelkova. Blaylock watched the two of them, wondered whether to see connections or coincidence. Dunn wasn't looking well. His rebuttal to Reed had been strong, his stage presence forceful, his logic turning Reed's syllogisms into loose and broken Tinkertoys. Up close, he was slumping, his eyes sunken in the dark holes of months of exhaustion. His responses to Zelkova were quiet, pared to minimal syllables. Zelkova gave up after a couple of minutes. Dunn's wife, held up by her clothes, not her will, fiddled with her place card. She turned it around in her hands, then picked up the bill of fare. "I don't know what half of these things are," Linda said. Her cheerfulness was as forced as a next-morning execution. The vellum slipped from her fingers.

Blaylock glanced at the menu. One of the appetizers was *Sea Urchin Soufflé in Aurore Sauce*. She wasn't sure what that was, either, but her mouth watered. By the time the main course arrived, *Truffled Saddle of Venison Wrapped in Irish Bacon, with Perigueux Sauce,* accompanied by, among others, a *Vegetable Medley in Parmesan Tuile*, she wasn't worried about definitions. Absolute power, absolute corruption, who cares, just let me eat this again. She kept her eye on Dunn while she ate. He looked at each dish as it sat before him, picked and nibbled, then lost interest. He held his cutlery in a loose grip, leaning the silverware against his plate. His eyes stared at the center of the table, glazed and haunted. By dessert, when his spoon hovered over his pristine *Raspberry and Poire William Bavaroise with Bitter Chocolate Sauce,* Blaylock felt the shame of waste. "Are you going to eat that?" she asked him. He looked up, pushed the dessert across the table to her. Linda spooned her bavaroise around, mashed it, didn't bring it near her mouth. "I liked your rebuttal," Blaylock told Dunn.

He shrugged. "Pre-sold audience."

Zelkova looked around. "Here?" she asked. Big disbelief.

"Some," Dunn said. "You. Him." He pointed to a rock star walking across the hall back to his seat. He wore his tux with biker boots and wraparound mirror shades. "Anyway, I doubt those who aren't converted were listening."

"At least they're fuming," Blaylock said. "That was a great hatchet job you did on Reed."

Dunn snorted. His eyes narrowed. Blaylock turned her head to see what he was looking at. The devil summoned, Reed was approaching their table. He clapped Dunn on the shoulder. "Impressive performance today, Lawrence." He was beaming birthday-bright. "Very impressive. You gave us all plenty to think about." He turned to Zelkova and Blaylock. "Evening, ladies." Blaylock smiled, sugar-sweet, but let him see shark in her eyes. His cat-with-canary look faltered a bit before he bowed and moved off.

"Some hatchet job," Dunn said. "How come he's not

pissed off?" He shook his head and turned to Zelkova. Desperation glittered in his eyes. "The President," he said. "Your husband. Why do they like me so much? Why are they *encouraging* me?"

Zelkova didn't meet his gaze. "I don't know," she said. Softly.

Dunn stood up and walked away from the table. His gait was rigid. Blaylock saw anger and fear twisting his body into quivering wire. Zelkova looked stricken. Linda glared at her. "Why are you doing this to us?" she whispered.

"I'm not." Zelkova was almost inaudible. She bunched her napkin, wouldn't meet Blaylock's eyes, either.

Blaylock excused herself and followed Dunn. She caught up to him by the narrow windows that looked out over the Center's parking lot and the Talstrasse. "Round and round we go," Dunn said. The protesters were gathering force in the lot. He looked at Blaylock. "Something I can do for you?" he asked, harsh from despair.

"I was going to ask you that."

Dunn rolled his eyes. "How? With a blistering op-ed piece? No offense, but I'm media, too. I know our limits."

Blaylock gambled, reached out. "I have other resources," she said, choosing her words. "And I know, for instance, that Salvatore Coscarelli had you jumping. Want to talk about it?"

"And have Sherbina slaughter my children? I think not." He stalked off. "Stay away from me," he called over his shoulder.

The march was much smaller than in Ottawa. Alloway tried to gauge the numbers as they moved down the Talstrasse towards the Congress Center. Three thousand?

Four? Maybe. There were tens of thousands back in September. But in the small space of Davos, the numbers seemed huge, a concentrated fist aimed at the WEF. The crowd was a swelling, bursting the seams of the road, blocking all traffic. They spilled, uncorked, into the park just west of the Center, flowed over the soccer field, reformed the fist in the parking lot. The Center's main entrance was uphill, on the Promenade side, but here there was room, and here the banquet hall windows were visible. There wasn't much to see—a blank face of glass in a wooden facade, half blocked by the building's concrete arms that jutted forward into the lot—but the target was visible, and the roar went up.

Barriers stood between the lot and the Center. Soldiers were on patrol. The protest had been expected. But the size of the protest, Alloway could see, had not. The body language of the police was jittery. The soldiers were calling in on their radios. Surprise, Alloway thought. More to come. Global Response was bunched together at the head of the crowd. Alloway, Grimson, Avery, Mark and Judy Liang, Faye McNicoll, all for one and one against the system. Chuck Bilodeau in the thick of it, too, whether he approved or not. Someone had brought a boom box and was blasting out Asian Dub Foundation anthems. Alloway felt the energy build. The weight of the bomb on his back was the comfort of power. The chants, multilingual at first, settled into English, the language of media, as soon as a couple of cameras and reporters emerged from the Congress Center. The crowd hit the barrier and began to push.

"Leave the poor man alone."

Blaylock turned around. Sherbina's face was kind, concerned. Nothing but Dunn's welfare uppermost in his mind. Sam Reed was at his side, Joe Chapel one step behind. The Company man looked like a dutiful dog who really wanted to be somewhere else. "What's this?" Blaylock asked. "You three going to make me an offer I can't refuse?"

Sherbina laughed. "An unfortunate misapprehension. The President simply expressed an interest in a formal introduction. Joe here," he cocked a thumb back, "doesn't want to let his master out of his sight." Sherbina had also picked up on Chapel as humbled canine. Chapel reddened.

"Stepan has told me a lot about you," Reed said.

"Oh? And Joe hasn't? We've been seeing a fair bit of each other lately."

"Too much," Chapel muttered. Blaylock batted eyelashes at him.

"Joe didn't want me to speak to you at all," Reed said. "He's feeling protective."

"And so he should."

Sherbina threw his hands up. "You crazy kids, you," he said, and moved a few paces away.

Reed stepped in close. "Is it true," he asked, "that women find power an aphrodisiac?"

"Only those who don't have their own." Blaylock glanced past Reed at Chapel. He looked ready to pounce, ready to take the bullet he was sure she was going to try to put in his President.

"One can always have more."

"Said the most powerful man in the world, right?" Blaylock cranked the sarcasm, made it unmissable. "What's the story here? You trying to buy me or screw me?"

Reed hesitated. "What would you like?"

Blaylock didn't answer the question. "You think I'm an irritation."

"But a very attractive one." He took in the scars. "In an intriguing way."

Blaylock gave him silence.

Reed's game dropped. His glass eye became his entire face. "All right," he said. "I don't know who you are. I don't know your angle."

"I'm believing you right now. You utter the words *national security* and you blow the ball game."

Reed's face in hers. "You think that's a joke? Do you? You don't think there are men who would put their lives on the line for the sake of those words?"

"Sure there are." One of them was standing behind Reed. "But not you."

"You think wrong. If you want to be a player, go ahead. But you're on notice. Don't be a problem." He stalked off, Chapel following.

The fist grew tighter, its movement more defined, more dangerous. The crowd pushed the barricades back. The police and army retreated in slow steps. Alloway felt the force of the protest's blow build as they inched towards the Congress Center. The crowd was very dense now. It was hard to breathe, harder to move, but the exultation was still there. Global Response was becoming separated, though. Alloway held on hard to Grimson's hand. He could just make out Bilodeau a few heads over to the left. He'd lost track of Avery several minutes ago. He wondered where and when he should set the bomb.

There was a change in the current of the crowd, an

eddy disrupting the flow. So packed, so tight, the crowd was primed for butterfly-effect chaos. Alloway shoved forward, breaking through to the very front of the fist. There were more soldiers in front of them now. A lot more. Reinforcements were pouring in from the north side of the Center for the countermove. The fist wouldn't be strong enough to break this wall. The chanting developed syncopation. The timbre shifted from triumph towards anger, towards outrage, towards meltdown.

Blaylock stood beside Sherbina. He was watching the confrontation, his forever-smile dancing over his lips as things began to go ugly. Blaylock thought of Grimson, worried, had no choice but to trust her friend's skills. To Sherbina she said, "And the purpose of that exercise was?"

Sherbina kept his eyes on the protest. "My wife likes you, and I can see why. You're a deeply unpredictable variable, and my fondest wish is to make Irina happy. But." He paused for a moment, and still that whisper of a smile ghosted his face. "You've a deft hand with steel poles, dear heart, but don't get cocky."

Once more unto the breach. The fist coalesced for the desperation offensive. The protesters rammed hard at the barricades. Soldiers raised guns. The tear gas grenades arced.

"There are true powers in this world," Sherbina said. "I wonder if you understand this. I wonder if you aren't the same kind of dreamer as, though it pains me to say this, my wife. And those people out there."

Alloway let go of her hand. Grimson pulled a cloth out of her pocket and tied it around her face. Someone banged into her stomach, and she stumbled back. She wrapped her arms around herself, protecting, and tried to move forward. The chants had stopped. People were yelling. The gas grenades landed, and the familiar hurt spread out. Grimson used her elbows, caught a glimpse of Alloway kneeling. He was fumbling with his backpack.

"These forces," Sherbina said, "are extremely powerful." He turned away from the window and faced the room. Blaylock followed his gaze. She saw a tuxedo filled to bursting by a giant.

Blaylock asked, "Who's the wall of muscle?"

Sherbina clucked his tongue. "Shame on you. Yevgeny Nevzlin is a financial wizard. And all too often a victim of just the sort of conclusion you leaped to." Sherbina nodded. Nevzlin reached inside his tux, pulled out a cellphone.

Alloway coughed. His vision smeared with tears. He rubbed his eyes. He needed to see. Just a few seconds longer. He could hear the tramp of boots closing. Just a few seconds and he could run. He tried to make out the flashing clock. If he could see just long enough to set the timer for ten minutes. A blast at the feet of the Congress Center would make them think. He gagged on the tear gas. His lungs filled with air made of broken saw blades. He stared at the blinking red smear. He couldn't make out the buttons. His hands hovered, useless. Retreating protesters banged against him. He thought he heard Grimson calling his name.

"These forces are like forces of nature. Hurricanes. Volcanoes. Tsunamis." Sherbina's voice was calm as ever, but there was an undertone. It was the three Kelvin background radiation of the universe, undetectable to all but specialized equipment, to all but Blaylock, who shared the wavelength. It was an electric hum of power building up anticipation and joy. Blaylock felt a full-body shiver of cold sweat, felt her heart beat loud and bad. A huge machine, which had been pulsing for months in her peripheral vision, hove into view, gears meshing, gears she hadn't slowed at all. For the first time in over a year, she felt a true and awful fear. "You don't stop these forces," Sherbina said. "You don't stand in their way."

Alloway rubbed his eyes, saw long enough to find the right buttons. He pressed them. The clock stopped flashing. The countdown pulse began. There. Ten minutes. In the moment between killing breaths, he thought, Your turn to choke, you bastards. He felt a flush of triumph, and it was ugly. He looked up, saw gas masks, saw truncheons blur towards his face.

Sherbina turned back to the window. His thrum was almost audible. Blaylock, iced by the worst kind of failure, watched Nevzlin. He raised the phone to his ear, and when he grinned, Blaylock knew the phone was not a phone. "Listen for the music," Sherbina whispered. Nevzlin moved his thumb.

Grimson gagged and stumbled in the haze of chaos and gas. She lost sight of Alloway as more protesters shoved and banged against her. A cloud of poison swirled past, and the air cleared long enough for her to spot him again. She saw him sink beneath blows. She was close. She took a step his way. Soldiers blocked her. Two of them grabbed her arms. She dug her heels in, strained forward, saw her husband screaming and bleeding. Alloway covered his head. He tried to crawl. He disappeared in a flash of heat and light and blood.

19

Blaylock faced the window and saw Sherbina's music. There was a massive blast at the head of the protest. The fireball itself was quite small, but the force was big, a ripple that tore out from the center and shredded. Body parts flew through the smoke. The Plexiglas windows rattled. The boom sucked up all the sound in the hall. Blaylock felt the explosion brush against the Plexiglas, try to reach inside. She saw what looked like yellow confetti settling over the square.

The elapsed time was seconds, less than seconds. But the time dilation was enormous. Blaylock had time to register each hell-tableau before the next one unveiled. The second bomb went off toward the rear of the parking lot. The third in the middle. The crowd went into full frenzy, an all-directions stampede. The soldiers opened fire. Blaylock could see their faces, and some of them were screaming. And *boom, boom, boom*, more blasts, but now the explosions weren't near the Center. Smoke and dust billowed up to the west. She heard more booms, but couldn't see the explosions. The hits made no sense. They sounded like the strikes of a random artillery bombardment. On the other side of the Talstrasse from the Center was a filling station. Another bomb went off beside the pumps. The explosion that came a second later was huge, an unfolding, expanding sphere of fire whose rise and triumph were those of an unleashed genie. And everywhere the yellow confetti.

Grimson flew, batted by the explosion. She hit the ground at a low angle, meteor-hard. Her left shoulder popped out of its socket on impact. Her forehead slammed into the pavement. The blow to her stomach was deep and final. Skin peeled as she slid. Something inside snapped. She screamed, and couldn't hear her scream. Her ears were full of roar and a high whine. The air was dust and fire and tear gas and fluttering yellow. She struggled to her knees. Pain kicked her back down hard. She was disoriented. She looked around, tried to see where Alloway had been, saw nothing through tears but running shapes, a dumbshow delirium. A piece of the yellow flutter landed in front of her. Even through the agony and the chemical blindness, she could recognize the doomsday radiation logo.

Pandemonium in the banquet hall. Blaylock was pressed against the window by the sudden crush. The gods of trade and politics bore witness, and they were terrified. They screamed, they moaned, they chanted, "Oh no, oh no, oh no, oh no." And they watched. They were still spectators. The explosions were on the other side of the Plexiglas movie screen. "What's the yellow?" someone asked. The question was picked up, turned into a refrain. Blaylock saw some soldiers glance at the yellow as it landed near them. They stopped shooting. They ran.

That silenced the banquet hall. Fear gathered its strength, prepared its blow. Some of the soldiers were talking on radios as they ran. Their communication looked like a last gesture of order in the maelstrom. Instead, it was the vector of contagion. Seconds later, cellphones rang all over the hall, tiny digital panic. The calls were answered. The whisper began: *Radiation*. A few seconds later, the connection was made, the meaning sank in. The whisper changed. *Dirty bomb*. The whisper became a chant (*dirty bomb, dirty bomb*). The chant became a chorus of full-throat screams. The paranoid fantasy made flesh: *dirty bomb*. The contagion took hold. The explosions did not reach inside the Congress Center, but the stampede fever did.

The gods bolted. They became a whitewater smash of black and silver. They roared through the hall, battering back tables and chairs. Those who stumbled, those who fell, were crushed. The wave turned into a hydraulic press at the exit. Pain shrieks and death howls fused with the choir of panic. Blaylock was knocked back. She fell over a table, crashed through porcelain and cutlery, had to fight her way back up through the trample. She struggled to the window, flattened herself against it. She watched the genius of the dirty bomb at work. Actual radiation poisoning was unlikely except in the immediate vicinity of the blast. To spread radioactive debris over a large area, to really go to town and contaminate several city blocks for centuries, the bomb would need to be the size of a truck. The dirty bomb's potential for widespread destruction was measured in belief, in fear, in the imagination. In panic. The yellow confetti had done its job. Faith in the power of the bombs was strong. The panic hit critical mass. Davos burned.

The banquet hall was not empty. A few people had not run, and were hanging back from the death-trap exit.

Zelkova sat on the ground beside an overturned table. She was weeping. Nevzlin still lounged against his wall. He'd pocketed his trigger, and had grabbed Dunn and his wife by their arms. They slumped in his grip, clutching each other. Sam Reed stood in a corner, surrounded by his Secret Service detail and Joe Chapel. Stone faces all, but there was a set to Chapel's expression. He was having trouble maintaining the stone. Sherbina was relaxed, arms-folded cool in front of a Ragnarok backdrop. He watched Blaylock. His gaze was a challenge. Because they were so close to each other, Blaylock could see the laughter at the far depths of his poker eyes. She thought about killing him. She thought about stopping his machine dead by snapping his neck. She thought about this. Then she noticed his stance. His feet were shoulder-width apart, grounded. He only looked relaxed. He was waiting for her to go for him. She wondered if she could take him. She itched to try, to replace that smirk with fear and pain and death. She doubted she'd complete a lunge before Nevzlin drilled her. Dead, she'd be no use to Grimson, who was out there in the hell. So Blaylock gave Sherbina a look that said, *Later*, and she crossed the hall to the Secret Service wall. She stopped walking as soon as they began to look nervous. She held her hands out, harmless. "Get us out of here," she said.

The contingent, to a man, looked left and right. Both exits were jammed with bodies, both struggling and still. People were screaming. "I'm sorry, ma'am," one of the agents began. "That's not possible at this—"

"What," Blaylock demanded, "you're going to sit here until the place burns down with you and your boss in it?" She pointed at the windows. "You're armed, aren't you? So lose that Plexiglas."

"A capital notion," Sherbina called out. He moved away from the windows and joined his wife behind a table. She wouldn't look at him, but when he put his arm around her shoulders, she didn't pull away.

"Do it," Reed told the agents.

Blaylock made herself a furniture barricade against ricochets and ducked low. The sound of the automatic weapons fire took over the banquet hall, drowning the screams and the outside roar of death. The windows shattered, and the roar stepped inside, the new king, the throat-howl of fire and panic. With the roar came winter. The temperature plunged. Blaylock stood up, felt her arms goosepimple as she ran to the windows. The drop wasn't big—one large story. There was a concrete edge below her, and a railing beneath that. Piece of cake, even in these stupid shoes. She thought about discarding them, decided she'd be more useless with frozen feet. She swung her legs over the sill. Her skirt flapped, torn during the panic, and set her movements free.

"This really is a mess," Sherbina clucked. He was beside her again. She hadn't heard him approach. "I think it's time to call in the cavalry." Over his shoulder, Blaylock saw Nevzlin reach into his pocket again. This time what he produced really was a phone. "Do let me help," Sherbina winked. He slipped out of his tuxedo jacket, offered it to Blaylock. "You'll catch cold dressed like that."

Blaylock stared at him. The gesture told her something crucial. Sherbina knew about art, too. Handing her his jacket was a finishing touch, the fillip that made his creation perfect. Blaylock absorbed the insight, noted just how formidable Sherbina really was. He was right. She'd been cocky, playing in the lion's den. She knew better now. All it had taken was the casual destruction of a town completed by an ironic gesture of chivalry. She pulled on the jacket. She climbed down, hung from the windows, and swung down onto the balcony beneath. She clambered over the rail, dangled, then dropped the last six feet. She ran for the parking lot. She didn't call. There was too much noise. Her voice would have been ripped away by the roar. If she was going to find Grimson, she would have to see her.

Those who could run had fled the square. The panic had spread its havoc onto all the streets of Davos. Protesters and locals mixed and ran and screamed together. The fires started by the explosions burned out of control. The contagion, hungry, jumped from building to building. Its greed fueled the panic. The destruction was a perpetual motion machine, fire and crowd pushing each other to greater heights. To the west, Blaylock could see an entire block engulfed. Not all the bombs were dirty, she realized. Some were incendiary. A cluster of hotels had become a torch shoving back the night. Blaylock was back in Bosnia, feeling Europe rip itself down to the bone. The coordination of the explosions was perfect. Blaylock had a vision of all the elements coming together, of Davos becoming a radioactive firestorm. No, she thought. Not even Sherbina would want that. He wasn't Pembroke, bringing the temple down on everyone's head, including his own. Davos' death was a means, not an end. Even worse.

She moved closer to the site of the first blast. The urge to flee was atavistic, hardwired into the species since 1945. She knew the risk was minimal. The contaminated area would be quite wide, but her exposure would be brief. Swaths of Davos would be uninhabitable, but the key here was long-term exposure. The contamination zone was still safe to move through. (She thought, she hoped.) She fought down the flight instinct, and began to look at bodies. Dozens of people lay on the pavement. Some had bullet wounds. Some had deep, pumping shrapnel holes. Blood pooled, little streams flowing along the irregularities of the surface. Some of the bodies were incomplete, limbs missing, halves missing, heads. Blaylock saw pieces. She almost stepped on a group of three severed fingers that had landed together. Twenty feet beyond, she found the thumb. She jumped from body to body, peering at the faces in the flickering light. The features, smeared with dust and blood, were hard to make out. Some of the faces were gone, leaving concave depressions in broken skulls. One of the faceless was a woman. Her hair was long, blond. Blaylock stopped breathing, started again when she saw that the woman wasn't pregnant. Another face looked familiar. Chuck Bilodeau. He was still alive. Almost. He coughed, and the sound was very weak and very wet. Deep black blood pumped out his mouth. His eyes were open but unfocused. "You'll be okay," Blaylock whispered, lying, then lying some more: "The ambulance is on its way." Bilodeau didn't react. Blaylock didn't think he'd heard her. But when she stepped away, he whimpered. She crouched back down, held his hand, and the whimpering stopped. She felt his fingers give a slight pulse, the closest thing to a squeeze they could manage, the awareness of comfort the only thing Bilodeau had left. Blaylock bit her lip, trapped, looked around at the bodies nearby. Ten feet away, she saw the shape of a woman. The shape twitched. Blaylock watched, straining to make out something more than a silhouette. She needed to see. She resented Bilodeau's claim on her humanity. She stayed. Bilodeau's fingers pulsed again, then gripped hard. Blaylock looked down. Bilodeau's eyes had focused. They were wide, terribly wide. They were looking beyond Blaylock, beyond everything, and glittered with the reflection of the fire and the awful recognition of void. The fingers lost their grip. Blaylock felt Bilodeau's neck. He was dead, but the look in his eyes remained. "I know," Blaylock whispered to the eyes, and she ran to the woman.

Grimson was curled fetal on her right side. She had her arms wrapped straightjacket around her belly. Her entire body throbbed with a rhythmic agony beat. Her face was strips and slashes and blood. Her nose was broken. Her eyes were closed in a wince as tight as her grimace. Her left shoulder was out of alignment. Blaylock sank to her knees beside Grimson. "Kelly," she said. She touched Grimson's hand.

Grimson's eyes opened. Their pain was big enough to swallow Blaylock's consciousness. Grimson licked her lips, and spoke the worst thing. "The baby's not moving."

Blaylock felt a bad pause as the world waited for her response. She had none. Everything was inadequate. "Can you stand?" is what she asked. She had to move Grimson out of the square.

"No," Grimson gasped. Her contractions were hard spasms.

Another pause. They were speaking to each other across a canyon, neither hearing the need of the other. Blaylock tucked her hand under Grimson's right shoulder. "You have to try," she said. She couldn't heave Grimson over her shoulder, not in this condition.

Grimson unfolded, slowly. She leaned on Blaylock, and managed to stand. She sobbed, a huge sound, as she straightened. "I'm all broken inside."

Blaylock took off the tux, draped it around Grimson's shoulders, and held her up. She looked across the parking lot. An apartment complex to the left of the gas station was burning. The last building on the block, the same peach color and boxy look, was isolated, untouched. Blaylock showed Grimson where they were heading. Grimson nodded, and limped forward. They had to sidestep bodies. Blaylock didn't recognize any other faces. The rest of Global Response had vanished. The wind whipped in from the Promenade, carrying ash and the tang of burn. The cold was a sick kiss on Blaylock's skin.

The building's doors were intact. Blaylock pushed them open and helped Grimson into the vestibule. The inside doors were locked. The power was off, but there was candlelight. A flashlight flicked on, caught Blaylock, then Grimson, in the face for a few seconds, then went off. When the dazzle faded, Blaylock saw an older woman on the other side of the door. Her face, taut with fear, was as gray as her hair. She stared at Grimson, then exchanged looks with Blaylock. After a moment, she nodded. She opened the door. Straight ahead, a staircase rose out of the lobby. The woman started up a few steps, then waited. "Stairs," Grimson groaned.

Blaylock said, "We have to find you into a bed. Can you do it?"

Grimson nodded. She raised her right foot to the first step, brought the left foot up beside the right. She paused, then repeated. It took two minutes to climb to the first floor. The woman led them down the hall to her suite and her bedroom. She helped Grimson undress and crawl into the bed. Blaylock thanked her. The woman nodded. She lit candles. She was still pale, but her face was pinched now with sorrow. She knew, Blaylock thought. She knew, too.

"Thirsty," Grimson whispered. Blaylock found some glasses in the bathroom, filled one with water. She sat on the bed beside Grimson and raised the glass to her lips. She let the water dribble in slowly, waiting for Grimson to swallow before easing in another mouthful. Grimson winced as another contraction hit. "I need your help," she said. The candlelight made shadows move in and out of the wounds on her face, flickering revelations of damage and pain. "Do this with me."

"Yes," Blaylock said. "Tell me what to do."

Grimson licked her lips. Blaylock gave her more water. "The baby might not be in the right position."

"How do I—?"

"Feel. Press my stomach. Hard if you have to."

Blaylock did. She found the head, facing the wrong way. She swallowed hard at the total stillness. Grimson told her to keep manipulating, to reposition the baby. Blaylock did that, too. She did everything Grimson said or whispered, gasped or sobbed. The labor was long, but not extreme. The baby was so small. The woman did her best with Grimson's wounds, sponging away the worst of the blood and dirt. But all she had was water and cloth.

During a pause between contractions, Grimson's attention shifted to the window. "What's going on?" she asked. The noise outside had changed. There were far fewer shouts. Now came the sound of order. The sound of marching boots. Blaylock left the bed to take a look. Night was full and deep over Davos, thick clouds turning the sky to starless pitch. Entire blocks were blazing, casting candleglow and brimstone hellsmoke over the rest of the city. Below, she saw men in uniform. Some were marching in platoons towards the fires. Some were herding people through the streets. Others were gathering corpses in the square. Blaylock didn't recognize the uniforms at first. Then their almost-but-not-quite Russian design registered. "Kornukopia's taking charge," she said. She returned to Grimson. "They probably have medical supplies. I can go down and ask."

Grimson shook her head. "Stay with me."

Blaylock stayed. She stayed through the entire chapter of pain. The knifepoint of the pain was emotional. The birth itself, just before dawn, was an easy one. (So small.) Grimson pushed, the baby came out, and Blaylock held the body in her arms. (So small.) Against hope, against reality, she cleared the mouth and nostrils. There was no breath. Blaylock had never held anything heavier.

"Boy or girl?" Grimson asked. Her voice was a gossamer whisper, crushed under the boulders of exhaustion and grief.

"Boy."

A breath, too weak to be either sob or sigh, but more expressive than either. "Let me have him." She held out her good arm.

Blaylock gave her the baby, umbilical still linking him to his broken home. "What's his name?"

Grimson gazed at what had been taken from her. Her fingers fluttered at the tiny face, as if to make the eyes open once, just this once, so she could see them. Her fingers stilled. "Jon—" Grimson started to say. She paused, choking off her husband's name. "Edward," she said. After her father. Her teeth began to chatter. Her body trembled with full shock.

Blaylock said, "That's a good name." She piled the eiderdown on Grimson.

Grimson nodded. She squeezed her eyes shut. Her trembling eased. In its place, her body began to twitch.

The rhythm was the same as when Blaylock had found her. But this time she was weeping. Blaylock moved away, giving space for the grief. The older woman, also crying, left the room. Blaylock sat down in the corner of the room beside the door, farthest away from the candles, farthest from the pain she could do nothing for, the pain that frightened her. She listened to the noise outside shift down with the passing of the night from chaos to aftermath. She listened to the sounds of Grimson's mourning, small sounds, a murmured keening. She listened to her own helplessness. She listened to the frozen-river cracks of her sorrow hardening into hatred. She listened to her darkness. The war machine made allegiance with savagery and its absolute promise.

20

This happened, too, two minutes after the bombs went off in Davos. In Geneva, Louis Lafone strolled down the Avenue de la Paix. Five hundred yards ahead was the WTO. Lafone was dressed in business suit and winter overcoat. He carried an attaché case. He knew he looked like a faceless bureaucrat, underfed variety. That was the idea. He felt the cellphone in his breast pocket vibrate once, and he knew that all was well. Nevzlin had given him the go. He unbuttoned his coat, felt inside for the phone, stroked it with a finger. He hummed *Bolero*, and each bar was metronome-perfect in its beat. He watched the intersection, and saw the van, and felt the precision of timing, and kept his choreographer's smile to himself. Driving the van, a VW of course, were members of Geneva's Lignes de Fuite du Peuple, homegrown protestors cut from the Global Response cloth, but big on poststructuralist theory and political art. They turned hard right and roared into the WTO's drive. They were armed with spray paint and ideals. They were going to turn the facade of the building into a piece called *Capitalism's Body Without Organs*. They had practiced their moves for hours. Lafone had watched them. While they worked on their art, he had worked his magic on the van. Now his finger found the detonator. Really big bang.

Sharks. Piranha. Grasshopper storm. When the media fed, the spectacle wasn't pretty. When the media gorged, the sensitive and the holy looked away. Flanagan watched.

He was in The Baying Hound, munching a plowman's lunch. The pub was plastic Olde England, was a few blocks away from InSec, and was where Flanagan had first seen Blaylock kill a man. The bar had been, for him, a site of trauma and blood. Since the Coscarelli pogrom, though, he'd been coming here a lot. When he sat at this table, in the very chair where Johnathan W. Smith III had died, face shot to porridge, he felt close to Blaylock. The Baying Hound had been transformed by her passage. Its air still vibrated with the echo of death. Flanagan's memories, superimposed on the present, turned the actual patrons into ghosts, lightplays hollowed out by the fact of undiluted force. On the television above the bar, images and words linked Flanagan to Blaylock still further. Geneva was big, where a van had Oklahoma City'ed the WTO headquarters. But Davos was bigger. Davos was a whole town. The networks and major papers, on-site for the conference, were in the bull's eye of the fun. The media feast was incandescent. The joy was radioactive. The dirty bomb attack, the terrorist scenario played out in a thousand hypotheticals by the punditocracy over the years, had at last come to pass. In honor of the event, the television's volume was turned up. CNN was beside itself. The central image was live destruction. The crawl was updated body counts. The anchor's voice was wire-taut with contained excitement. The reporters, those who had survived the stampede from the Congress Center, walked the razor line between excitement and hysteria. The spectacle was top-flight, the location and players were known and recognizable, but the setting was far from home. The news was fear without paranoia, the perfect horror movie thrill. Flanagan wondered what Blaylock's part in the film was. His stomach was tight, but he was still able to eat. Faith kept him grounded, faith that the destruction was too indiscriminate to be Blaylock's, faith that she was still alive. She had called him once to tell him where she'd be staying, but he was resisting now the urge to check up. The faith was that strong. Beneath his shock, he felt a buzz as he watched the news. The buzz disturbed him and shamed him. But not enough.

The anchor said *Kornukopia*. Flanagan stopped eating. The anchor said private security forces were restoring order, stealing the march on the Swiss army, which was only now, as it tried to organize, realizing how many men it had lost in the hours leading up to the explosions. The anchor began to say things like *coordinated attack,* but Flanagan was still stuck on the Kornukopia reference. He thought about West's suicide. Connections snarled.

On the screen, the President appeared. Seeing him in full dignity, surrounded by destruction, the camera decided that it liked Sam Reed after all. He spoke about the need for calm and resolve. The crawl flashed a statement from the Secretary for Homeland Defense. The terrorist forecast was not being upgraded to orange, underlining Reed's calm. Flanagan felt a quick flash of surprise, but then tuned the news out, still trying to see where the equation of Davos+Kornukopia=West led him. It took him nowhere but to worries. He had to talk to someone. He stood up, borrowed the bar phone, and called Dean Garnett.

Charlotte Taber media-surfed. Her office held a bank of

television screens, the images shrieking but the audio silent. On her supersized desk were a radio, a computer, and the day's major papers. She skimmed op-ed in print and on the Net. She hummed, happy. The papers were a consensus of solemnity. TERROR MUST BE CONFRONTED HEAD-ON. THE WAR ON TERROR IS A REAL WAR. Stirring sentiments without a whiff of implementation. Good stuff. As she read, Taber kept half an eye on the screens. When a story on one of the networks or cable news channels looked promising, she would turn the sound up. The promising stories had pundits. The really promising stories featured a logo her office had designed. In the weeks leading up to the WEF, she had released a short ad to the networks. The campaign was an uncomplicated montage of smiling melting-pot ethnicity and cooperative prosperity. At the end of the warm-and-fuzzies came the message: *The WTO. It's us.* The spots had played in the background noise until now. Reed's big speech and the big boom paid off in a big boost. Taber watched the spin develop. The legions had been sent out from the strongholds of Taber & Hackbarth and of Public Diplomacy. They did their work well. Taber saw the WTO turn into a paragon of grassroots democracy, and knew that all was good.

"You're implying West knew this was coming?" Garnett said.

They were in Characters, and Flanagan was fighting the queasy sense of history coming back at him on an electric loop. Characters, nondescript but familiar, was his local bar. It was on Albany, a block down from his Hudson Tower apartment. The Baying Hound was where he had seen Blaylock kill, and Characters was where, that same night, he had met her, and crossed her event horizon. Garnett had suggested meeting here at ten. Flanagan had agreed. Garnett's gesture, seeing Flanagan on home turf, was a nice one. But doing both pubs in the day, and linking both to the bad game, gave Flanagan déjà vu jitters.

"I don't know if West knew," Flanagan told Garnett. "These are just dots I thought you should know I can connect."

"You should leave dot-connecting to the professionals," Garnett said. He smiled, turning the chiding into banter.

"That's why I called you." Thinking, *You professionals did a great job of keeping track of Pembroke, didn't you?*

"And I'm glad you did. I'll look into it." Garnett's tone was friendly, but Flanagan read condescension in the words and bristled. "I wouldn't worry, though. You saw the terror alert?" Flanagan nodded. "There you go," Garnett went on. "No upgrade, so no credible threat. You can relax. Tell me yes."

"But how can you know that?" Flanagan demanded. "You can't, unless—" He caught himself.

No reaction from Garnett. "Unless what?" Perfect innocence.

Unless you had advance knowledge. Unless you were in on it. Flanagan worked to keep the tremor out of his voice, to keep his face poker. "Nothing," he said, and judged his performance awful. "You're right."

"There you go," said Garnett. He popped a peanut, Mr. Relaxed. His eyes flicked for a moment to something over Flanagan's right shoulder. Flanagan didn't look. "So go home," Garnett continued. "Get yourself some sleep, and leave the worrying to those what get paid to do it." He grinned.

Flanagan grinned back, rabbit trying to bluff. "Thanks,"

he said. "That's a load off my mind." They were both playing a game now, lobbing lies back and forth, marking time. End it, Flanagan thought. He stood, amazed his knees didn't give out, tossed some bills on the table. He turned around and, as he walked to the exit, scanned the bar. He saw two men at a table near the door. They were paying their tab, the only other customers preparing to leave. They looked relaxed, very. Just like Garnett. Their suits were sharp. They might just be Street players. They also looked fit. Hard fit, not gym fit. They didn't even glance at Flanagan as he passed by.

"How much do you have riding on it?" one asked the other.

"This is me pretending you didn't ask that," the other replied.

Look like players, sound like players. You're being silly, being paranoid. (But hard fit.) Flanagan stepped out onto the street. Albany was quiet. There was no one else on the block just now. He headed home, tried to stroll. He wondered if he appeared relaxed. He doubted he would fool trained eyes. Behind him, he heard the two men. They were still talking deals and risks. One of them laughed. Flanagan's shoulders twitched nervous at the sound. The laugh bounced, echoing crow, off the sides of the buildings. Flanagan didn't look back. He wondered if he should, if not checking to see who laughed was the giveaway, the unnatural thing to do. He knew they were walking in the same direction he was. Their voices didn't recede. They didn't come closer, either. He caught flotsam of conversation as it drifted his way on the crisp air. He was half a block from home.

"So what did you do?" he heard.

"Said I'd kill him."

"Will you?"

"What do you think?"

Laughter (*caw, caw, caw*). They're playing with me. (No. Why would they?) Because they can. There are no coincidences. You know this. You know this. But he didn't run. He pretended. He reached the main entrance.

"Now?" he heard.

Flanagan looked. The men were still walking, still casual. He lost it and bolted through the door. He blew past Bernie Walmsley. The doorman jumped back. "Mr. Fla—" he began, but Flanagan was already taking the stairs, too frightened to wait for the elevator. Eight floors at full tilt. He stumbled into his apartment, wheezing and sweating, locked the door and threw the chain. The lights went on behind him. He whirled. Another man, another suit, another hard fit. He was standing at the entrance to the living room. He wasn't holding a gun. "Mr. Flanagan," the man said, death-cold polite, "I'd like you to come with me."

"Who are you?" Just like he didn't know.

The man ignored the question. "This is a matter of national security."

Of course it goddamn is. Terror alert gone from yellow to red, but only in the home of Michael Flanagan. Play for time. "Where are we going?"

"I'm afraid I can't tell you that, sir."

"Will we be long?"

"Please pack for a few days."

And don't forget your pennies to pay the Ferryman. Flanagan nodded. "Okay," he lied. The man smiled, and his stance shifted. Flanagan hadn't even noticed he was in attack mode until he relaxed. His fingers hung more loosely, safety on. Flanagan walked to the bedroom. He eyed the window. He heard a footstep behind him. He glanced over his shoulder. The agent stood halfway down the hall, watching him. No escapes, then. Why not kill me here? he thought. Because there would be no mess if he was taken for a drive. No imediate search, either, if he left carrying a suitcase.

He went down on his hands and knees, and reached under the bed for his suitcase. His hand closed on the handle. Beside the suitcase were the pistol and the shotgun. Flanagan hesitated. They were loaded. He'd objected when Blaylock had made him stash them that way. "You don't have kids," she'd told him, chambering a round in the shotgun and loading the cartridge with five. "You might have enemies." He pulled the suitcase out, then reached under again. He touched the Saiga. He wondered if he could do this.

"Do you need help?" the agent asked.

"I'm okay, thanks," Flanagan said. What if I'm wrong? he thought. Better him than you, said his fear. He yanked the shotgun towards him. The barrel caught on the bed frame. Flanagan turned his head, saw the agent launch himself forward. Flanagan fought the Saiga out, spun it towards the agent, and fired. Point-blank, he couldn't miss. Buckshot blew out the man's stomach. His attack died. Momentum carried him forward two dying steps and he collapsed against Flanagan. Blood burbled from the agent's mouth into Flanagan's face. The man's eyes glazed.

Flanagan was on his back. The body was heavy, two hundred pounds of massively trained dead weight. Flanagan's arms were free, but the leverage was bad. He was about to let go of the shotgun when the apartment door was kicked in. Flanagan didn't look, didn't aim, just fired down the hall. Twice. He raised his head. He saw one of the two men from the bar slump against the wall and slide to the floor, smearing a thick and glistening arc of red as he fell. The other man was behind him, silenced pistol out. He fired. The bullet thudded into the corpse on Flanagan, struck bone, and remained in the body. Flanagan screamed and pulled the trigger, screamed and pulled, screamed and pulled. The corridor exploded with lead, plaster, and blood. The last agent flew back, face and torso shredded mulch in the hail of buckshot.

Flanagan kept screaming. He kept pulling the trigger. The shotgun clicked. Screaming, Flanagan dropped the gun and shoved at the body. The man wouldn't move. Screaming, Flanagan squirmed and pushed, tendons straining. The body, dead whale, rolled off. Screaming, Flanagan stood. He was soaked with blood. It was warm, it was everywhere, it tasted like the last supper. His mind stopped shouting *kill*. Flanagan stopped screaming. His mind began to shout *run*.

The view was spectacular. Sam Reed had the penthouse suite of the Bellevue. Chapel had a vulture's perspective of the length of the city. Fires still roared in a few buildings, but the worst of the burn was out. Smoke rose black, dirtying the dawn. Power was back on in the areas furthest from Congress Center. Emergency vehicle lights pulsed. Helicopters flew aid in, and the injured out. There were more soldiers on the streets now, taking over from the Kornukopia forces. Sherbina's men had been clockwork impressive, Chapel gave them that. They still guarded the Bellevue. They were working lover-tight with Reed's Secret Service detail. Chapel wasn't sure how he felt about that. Reed wasn't bothered. Chapel turned from the city to look at his President. They were both sitting in armchairs at the window, angled slightly toward each other. Chapel waved at the city. "Did you know this was coming?"

Reed didn't answer. Calm, assured, he faced Chapel. He seemed to be giving Chapel the chance to withdraw the question. Chapel didn't. Reed said, "I had no idea I would be witness to such destruction tonight. And that's the truth."

But not an answer, Chapel thought. He let it go. "Sherbina's going a bit over the top, don't you think?"

"The situation is certainly very fluid." Reed smiled. Chapel wished he hadn't. Chapel recognized the smile. It was the *Hell, can you believe this mess?* smile Reed sometimes used at press conferences. Chapel didn't begrudge Reed the politician's tool kit. He just didn't like having the tools used on him. He wanted to believe Reed, though. He needed to. For the country's sake. Reed leaned forward, and his smile faded. His eyes turned hard, and Chapel relaxed. He was looking at a leader now, not a politician. "You realize how serious this attack is."

"Ember Lake II," Chapel said.

"The world economy can't take another hit like that. But there are no problems. Only challenges." The platitude sounded like a good truth won from bad wars. "The challenge here is to see that something good comes of this disaster."

Outside, the smoke was turning into a pall. Silver linings looked like a fetishist's lie. "You see something?" Chapel asked, hopeful.

Reed said, "You've heard the same reports I have. You saw the same thing I did. This was the anti-globalization movement's big kick at the can. I think it should be their last."

"You want me to make sure."

"All Sherbina did was give them enough rope to hang themselves. I want you to tighten the noose. Make sure justice is done. I want the people to know who these fanatics are, what they've done, why they need to be stopped, and how we're going to stop them."

Chapel nodded, message received. *The anti-globalization forces are responsible. That's the story. Make it stick.* "There are risks involved," he said. No story was perfect. If someone found a flaw, and cracked this one open, the blowback would be epic.

"I know. The end will be worth it. Do you trust me?"

"I do." You, yes. Sherbina, no.

The ache woke her. Not the ache of the body bruised and bones broken. That pain brought back the old training instincts she thought she'd left behind in Bosnia. That pain was nothing. She wasn't woken by the aches of labor, either, or by the pressure in her breasts as the milk built up. The other ache woke her. The ache was a mahogany fist, punching her gut with the rhythm of her heart. It was also an echo chamber, the void ringing with a name never to be spoken except in anguish. She hurt. Oh, Christ, she hurt.

She opened her eyes. Dawn filtered through the curtains, turning the bedroom into a huddle of gray shapes and shadows. In the far corner, the shadows had pooled into concentrated dark. Grimson blinked, saw that the blackness had a shape, had substance. She grunted, startled. The darkness rose, drawing tentacles of shadow across the floor towards itself. The tentacles whispered against the floor. The darkness breathed. Grimson gasped. In that second, childhood fears were true. There were monsters under the bed and in the closet, and if you saw them, they came for you. Then the darkness was touched by the weak light from the window, and became Blaylock. The tentacles were the tatters of her skirt, gathered in as she stood up. Grimson swallowed, felt stupid, then felt nothing but the ache again. "Were you there all night?" she asked.

Blaylock nodded. "How are you?"

Grimson tried to speak. Words bunched up in her throat, inadequate, flattened by the ache. She shook her head.

"You need a hospital." Blaylock drew back the curtains. "Looks like help is here." She moved to the door. "I'll have you airlifted out." She paused with her back to Grimson. "Kelly," she said, "will you tell me why you changed your mind about the name?"

The ache, bigger yet. Poison at its edges, curdling good memories, making everything bad. "There was a bomb in Jonathan's backpack."

A long silence. "Did he know?"

"I'm not sure. He was up to something in Geneva." She saw Blaylock stiffen. "And he was fiddling with the bag just before..." Blaylock nodded, still facing the door. Grimson felt the coldness of judgment radiate from her posture. "Jen?" Grimson said.

Blaylock turned around. When Grimson saw her face, saw the promise and the war written there, she felt the fear again. She understood what little Jenny McNicoll had seen, what had made her scream. Children were right. There were monsters. The darkness let herself out of the room.

21

The Davos Sports Center, a massive, four-cornered dome, had become triage central. The airlifts left from the adjacent soccer field. The town was a crazy quilt of smoke and soldiers, paramedics and the dead. There still wasn't enough order for mourning to begin. Blaylock watched the helicopter carrying Grimson and other transportable wounded take off, then walked through the damage, taking in the sight of a town dealt a mortal wound. Even where there was no physical damage, she could sense spiritual bleed. She could see it in the eyes of the few locals who were out on the streets. The fear had come. It would never leave, so the people had to instead. All changed, changed utterly, by the birth of Sherbina's terrible beauty. But when Blaylock reached the Bellevue, she found on the terrace not change, but grotesque continuity. The old circus was back like it had never gone. The show must go on, and go on it did, with Sam Reed the grim ringmaster, surrounded by the captive audience of microphones and cameras. Roll tape, and feel the spin. Blaylock muscled her way in as close as she could to where the press conference podium had been set up. Chapel stood in the background, glaring at the cameras. "This will not stand," Reed was saying. He didn't need to add *Not on my watch*. The pundits would do that for him. "If these terrorists think they have shaken us, we are going to show them how mistaken they are." Pause here, for a burning look of strength, determination, and holy anger straight through the camera lenses and into the living rooms of the world. Then the set of the lips turned into a grim smile. "Already," said the President, "the guilty are facing justice." Another pause, just long enough for the questions to explode. The grin grew broader, Reed shook his head, and brought Chapel up to the mike.

Chapel waited while Reed sang his praises, and Blaylock stared hard at him, willing him to look her way. Chapel did. Reed finished the set-up. Chapel spoke, eyes locked with Blaylock's. Chapel said, "I can confirm earlier reports that arrests have been made." Blaylock turned up the intensity. Chapel looked away. Blaylock watched him sweat the spotlight, spook out of his natural element. Then she left.

She went up to her room, changed out of her rags and into dark clothes. Then she turned the TV on to see what story the circus was telling. Twelve hours since the bombs had gone off, and the narrative was well in place: the anti-globalization movement had gone berserk. On Fox *News*, scowling white men in suits told-you-so'ed. A spokeswoman for the American Enterprise Institute had trouble keeping the glee from her voice as she spoke the words *completely discredited*. Charlotte Taber, the guest on the panel, concurred, but also spoke with iron seriousness but quiet awe about the President. She called him *the Unbending Reed*. The stench of a new catchphrase wafted from the screen. Then fresh-from-the-scene tape rolled, and on Fox, on CNN, on the BBC, familiar faces appeared, and a familiar name was spoken. The familiar faces were Judy Liang (eyes puffy, forehead cut), husband Mark (arm in a sling), Faye McNicoll (black and blue). They were all in handcuffs. The name on the screen was *Global Response.* Alloway would have been thrilled, Blaylock thought. Recognition at last. After the demonization, more evidence of evil, and the thing Blaylock hadn't known about: the WTO headquarters, facade evaporated, structure slumping. Verbatim on all the news channels: *In a tragic irony, the attack on the WTO came mere hours after President Reed's speech.* Cut to the Reed clip. *There is no more effective a body for bringing nations together in trade than the World Trade Organization.* Blaylock saw the story, saw the spin, saw the brilliance. Victim/hero: WTO. Villains: protesters. She knew the story played out to the WTO's benefit, but not why. Why the WTO? Why the collusion between Reed and Sherbina?

Her phone rang. She muted the TV and noticed, as she answered, that the message light had been flashing. "Thank God you're still there," Flanagan said. "I've been trying and trying . . ." There was a steady noise, hum and whine, behind his voice.

"Mike? Where are you calling from?"

"From a plane."

What the hell? she thought, but didn't say. She said, "Then you should speak calmly and carefully."

She heard him take a breath. When he spoke, he wasn't gabbling, but there was still a tremor in his tone. "I'm coming to Switzerland."

"And you'll tell me why later."

"Okay."

"Did you need to come?"

"Yes."

"For whose sake?"

"Mine."

He's in trouble. Why? Not over the phone. "You can't come here. Wait for me in Zurich. Go see Kelly Grimson at the University Hospital. Stay with her." She thought for a moment. "Take care," she added before she hung up.

The television screen caught her eye again. Sherbina was holding forth. She didn't give him volume. She could guess what he was saying. The important data was the dateline: Geneva. Bastard had already flown out of here. Had Zelkova? Blaylock called her room. No answer. She tried the front desk. Zelkova hadn't checked out. Blaylock went looking.

She found her inside the Sports Center, the first place she tried. The wounded were laid out on mats. Zelkova moved from victim to victim, a first-aid machine, but she looked like she was wearing down. She hadn't changed, and her gown was blotched dark with blood. Her eyes were red and sunken, beaten by tears and lack of sleep. Blaylock waited until Zelkova sat down on a bleacher with a cup of coffee before she approached. Zelkova stared at the coffee as if she wasn't sure what it was for. Her hand trembled with fatigue. Blaylock sat down beside her, said nothing. Zelkova looked at her, and Blaylock saw etchings of pain deeper than fatigue. "Your friends?" Zelkova asked. Her voice was a croak.

"Some dead. Some hurt. Some arrested."

"And Kelly?"

"She'll live."

"The baby?" When Blaylock didn't answer, the etchings on Zelkova's face grew deeper. "You said some were arrested?" she asked after a minute. "The police think they were responsible?"

"Do you?"

"No." Zelkova turned her head to face the rows of mats and gurneys.

Blaylock probed. "Then who was?" How much do you know? she wondered.

"I don't..." she trailed off.

"Have you seen the news today?"

Zelkova shook her head. She gestured at the wounded. "Just so many," she whispered.

"Your husband and the President are singing from the same hymn book."

"What are you suggesting?"

"I'm just asking what you think happened."

"I don't know."

"Do you want to?"

The pause was a long one. "This is off the record." She waited for Blaylock to nod. "I do not want to. But I need to." Blaylock heard an enormous wrench in Zelkova's voice. The sound of love that was not blind, but wished it could be.

"What will you do when you know?"

Zelkova said nothing. She continued to gaze at the victims of her husband's art. You know he did this, Blaylock thought. You know it. She stood up, put her hand on Zelkova's shoulder, gave a squeeze. She made her way out of the complex.

She didn't go far. She hovered near the Sports Center, never staying in one place long enough to draw attention, but never losing sight of the entrance. She waited. She was patient. She saw the day out. She was rewarded. Zelkova left as the light failed. Blaylock watched her stumble as she stepped outside. She put out a hand to steady herself. Blaylock expected Zelkova to head back to the Bellevue. Instead, she straightened, appeared to gather strength, and made her way first to the Talstrasse, then took it west, towards the Davos Platz station. Zelkova slowed as she approached the train station. The street widened here, and was still clogged as medical personnel and soldiers arrived, pouring off each new train that pulled in. Zelkova wasn't interested in them. Her attention was focused on the Kornukopia train. It wasn't letting people off. With the arrival of the Swiss army in full force, Sherbina's private force was relieved. Duty done, order restored (and anarchists arrested? Blaylock wondered), they were boarding. Blaylock thought about her weapons cache, still uselessly bundled beneath the ornamental coal tender. She had been prepared to write the arms off, start fresh once she reached Zurich or Geneva. But Zelkova's interest in the train piqued hers. She watched the troops haul packs, weapons, and ammo onto the train. She paid careful attention to the uniforms for the first time. They weren't camouflage. Visibility had been the goal in Davos. They were dark, expensive, Kevlar-padded. And smart. And imposing. They had a style, a flair that didn't impair effectiveness but went beyond the call of the necessary. Sherbina's attention to detail, Blaylock knew now. There was an inspiration here. She didn't like what she saw: the lessons of the Nazi esthetic well learned and adapted.

Zelkova entered the station, took the underground passage to the Kornukopia train's platform. She and Blaylock were the only women on the platform, and Blaylock had to hold back farther. Zelkova stared into each window as she walked past. Now and then she shook her head, as if arguing with herself. She worked her way all the way to the locomotive, then headed back. Blaylock had to retreat partway down the stairs to the underpass to avoid being made. She studied Zelkova's silhouette as she drew nearer. She was still looking at the train windows, but she was slumping, the last of her reserves drained. She wasn't finding what she wanted. At the last car, the car with the turret, she stopped. She was standing under one of the station lights, and Blaylock saw her eyes widen. Zelkova's face twisted. The expression was one Blaylock hadn't seen on her before. There was big shock, and there was huge anger, and bigger than both was a sick despair. She wobbled, the emotion teetering her between collapse and the energy of rage. The rage won out. Zelkova hammered on the car's first window. She shouted something, but there was too much commotion for Blaylock to make out the words. Zelkova gestured, furious. She paused for a moment, then gestured again. Summoning. Imperious. She was obeyed.

Darryl Avery stepped off the train.

Blaylock made fists, sank her nails deep into flesh. The pain was the only thing that kept her where she was, that stopped her from launching herself across space to kill Avery. With her teeth. And liking it. She felt her face mirror Zelkova's. She watched Avery smile, and she wanted to be right there with a straight razor. Zelkova yelled. Avery took the rant, impassive. He said something, so quiet his lips barely moved. His shape was immobile, a monolith of calm. Zelkova hit the stratosphere. She beat Avery's chest. Avery took hold of her wrists, pushed her hands away. His movement was gentle, slow, controlled. Zelkova struggled in his grip. He let go, and she backed away. Avery spoke again. Zelkova wilted. She stumbled away from Avery, one hand holding her head, as if to keep the grief inside. Avery climbed back onto the train.

Blaylock promised him great things, and backed off before Zelkova spotted her.

Blaylock went east for a block down the Talstrasse, then ducked behind a supermarket. There was a concrete barrier between the rear of the store and the track. Nothing more than kid-deterrent. She went over, dropped low, checked for witnesses, then scuttled across the rails. The train's headlamp was a blurred glare in the fog. Blaylock found a hollow next to the track. She huddled down, face to the earth. Her breathing slowed. She became stillness, became night on night. Fog swept over her, blanket. Blind, she smelled earth and oil. She listened to the sounds, heard rhythms, patterns of noise and movement shaped into tides. Helicopter blades were the background, the white noise of the rescue efforts. The next layer of sound, closer, was the conversation, laughter, and banging equipment of the loading going on at the station. Closest yet, tiny shiftings of the earth, subvocal hums on the rails, the predator's beat of her pulse. She keyed into the sounds that came from the station, blotted the others out. Time passed, but was irrelevant. Her muscles began to cramp. She tensed and relaxed, tensed and relaxed, but didn't move.

The change she was waiting for arrived. The station grew quiet. Deeper thrums traveled down the rails. A machine gathered strength. Blaylock prepared to move, shifting from still to taut, rock to straining spring. She heard a blast of steam. Even without Sherbina aboard, the train stayed in character, the phony period detail a last spit in Davos' wounded eye. *Chuffff*, said the train, and it began to move. Blaylock listened to the approaching rumble. She looked up as the front end of the locomotive passed her head. The train was still slow. Blaylock moved to a crouch. The speed built. The coal tender came up. Ornamental, it carried real never-to-be-used coal, and was girded by a railed walkway that kept the access between the locomotive and the passenger cars open. Blaylock jumped. She grabbed the railing and swung herself onto the walkway. The train moved faster, windchill on her cheek. The fog was thick now, the world disintegrating into blurs of deep black, harsh white, and hints in grainy impressionism.

Blaylock crouched low, moved right towards the locomotive. At the corner of the walkway, she climbed back over the railing, hooked an arm around it, and dangled over the edge. The ground raced by, eager for a slip. She rocked with the motion of the train, came a death's head kiss away from the wheels. She steadied herself, and reached underneath the car. Her fingers fumbled around, felt nothing. She wondered if she'd played and lost. Then she snagged the handle. She hauled hard and fast, swinging her arm up, and her kit bag arced up out from under the car and onto the walkway. She climbed back over the railing, loaded the firearms. She undid her jacket, slipped the SIG inside, kept everything else in the bag, and carried it over her shoulder, casual. She walked straight and crossed into the locomotive. Zero stealth, own-the-place attitude. She moved quickly down the length of the engine and into the cab. The driver turned to face her, startled. "I need you to call Avery down here," she said.

The man muttered something in Russian, then demanded, "Who are you?"

"A friend of Stepan's." She used the first name deliberately, implying intimacy. She hooked her thumb over her shoulder. "I'm in the passenger car." She'd noticed that none of the troops had boarded the luxury end of the train, preserving the sanctity of Sherbina's space. "Now call Avery." She gave the driver full steel. He was military, he knew an order when he heard it, and he obeyed. But when he turned away from the intercom, his face was suspicious again. He stared at her bag. Blaylock saw him put pieces together, realize that her story made no sense. He reached for his holster. Blaylock swung the bag at him, hammered him in the shoulder, and knocked him off his feet. She pulled the handgun out of her jacket and shot him.

She opened the cab's outside door, took the C4 bricks out of the bag, and lay on her stomach, her torso hanging down the right-hand side of the locomotive. She could just reach underneath a ledge. Not perfect, but she had overkill explosive for what she had in mind. She checked that the remote and the blasting caps were happy and talking to each other, then inserted the caps into the bricks. She stuck the C4 to the underside of the ledge. Entire bricks. Three of them. When she was done, she pocketed the remote and headed back through the locomotive.

Her timing was off. She was just reaching the rear door when Avery stepped through. He almost hit her with the door, and she stumbled back. He stared for a moment, jaw slack in surprise, then recovered and charged. A battering ram took her and slammed her into the rear of the diesel engine's wall. The impact rattled through her frame. She saw stars. She let herself slump. Avery loomed over her. His size was all aggression now, all hurt. Blaylock felt, through the haze of hate, a sliver of admiration for how convincing his mask of harmlessness had been. He leaned down and one of his hands, meat and steel, grabbed her by the throat and lifted her. Blaylock's head rolled. She felt her air passages squeeze shut. She fought the gagging, fought the panic instinct, won. Avery smiled and held her out at arm's length. His arm was straight, an iron rod. Show-off, Blaylock thought, and snapped out of possum. She shot a hand up against his elbow, felt that good break. Avery howled and dropped her. He stumbled away, his right arm angled wrong and hanging useless.

Blaylock came at him. She kicked him in the stomach, then kneed his chin as he doubled over. His head jerked back, teeth clicking shut *clack* right through his lower lip. She grabbed his broken arm, twisted it until he screamed and she felt his limbs go rubbery. His balance was hers now. She spun him around, bashed his head against the doorway, held him there, slammed the door against the other side of his skull. Avery crashed to the ground. He tried to crawl away, and Blaylock kicked him through the door. He fell, legs dangling off the step between the locomotive and the coal tender. One more good blow and she would knock him under the train. He groaned, eyes glazed.

Blaylock knelt beside him. "Wake up," she said. She squeezed his smashed elbow. Avery's eyes popped open and he shrieked. *Chuff chuff chuff,* said the phony steam engine, enough to cover screams twice as loud. "Why did you do it?" she asked.

"I didn't do anything."

She made him scream again. "We can keep doing this," she said. "I like it."

"Screw you, bitch! *I didn't do anything*. Jonathan did it to himself."

"He didn't know he had a dirty bomb. You tell me he did and I start working on your eyes."

"No, man, but he knew he had a bomb. He told me to get him a bomb." Avery was rationalizing, shifting blame, but his tone had the whine and sniffle of truth.

"So tell me what the game is," Blaylock hissed. She grabbed Avery's chin and forced him to look at her.

"I don't know!" Avery's eyes shone fear and pain. "Sherbina doesn't tell me his big plans."

Blaylock snorted in frustration. She smashed the stock of her C7 against Avery's cheekbone. Avery howled. Blood poured out of his mouth. He held his good hand against the side of his broken face as he writhed. "Don't stall again," Blaylock told him.

"I'm not." He spoke quickly, before she had a chance to hit him again. His words were slurred. "Orders were to cozy up to Jonathan, make sure he goes over the edge, turns fantastic bomb-happy, then help him find what he needs."

Blaylock thought about the number of explosions. "You weren't the only one."

Avery shook his head. "Sherbina must have done psych profiling. There were all these other guys out there, every place there was a group that could turn violent."

Blaylock moved her face close to Avery's. "Now tell me why you did it. I need to know why you could do that to your friend."

"My friend?" Total disbelief. "That asshole?"

Blaylock blinked, startled by truth, and of course Avery was right. She felt herself pause, knew at the deep level that she was making a mistake, but it was too late. Avery hit her in the face, very hard. He was strong and he had surprise and she flew back inside the locomotive. The remote flew out of her pocket, skittered across the floor. Avery was up and ready to run, but he saw the remote. He stormed into the locomotive. Blaylock sat up, groggy. Avery kicked her in the head, and the red haze in her vision went black. Her eyes cleared, and she saw Avery pick up the remote. She was sitting on her C7. She yanked the SIG out of her jacket as Avery turned on her again. He threw himself down and right as she fired. He screamed as he landed on his broken arm. Blaylock's bullet whined and pinged multiple ricochets. Blaylock shook her head, cleared it, sighted, but Avery was up and running. She jumped to her feet and followed. He was already three quarters of the way around the coal tender, yelling holy hell. He was crossing into the passenger car before Blaylock could fire a burst from her C7. She saw one bullet smack his shoulder, but he kept going. She cursed, ran after him.

He moved fast, staying one car length ahead of her. Blaylock paused between the two empty passenger cars. A few more seconds and she was going to run into the concentrated gunfire of the troop transports. She scrambled up the ladder at the end of the car. The roof was deep limbo. The fog was thick, a white stream flowing past Blaylock's feet, fading to invisible black a few feet beyond the lights of the train. The night was wind and the rush of blindness. Blaylock could barely see the roof of the car. She kept low, spider-walking on all fours, zigzagging with the rocking of the train. Just as she reached the end of the car, her scalp prickled. There was a whoosh above her head, her ears popped from a pressure change, and the train was in a tunnel. Blaylock froze flat, waiting the tunnel out, giving Avery another fifteen seconds to pull ahead, the Kornukopia troops another fifteen seconds to prepare her greeting.

The train roared out into the open. Blaylock stood and leaped in one movement. A bullet whizzed vertical past her cheek. She landed on the roof of the first of the troop cars. She scrabbled forward, heard shouts and movement inside, but no gunshots through the armored plating. She heard someone open and close the car doors as she neared the gap. Avery was still going for the rear of the train. She reached the next leap. She fired a burst from her C7 between the cars, clearing the passageway this time before she jumped. At the next car, the same pattern: crawl, fire, leap, crawl. And then again. By the fourth car, she was feeling lucky. She would have expected rooftop company by now. As she jumped to the fifth car, the luck curdled. The train hit a curve. She landed off the center and off her balance, right foot first. She fell, slid, saw the edge of the roof come up and kicked out, rammed her heel against the guide rail. She stopped moving, but was a splayed turtle on her back. She heard voices, and they weren't coming from inside the train. She looked forward and back along the length of the train, but couldn't see more than a car length. Someone fired from the direction of the locomotive, but the burst was random shots in the dark, the blind looking to hit lucky. Blaylock held fire, righted herself, crawled forward. If they were shooting from the front of the train, she could count on the way to the rear being clear. The enemy would avoid friendly crossfire. She was less certain if Avery was still moving this way. She'd lost track of him.

The shooting stopped. The voices stilled. Blaylock jumped to the last car. Mid-air, she felt the prickle. She slammed down, her hair ruffled by the tunnel roof. While she lay still, she heard a noise of big gears. Ahead of her, there was movement in the dark, a suggestion of plate-metal petals parting, black rose blooming. The turret guns opened up as the train left the tunnel. The muzzle flashes were huge and bright. Rounds marched down the armor-plated roof of the car, screeching off chunks of metal. Blaylock rolled right, let her legs embrace the void. She slid from the roof as the heavy fire reached her position. She grabbed the guide rails, last-second save. She felt the yank in her shoulders. Her legs swung, bounced against the side of the train.

The machine-gun fire walked the length of the train, then started back, zigzagging over the roof. Blaylock worked her way to the right. Her boots found no hold. Her hands took all her weight. The metal was slick with condensation and cold. Her hands went clumsy numb. She tightened her grip, was squeezing the metal more than she was holding it, and felt cramps begin. She moved her arms, right one, left one, right, left, swung her way closer to the rear of the train. A window opened beneath her and to the left. She put faith in her strength, let go with her left hand. She dangled a bouncing diagonal, starfish on the rack. Her shoulder screamed. She fumbled her C7 into her left hand, sprayed the window, heard the sounds of death. She snatched back at the guide rail just as she felt her fingers begin to slip.

The fog went from black to white to black again as the train burned through Klosters. The turret fire marched back over her position, hit the limit of the guns' down-angle, then started back again. All the windows on Blaylock's side of the train opened. She heard the click-clack of an execution line of assault rifles, knew bad odds. She lifted herself back onto the roof as the walking fire passed over her again. Micro-shrapnel sprayed into her cheek. The soldiers below cut loose, metal rain shooting skyward. A bullet took out a chunk of her right boot-heel as she hauled ass out of the line of fire.

Seconds that were hers, now, the seconds it took the turret guns to rake the roof all the way to the front and work back. She stood and duck-ran, legs spread, back bent, leaning against the wind that wanted to push her face-first onto the roof. She was spotted. The turret guns dropped suddenly, racing to catch her in their sights. She won the race and ducked beneath the barrels. She worked her way around to the side of the turret. The guns whined as they searched up and down for the vanished target. She crawled to the top of the dome, and was too high now if another tunnel came. She yanked open the observation hatch and aimed the C7 inside. Avery was seated beneath her. He looked up, his face a pathology of panic and rage. He brandished the remote with his good hand, thumb hovering over the detonator. "I will," he warned.

Blaylock said, "Okay," and gutshot him. Avery jackknifed forward. His hand tightened in pain reflex over the remote. Night flamed day at the front of the train. The locomotive flipped over left and hauled the train after it, doomsday chain. Blaylock crossed her arms over her head and jumped into the dark. She threw her body straight out from the train, had a second in the air to anticipate the blows. They came. Branches hammersmashing her arms, bushes clawing her face and clothes. Bonecrunch rattle of hits, blur of the earth and forest beating her and the pain was all one, a stoning to death. She hit the ground straight and rolled, a battered log. She came to a stop, would have blacked out, but the adrenaline of war kept her moving through the agony. She needed to see, couldn't see for the wet in her eyes, the wet that was everywhere and was warm and stung like salt. She wiped at the torrent of blood, animal anger-moan in her chest the only sound she could still make. And then she saw. She saw the train roll and coil down the near-vertical slope of the mountainside. She saw the whiplash snap trees and hurl them high. She heard the beast-roar of tortured metal. She saw the train disappear into the night. She heard the big impact of metal against stone and the hiss of fire in water as the train slammed into the narrow stream at the base of the valley. She heard the blast of secondary explosions. She saw the fog burst orange and red. She saw her burnt offering to a reptile god.

22

Geneva. The night after being evacuated from Davos. Lap of luxury in the Hotel President Wilson. All needs tended. Lawrence Dunn didn't notice. Nor did Linda. They ate in the hotel. They didn't go outside. They didn't watch TV after the first couple of hours. They sat in their room. They phoned home a lot. The kids were fine, were still fine twenty minutes later, and ten minutes after that. Dunn and Linda stared at each other. They waited. Dunn said, "I'm sorry."

"I know. Doesn't do us much good, though, does it?"

He looked away. The bitterness in her voice was scalpel-cold. It was the anger of a life destroyed. He couldn't blame her. He twisted his fingers, feeling the bad knowledge sink in. However the game played out, he had lost. His family wouldn't be coming back.

The phone rang. Linda said, "Do what he wants and get it over with."

"I've been trying to," Dunn answered. He picked up the phone.

The voice wasn't Sherbina's. "Are you ready to serve your country?" asked Sam Reed.

"When is Mama coming home?" Inna wanted to know. She and Sherbina were sitting cross-legged on the floor of her bedroom. They were arranging her plastic farm animals. Inna held a sheep in her fist. Her fingers tightened with the worry of her question.

"Soon," Sherbina answered. He had just finished assembling a fence around the farmhouse. He kept fiddling with the fence. He didn't meet his daughter's eyes, but he didn't think he was lying. He would not accept that possibility.

"But when?"

He looked up now. Inna's face was tight as her fist. "As soon as she can. But a lot of people need her help right now."

"You came home."

"Mama's better at that sort of thing than I am." He made his lower lip tremble in cartoon grief. "Should I have stayed away, too?"

"No!" Inna scattered the farm as she threw herself into Sherbina's arms. "You have to stay. Both of you." Her frame trembled. Sherbina stroked her hair and rocked her, tried to soothe the shadow away, wondered what had cast it.

Sound of car wheels on gravel. Someone pulling up to the house. "Do you hear that?" Sherbina asked. "Who could that be?"

"Mama!" Inna shouted, and Sherbina regretted, snap, that he had given her the same hope he felt. What if it isn't her? he thought as he followed Inna downstairs, Inna stomp-running in full delight. And then the doorbell rang. Inna slumped in disappointment. She still opened the door. "Hi, Uncle Yevgeny," she said, voice too quiet, and Sherbina winced.

Nevzlin patted Inna on the head, but said nothing. His face was the shade of harsh tidings.

Inna in the living room, watching *The Iron Giant* with Nevzlin, and Sherbina running for his study. Sherbina, blood iced. Sherbina, feeling that new and awful thing, fear. Sherbina, retaining only one detail about the train wreck, only one item that had any meaning right now, the terrible ambiguity that no bodies had been identified yet. Sherbina, seeing that one worst image in his mind's eye. Sherbina, scrambling for the phone, clumsy-shit fingers hitting the wrong buttons, trying again, getting though to Davos, to the Bellevue, croaking Zelkova's room number through a throat clenched to silence by the possibility of the worst, the worst. And then Zelkova answered. "Oh God, Irina," Sherbina gasped.

"Why are you calling?" Frost. No thaw since they'd parted.

"There's been an accident. The train derailed. I was worried—"

"That I might be on it with your goons? When there's still so much of the blood you spilled here to be mopped up?"

"Please, don't—"

"Then don't call me. I can't speak to you right now. This is just too awful. I don't know if I can do this anymore."

"The chaos is almost over. Trust me, please. The stability that comes next—"

She cut him off again. "Will make this worth it somehow? How can you believe that? How can you expect *me* to believe that? How can . . ." She trailed off.

Sherbina heard a television in the background. "What is it?"

"What are you up to? The news just said you're offering the Kornukopia headquarters to the WTO."

"It needs a new home. Please come back to yours."

"So you can bring me in line?"

"Because Inna and I need you. I love you."

Zelkova sighed. "I . . ." she said, but didn't finish. She hung up.

Sherbina put the receiver down gently. He leaned back in his chair and felt his limbs go weak as adrenaline was leeched out by relief. His mind, freed of the fear tether, turned back to the train and worked through the consequences. Nothing too drastic. He had plenty of manpower. The implications bothered him more. Someone had hit him hard. The novelty was unpleasant. He thought about Zelkova's pet journalist. The woman was present at more massacres than he was, and believing in coincidence was a fine way to die. He felt twinges, worry that turned into poison-fanged anxiety. The thrill of playing danger games with Baylor was gone. He hadn't taken her seriously, had shark-flirted with her instead of looking for the organization she must be working for. So. No more games now. Identify the enemy. Take out insurance. Deal with Baylor, but don't alienate Zelkova any further.

Come home soon, he begged.

Grimson had a six-inch television set suspended above her hospital bed. Flanagan sat beside her and they watched the news. The coverage was still wall-to-wall Davos. The media was having a happy happy day adding the Kornukopia train wreck to the story. When the wreckage flashed onto the screen, Flanagan and Grimson both said, "Oh, Christ," and then Blaylock walked into the room. Flanagan barely recognized her for the wounds. Her face was a chainsaw cross-hatch of bruises and cuts. Zigzag stitching held a half-dozen of the bigger slashes shut. The discoloration turned her flesh into red and purple camouflage. "Are you all right?" Flanagan asked, and Blaylock grinned. Flanagan was surprised to see her teeth were still there.

Blaylock limped to the left side of Grimson's bed and knelt beside her. "How are you doing?"

"They're releasing me tomorrow."

"That doesn't answer my question."

Grimson shrugged. "I'm patched up," she said, equivocal and flat. She nodded at the screen. A spokesman for Kornukopia was getting weepy over the deaths of heroes. "Was that you?"

Blaylock said nothing.

"I don't want revenge," Grimson stated.

Blaylock looked at her. Sharply. The tableau struck Flanagan. Two soldiers, both wounded, long comrades, long on different paths, at last coming to terms with just how different the paths were. "Really?" Blaylock breathed.

"Yes. Can you understand?"

"No."

Neither could Flanagan. He remembered his rage when InSec had killed his sister and nephew. No revenge would have been enough.

"No," Blaylock repeated, shaking her head. "You can't tell me you haven't thought about—"

"Of course I have!" The sudden pain in Grimson's shout made Flanagan flinch. "I've had forty-eight hours to think of nothing else. You think I don't imagine the bastards who did this roasting on slow spits? Do you?"

"So?" Blaylock prompted.

"So I've also thought about what revenge would do to me. To everything I've spent years working for and believing in. I won't do that to myself. I have ideals, I have ethics, and I'm going to be true to them."

"Good," said Blaylock.

Grimson paused. "You understand now?"

"Completely."

"You respect my decision?" Cross-examining.

"Absolutely."

"So you'll stop what you're doing."

Blaylock snorted and stood up.

"Jen," Grimson sounded desperate. "Please."

"Kelly," Blaylock responded, but quiet, not unkind. "Let it go."

Silence for a minute. Then, "Why won't you stop?"

"Would you believe me if I said so you can have the luxury of rejecting vengeance? Would you believe me if I said that somebody has to be damned fighting these bastards with their own fire, and that might as well be me and not somebody else? Would you believe me?"

"No," Grimson answered, but not right away.

Blaylock shrugged. "Fine. Then let's just say it's what I do."

"What if you do these things because you like to?" Flanagan asked.

Blaylock glared. "That a problem?" Her voice hissed, shocked.

Flanagan said nothing. He'd felt a tingle of awe when he saw the train wreckage. He would not stop her. He knew he couldn't. He knew he wouldn't want to.

Blaylock rested a hand on Grimson's shoulder. "Where will you go tomorrow?"

"Home."

But home was cinders, Flanagan knew. Grimson had told him.

"Your parents?" Blaylock asked.

Grimson nodded. "For a while."

Blaylock knelt and kissed Grimson's forehead. "I'm sorry," she whispered, encompassing worlds.

She made sure they weren't tailed, then chose a hotel a few blocks from the Gare de Cornavin. She gave Flanagan cash, had him check in after she'd talked him through the steps of fudging his identity. She loitered on the sidewalk, watching through the windows until she saw him leave the desk and head for the elevator. Then she trotted in, keeping her noteworthy face away from staff. Their room was on the seventh floor. Its window overlooked a Salvation Army residence. On the street, a drunken man was screaming about foreigners. Blaylock collapsed on the bed. She left room beside her for Flanagan. After a moment, he climbed onto the mattress, but didn't lie down. He sat with his legs stretched out, pillows behind his back. Blaylock reached out a hand, tentative, and tapped his leg once with a finger. "Tell me why you're here," she said, and he did. He told her a story about an Agency player named Garnett and dead men in his apartment. "You did well, soldier," she said when he'd finished.

"I'm scared shitless."

"I don't blame you. You'll have to hide until this war is over."

"And what is this war?"

"Still working on it."

"Jen," Flanagan said after a minute, and she liked the

way he spoke her name. "I'm glad I'm here. With you, I mean."

"Good," she whispered, scared to read what she wanted in what he said.

"And not just because I need you to save my ass again."

She twisted her head on the pillow so she could look up at him. "For real and for true?" she asked, trying to sound flip, but the tremor in her voice on the last word gave her away. Flanagan shifted down on the bed and embraced her. She made a sound, an involuntary *hnh* of relief, of joy, of letting go. How long since she had felt arms around her? She felt something wet at the corner of her eyes. She shut them, felt Flanagan kiss her. Her sigh shuddered. Then she had to ask, not flip at all, "How are you dealing with the blood and fire?"

"Better all the time."

She didn't know if she wanted him to. She didn't know if she wanted him on this path. She didn't know if she could handle the guilt. She did know that now, here, this moment, this place, she couldn't fight. She clutched Flanagan hard when he kissed her again.

He held her while she slept. He'd never done that before. He turned on a bedside light so he could look at her. She stirred but didn't wake. He stroked her hair, gazed down at the face of war in repose. Earlier, he'd felt the roughness of scabs when he kissed her, and she pulled away for a moment when his lips brushed over the tickle of stitching.

Fingers to her face. "Christ, what do I look like?"

"Jason Voorhees."

She laughed and agreed, but the joke was a big lie, and he almost woke her now to tell her how much of a lie it had been. He could see her aquiline beauty pushing to light like a developing photograph through the purple and the swelling. The lines, the bones, the will. They were too strong to hide. Her body was the same. When he'd undressed her, her movements had been stiff, and he'd winced at the scale of the bruises. She'd gasped when he touched her breast. "Does it hurt?" he'd asked.

"No. Make it warm." With hunger, her power had reasserted itself, and she'd moved again like flowing iron.

And now? Now the iron rested. Now the power slept. Now Flanagan looked for softness. There was none left.

Morning. Flanagan watched Blaylock exercise, enjoyed the sight of limbering pistons. "You heard about Kornukopia's generous offer to the WTO?" he asked.

She paused in mid-push-up. "No. Missed the news yesterday."

"Brand new headquarters."

Blaylock's next push-up was very slow.

Flanagan asked, "Does that help? Do you know what he's up to?"

"I'm getting an idea."

Flanagan kept quiet while she finished working out and took a shower. "What now?" he asked as she toweled off.

"You need a workable ID to hide behind."

"Where am I going to get one?"

"Amsterdam."

"How do I go there without picking up company?"

"You don't. I go. I need some more names myself. Give me your passport and I'll take care of it. I can be there and back again by tomorrow." She dressed. "I need to pick up some more weapons, too."

"I don't think I can help you anymore. My password's probably canceled."

She smirked. "Ten bucks says it isn't. Ten bucks says they'd love you to log in so they can track what you're up to." She shook her head. "Not worth the risk. Anyway, you shipped me plenty of toys. My supplies here are still good."

"Is there anything I can do to help?"

"I don't know what I'm going to do yet."

"But when you do know?"

She let the question hang in the air for a minute. "Mike, think about what you're asking. Think about what it means."

"I have."

She sat beside him and took one of his hands in hers. "Tell me how you felt after you killed the men in your apartment."

"Sick. Scared."

"Anything else? Anything good?"

Flanagan said nothing.

"Good." Blaylock kissed his neck. "Stay uneasy." Another kiss. "And stay safe. If I know you're okay, I can focus."

"I feel like a child."

"No. A human."

They were waiting for her outside the hospital's main doors. There were three women and a man. Two of the women were nurses. The third was a power-suited doctor. Her hair was steel gray and brush cut. The man was an orderly, wheelchair at the ready. There was a private ambulance parked at the curb. "Ms Grimson?" the doctor asked. She didn't wait for an answer. "We're ready for you."

Grimson tensed as the two nurses circled behind her. "Thanks, but I'm fine." She turned to go back into the hospital.

One of the nurses clasped her upper arm, smiling, friendly. "Of course you're fine," said the doctor. There was a black undertow of steel humor in the woman's voice that could have been Blaylock's. Grimson felt a sharp prick in her arm. Her vision tunneled to black.

23

Hurry up and wait. Wham, bam, and back from Amsterdam with a fistful of passports. Then a week went by. Blaylock newsbinged, saw nothing new. She kept busy, set up a Right Bank apartment as a safe house and stashed Flanagan and herself there. The place was in an anonymous ten-story pile on the Rue de la Servette. It was a furnished one-bedroom with a kitchenette the size of a closet. Blaylock carpeted the floor with newspapers as she searched for the new thing, the evidence that the Davos gambit was bearing fruit. She watched the perimeter of the Kornukopia complex, saw the phalanxes of bureaucrats moving files in through the gates. She rented a car, drove into the mountains, and spent hours gazing at Sherbina's house through binoculars. She saw father and daughter at play. She saw Sherbina enjoy the life he had denied Grimson. She was none the wiser.

Another week. She was in the bathroom, leaning on the sink and eyeing bruises. They were fading well. She wasn't a grotesque anymore, though she still attracted pitying looks on the street. Flanagan called from the living room, voice urgent. Blaylock rushed in. The television was set to BBC *World*. The scene was a press conference on the White House lawn. The Unbending Reed was holding court, serious face just barely holding back shit-eating grin. "The terrorists have failed," he said, and Blaylock whispered, "Oh shit."

"Wait for it," Flanagan said. And then it came. The latest round of the WTO talks had been completed. The Davos attacks had triggered a fast-track frenzy. Blaylock wondered if Grimson was watching this back home, and, if she was, how much salt was pouring into her wounds. Then she heard Reed use the word *enforcement*. She blinked. She started to say, "He can't mean—" and so she almost missed Reed say *new powers*.

Blaylock's legs went numb rubber. She reached behind her, felt for the arm of the sofa, lowered herself down beside Flanagan. "Jesus," she whispered, over and over. "They've done it." There were darker thoughts. They've won. You've lost. The war's over.

"What have they done?" Flanagan asked.

Blaylock laughed, blood-bitter. "The utopian goal. The dream of the ages. World government. Imposed not through force of arms, but force of trade." She turned to face Flanagan, gave him a twisted smile. "Do I sound paranoid enough?"

Flanagan didn't laugh. "I don't follow."

"The WTO runs the show. Reed and Sherbina run the WTO." Flanagan said nothing. Blaylock asked, "What?"

Flanagan sighed. "I don't know. Yeah, maybe you are paranoid enough. I feel like you're going to talk about black helicopters next."

Blaylock spread her arms, taking in the living room. "This look like your apartment, Mike? You feeling right at home? You want to call your good friend Dean Garnett?"

"That's not what I meant. I know there's collusion going on, at least between the Agency and Kornukopia. But . . ."

He paused, shook his head in frustration. "You're making trade the boogeyman again. The goal of the WTO—"

"Is to rationalize, standardize, regulate, level the playing field, blah blah blah, I've heard it before. That's not the point. Tell me, is organized crime your idea of how the holy-holy-holy invisible hand should operate?"

"Of course not . . ."

"Then what do you think Sherbina making the WTO dance means?" Nothing from Flanagan. "You heard what Reed said. Think it through. Think about how all the member states have surrendered sovereignty to the WTO rulings. Think about what happens when Sherbina and Reed control what those rulings will be."

"But how?" Flanagan objected. "How would they control it? If it were that easy the US would never have lost a Dispute Settlement Board ruling, and we have. Plenty!"

"I don't know." But somehow they've won.

Two more days. Forty-eight hours of defeat that tasted of bile and felt of eyes-open nights. Flanagan wasn't buying. Then why Davos? Blaylock asked. Something else, Flanagan evaded, vague. Two days of pointless surveillance. Two days.

The eureka wasn't carried on the front page, but was big enough to play editorially. The whole spectrum from the *Guardian* to the *Wall Street Journal*, from *Libération* to *Le Monde* to *Le Figaro* to the *Daily Telegraph* to the *New York Times*, all thought well of the appointment. Blaylock had never seen unanimity on that scale. But why not? A few months ago and she would have been nodding her head, too. Nothing wrong and everything right with Lawrence Dunn becoming a member of the WTO's Appellate Body.

Except.

She had seen him in Davos. She had seen a hunted man. She had seen Reed and Sherbina fawn over him. And then there was the thing she had never seen. She had never seen the Appellate Body's membership made public, let alone an announcement made media-wide. The chain of cause and effect was so tidy it was ornamental. Anti-globalization terrorism backfires, leading to increased WTO authority. The WTO shows deep sensitivity by taking one of its biggest critics into its very heart. *Lawrence Dunn will keep the WTO honest,* said the *Guardian. The WTO proves by this action that, despite the bleating of the misinformed, it is not the devil's tool,* opined the *Journal.* You're good, Blaylock thought, tipping her hat to Sherbina. Take out the fact that somehow you have leverage on Dunn, and the picture is Hallmark-rosy. She gathered up the papers and made Flanagan read them. When he was finished, he didn't look happy. "What about the other members of the Appellate Body?" he asked, more worried now than argumentative.

Good question.

Four days ago, Zelkova had returned from Davos. The media had left long before, lingering wounded and slow reconstruction losing their appeal. Blaylock saw Zelkova's arrival home through the binoculars. She saw Inna run out of the house, throw herself into her mother's arms. She saw Sherbina hang back near the door. The body language between the two adults was tentative, with Sherbina uncertain, Zelkova wary. Today, from a pay phone, Blaylock called Zelkova at her UN office. Zelkova sounded glad to speak to her. She also sounded exhausted. Still.

Zelkova asked, "Have you filed your story yet?"

"Still working on it. It's becoming big. I'm talking to *Harper's* about it." Blaylock wondered why they went through the charade. But Zelkova continued going through the motions, as if she needed to maintain the fiction rather than imagine the alternatives. "Did you find out what you needed to?" Blaylock asked.

Zelkova's silence stretched long. "I would rather not talk about that," she said finally.

Blaylock decided to push. Not for information that she already knew, but to challenge Zelkova. "That sounds like a cop-out."

"Yes, it does."

"Is it?"

"It isn't meant to be. I am still . . ." Pause again. "Deciding." The word was final. Subject closed.

"All right," Blaylock said, letting her squirm off the hook for the time being. "What do you think about the Lawrence Dunn appointment?"

Another long silence.

Blaylock began to feel she was speaking to a dead phone. "I thought you'd be pleased," she continued. "You and he are on the same page, after all."

"Ostensibly."

"Meaning? Do you think he's been compromised?"

"There is nothing I wish to say." Suddenly formal, as if remembering she was speaking to a member of the press.

"Then perhaps you might comment on how well you think he'll work with the other members of the board."

"The other . . ." Zelkova trailed off, confronted with new things to think about.

Blaylock asked the big question. "Do you know who they are?"

"No." The tone less formal now, more interested, more speculative.

"Can you find out?"

Sherbina knocked on the doorway of Zelkova's study. Her workspace was at the top of the house, where the roof peaked. Her desk was set up in front of the window, but there was still room to squeeze past. Zelkova was leaning on the sill, looking out at the night. The mountains were the deeper, starless black under the sky. "What is it?" she asked without turning around.

Sherbina glanced around at the strewn files. "Am I interrupting?"

"Not really."

He walked around the desk and touched her shoulder. Her frame was steel-rigid. He pretended not to notice. "I'm glad you're home," he said.

"Mm," she said, noncommittal.

He leaned in to kiss her neck. It was like kissing a lamppost, but twice as cold. He ran his hand down the back of her blouse, found nothing but marble. "Irina," he said, tried to keep the pleading from his voice, failed.

"I can't," she said. "Not now."

"Not ever?"

"I didn't say that." Now she turned her head. Her gaze was steady, cold, sorrowful. "I don't know. I came back home because of Inna. More than that . . ."

"You'll have to see."

"That's right."

Sherbina folded his arms, felt his own muscles tense. "I don't understand what's different. You never had trouble loving the sinner before."

"Scale is different. And I never had to bear witness to his sins before."

"I told you that after this—"

"Yes, you did. Wonderful stability." She stabbed venom into each syllable.

Sherbina eyed the files again. Zelkova's mood was darker than when she'd arrived, the stiff chill dropping to absolute zero. He wondered what she'd found. The papers were too jumbled. He couldn't tell from a quick glance. She would tell him or she wouldn't. She would come back to him, or . . . He shut off the thought, denying the possibility.

He started out of the room, paused at the doorway, and drummed his fingers against the doorjamb. "By the way," he said, "have you seen Jen Baylor recently?"

"Why?"

Because if that's her name and she's a journalist, I'm the Pope. Because she's at war with me, and I know now that she's dangerous. "Just asking." His marriage felt fragile. He was not going to apply any more pressure. He still didn't know who Baylor was working with, and he would say nothing until he did, if then. He didn't want Zelkova to witness anything else. And still he was going to have to skate out onto thin ice, apply the very pressure he wanted to avoid, one more time, and hope he didn't fall through into the cold and drown. "If you do run into her," he said, making the neutralization casual, "could you pass on a message?"

Flanagan, bouncing off the walls, in touch with his inner cabin fever. He had crossed the threshold of the suite precisely once, when he'd entered. The door might as well be a wall now. He stayed away from the window, too. The outside world existed only as filtered pixels on the television screen. He wanted to go out. He wanted to breathe fresh air. He wanted to walk more than a half dozen strides in a straight line. He wanted to take action. Like Blaylock. She was out again, taking action again. He felt jealous. He felt useless. He was the complicating bystander. He was in her way.

He thought that now. He had thought that yesterday, too. Every day for the last week, in the heart of the shapeless and eternal afternoon, had come the clockwork torture refrain. The mechanism tick-tocked through the same gears each time. Tick: I'm in her way. Tock: So leave. Tick: I'm afraid. Tock: So is she, for you. Tick: If I leave, I've had it. Tock: If you stay, you might die anyway. Tick: If I die . . . Tock: You'll free her. Tick, tock, tick, tock, back and forth and nothing to show for it but the slow buildup of bad. And then Blaylock would come back, anywhere from early evening to late dawn, and when she did, the thought of freeing her of responsibility evaporated. When she looked at him, he didn't see responsibility in her eyes. He saw need. For an anchor. For contact.

For him?

Maybe. And tick: What do you need? Tock: Her. Tick: Just her? What about the thrill that frightened him and hooked him? What about the pulse-surge he'd felt at the sight of the shattered warehouse, graveyard of a Mob family? The surge again with the news of the train? Oh sure, he'd felt all the good emotions alongside Kelly Grimson, the stomach-dropping horror at scale and savagery, the wonder at the cost (what is this doing to you, Jen?). Very moral. Very correct. But . . .

When he'd teased her about looking like Jason

Voorhees, her reply had been: "You should see the other guy." And he had. He'd seen the charred and mangled corpses on the news. If Blaylock came through a fight looking rough, the other guy wasn't coming through at all.

Tick: Look at what she can *do*.

Tock: You've killed. You liked that? You want to do it again?

Tick: No—

Tock: And again? And again? Like Jen?

Tick: No.

Tock: Just being *near* her has a price.

Tick: I know. But look at what she can *do*.

Tick. *Tock*.

Zelkova wanted to meet. Her voice on the phone had been grim with news, guarded with wariness. The Maison Tavel, Zelkova had said. See you there. Blaylock found it on the Rue du Puits-St-Pierre, a tiny narrowness in the Old Town, a block away from the cathedral. The building was the oldest in Geneva, a twelfth-century home, now a museum of the city's history. Middle of the day, middle of the week, and the place was deserted. Blaylock took the elevator to the attic, stepped out into a huge room in perpetual twilight. In the center was a gigantic relief map. A scale model of Geneva spread out before Blaylock. The love and obsession the map embodied took her breath away. Zelkova was walking around the map, running her left hand along the metal railing. Her right hand held a briefcase. She barely glanced at Blaylock. "Tell me what you notice about this," she said.

Blaylock joined her at the model's periphery. "The

detail," she said. Every street, every house, had its own identity.

"The detail is important, yes. That is where you see the love. Auguste Magnin loved his city. What else do you notice?"

Blaylock wondered where Zelkova was heading. "The fortifications." The city was contained by concentric walls and ditches that radiated in aggressive salient angles.

Zelkova set the briefcase down. She nodded. "Magnin worked on his map for sixteen years. He began it in 1880, but the Geneva he was building was from 1850. The fortifications were gone by the time he began. Do you know why he chose to represent the past rather than his present? Because he felt the fortifications defined the Geneva he loved. There were good reasons for destroying them. The city was being constricted by them. It could not grow. It was stagnating. There was no point to the walls anymore."

"But they protected his memory city."

"Yes." Zelkova pursed her lips against pain. "His dream city." Her voice began to shake. "Look at the detail. So exquisite. And it is accurate. Everything he loved about the city was true."

"Just not the whole truth. Not in the present."

"Do you think that portion of the truth might be good enough?" Zelkova gripped the railing hard. "Was it wrong for Magnin to live in this version of Geneva for so long?"

"No," Blaylock answered. "Because doing so did no harm."

Zelkova's arms trembled. "Four of the current members of the Appellate Body are sheep," she whispered. She knelt, opened the briefcase, pulled out a file, and handed it to Blaylock. "They know nothing."

"About what's going on?"

"About anything."

"So they're just cover? They'll dance to the tune of the other three?"

Zelkova ignored Blaylock's question. "The other three are Lawrence Dunn, Yevgeny Nevzlin, and an American I do not know: Dean Garnett."

The picture came together with the snap of a mousetrap. "Garnett is CIA," Blaylock said. The assault on Flanagan clicked into place. Blaylock granted the seamless perfection of the scheme a moment of admiration. There would be four years of Garnett and Nevzlin calling the shots for Reed and Sherbina. If they had a grip on Dunn, they would have the other four in headlocks, too. Four years of power consolidation. When the term was up, Blaylock doubted the new faces would make a difference, if there were any new faces at all. She flipped through the file, memorized pictures.

Zelkova was still staring at the model. She wasn't blinking, as if force of will might allow her to shrink and enter the protected, unchanging world of the map. "What are you going to write about Stepan?" she asked.

"What does it matter? A couple of black articles are going to hurt him? I don't think so."

"He's a good husband."

"As long as you make believe about the fortifications."

"No. No. He is a good husband and a good father, without conditions."

"I'm happy for you and Inna." Blaylock keeping things cold and neutral. No sarcasm, no sympathy.

"He likes you, too."

Blaylock snorted. "I noticed. I think he and I have an understanding." No keeping the humor, blacker than hate, out of her voice.

"He was asking about you last night."

"Was he, now?"

"He thought you might be worried about your friend."

"My . . ."

"Kelly Grimson. He wanted me to pass on that she is resting comfortably at the clinic."

24

When she calmed, the raging friend was subsumed by the war machine. She was half aware of Flanagan watching her, keeping his distance. She sat on the floor of the bedroom, back against the wall, head tilted back, eyes locked on the blandness of the ceiling. She considered the state of the campaign. She totaled up the respective assets, acknowledged Sherbina's overwhelming strength. She examined her goals. She evaluated actions and consequences, targets and their benefits. Taking Sherbina out was the big objective, but not enough. The machine he and Reed had set up would run without either of them, could run forever. Flanagan's problem wouldn't be solved either.

Blaylock considered Grimson. Anxiety flared, then retreated under discipline. Blaylock made herself think, not as a friend, but as a strategist.

Kornukopia's private clinic was on the Rue des Granges. The street was the cobbled home to eighteenth-century mansions. The stone facades were an ochre stained dark with pollution's age. Behind the fifteen-foot walls were courtyards and the mansions themselves, their luxury a secret from the street, but hinted at by the distance between each address. The door in the clinic's wall was a polished oak twice Blaylock's height. There was no sign with the clinic's name. There wasn't even a brass plaque, however small, however tasteful. There was the street number, and that was all. Blaylock wouldn't have known where the clinic was if Zelkova weren't standing in front of the door, ringing its bell. Zelkova glanced around. Late afternoon and off-season, the street was deserted. Blaylock stepped back out of sight around Granges' sharp right corner. She didn't think Zelkova had seen her.

The thing that bothered her, that really stuck in her craw, was that the clinic was a minute's walk from the Maison Tavel. She'd been that close to Grimson. The combination of her ignorance, the proximity, and the coincidence nagged, loose tooth.

She checked around the corner. The door had opened. Zelkova walked in. Do this thing, Blaylock commanded. Do it.

A drizzle began.

Dr. Isabelle Sourial said, "Ms Zelkova," and came up empty. She ran her hand over the wire brush of her hair, flustered. She exchanged a look with the orderly who had opened the door. The man was brick-square, a tower of obedient muscle. He didn't look happy, either. He had retired a respectful distance from Zelkova, but still blocked the way through the vestibule to the courtyard and the clinic beyond. Sourial tried again. "We weren't expecting—"

"That's all right," Zelkova reassured her. She swallowed to wet her dry throat. "I'm not—" she began, realized that nerves had made her switch to Russian, stopped herself and started over in French. "I am not expecting a tour. I am here to visit a patient."

Sourial frowned. "Most of the clinic is undergoing renovations. We aren't really functioning right now."

"But you do have one patient," Zelkova insisted. She was careful to make the sentence a statement, not a question. She was speaking from a position of knowledge, and a denial wasn't going to fly. It was important that they know this.

Another non-verbal exchange between Sourial and the orderly. The orderly crossed his arms, looked stubborn and dangerous. Sourial's face darkened. "We do," she said, a world of suspicion in two syllables.

"I have come to see her." Zelkova emphasized the gender. *See? I know who's here.*

The orderly spoke. "Does Mr. Sherbina know about this?" His tone was the sullen essence of skinhead and Swiss People's Party.

Zelkova turned to him, kept her gaze even, cold, stone. She let the silence become long before she spoke. "Shall I tell him you asked me that?" She kept up the stare, and her pulse hammered with worry. What standing orders had Stepan left these people with? Would his absence still override her presence? At worst, she knew the orderly would show her back out the door. But then what? Hustle Grimson away before Zelkova could mount a second offensive? Dispose of her?

She rememberd Baylor pleading: "You have to help her out of there." Baylor insisting: "Prove to me that you're more than his outsourced social conscience." Zelkova was still stinging from the jab.

The orderly wasn't buying. He took intimidation from

only one person, and that was not her. He dropped his arms and took half a step forward. Sourial was still looking at Zelkova, though, and she bought. "That won't be necessary," she said, unhappy and cold. She gestured for the orderly to move aside, and the combined hierarchy of the two women was enough. He glared at Zelkova as he let her pass.

Sourial led her through the courtyard. Zelkova saw scaffolding on the main building's walls. Inside, tarps covered the floor. Zelkova's nostrils were hit by a dust and paint combo. There was no one at the reception desk, and most of the lights were off. Renovations were going on. But there were no workers. The tools and the ladders were abandoned. The clinic felt dead. A few guards and a prisoner, Zelkova thought. No one else to know or care. Grimson's stay could be indefinite.

Sourial walked down marble steps to the basement. She stopped outside a heavy wooden door. The orderly moved forward, selecting a brass key from a huge iron ring. "Is the patient violent?" Zelkova asked.

Sourial looked startled. "No."

"Then why is it necessary to lock her in?"

Sourial didn't answer. She wasn't playing the game anymore. The orderly opened the door, and Zelkova brushed past him. The room was fluorescent-sterile and had no windows. Grimson was in a metal hospital bed. There were straps on her arms. The straps were loose, but tied her to the bed, and there was a lever at the foot of the bed that would tighten them back down. An IV fed into her left arm. A nurse sat in the far corner, hands folded, doing nothing but watching Grimson. She looked up sharply as Zelkova walked in. Grimson turned her face Zelkova's way. Her neck wobbled, and she blinked slowly, frowning as she tried to focus. Zelkova approached the head of the bed. Grimson's pupils were dilated big and stupid. "Kelly?" Zelkova asked, and Grimson blinked some more. Her frown became epic. She nodded, too emphatic, her head's momentum beyond control. Zelkova was about to tell the others to leave, decided not to. She didn't want them out of her sight. She bent close, whispered into Grimson's ear. "Do you want to be here?"

No reaction at first. Zelkova wondered if Grimson could understand her. She was going to ask again, louder, when Grimson's body trembled. She took a huge breath that grated stone as it shuddered into a sob. Tears formed at the corners of the huge black eyes. Zelkova reached out for the drip. Sourial's hand closed on her wrist. Sourial, with ice and command: "What do you think you're doing?"

Zelkova responded in kind. "What do you think you are?"

Standoff. Sourial had reached the wall. This fa, no further. Zelkova pried Sourial's hand away. The orderly blocked the door. Zelkova yanked the drip out of Grimson's arm before Sourial could stop her again. Grimson's body jerked. Zelkova began undoing the straps.

"You're not taking her," Sourial stated.

"How will you stop me?" She put her arm around Grimson's shoulders and lifted her to a seated position. "We have to go, Kelly," she said gently. "You have to help me." Grimson shivered with struggle, tears flowing. Her legs wiggled, but nothing more. She wouldn't be able to support her own weight, Zelkova realized, let alone walk. She faced Sourial. "Not only am I taking her," she said, "but you're going to help."

Sourial didn't smile. Zelkova didn't think she could.

But her lips tightened in a thin, bad line of contempt and a corpse-shell of amusement. "Charles," she said, and the orderly moved forward. He stepped into Zelkova's space, moving her aside without touching her. He placed a hand the size of a dinner plate on Grimson's chest and pushed her back down. Grimson whimpered. Her head shook back and forth like a gasping fish. Charles kept his anvil hand pressing her down. He could grin, and he did, showing Zelkova big teeth. Sourial asked, "Are you going to overpower Charles? No? I don't think so. I *do* think it is time for you to go." She gestured toward the door, pressed her lips together again. The nurse picked up the IV needle.

"Let her go," Zelkova told Charles. He didn't move.

"We will not hurt you," Sourial said. "We all know that. But we can outwait you."

Zelkova had never kicked against her husband's commands before. She hadn't realized how high his walls were, how thick. She looked at each of Grimson's captors in turn. Sourial began to tap a shoe against the floor, syncopated metronome. Her lips were still thin and tight with victory.

They met under *United Peace*. The wind picked up and the stabile shifted on its pedestal. Raindrops rattled against the sculpture's metal. The forecourt of the US Mission to the UN was turning slick with the freezing drizzle. Chapel's mood was darker and colder. "Welcome to Geneva," he said to Dean Garnett. He didn't spit the words. He just sent them out flat to die.

Garnett grimaced. "Thanks," he said, and gave a peace-offering smile. He still shone innocence and sun.

Chapel kept his expression as flat as his words. He faced

Garnett and let the rain come down on them. Neither man was dressed for wet. Chapel didn't care, and he was glad to see Garnett did. Water trickled down Garnett's hair and under the collar of his coat. He shifted, sighed, put his suitcase down. "Look—" he began.

Chapel cut him off. "How long?"

"How long what?"

"How long were you and the President operating behind my back? How long have I been played? How long have you been on Sherbina's payroll?"

Garnett held up a hand, angry now. "Don't you *ever* question my loyalty to my country."

"How long?" Chapel repeated.

"Can't we go inside?"

"No."

Garnett puffed out his cheeks. "Sam—" he began.

"The President," Chapel corrected. He resented the familiarity Garnett had started to throw in his face.

"Fine. The President only approached me a couple of months ago."

Chapel tested the chronology. "Before or after he made me DDCI?"

Garnett said, "After," but there was a micro-hesitation, as if he was deciding between versions of the story, debating which version would offend Chapel less. The hesitation turned the answer into dismissible lie. When Chapel didn't respond, Garnett tried again. "Joe, he only picked me *because* I work for you."

"Meaning what?"

"We know each other. We know what's what. He knows we're loyal, to him, to the country. And to each other. Tell me yes."

Chapel snorted.

Garnett blew up. "Goddamn it, man. You'd think you'd never heard of plausible deniability."

"What?"

"Would knowing what Sam ... what the President had in mind for me have helped you ride herd on the Davos story? Christ, I thought you'd be happy to see me. What do you care who's on the Appellate Body so long as our interests are protected? Well, now you know they are! We finally have this damn organization tamed."

"For whom? America or Kornukopia?"

"You think the President's wrong?"

About Sherbina, probably. The right President had been brought down or badly hurt before by making the right move with the wrong people. Watergate. Iran-Contra. Chapel didn't want a sideshow to burn down the circus. "Let's go inside," he said, easing up on Garnett.

They crossed the slippery forecourt and entered the main building. "How's the spin going?" Garnett asked as they took the elevator to the basement.

"Not bad. The Global Response group is one of the most promising. They had profile, they had one of the bombs, and they're not American domestic." He turned down a blind corridor. There was a door at the end with a guard posted outside. Chapel nodded to the guard, who unlocked the door for them. "The best is we have some of them." Inside was a small, dark room with two office chairs, a console, and a wall of one-way glass. A woman sat at the console and nodded when Chapel walked in. On the other side of the glass was another room, stark white, with no furniture. Slumped on the floor were a man and a two women. "Judy Liang," Chapel said, pointing. "Husband Mark. Faye McNicoll."

"Nice," Garnett said.

"Boring," the woman corrected. She was in her fifties, had seen it all twice and not been impressed the first time.

"Dean Garnett, Loo Meacham," Chapel introduced. "Anything new?"

Meacham shook her head. "Same old. Same as all the other protestors we picked up. Bunch of morons who didn't even know their own buddies had bombs. These three keep going on about Scary Lady, though. You like her for the train thing? Should I give her to Charlotte?"

Taber's instructions from Chapel had been categoric: deal with the derailment. Neutralize it or add it to the story so it works for us, anything, but keep it under control. "Not yet," he said. "She's too much of a variable while she's loose. I don't want her knocking the spin off its axis."

"Who is she?" Garnett asked.

Chapel told him about Baylor. Meacham added, "We don't know where she is." She poked at Chapel with a pencil. "I say she's great for the train. She's Global Response's Osama bin Laden, still on the loose."

"We don't know which way we want to go with the train," Chapel answered. "Might be better if that was their last gasp, planted ahead of time."

"Not by these idiots. They couldn't plant a weed without a leader. I make Scary Lady for that."

Chapel thought about the rage on Baylor's face when the bombs had gone off. "No," he said. "At most she Trojan-horsed them."

Meacham still wasn't happy. "Sure as shit is no reporter."

Garnett asked, "Are you looking for her?"

Chapel nodded. Meacham asked, "What do we do

with these three? We're not going to pry anything useful out of them."

"Not yet."

"Not ever. Why don't I just give them to the Swiss? They need to give the public some bad guys' blood."

"No," Chapel said after a moment. "We need the blood, too. Ship them to Guantánamo."

"Swiss are going to howl."

"Screw them. They may be Swiss but they're still Europeans. I don't trust them not to let the suspects go and lose the asset. We can keep a handle on the story better. These jokers are going to Cuba. The word is that America nails terrorists." Chapel watched the prisoners for another minute. "We're not shipping them out for another week," he said to Meacham. "Cycle them through a few more times, see if they cough up anything else at all useful."

"The other groups, too?"

"No. Focus on Scary Lady." He walked out of the room, trailing Garnett. He was quiet on the way from the basement to his temporary office on the seventh floor. Still quiet, he took off his coat, hung it up, sat down behind his desk. He didn't invite Garnett to sit. Instead, he folded his arms, assumed the authority of his rank and his desk. "Mr. Garnett," he said, slow and ice-dagger clear, "so we understand each other, you report to me. You do not decide whether or not I'm in the loop. I am always in the loop." Garnett nodded, said nothing. He didn't say, *Like we keep Director Korda informed,* and that was a smart move. "Now," Chapel went on, "you want to tell me why it is that the only two Ember Lake survivors keep showing up in weird ways on the radar?"

Garnett looked sheepish. "You heard about what happened with Mike Flanagan. Please tell me no."

"I heard about a monumental cock-up with dead men all over the place. What the hell was that?"

Garnett scratched the back of his head, on the spot and not his sunny self, no, not at all. "I don't know what to tell you. He gets the wind up about something, I send a team to bring him in for protective custody, he goes berserk and ices them all."

"You're sure it was him?"

"No, but within hours he was on a flight to Geneva, and then he disappeared."

"He and Baylor are not coincidences. I want him found."

Sherbina walked along the observation platform of the telecom mast. He was outside, catching the wind. Drizzle or not, Sherbina could feel the weather turning toward mild, the half-hearted European winter making tracks. Up here, though, the wind still had teeth. Sherbina enjoyed matching wills with it. When it blew strong, and the air was damp, the wind thrust into his core, dared him to face it. His facial muscles pulled back into a defensive grin. But there was an exhilaration, too, and the purity of sensation, of him and the wind and no one else coming to terms at the top of his world.

The WTO's move was almost finished. The complex had a heartbeat and circulation now. It lived, and was both host and parasite to the WTO. Kornukopia One was a home with cameras in every room, some visible, most not. The command center, at the heart of the Security dome, recorded every breath and gesture of the life in the complex, anatomizing the WTO's existence and spreading it out for Sherbina to play. When he was up on the mast, digest sitreps ran on the monitors of his private lounge. They were updated every five minutes. Sherbina hadn't glanced at them all day. With the last of the Appellate Body appointments confirmed, he shouldn't even need the monitors anymore. He would know the WTO's thoughts and commands before it did. He leaned into the wind, felt it yank at his hair with cold talons. He looked down on his works, and saw that they were good.

The phone in the lounge trilled, its cry broadcast out onto the platform. Sherbina pulled open the door to the lounge and stepped inside. He slapped his hands together, banging away numbness. He picked up the phone.

"I'm at the clinic," his wife said.

Grimson woke up. For the first time in weeks, she woke up properly. Her thoughts weren't trapped in flowing amber, her eyelids weren't heavy shutters, her movements weren't held back by lead blankets. Her throat was a jagged pain, acid over rusty metal. Her head throbbed with the toll of a giant, muffled bell. And the light was stiletto jabs into her eyes. But she was awake. She was lying in a queen bed, not the narrow plank at the clinic. The eiderdown was smooth luxury. Grimson squinted hard and opened her eyes a crack. She let them adjust to the light before opening them the rest of the way. She didn't recognize the bedroom, but it felt like someone's home, not a hotel. There was a painting of what looked like a Moscow street scene on the wall to her right. The painting was an original, not a print. The room's gentle oaks and whites felt like comfort. There was a water glass on the bedside table. Grimson raised herself up, groaning, and drank. When swallowing didn't hurt anymore, she called out.

Sounds of someone moving around below her. Someone on stairs. Someone in the corridor. Zelkova opened the door. There was a rocking chair beside the bed and she sat in it, hands clasped, eyes deep with concern, brows furrowed with guilt. Grimson said, "Are you going to tell me where I am?"

"My home."

Mull over that for a bit. "Why?"

"To keep you safe."

"From whom?"

"My husband."

The logic wasn't working for her, but she still felt groggy. "I want to go back to my home."

"You can't," Zelkova said, her sadness genuine. "I think you might be killed if you leave."

"*Why?*"

"That is what I want to ask you."

Blaylock sat in the lobby of the President Wilson, feeding on anger. She gnawed at the afternoon's memory, sucking hatred from the marrow of its bones. She'd waited outside the clinic until she saw Zelkova emerge, until she saw Grimson carried by the orderly and dumped into Zelkova's Alfa Romeo. The orderly's movements were contemptuous, a man disposing of garbage. Grimson lolled like garbage, her hands twitching uncontrolled distress. Zelkova drove past Blaylock. Her eyes were fixed on the road. Her face was pale. Grimson was slumped against a window, and her face was loose, a flesh sack both upset and blank.

Now Blaylock waited for Lawrence Dunn to appear. She promised Sherbina better than payback. She promised him pain.

Dunn and his wife stepped out of the elevator a little before eight. Blaylock scanned the lobby, saw a wiry man slouching by the main entrance, watching the Dunns. His suit was expensive. His posture was goon trash. His eyes tracked the couple until they went into the restaurant. Boredom slammed down on his face and he stepped outside, lit up a smoke. Keeping Dunn in, Blaylock decided. Not protection. Good. She hit the restaurant. She spotted Dunn and Linda beside a window looking out on the Wilson's terrace and, beyond it, the Quai Wilson and Lake Geneva. They studied their menus, then stared at the lake. They didn't speak. Blaylock watched them from just outside the restaurant entrance for a couple of minutes, then strode in. She waved the maitre d' off, snatched a chair from an unoccupied table, and sat down at Dunn's table. He and Linda jumped. "Remember me?" Blaylock asked.

Dunn swallowed. "This is not the time for an interview."

"No, it isn't," Blaylock agreed. "But before long, it will be. Not with me, though. I believe, *very strongly*, that very soon you should be holding a press conference. And at that press conference, you're going to explain how Sherbina and others are blackmailing you into carrying out their agenda at the WTO. You're going to spill that story, all of it, every sleazy detail, and you're going to name names."

Linda had a hand at her mouth, suppressing a whimper. Dunn was gripping the edge of the table. "Who are you?" he whispered.

"I can help," Blaylock said. "Whatever Sherbina has over you, I can help."

Linda was shaking her head. "No. No, you can't. You'll only make things worse."

"Try me. You know, Sherbina can't use his leverage when he's dead."

Dunn made a sound. Blaylock couldn't decide if he'd laughed or grunted in pain. "You think that would make a difference?" he asked.

No. She'd known that executing Sherbina wasn't going to be enough. But a girl can always dream. Blaylock thought for a moment about what she was going to say next. She gave herself the chance to change her mind, to think of another way, a way that wouldn't soil her. The moment passed. "Salvatore Coscarelli used to frighten you, didn't he?" she said. Dunn nodded. "He doesn't anymore, does he? None of the Coscarellis do. In fact, it's hard to find a Coscarelli with a pulse these days." She lowered her voice. "That's because I'm worse than the Coscarellis. I'm worse than Sherbina. The people who might hurt you are going to be too busy bleeding to bother with you. Fair warning. The Appellate Body comes clean, or it goes down. That means Garnett, that means Nevzlin, that means you." She stared at Dunn until she could see the new terror sink roots and grow. "Do the right thing," she said, then stood up and left.

25

The Parc des Bastions on the Left Bank. Long gravel alleys, bordered by chestnut trees. Giant chessboards and old men. The Mur de la Réformation, Calvin and the fun team in frozen stone overlooking the skateboard thrasher moves. Facing the wall, on the other side of the park, the university. In the Aile Salève, the library. In the library, Blaylock doing research, moving off the incomplete computer catalog to the cards, going back, acquiring target. Blaylock's lip, curling. Coming together: the lesson in pain.

Blaylock said, "Don't go outside."
　Flanagan, looking at the bags of groceries Blaylock had brought into the apartment, asked, "How long are you going to be gone?"
　"A few days."
　"And if you're longer than a few days?"

The evening of her first day in the house, the moment came and Grimson was alone with Sherbina. Inna was in bed. Zelkova had gone to fetch coffee. Sherbina grinned at Grimson and waggled a finger. "You women," he said. "Have you nothing better to do than render a poor man's life complicated?" He winked to show he was joking. Then, in the moment before Zelkova came back to the living room, his smile vanished and his presence became power and a warning. As Zelkova sat down, he tossed off his drink and became sparkling charm again. "I shall leave you two to your conspiracies against me," he said. Exit with theatrical bow.

Zelkova asked, "Did he say anything to you?"

"I think he was just making fun." Bad fun, Grimson thought. Cat-with-mouse fun.

"I am sure he was. I apologize."

"Don't." One more abject apology from Zelkova, already brittle-faced from guilt over Grimson's house arrest, and Grimson might apologize, too, for holding back when Zelkova had asked why she was in Sherbina's crosshairs. Because of the bomb, Grimson had guessed. Because she knew her husband did not have a martyr complex, and though she believed (feeling sick) that he might have gone out to find a bomb (*What did you do that night in Geneva, Jonathan?*), the rest made no sense. Because, still guessing for Zelkova, she was the only member of Global Response who had not been caught in the anti-terror drift net, and so was uncontrolled. She told Zelkova all of this. She didn't tell her the last guess, that Sherbina moved against her because of Blaylock. She wasn't sure, and she wasn't sure how much Sherbina and Zelkova knew about Blaylock. If she came up in conversation, everybody still called her Baylor. Sherbina had looked guarded at dinner when Zelkova mentioned trying reach her, but he had also seemed uncertain, and Grimson sensed that condition was black-swan rare, and should be nurtured.

Zelkova handed Grimson a cup of coffee. The brew was delicious, but scouring. Zelkova said, "If you were not . . . if this were not happening, what would you do?"

"I'd go home to Canada."

"What would you do there?"

Grimson sipped, said nothing, knew her expression gave her away: *I don't know.* Home burned, husband dead, baby dead, friends dead or arrested. Howzit goin', Kelly? Like your options?

"Can you still fight?" Zelkova probed.

Exhaustion at the mere thought of more struggle. She pictured Blaylock, mocking and cynical: *Your fights have all turned out so well, haven't they, Hippiechick?* But under the fatigue, under the despair, she thought she felt the shape of her old anger and hope. So she said, "Yes. Why do you ask?"

"Would you like a job?"

"To make my incarceration less onerous?"

Zelkova winced. "No. This will not last." Her expression was sour. "I know my husband. He will . . . consolidate, and soon be beyond the possibility of threat from you. Stay here and work with me. I have considerable resources."

In other words, Sherbina's resources, co-opted and re-tasked. The hint of vengeance appealed to Grimson. So did the perversity, and, for a moment, the Sherbina-Zelkova marriage made perfect sense. "There's something we should fight for now," she said, making Zelkova smile.

"What's that?"

"You freed me. I want my friends released, too."

Chapel said, "You might as well meet the new partner."

Garnett said, "You sound like somebody pissed in your soup."

Sherbina loved English. He loved traveling the circumlocutions, teasing weapons out of formality. Speaking English was both play and control. Mastering the language in his early years with the KGB had been more than a strategic necessity. He'd found the joy of learning an instrument. English had become a physical object to capture and deploy. It had a luster for him that Russian didn't, because Russian was instinct, was breathing, had always been there. English was the conquered land, the opposition's domain that he knew better than the natives.

Then there was the edge. Anglophones never adjusted to him, couldn't process the fact that he owned their language in a way they couldn't. When he opened his mouth, they tensed up and never relaxed. Joe Chapel, case in point. They could meet and discuss nothing but weather, and Sherbina would be well satisfied. Showing up was half the humiliation for Chapel. Sherbina worked that now. He was in Chapel's office at the US Mission. Chapel sat behind the desk. Dean Garnett leaned against the wall behind him, arms folded. The set-up of the room amused Sherbina. The psychological purpose of the furniture was so obvious the result was high camp. Chapel's desk was enormous, a monolith of oak that shrieked its authority with all the subtlety and lack of affect of a drill sergeant. On its surface, nothing but a phone (black) in one corner and a pad and pen in the center, emphasizing the immensity. Chapel's chair was high-backed leather. Sherbina's was small, humble, fabric over a wooden frame. It was the seat of the supplicant, of the cowed subordinate. Sherbina stretched out his legs, clasped his hands over his stomach, and sank low, countering the chair's Calvinist intent with languor. He wanted Chapel annoyed, off-guard, and misreading. "My darling wife," he said, "is deeply troubled about the fate of three earnest Canadians we understand are in your custody."

"I'm not at liberty to confirm the identity of *anybody* we might or might not—"

Sherbina waved a hand, cutting him off. "Joe, Joe, Joe," he chided. "This is me. You know what I know. Can we dispense with the usual intelligence evasion and casuistry? Thank you." He hardened his accent into Hollywood Thug. "We knows ya gots 'em, an' we wants 'em out." No, he didn't, but he'd gone through the motions for Zelkova.

Chapel's disgust was naked. Sherbina clamped down on a laugh. Chapel said, "We don't give up suspected terrorists just because someone's wife would like us to."

Still holding the line on the terrorist story, Sherbina noted. Interesting. Chapel was committed to the narrative in a way that even Reed wasn't in private conversation. Sherbina wasn't sure if he approved or not. He still wondered if Reed had chosen well. He didn't know if he could work with this man. "And if there were more compelling reasons for them to be released to the knowing care of a trusted partner?" Acid test.

Chapel's lip curled. "Hilarious."

"That, I take it, was a no?"

"My President feels that it is in the nation's interest that we cooperate with you. That doesn't mean we're friends, and it sure as shit doesn't mean I trust you. You work with me, you work on a very short leash. First hint things are out of control, I yank you in."

Singsong in Sherbina's head: *How far will little Joey play ball? Not very far, not far at all.* "Woof," he said, then shook his head with the sadness of Victorian melodrama. "I can't account for your hostility." He wiped away an imaginary tear.

"You're a criminal."

Sherbina roared. By the time he had himself under control, the tears on his cheeks were real. "And you're not?" he gasped out.

"Show him out," Chapel told Garnett.

And as Garnett led him out to the Mission forecourt, Sherbina said, "So it's Saturday, then, that they're off for the Cuban holiday?"

The light in the room never went off. Judy Liang's eyes were dry. Her vision was bleached fluorescent. Her head throbbed with the just-audible hum of the lights. She hadn't slept more than an hour at a time since Davos. She didn't know how long ago that was. They had taken her watch away, and time was a meaningless limbo of white walls, white floor, whiter light. Meals were rare, random and supervised. Only one of the prisoners was allowed to eat at any one session. The other two had to watch, crave, and hope the next time would be their turn. Last time, Mark had eaten. Before that, Faye. That didn't mean Judy would be up next. Her chances were always one in three. Sometimes she had two meals in a row. Other times, she missed four. Stomach sore and gurgling, she was curled into a corner of the room. Mark and Faye had each taken another corner. No one wanted to huddle together anymore. Misery and fear had flattened out to dull despair, had turned inward to fetal selfishness. She waited for the torture of the white nothing to be replaced by the torture of the angry interrogations. She hugged her shoulders, trembled, tried to curl tighter. In her mind, halfway between a thought and an instinct, a curse circled, a numbed and debased refrain against Kelly Grimson's friend, the dark woman with whose arrival had come fire and death and nightmare.

The door of the cell opened. Judy looked up, expected the angry woman who ran most of the interrogations. Instead, she saw three men she didn't know. Two big men, one of them holding a medical bag, stood behind the shorter one. He was smiling, happy, and the harmlessness of his face gave Judy a pang of hope. "How are we all doing?" the man said as one of his colleagues closed the door. "Ready for the big trip? Tell me yes."

"We're leaving here?" Faye croaked the question before Judy could loosen her own throat.

"You certainly are," the smiling man said. The man with the bag opened it and pulled out a hypodermic.

"Where are we going?" Judy noticed that the man's left ring finger was missing.

"Home. You're going home. You just need a little shot of something to help you make the trip."

Mark said, "A shot of what?" But he rolled up his sleeve and held out his arm as the big man approached him.

"It's nothing, really," said the smiling man. The big man snorted. He took Mark's wrist and aimed the needle at a vein. The joke clicked, and Judy screamed her husband's name. There was nothing in the hypo. Just air. Mark jumped. The man's grip was granite, and the plunger went home.

Judy, screaming. Faye, screaming. Judy and Faye, on

their feet and pounding on the one-way glass, shrieking for someone, anyone, the angry lady, the dark woman, anyone, anyone. The big man who was standing by the door grabbed Faye. He pinned her arms behind her back. The hypo man stepped towards her. Judy jumped on his back. He shrugged her off, not even irritated. She landed beside Mark. Mark was already convulsing as the air bubble in his blood hit his brain and did its thing. Eyes too dry for fear or grief, Judy tried to stand. The smiling man pressed a gentle hand against her chest, forced her back down, caring parent and hydraulic press. "Shhh," he said. He was calm, comforting. "It's all right. It's all right." Faye was given her bubble.

Judy's sob was dry. Faye screamed and struggled a bit more, but not much more before she went flopping fish. "See," the smiling man said. "Everything's fine." The needle headed Judy's way. She tried to twist out from under the smiling man's grip. He chuckled, indulgent, and held her. "There, there," stroking her hair, "there, there." A huge hand took her arm. As she felt the pinch of the needle entering, she turned her head and met the smiling man's eyes. His smile didn't falter, his mood stayed sunny, but he looked away. Then pain was a black and swelling fist behind her eyes.

It was time to acknowledge the ghosts.

There were good days to be an old man. They were rarer in the fanged depths late in a Moscow February, but he found them even then. When there hadn't been a snowfall for a while, and the sidewalks were clear, and the sun shone, not with warmth, but a hard purity of light that only came with winter, those were good days. He walked every day, and if he didn't hit any ice patches, if he didn't once feel that he might stumble, that lifted his mood past the encrusted ache of his joints. The sun shone today. His gait felt younger today. A good day.

His walk took him along the banks of the River Moskva, on the Kreml'ovskaja. This was the core of his ritual. He had strolled this route the first time over sixty years ago, when he moved to Moscow to begin his career. His first walk had been a tourist's gawp at the river on one side and the Kremlin on the other. Hick kid flattened by metropolis awe. The Kremlin, a green-roofed, white-walled, squat massiveness, rose behind its park and its walls, a seductive majesty, a stern welcome. The second meaningful walk had been less than a year later. The novelty had worn off, the job was stressful, decisions needed to be made. He'd stared at the river until its current had taken his thoughts. Surrendering to the flow, he'd made his choice. Now, he nodded to the river, nodded to its expanse of ice, glare-white in the sun. He nodded to absent friends and colleagues, the ghosts embedded in the cold.

He headed home. Each year, the walk covered less distance and took more time. It had shrunk to its bare bones of apartment, river, apartment. Still, he could walk. More than he could say for most of his peers. Still, he could breathe. More than he could say for most of his peers.

Home had been the same apartment on Janševa, just off Kalinin Avenue, since 1946. He and Anna didn't need to stay there. The plumbing worked but wore its age. Their suite was on the eighth floor, and the elevator worked on a random schedule. The wind found its way through the thick walls. Mildew blossomed. They didn't need to stay. They had money. They had offers. They had prospects. They had a stock of brochures slick with glossy luxury, courtesy their son. But they also had inertia. The apartment and the neighborhood were in their marrow. Removal would be fatal. Home was the familiar. It was the stability of routine, the elimination of surprise. It took decades of living with surprise and uncertain routine to teach an appreciation of tedium.

He reached the building. The elevator, the little exercise in expected surprise, came when he called, and clanked him up. Unbuttoning his coat, he shuffled down the corridor to the corner apartment. The corridor was windowless and dim, yellow hall lights creating shadows but little else, and he was focusing on a button he was having trouble with, so he was almost at the door before he saw that it had been kicked in. His fingers froze on the button. Shadows bled from the open maw of his home. He stood still, listened. Silence, the bad silence of no movement. He sensed something clawed, in the shadows or of the shadows, reaching for him. It was reptile, and would show him no pity. He begged anyway. He spoke one word, his prayer, into the darkness. "Anna?"

Beats, then, an executioner's ticks on the clock. One second, two, three, four. Silence. The clawed thing, name still shrouded, slithered closer. He prayed again, felt the union of desperation and despair. "Anna." Beat one, two, three, four, five. Then, "Petr." Her voice a tremble of parchment, a torn spiderweb, and in her tone a very great fear. He walked into the apartment, into the shadows, toward the advancing, hissing thing. All the curtains had been drawn. The apartment was never bright, but now the monster could be anywhere in the play of gloaming and pitch. He moved down the hall. His footsteps crunched. He glanced down. Broken glass on the floor.

All the frames, all the pictures of the past and its honors, of him shaking hands and standing next to ghosts, had been ripped off the wall and smashed. The photographs were torn, some impaled on larger shards. He felt the clawed thing close in, began to guess at its name.

Kitchen empty. He crossed the twilight expanse of the living room. His cabinet of awards was destroyed. His and Anna's wedding portrait, on the ornamental mantelpiece, was untouched. The reptilian name was very close. He fought down a moan as he stepped into the bedroom. Darkest shadows here. He barely made out Anna. She was huddled on the bed, her back against the wall, her hands up in defense. She was shaking. Her eyes and mouth were wide skull-shadows of terror. He spoke her name again. Then the shadows behind him hissed. He started to turn, and his peripheral vision caught the uncoiling of a sudden serpent. Hands grabbed him by the collar. They dragged him down the length of the bedroom and threw him against the curtains. He felt the window smash. He felt the glass cut through his coat. He heard Anna scream. The curtains tore and the sun stabbed into the room. He felt gravity snap its jaws around him and pull him over the windowsill. He heard his own cry.

He saw the eyes of the woman.

He fell. The light was cold. The wind shrieked past his ears. The city spun and blurred. But the only thing he knew in the seconds before the pavement hit him was what had been in the woman's eyes. He had seen the monster that had slithered out of the past to snatch him and take him to the ghosts no longer satisfied with a nod of the head. He had seen its name.

Justice.

26

Are you proud of yourself?

Flanagan jolted awake, sat up in bed. There was a presence in the apartment. He tiptoed out of the room, felt his way through the dark, shaking with fight-or-flight adrenaline. The curtains over the living room window were thin, and enough moonlight filtered through to show Blaylock's silhouette. She was seated on the couch, motionless. Flanagan let a breath out. "I didn't hear you come in," he said. He turned on a light. "Where have you been?" he started to ask, but then he saw her face.

Top of the world. Sherbina stretched out on a couch in his lounge in the Kornukopia spire. He had Chapel on the speakerphone. He worked on letting just the right level of mockery leak into his tone. "Your situation does bespeak a certain carelessness, don't you think? I mean, losing all three of those dangerous terrorists? Not impressive, old boy, not at all."

"Cut that snob shit. What did I tell you? I told you a short leash."

"What makes you think I had anything to do this?"

"Coincidences are bullshit."

"My wife wanted them out and free, not out in coffins."

"Whatever. Why did you do this? How do you benefit?"

The same way you do, you idiot, Sherbina thought. Dead terrorists can't prove their innocence. They were awkward, and who knew what legal contortions might have sprung them at some point down the line? "Remember what your President wants you to do." Sherbina chided. "Protect the project." Which is exactly what I did.

"I am," Chapel snapped. "But I also protect my nation. I'm yanking your leash." He hung up.

Sherbina snorted. Chapel's leash bluster was good chuckles. The phone rang again. Sherbina blinked. Chapel calling back? Too hilarious. He tapped the speaker. "More thoughts about my leash, Joe?" he asked.

"Stepan?" The voice frail, and filled with something awful.

"Mother?"

Are you proud of yourself?

Grimson stood beside Zelkova's chair and looked over her shoulder at the computer screen. Zelkova took her through the UN flow charts, summarizing each body's theoretical function and its political realities, indicating where pressure was working, where they were going to need more leverage. The office door slammed open. Grimson jumped. Sherbina stormed in with Nevzlin hulking behind. A few steps back was Zelkova's secretary, terrified and over her head. Grimson stared at Sherbina. His Euro-cool was shredded. His face was wild. She saw tears on his cheeks. Nevzlin looked as frightened as the secretary. Sherbina stabbed a finger at Grimson. "Take her out of here," he told Nevzlin. Grimson stepped away from the desk. Nevzlin grabbed her arm and hauled her out of the office. She looked back and saw Zelkova, stunned, turning pale, open her mouth to ask a question. Then she was in the outer office and Nevzlin shut the door with a bang. He pushed her and the secretary down into chairs, then turned back to the door. His hand hovered over the doorknob, uncertain, then froze. A noise began on the other side of the door. The howl started in the low timbre of rage. It climbed to an animal shriek of bleeding grief.

It was night when Chapel left the Mission. Sherbina materialized by the main door. He and Nevzlin fell into step beside Chapel. Sherbina didn't say anything at first. His face was rigid planes of steel. It was the first time Chapel had seen him without the my-shit-is-gold grin. Sherbina didn't say anything. They reached the Route de Pregny. Chapel unlocked the door to his car, a nondescript Renault rental. Sherbina still said nothing. Chapel opened the door. Sherbina slammed it shut with the flat of his hand. He glared at Chapel. "What?" Chapel demanded, bored and curt.

"So that's how you yank a leash." None of the snot-toned fancy talk, Chapel noticed. He didn't know what Sherbina was talking about, but he said nothing, waited to see where this would go. "You're asking for serious escalation." Something bad had happened, and Sherbina blamed him. Chapel decided to play along, take the credit and grab the leverage he sniffed close by.

"Sounds like a threat," he said. "You know what a threat signals to me? Impotence. A problem I don't have. I can act. I do whatever I deem necessary."

Sherbina went very still. His breath, which had been misting the night air like a pre-charge bull's, slowed and quieted. Chapel noted the self-control, grounded his stance for an attack. He kept the car at his back and Nevzlin in his peripheral vision. Sherbina said, "You want to die now? Here?"

Chapel smiled. He didn't know what had happened to reverse their positions since the morning, didn't care. He'd drawn a headache by spending the day trying to work out how to hamstring Sherbina. And now, pure gift, he felt the power flow's current shift, surge his way. Life was good. "You want to dance? Fine. Let's dance. And say I die. You think the President will still be in bed with you tomorrow?" Chapel shook his head. "You're useful, but the project doesn't need you anymore." He glanced at Nevzlin. "You only have one vote to our two in the Appellate Body." He yanked the door open, shoving Sherbina aside. "Through talking tough? Good." He sat down.

Sherbina grabbed the door with one hand, stopped Chapel from shutting it. He held onto the roof with the other hand, leaned forward. He was anger in silhouette. "You think you can just have my father killed?" he said. "You're going to burn, but first your bitch is dead." He was starting to breathe hard again. "You can tell her if you want. Warn her. That'll make it good. Just so she knows. She has less than twenty-four hours."

Chapel stared back, processing the pieces fast. Bitch? Baylor? Had to be. Sherbina thought she was Agency? Let him, as long he stayed off-balance and directed his threats at useless targets. And if he nailed Baylor, there was another headache gone. Chapel's shrug was slow and elaborate. He leaned forward, grasped the door handle. "Excuse me," he said, smiling and polite and treasuring each second of ramming Sherbina's attitude right back down his well-bred asshole throat. "I have useful places to be." He pulled the door shut and started the car. Before he drove off, he mimed pulling a leash around his neck. He started to laugh.

The tail lights disappeared. Sherbina stopped yelling. Nevzlin stayed a few steps back, hoping not to be noticed before Sherbina was calm again. The boss turned around to face him, eyes bad and glittering. He looked like he'd never be calm. But when he spoke, the night iced. "You heard what I said?" Nevzlin nodded. "Then make it happen. Tap everybody. Someone will have seen her. Locate her."

"Finish her?"

"No. Just let me know where she is." Sherbina glanced in the direction Chapel had gone. "I want to make sure the lesson sinks in. And call Lafone. Tell him I want the warning sent."

Are you proud of yourself?

Blaylock following, keeping tabs, playing hunches and improvising. Blaylock keeping her mind busy. She'd made her nervous cab driver follow Sherbina from Zelkova's offices at Place des Nations. She watched, a hundred yards up the road, the confrontation between Sherbina and Chapel. She saw Sherbina yell and scream, no cool left. Good. More pain to come.

Chapel seemed calm. Maybe even happy. She wasn't sure she liked that. She wasn't waging war on Sherbina to hand Chapel and his master a victory. She needed to slip him the gears, too. She had the cabbie follow Chapel's car, and watched for the opening, the opportunity to spread confusion, fear, pain.

Chapel pulled into an underground parkade beneath the Hotel de la Ligue, on the Quai du Mont Blanc. Blaylock paid off the cab. She stood before the entrance to the sprawl of neo-classical luxury. She waited for the muse. Stir things up, make trouble for Chapel. Make him bare his fangs like Sherbina. What would look like a Russian strike? Short of killing Chapel. She wasn't at that point yet. After a moment, the muse whispered in her ear. She started forward. The doorman opened the door to her virus. She moved through the marble lobby just as a tour group poured in through the side entrance. The set of *Grand Hotel* was invaded by gold-carded trailer trash. Blaylock shouldered through the snob-label jeans and Tiffany-priced running shoes. She took the stairs down to the parkade. She ran her eyes over the rows of cars, scanning for the memorized licence plate.

She heard the clunk of metal. Fifty yards ahead, next to the elevator bank, a man's legs were sticking out from underneath a car. Blaylock padded in, spotted the licence plate, had her target. She stood by the man's feet and cleared her throat. He shot out from under car. He sat up, reaching inside his windbreaker. She kicked him on the chin. His head snapped back and smashed against the rear bumper. The sound was hammer on coconut. The man sprawled, lights out.

Blaylock knelt and felt inside his jacket. She found the gun he'd wanted, and his wallet. She checked his ID: *Lafone, Louis.* She eyed him, a pile of gangly limbs and too-long-in-the-basement pallor. She sniffed dangerous geek. She pushed him out of the way and crawled under the car. The bomb was obvious, and it was on a timer, not a trigger. A warning, then, not a hit. She and Sherbina were reading each other's minds. The timer was counting down from five minutes.

Out from under the car, Blaylock checked the parkade. There was no one else around. She noticed that the doors to both elevators were open. She peered inside. Lafone had disabled both cars, ensuring no unwanted company from that quarter. Good. She sauntered back to the stairwell to keep the parkade quarantined. She sheltered behind the car nearest the exit door and counted down the seconds to the blast. She wondered if Lafone would wake up in time.

He didn't.

Home. In the study, door shut, TV off, distractions banned. Inna in bed, Zelkova working upstairs. The house silent. Sherbina in hardcore thought experiment, testing out each action, tracing out probable consequences, weighing costs and benefits, vengeance and profit, anger and reason. Two things above all: preserve the Davos accomplishment, and preserve the marriage. In the wake of his father's death, Irina seemed to have forgiven much. That was the only balm in the day's pain.

First objective: kill Baylor. He still didn't have firm

data on her, but that absence itself said CIA. He should have realized. Stupid to have fallen for her cover. The left-wing journalist pretending to be right-wing was such a basic ploy, easy double misdirection, but it had worked. He'd been cocky and missed the signs, the too-many coincidental and convenient appearances, Baylor first showing up around the time Reed brought Chapel in on the game, Chapel's up-front hostility. Obvious now. On his desk, three sheets of paper. Three letters received at the WTO's new address. They'd been sent to Dunn, to Nevzlin, and to Garnett. The same sentence on each: *Expose the Appellate Body, or listen for the music.* Sherbina's whisper to Baylor at Davos, thrown back at him. Posturing, he'd thought. (Idiot.) He'd laughed when he'd read the letters. (Idiot.) He didn't know how she knew what she did, but she was one woman. She had no leverage, he thought. No angles. (Idiot.) He should have triangulated, should have seen her as Chapel's proxy. (Idiot idiot *idiot*.) He shouldn't have played games in Geneva. When the first hit team missed, he should have had her executed on the train. Should have this, shouldn't have that, the regrets of a thousand *if onlys*. (*Father, I'm sorry*.) No more *if onlys* now. He'd made the calls. The mad bitch was going to be put down.

Second objective: maximum, *instructive*, damage to Chapel. Done and done. Take out Baylor, and send a second message through his car. The explosion was all over the news. Sherbina wondered why Lafone hadn't called in to confirm, decided to ream him out tomorrow. Meanwhile, focus on Chapel. Make sure the message was received. More to come if he ignored tonight's warning. Sherbina would show him a thing or two about leashes.

Tactical consideration: should he tell Zelkova who had

killed his father? No. Don't risk disbelief. Much safer never to mention Baylor again. Possible contingency: Zelkova finds out about her death. Solution: establish groundwork so that her suspicions go Chapel's way. One more reason, then, to maintain the fiction that Baylor wasn't CIA. How to direct Zelkova's suspicions? Create the precedent of the CIA eliminating awkward dissenting voices. He already had the example he needed, an unexpected bonus of last night's operation.

He left his office, walked slowly upstairs to find Zelkova in hers. He didn't need to work to make his face grave. He felt his father's death as a repeated stabbing, in rhythm with his pulse. Zelkova turned from her computer as he walked in. She reached out a hand. He knelt in front of her and she hugged him, didn't let go. He closed his eyes, and, in the comfort of her embrace, the stabbing slowed and dulled, and he almost forgot to tell the lies. "I have some more bad news," his whispered. He felt Zelkova tense. "Your Global Response friends have died in CIA custody."

Intake of breath, followed by bitterness. "Natural causes, I suppose."

He matched her bitterness, let her feel the outrage he shared. "What else?" Now he hugged her, comforting her now, but also clutching, scared she might pull away from him. She didn't. She squeezed him back, and he felt her tears on his cheek. He kissed her neck, and began to weep, too.

In gratitude.

Are you proud of yourself?

"Lawrence?" Linda called. Tension twanged in her voice. It always did, now. Every time she spoke, her vocal chords were plucked harpsichord strings, their music pinched and thin. Dunn knew he was no better. He couldn't lose his clenched throat. He finished brushing his teeth, stepped out of the bathroom. Linda, in her nightgown, no longer looking sleepy, held an manilla envelope. It was addressed to him. "Someone slipped this under the door," she said.

After midnight? Not sleepy either now, he took the envelope. Inside was a sheaf of printouts. The top one was from the on-line edition of that day's *Moscow Times*. The article's headline was *90-YEAR-OLD THROWN TO HIS DEATH*. Dunn glanced at the picture, shuddered, passed the sheet to Linda. The other pages were biographical data, replete with footnotes. The entries were the cold lines of a black, fairy-tale career. Once upon a time, a teen did his bit to make sure the Ukrainian famine did its good work. Officialdom took note. The subject became a young enforcer for Stalin, his rise through the ranks of the *nomenklatura* matched by an enviable longevity. That longevity came at the expense of associates, colleagues, friends, even some family, bureaucratically dispatched to the murder machine. Show trials, gulags, executions, as his master bid or whimmed, so did the loyal servant. At age forty-five, up to his armpits in blood but politically spotless, the subject married Anna Vlasova, fifteen years his junior, whose dowry was strong family connections to the *vory v zakone* crime organizations. One child five years later. Happily ever after. Dunn frowned, couldn't see why he was supposed to be reading this.

"Oh God," Linda said. Dunn looked up. Linda asked, "Didn't you read this?"

"Just the headline."

"Are you blind? Look at this!" She jabbed a finger at the final paragraph. Waiting like a bad surprise was an asterisk, drawn in black ink next to the sentence, *Police have not yet released the name of the victim.* Dunn looked, couldn't see where the asterisk led. Linda turned the paper over. On the blank side, in neat, angular printing, an asterisked name: PETR SHERBINA.

Blaylock in the hotel lobby, following through. She'd chosen a black road, pointless to try a U-turn. She was so dirty now, what was a bit more filth? Waging psych war on Dunn and his wife was big filthy. But she needed them to fear her, to believe the worst. She wanted Dunn to still feel her pressure after she had removed Sherbina's. She wasn't going to chance his retreat into discretion if he thought the nightmare was over. She waited until she thought Dunn and Linda had had enough time to read and tremble over the envelope's contents, then she picked up the lobby phone and called their room. When Dunn answered, she asked, "Ready to do the right thing?"

"Leave us alone. I can't—"

"Shop the Appellate Body? Of course you can. And you will."

"He's going to kill you."

"Who? Sherbina? You think he can? You think he isn't afraid of me right now? You think he isn't afraid for his wife? For his child?" She paused, let Dunn think about that for a minute, apply the same threat to himself.

"I could tell them about you. I could tell them what you've done."

You really think he doesn't know? Blaylock thought.

Perfect, then. Plant the seeds. "Go ahead. Please. Phone Nevzlin. Tell him this demon whore is blackmailing you. I don't mind. We'll see how the game goes." She hung up. She waited, following through.

Nevzlin wasn't going to Sherbina with this one. The boss didn't need Dunn bothering him. Not right now, and not for this reason. Dunn had been raging over the phone, yelling about Sherbina's father and pictures and a woman and blackmail, and was about to spew project details all over an unsecured phone line before Nevzlin shut him up. "She knows!" Dunn had repeated. "She knows all about it!" So now, like the day hadn't been bad and long enough, like he didn't have an all-nighter's worth of work clearing the accounting decks in preparation for the floodtide of material that was going to head his way courtesy the Appellate Body, like there weren't enough serious and bad worries with Chapel refusing to play on the team, he had to talk Dunn down from hysteria's high. He strode through the President Wilson's lobby to the elevator, organizing his calming mantra. We know about the problem. The problem will be dead by tomorrow. There is no problem. Nevzlin was just a bit disturbed, though, by how much Baylor did know. For all the good it was going to do her. For all the harm it was going to cause her.

Down the hallway to Dunn's penthouse suite. Nevzlin knocked on the door, gave it a good full-fisted *wham*, letting Dunn know that nonsense was over and strength was back. Dunn opened the door. He was dressed in flannel pajamas and a terry bathrobe. He looked frightened, but angry, too, as if he might actually fight back. Linda was on the couch, legs curled under her, hands clenched tight. "Listen," Dunn began, "you people put me into this. You have to get me out. I don't know what—"

Nevzlin slapped him. Tiny tap, really, quick flick of the fingertips. Good noise, though, *whap*. Good satisfaction. Hard fist to the whiner's nose would have been even better, but Nevzlin kept his restraint and took what he could. Dunn staggered back, hand to his cheek. Nevzlin folded his arms, made his suit jacket strain around his size. "We know about the problem," he said. "The problem will be dead by tomorrow."

Pain.

Crack. The top of Nevzlin's head blew off. Red and bone burst up, staining the ceiling. Droplets and bits splatted against Dunn's face. Nevzlin stood still for a moment, one eye on his cheek. Then his knees buckled. He went down boom, felled redwood. Behind him, in the doorway, holding a gun, was the woman. Dunn could feel the straining of his jaw tendons, knew his mouth was wide open. He could feel a scraping in his throat and chest, knew he was screaming. He couldn't hear himself. He could hear *crack* of shot and *thud* of body, looping infinitum. Everything else was cotton lead, thick, enveloping, heavy, numbing. The woman brought a finger to her lips. Dunn felt his mouth close. She spoke, and he heard her, heard the refrain she was granting his nightmares. "Do the right thing," she said. She disappeared down the hall.

Are you proud of yourself?

27

The phone call didn't wake him. Zelkova was asleep. He had listened to the change in her breathing, felt her small movements, had drawn some comfort from the reality of her presence and her sleep, but not enough comfort. He lay still, eyes open, waiting. He had left orders. The instant what he had commanded went down, he was to know about it. He wouldn't be able to sleep until his counterattack was underway.

He slid out of the bed when the phone rang. Anticipating news of his strike, his movements had reverted to Spetznaz fluidity, and he barely rippled the sheets. Zelkova didn't stir. He glided down to his study, heart beating with the eagerness of war, and took the call. When the voice on the other end turned out to be Dunn's, his fist clenched so hard his nails drew blood from his palms.

She walked home. She was covered in filth. She could feel it crawl over her skin and through her gut, worms and teeth and squirm and writhe. The bad fun of the Coscarelli wipeout was long gone. The hunger and the anger were still there, but they were taking a serious hit from the guilt. The memories of eyes hurt her. The eyes of an old man and his wife. The eyes of Dunn and Linda. Eyes gone animal with the purity of terror, eyes widewidewide as they took in the finality of the predator. Eyes that held up a mirror to the monster.

She was on Servette, less than a block away from the apartment. The guilt mounted a big offensive. Its weapon was a shock wave of self-loathing. The wave hit, and Blaylock staggered. She reached out a hand to steady herself against the metal shutters of a stationer's. She took deep breaths, tried to edge out of the guilt's targeting lights, back into the night. She made herself think the word *necessary*. She whispered it, inhaling the word, exhaling it, narrowing her consciousness to this one thing, this one reality, this one truth.

Necessary. I have to frighten them. Better they fear the person who won't really hurt them.

Necessary. The old man had it coming. He murdered more people than his son has.

The guilt hit back. *Is this the only way?* (*Necessary*. The only way I can think of.) *Why that old man and not another?* (Target of contingency. Necessary. Sherbina needs to feel pain.) *Was that justice or revenge that threw the old man out the window?* (Both. Either. Doesn't matter.) She pushed herself away from the shutter, straightened up, and kept walking. She swallowed the guilt, acknowledged its tight fist of bile, and accepted the filth. This was the price of war. She'd known this since Ember Lake. She couldn't complain, and she couldn't stop. (*Necessary*. I am the necessary monster.)

The last thought, the reminder, helped. She walked the rest of the way without staggering again. She took the elevator up, and the closer she came to Flanagan, the closer she felt to a balm. He hadn't fled when she'd told him about Moscow. He *had* judged— she'd seen her trial and conviction pass over his face. But he hadn't run. He hadn't pushed her away. He had held her. He had judged and stayed.

She unlocked the door and stepped inside. Flanagan was sitting on the couch in front of the television. He didn't react to her entrance. "Thought you'd be asleep," she said. He said nothing. "Mike?" She sat down next to him. He didn't look at her. He didn't move at all. His breathing was slow, heavy, strained. Blaylock reached for her gun. The blow to the back of her head slammed her into blackout.

The phone rang a second time. This time, Sherbina heard what he wanted. "Squeeze her dry," he ordered. "Any way you like, but she doesn't have a secret left by the time you're done."

"And then?" Asking for permission.

And then? He thought about Nevzlin. They had known each other since the KGB. Nevzlin had been on the ground floor of Kornukopia. He had been first-class muscle, but his real gift, the one Sherbina had spotted back when they were still employees of the state and loyal Soviets all, was numbers. Kornukopia's financial records were high art. Nevzlin had known every angle, had created new ones every day. The finer details of the WTO project were all his, and he'd been auteur-proud of his work. He was going to be the center of the Appellate Body, the conductor leading the world symphony to his master's pleasure. He was going to—

Was. No. Had been.

And then? He thought of Nevzlin. He thought of his father. The answer came easily. "Kill her. Slowly. If she lasts less than twelve hours, you'll last twenty-four."

More blows brought her around. Someone was kicking her in the ribs. Blaylock grunted. Her head was a throbbing bruise. The pain was lead, alternating solid and molten. She was on her knees, embracing the toilet. Her wrists were bound to the tank by plastic straps. There were more straps around her ankles. Her legs were already cramped. The hard ceramic tile of the floor dug into her knees. She turned her head, and the kicks stopped. "That's enough, Larry," said a voice. She squinted until she could focus. A huge man in suit pants and shirt sleeves stood over her. His brown hair was cropped just shy of a buzz cut. He wore wire-rimmed glasses. He had a face like an Easter Island bureaucrat. He looked down at her, expressionless. Then he stepped aside and let the man who had spoken into the bathroom. Blaylock recognized Dean Garnett from his picture. He smiled at her, Mr. Sunny Sunny Day, and crouched down. "Bet you must feel pretty sore," he said, and grimaced. He felt her pain. "Tell me yes." He waited for her to respond. She said nothing. Garnett pursed his lips, thoughtful. He said, "Silent treatment? Okay, maybe we deserve that. Larry does overdo it sometimes, but what can you do." He spread his hands. So hard to find good help. "I hope we can move beyond this and have a reasonable, adult conversation, or Larry's likely to overdo things again." He lowered his voice, confidential. "Then there's Al." He shook his head at the sorrowful prospect. "I really don't know what to tell you. Al scares me sometimes."

"And you're good cop?" Blaylock croaked.

Garnett clucked his tongue. He backhanded her hard against her cheekbone, smashing her skull against the toilet bowl. Her ears rang. "Actually," Garnett said, still just as conversational, "sometimes I scare Al." He stroked her hair. "Poor thing," he murmured. He grabbed a handful of hair and yanked her head back whiplash fast. Her throat felt like it would tear. "There, there," Garnett said, smiling comfort and concern. "There, there. Everything will be okay. You'll see." He let go of her hair and stood up.

"Disappointing," Blaylock muttered.

"Say again?"

"So Joe's fobbing all his wet work off on proxies? That takes guts."

Garnett and Larry looked at each other. Garnett nodded, and Larry left them alone. Garnett watched her closely. "You think Joe would do a better job than me?"

"Can I comparison shop?"

He smiled. "What's with the lip? Are you trying to get my goat? What kind of a strategy is that?" He sounded pleased. Blaylock realized she'd made a mistake. "Still," he continued, "you just answered one of my questions. Keep it up."

"Happy to please. What were you going to ask?"

"Stepan thinks you're working for Joe. I didn't think you were, but I had to check."

So she'd cleared that up for him. Big deal. He'd fed her something now, too. Garnett working for Kornukopia over the CIA. Interesting. (Sure, girlfriend, if you can get away from the toilet.)

Garnett looked around. "You call this a safe house?" he asked. "Sister, you have to stop dealing with shady characters for your IDs. You might be able to hide from Joe, but once Stepan puts the word out on the street, I'm sorry, but the street gives you up."

"Noted."

"Good. Now, since we're so friendly and all," Garnett said, "want to tell me who you are working for?"

Blaylock said nothing. She weighed options. Saw ten roads of shit, none of gold.

Garnett drummed his fingers against the door frame. "Here're the options. We could work you over, but a little voice tells me that'll take way too long before becoming productive. We could drug you, but that's a long pain in the ass, too, wading through all the useless bullshit that comes out. Agreed? Good. So let's be expedient." He paused for a moment. "I have a family, you know."

Blaylock thought, Oh shit.

Garnett said, "I'm not proud of this option, but it does the job. Larry and Al are with your boyfriend. He is your boyfriend, right? I thought so. Can't say that I figure you and Mikey there, but hey. The heart's a strange country, isn't it? Tell me yes. Anyway, if Larry and Al don't hear me sounding happy in here, then Mikey's going to start hurting." He stopped smiling. His eyes, serious, met Blaylock's, one professional to another: we both know this is how things are. Blaylock stared back, putting threat into her gaze, trying to keep the fear for Flanagan out. Anxiety flexed her fingers. Her left hand touched the hose that ran from the base of the toilet tank. Garnett said, "One more time. Who are you working for?"

No good options. Pray for time and tell the truth. "No one." She twisted her hand. With thumb and index finger, she could just grasp the flange that linked the hose to the toilet.

Garnett sighed. "I hate it when people don't take me seriously." He ducked his head into the hallway. "Larry," he called. Flanagan screamed. "Volume knob," Garnett said. Flanagan's shrieks were muffled. Blaylock heard choking: a gag.

The nausea was a dagger-stab of terror and of a hatred for herself greater than anything she could feel for Garnett. Her body convulsed, and she lost her grip on the flange. "I'm telling you the truth," she whispered. The sound of Flanagan's pain was derailing her thoughts. Her mind was a landscape of wreckage.

Garnett nodded his appreciation. "You're very good. I like the desperate tone. Very convincing." He clasped his hands. "Body language, facial expression, eye movements, you have the whole ball of wax down. All the signs say you're being straight with me." He sighed. "Only thing you're messing up is plausibility. If you put yourself in my place, you'd realize how ridiculous you sound. I mean, wasn't this covered in your training? This is why this method works so well. Basic stuff. You can't think straight when the loved one is suffering. You can't come up with plausible lies."

He was right. "Not lying," she muttered, pleading now.

"Boring," Garnett said. He slapped her, again. Hard. "Be right back." He walked down the hall.

Flanagan tortured, Flanagan bleeding, Flanagan dying, her only thoughts and only fears, wall-to-wall and darker than God. No focus now. She grunted animal panic, writhed against the bonds. The plastic sliced into her wrists. She bled. Her fingers banged against the flange again. She grabbed it, life raft, and made it her world. Her fingers, sweat-slicked, slipped. She seized the flange, twisted, felt the metal slice into her flesh, gripped harder on the world's last real thing, twisted, twisted.

The flange moved.

In the living room, something bad. Piercing through the gag, a howl of pain and outrage.

The flange moved. She felt liquid that wasn't sweat or blood begin to run down her fingers. Droplets first, then a stream as the hose came loose. Water poured out of the tank, soaking into her clothes, flooding over the tiling.

Garnett came back. He splashed into the puddle, looked down at the floor, frowned. "There a point to this?" he asked. "Tell me no." He crouched down next to her, face in hers. He held up his left hand. He twitched the stump of his ring finger. "Looky looky." His smile was so sunny, so kind. "Found a replacement." He waggled a severed finger, Groucho Marx with cigar. Blood dripped from the ragged end of the finger. Garnett dropped the finger. It slid into a groove between two tiles. He pulled a combat knife from his belt. He pricked Blaylock's forehead with the tip. "Tell me your story," he said. "If it's the same one, or another story I don't like, I'm coming back with one of his balls." He stood up. He placed one foot on the finger, rolled it under his shoe. "So?"

Blaylock moaned. The sound bounced off the bathroom walls. It was dragon's hatred and wolf's anger. "Shut up," Garnett snarled. He leaned forward. She kicked out against his ankles. His feet slipped on the slick tiles. He fell. Blaylock screamed, covering the crack his head made against the toilet tank. Garnett blinked, dazed. His face was inches from hers. Their eyes met. Then Blaylock's moan was muffled, because she sank her teeth into his throat. She closed her eyes, closed her mind, did nothing but force her teeth together. Garnett started to scream, started to struggle. His heels slid on water, found no grip. His voice was strangled. Blaylock tasted flesh, then blood as she clamped down. She heard tearing. She heard a wet crackling and tried not to think *gristle*. She heard the clatter of the knife against the floor. She felt Garnett's hands beat against her head in a broken-wing spasm. She heard a *click* through her skull as her teeth met. She pulled her head back, yank and rip. Garnett gurgled and showered her with the salty warmth of his blood.

Blaylock spat out what she had in her mouth, heard it drop into the toilet. She retched. She opened her eyes. Blood stung and blurred her vision. Garnett's face was still close to hers, mouth and throat gaping. One of his eyelids twitched before freezing open. Blaylock moaned and whimpered, keeping up appearances for listeners in the living room. She looked down for the knife. It had fallen not far from her right hand. She stretched out her fingers. Her little finger grazed the blade. Blaylock almost held her breath, almost forgot to moan. She stretched further, gained the breadth of one hair, then another, and touched the blade gently. Her finger was sticky with blood and sweat, and the blade stuck. She twitched her finger in. The blade lost its hold, but rotated her way. She stretched again, and this time touched the knife with two fingers. She had it.

Blaylock pulled the knife in, grabbed it by the handle, and cut through the plastic. She slumped away from the toilet and freed her ankles. She stood up, moved to the bathroom door, and started to scream.

"Boss?" came the call from the living room. "Think you should keep it down a bit."

Blaylock paused for a moment, then screamed again. She heard an exasperated "Oh, for Christ's sake." She raised the knife. Footsteps coming down the hall. Larry turned into the bathroom. "Boss," he began. Blaylock slashed him across the throat to shut him up, then pistoned her arm, driving the blade through his glasses, through his eye, hilt-deep into his brain. Larry fell. Blaylock opened his vest, found a shoulder holster. She took his gun and silencer.

Blood-drenched, she hit the living room. She saw Flanagan tied to a chair, writhing, bleeding, but alive. Al was sitting on the couch. He had the good sense to look frightened before Blaylock shot him.

28

Flanagan's first question when he came to was, "Are they dead?"

He'd passed out when Blaylock was untying him. Now consciousness was back and he was in a hospital, another goddamn hospital, and his left hand hurt like it was being gnawed by hell's own pit bull, and there was just that one thing he wanted to know. Were they dead? All of them. He looked at Blaylock, sitting next to his bed. She nodded. "Did it hurt?" he asked.

Her cheek twitched. "Garnett had a pretty good world of pain, yeah."

"Good." His phantom finger throbbed. His conscience did, too, for a moment, then subsided, retreating before a new, crawling sensation. Flanagan thought the slither was understanding, a brush of the reptile epiphany that had enveloped Blaylock years ago. That Garnett was dead, and that he had suffered, this was good knowledge. He liked owning it. When Blaylock had killed Pembroke, Flanagan had watched, and had felt horror, not gratification. Pembroke was the reason Flanagan's sister and nephew had died, but in the slaughterhouse of Ember Lake, all Flanagan had wanted was to escape the killing. Now he knew different. Now he knew what a bad wish and a false hope that was. The jackals would keep coming, and the only thing they respected was the bigger, better predator. Outside the warehouse that had become the Coscarellis' mausoleum, he had felt a sick slick of admiration and excitement. But the pleasure was one of distance. The deaths had no bearing on his life. *Wrong*, he thought. *Those were that many jackals who would never hurt him or other weak animals again. Now the jackals who had bitten him were gone. Good.*

He felt himself sliding down a slope. He knew, if he wasn't careful, that he'd hit a big drop. He didn't care. He liked the ride. "What now?" he asked.

"You heal." She touched his bandaged hand. Throb. "Oh God, Mike. Oh, God. I'm so sorry." Her face cracked. "My poor soldier."

He didn't want to ask the next question. "Can they reattach . . . ?" He trailed off when he saw Blaylock sag with guilt.

"If you weren't with me," she whispered, "this wouldn't—" And then her voice caught.

"Don't," he said. "Don't. I'm with you, and I don't regret it." He let himself slide further down the slope. "You're taking Sherbina down, aren't you? I want in."

He didn't understand the look Blaylock gave him. Her eyes flashed from a nanosecond of joy to deep horror and grief. "No," she said.

"Why not? I know I'm not much use for combat, but there must be something—"

She cut him off. "I said no. You don't know what you're asking."

"I know damn well what I'm asking. I want to—"

She shushed him with a finger to his lips. "I know

what you want. But I don't think you do. There are things I have to do that no one else should. Ever."

"If you mean killing, I'm better at dealing with that, now."

"That's the problem."

"Christ, stop patronizing me! I'm not a child who needs shielding from life's hard realities."

"I'm shielding you from *being* one of those realities."

"How very messianic."

She flinched. Flanagan knew he'd struck home, regretted it. Blaylock shook her head. When she spoke, her voice was very soft, very tired. "You think you understand, but you don't. You really, really don't. There's more than killing. There are other things. I'm dirty, Mike. I'm so filthy I have grime inside my bones. You can't become like that. If you did, then I don't know what I'd..." She stared into the middle distance, gathering thoughts. "Remember, in New York, when you called me down. You said what I was doing was wrong. You were mad at me. You were horrified." She swallowed. "You were right. You were human. Don't lose that." Her face pinched with worry and fear.

"And if I think you go too far?"

"Then you'll have a decision to make." She stood up.

"You're going?"

"Have to. Don't worry. You'll be safe."

"How?"

She smiled. The smile was twisted and anticipatory. "I made some calls."

The calls while Flanagan was unconscious. One was to Zelkova, invoking protection, blocking Sherbina with his own force. The other was to the media.

The police cordon kept Sherbina away from the apartment for a full minute. It took him that long to track someone down on the phone who could give orders and knew enough to be frightened of him. He brushed past the cameras of a disgruntled media, hustled out by the police after having the initial scene to themselves. They saw the site as their turf now. The police could go blow. But the police had muscle, so the media was out. Sherbina had more muscle, so he was in.

Dead man in the living room, couch upholstered in exit-wound red. Slaughterhouse bathroom. The medical examiner glanced up at Sherbina, then averted his eyes and went back to work on Garnett's body. The room smelled of humidity and meat. We had her, Sherbina thought. He saw the severed plastic restraints on the floor beside the toilet. He wanted Garnett alive so he could kill him again for incompetence. He kicked the anger away and evaluated the damage. Baylor gone, three men dead, and she'd been neutralized when Garnett had called. Chapel must have caught wind of what was going down and sent in the cavalry.

Chapel was winning the war, Sherbina thought. Sherbina was still running to catch up with the bastard. Chapel had been hostile to him from the first day Reed had brought him into the loop, and Baylor had been the perfect stalking horse, drawing his attention from Chapel, confusing him with notions of a one-woman death squad training her sights on him for no obvious reason. The ploy had worked. He'd missed any trace of Chapel's teams around the train wreck. And now Nevzlin and Garnett dead. Lafone meat-whacked by his own bomb. Pushing Dunn to the media was a front. Sherbina was being squeezed out now that the WTO takeover was complete. Garnett's CIA exposure was more of the same blind alley as Baylor's politics. The slaughter made it seem like the CIA was out of the Appellate Body. But who was dead? Sherbina's boys.

Squeeze me out? he thought. I'll show you squeezing.

Big joy in Chapel's Mission office. "Do you have CNN on?" the President asked. Chapel did. The TV stood on a mobile stand at the other end of the office. "Because you know what I'm seeing on my screen?" Reed went on. "I'm seeing what we call a developing situation."

"Yes, sir." Chapel's grip on the phone tightened. The situation was developing all right. It had been developing like a mushroom cloud all day. Dean Garnett, his identity blown as wide open as his throat, had had the media on his corpse like blowflies a good half-hour before the police arrived. But at least the police placed second. Who was last in the race, last to know where Garnett was and what had happened? Joe Chapel and the CIA. Chapel's mood was black. The questions he had were even worse. Having them voiced by Reed was a knife-twist.

"Joe, are you on top of things over there? Do you really know what's going on? Because if you do, then how is something that should be an opportunity for our country and for the world turning so sour?"

"I'm all over it, sir."

"I hope so. A lot of work has gone into this project. America can't afford to have it go wrong."

"No," Chapel agreed. Doubts, now, though. Had Reed thought this through all the way? The ends made sense, but were they using the right means? Of course not.

"What was Dean doing in that apartment?" Reed asked.

I was hoping you could tell me, Chapel thought. You're the one who had the side deal going with him. "Sir, I mean no disrespect, but are you sure you don't know?"

Frozen hell silence.

"Because if you don't ..." Chapel hesitated, careful of the phrasing, even on a secure, multi-encryption line. "If he wasn't acting on your ... on our behalf, however indirectly and misguidedly, then he was working for someone else."

"Tell me what you mean."

"This project has another ... principal investor." And I'm at war with him.

"You think he might have a different agenda?"

"I think he wants to be the majority shareholder." So says my car. So says whoever that was who died in the explosion.

"Don't let him." Reed hung up.

Chapel replaced the phone in its cradle. He picked up the remote, turned the volume up on the TV. The bad news went loud again, turned into background roar as he thought. He'd told Garnett to find Baylor and Flanagan. No joy from him, and then this. Had they been there? From Sherbina's train being derailed to Garnett dead on a toilet, the WTO takeover was unraveling. A third force in play? Maybe. In the meantime, he could use the chaos to pull Reed away from Sherbina. Cut out the mobster, keep the Appellate Body control in-house.

Irina Zelkova's face drew his attention back to the screen. She held up papers, and stormed against CIA presence on the Appellate Body. Chapel watched the story go from big to huge, wondered what the hell Sherbina was up to, then realized that Lawrence Dunn was the only American presence left on the Appellate Body. He saw a picture form. He saw red.

Then he saw Jim Korda. He blinked a few times, sure he was imagining the CIA Director before a bank of microphones, sure the statements he was making, the yes-yes-yes guillotine admissions, were worst-case hallucinations. But Korda didn't go away. He stood there, solemn as the Pope, and did his damage. Yes, Dean Garnett was CIA. Yes, he'd been appointed to the Appellate Body. A reporter asked why. Chapel thought a smile flicked over Korda's face before he answered. "I don't know," he said. "Dean Garnett was engaged in activities under the purview of the Directorate of Operations. These activities were not sanctioned by my office. A full internal investigation is underway."

"Son of a bitch," Chapel whispered. He admired the move even as he wished death and hell on Korda. Chapel had just witnessed the digging of his own grave. The only question was whether Korda would push him in now or hold the threat over his head. The man was good. Damn. *You two aren't levering me out*, he'd said. Now Garnett was dead, and the ax was tickling the back of Chapel's neck. Chapel felt a panic urge to fly back to Washington and take Korda out, by game or by force. Duty called him back to reason. Korda played games, he didn't. He did his job, and his job was to save the project. For his President. For his country. Screw Korda.

It was after midnight when he left the Mission. He stepped out into rain. This wasn't the drizzle of a few days ago. It was the full-on misery of spring, chilled with the departing season, beating down with the promise of future storms. He opened his umbrella, and the wind turned it inside out. Chapel cursed, wrestled the umbrella closed, accepted the soaking. A block down from the forecourt, a man was standing on the sidewalk, arms crossed. He stood beyond the range of the street light. Chapel sensed from the silhouette's stance that the man was looking his way. He walked towards the man, swinging the umbrella. It's been a hell of a day, he thought. So give me a reason to hit you. Hell, an excuse will do.

He had almost closed the distance between them before he recognized Sherbina. The Russian dropped his arms as Chapel drew near. He was wearing a leather raincoat. It was hanging open, and his suit underneath was high-end sponge. His hair was flat and dripping over his skull. He looked like he'd been standing in the rain for hours. Chapel's lip curled. Lost your pretty-boy Nazi looks, he thought. But Sherbina didn't seem bothered. He cocked his head. His face was expressionless. Chapel thought about Zelkova's press conference, decided Sherbina was here to gloat. Chapel was glad. Korda wasn't here, but Sherbina would do fine. Chapel saw his duty and his satisfaction converge. "Think you're pretty clever, don't you?" he said.

Sherbina appeared to shrug with one shoulder. His sleeve rippled. His right hand had been empty. Now it held a crowbar. Chapel was only halfway to surprise when the bar broke his cheekbone. He staggered. Sherbina swung the crowbar in from the other side. Chapel felt his jaw go. Sherbina was two hard hits up. Chapel stepped into the next swing, cutting Sherbina's reach advantage. He brought his hands up in a double block, slamming Sherbina's arm at the wrist and elbow. Sherbina dropped the crowbar and danced to the side before Chapel could grab him. Chapel turned, following, slow and groggy. He jabbed at Sherbina's chin with the heel of his palm. Sherbina sidestepped, kicked from the side. Chapel's knee made a sick pop as it left its socket. His leg folded useless and he went over on his back. He lay with his legs on the sidewalk, his shoulders in the gutter, blocking the stream of rainwater. Chapel raised himself on his elbows. Sherbina looked at him for a moment, then picked up the crowbar. Chapel dragged himself back, had time to wonder what the hell he was hoping for before Sherbina broke both his arms. He slumped into the growing puddle. A car drove by, slowed down. Sherbina stared at it. The car sped up.

Sherbina walked around Chapel, tapping the crowbar into his palm. Then he started swinging again. Legs, ribs, hands, collarbone. Sherbina broke Chapel's anatomy down into shattered crockery. Chapel's senses began to shut down, individual pain clusters merging into a blanket of agony and darkness. Sherbina's boot smashed his nose flat. Chapel's vision grayed. Sherbina crouched down. Water dripped from his coat collar onto Chapel's face. Sherbina asked, "Am I making myself clear?" Then he stood up and went back to work.

Chapel lay in bad angles. He'd passed out before Sherbina had finished the second pass on the legs. Sherbina felt his pulse. Weak but steady. Blood bubbled at the corner of Chapel's mouth as he breathed. Sherbina poked at his body with the crowbar. Chapel was a bag of soft and moving fragments. Sherbina found a straight, unbroken line of bone in the left arm. He smashed it.

The ambulance arrived. The driver rolled down his

window. Sherbina eyed Chapel, crumpled in deepening water. "Keep track," Sherbina told the paramedic. "If it looks like he's going to die, load him up. Otherwise wait an hour." He walked away, tucking the crowbar back inside his raincoat. He hoped Chapel would appreciate the two great courtesies Sherbina was extending him. He was letting Chapel live. And he'd delivered the message in person. He hadn't delegated. He'd addressed Chapel as one commanding officer to another. More, he thought, than the man deserved. Sherbina stretched his neck. He felt better, some of the frustrations worked out of his system. He still had Baylor to find, that loose end to snip, but he'd communicated some of his displeasure to her master. He didn't know if Chapel was acting for Reed or on his own hook. If Chapel was taking orders, Sherbina didn't want him dead and replaced with a new, fresh player. He wanted fear and the lingering lessons of pain in the opposition's camp.

He splashed through puddles on the sidewalk. He thought about his father, felt the sharp message he'd been sent, didn't understand it. There was no angle but cruelty in killing him. Chapel taking a bit too much pleasure in sticking the knife to him? Maybe. He'd wait until Chapel was out of rehab, wait until he was sure the messages had been sent, received, and acknowledged, and that the squeeze play was dead. Then he'd kill Chapel.

He looked up, let the cold sting of the rain wash over his face. Time to finish the squeeze.

New York, six time zones earlier. Spring had sent a reconnaissance in force, courtesy of global warming, and the first short-sleeved day of the year had arrived. Angie

Dunn killed time before her evening class at CUNY. She sat on a bench in Washington Square, grabbing every second of the sun. "I'm toast," Pauline Jerden said. One hundred and thirty-second time today.

"You're not," Angie told her, for the hundred and thirty-first time. If she'd been quicker off the mark for the first, Pauline might have let it go. Problem was, Pauline was right. But she was the one who'd been stupid enough to choose Calculus as her science credit to complete her BA. Her marks were going flatline. That was Angie's fault? No. But someone had died and made her Pauline's perpetual crying shoulder.

"What am I going to do?"

Try studying for a change, Angie wanted to say. Wanted to. Couldn't. Pauline screwed herself, boring as clockwork. She didn't study, then she whined. Drove Angie nuts. She had her own exams coming up. But. Pauline was a friend. Suck it back, Angie, and don't let the impatience show. "Have you thought about a tutor?" Offering the constructive suggestion. Like Pauline was even listening.

She wasn't. "Isn't that your brother?" she asked.

"Yeah." She thought freshman Jake had headed home hours ago. He was walking towards them. Three men, big, in tailored overcoats, followed.

"Hey," he said. His voice cracked. He looked pale. "These guys say Mom and Dad want us to go with them."

"Bullshit."

Jake's eyes widened. "Angie," he begged. Angie felt her mouth dry very fast. The men didn't say anything.

"I'm not going anywhere," Angie said. Already she heard pleading in her voice. "I have a class."

One of the men took her by the arm and hauled her up off the bench. "So miss it," he said.

"What the hell do you guys think you're doing?" Pauline demanded. She stood up, spitting New York fire. Angie remembered why they were friends.

The man in the middle, the one with scars all over his nose, pulled a gun out. In the open, in public, the most natural gesture in the world. "We're doing our job," he said. He had a bad voice. "Siddown."

Pauline sat down.

Blaylock prowled, probing for weaknesses. Sherbina had thrown up steel-mesh security around the Wilson. The Kornukopia soldiers were dressed in civvies but still had a stormtrooper arrogance that set them apart from the legit tourists. They were everywhere. She couldn't approach any closer than the lake side of the street without running into goons on hair-trigger alert. She thought about an assault, pictured bystanders scythed like wheat in the crossfire, and remained in the night's shadows. She couldn't just saunter in. She was known now. Christmas would come early to the man who brought her down.

She moved north up the Quai Wilson, toward the Parc Mon Repos. She leaned against a tree, pulled a scope from her pocket. How do you storm the castle, girl? How do you reach Dunn? She trained the scope on the top floor of the hotel, looked for Dunn's room window. The lights were on, the curtains drawn. She discarded the idea of attempting a climb. Too visible, and the facade of the new wing was sheer glass and steel. Not a chance.

Shadows going back and forth behind the curtains. The movements were quick, some frantic. There were more than two people in the room. Had news of Garnett made it to Dunn? Was she seeing panic?

The lights went out.

"Shit," Blaylock whispered. The laws of unintended consequences weighed heavy. She kept watching the hotel. Blaylock at bay, feeling a lost opportunity slip further and further away. Blaylock in the dark, all information cut off.

Then the information came, and it was bad. Cars pulled away from the Wilson. The parade passed her by, a bulletproof phalanx, and *Who, girl, do you think is in that limo in the center?* She turned her head, saw Sherbina's communications mast blinking its light, winking at her. She watched her targets disappear in the direction of Fortress Kornukopia.

29

The first part was easy. She knew she was heading for big obstacles. Because of them, she felt a premonition. She felt the fluttering twinge in her gut, the anticipatory recoil from further filth. No good decisions ahead. Nothing but damnation, accumulating wide and deep. Deal with it, she thought. Live with it. (Rising from her core, the suspicion that what she was feeling wasn't revulsion, but excitement. More war. *Are we having fun yet?*)

But the first part was easy. One-stop shopping at an Internet café, where she Googled the Kornukopia complex. Plenty of hits, most of them outdated Web sites still trumpeting the grand opening and advertising the concert. Blaylock made her way through four pages of search results before she found what she wanted. The general contractor for the complex was S. Farquet et Associés. The firm had an address on the Rue du Rhône. Right at hand.

The Rue du Rhône, on the Left Bank, ran in a straight line one block off the riverfront. The streets leading off it went uphill, into the Old Town. The Rue du Rhône was modern Geneva, big money Geneva. The shopping was expensive. The jewelers were top-flight. And the bank buildings weren't anonymous. None were over eight storys high, and they weren't the futuristic Jetsons fantasies of Shanghai or Hong Kong, but they didn't mutter their names in little door plaques, either. They shouted their presence in neon rooftop signs. The facades, though, returned to discretion with windows tinted amber, tinted black, tinted mirror. The Farquet offices were in the block that belonged to the International Bank of Commerce and Industry, another Kornukopia fiefdom. Just before four, Blaylock, dressed executive, toting briefcase, marched into the building and took the elevator to the seventh floor. She received a few odd looks. Her face had healed, but the scarring was there. She knew she didn't look like she spent her days captaining Power Point presentations. She returned the stares, walloping back with authority. The curious turned back to watching the floor numbers climb.

The doors to Farquet et Associés were clear glass. She walked down the hall towards them, wondered about an alternative course of action, saw none, and pushed through into the reception area. The room was large, with float-mounted paintings of Farquet projects on the walls. The secretary's desk was a vast, circular island in the middle of the muted brown carpet. The woman was middle-aged. There were drafting-table lines to her clothing and her hairdo. She had a nice smile for Blaylock. Blaylock said goodbye to the easy part.

Zelkova pulled into the drive. Back home and fed up to here. Today had been worse than useless. Diplomacy and negotiations had screeched to a halt as the Appellate Body train wreck unfolded. She might as well have stayed home and taken up performance art for all the headway she'd made today. The phone was ringing as she walked into the house, and it was Sherbina with a request that made her angry: "Would you come to the complex?"

"Why?" she demanded.

"To stay."

"You will not pull us into your war."

"Other people might. I have untrustworthy partners. Someone pulled my father in. I want you to be safe."

"Stepan, I'm not going to live in your high-tech cage."

"Please, just for a little while. Just until this is over."

"You keep promising that things will soon be over."

"Please." There was frustration in his voice, and more, a tremor. But he was still asking. She knew he wouldn't force her. Then he played a trump. "Think of Inna."

"Bastard," she said, and hung up. She watched her daughter arrange her farm. Grimson was absently rolling a sheep around in her palm. She was looking at Zelkova. *Bastard,* Zelkova thought. *Bastard. What have you done to us?*

Beyond the secretary's desk, there were closed office doors on the left and the right. The one on the left had a plaque that read *S. Farquet*. "I'm here to see Mr. Farquet," Blaylock said, speaking French.

The secretary's smile stayed put, but her eyebrows creased in the beginning of an apologetic frown. "Mr. Farquet doesn't have appointments today."

Blaylock gave her a curt nod and a haughty gaze. *Placate me, lady. I'm difficult.* "I'm sure he doesn't. But I'm here on behalf of Irina Zelkova."

The bluff worked. The secretary was on her feet, face a clash of pleasure and alarm. "Of course," she said. "Please come this way." She led Blaylock to the left-hand door. She knocked twice, paused two seconds, and opened the door. "Someone from Ms Zelkova," she said, ushering Blaylock in.

S. Farquet was a small, round man in his early sixties. His white hair was a monk's fringe around his bald dome. His mustache and goatee were precision-trimmed. His skin was deeply tanned leather, but uncreased. He bounced up and around his desk, hand out, beaming. His smile was shy, but his "How do you do?" boomed. Blaylock shook his hand, which pumped up and down like a squirrel's heartbeat. "Won't you sit down?" he asked, but Blaylock turned to the secretary.

"Please stay," Blaylock said, and steered the woman into the chair Farquet had offered her. The secretary and Farquet paused, nonplussed by broken protocol. Blaylock shut the office door, locked it. "I really am very sorry," she said, and meant it. She pulled out her SIG.

Make yourselves at home. Feel free to explore.

Home was more sterile luxury. The apartment was deep inside Kornukopia One. It was furnished. Living room, two bedrooms (one with a king bed, the other with two twins), kitchenette. The look of the place was pure showroom, the furniture smelling of fresh-from-the-box, the carpet still outgassing. All the lines were sleek and tasteful. There was art on the walls, abstract blendings of pastel colors crossed by bold black slashes of phony ideograms. The paintings didn't stand out. They set off the walls. They were esthetics become functional. The suite had all the individuality of a tongue depressor. There were no windows.

Make yourselves at home. Feel free to explore.

At 11:35 a.m., Lawrence Dunn saw his entire family in one room for the first time since leaving New York. Sherbina sauntered into the quarters assigned to Dunn and Linda. He had his arms around the shoulders of Angie and Jake. Dunn's children, old enough to vote, didn't look like adults. They were wide-eyed little children who had been snatched by the boogeyman. "Look who's here!" Sherbina crowed. "Isn't this just the most delicious surprise? No? Of course it is." He ruffled Jake's hair. "I said to myself that here is a family that has been too long apart. Surely they've been worried about each other. Well, worry no more! Here you are, all together, safe and snug as bugs in rugs." He laughed, but Dunn thought his laugh sounded more forced than usual. Sherbina's expansive good humor was an act. The performance was strained, hit harsh notes. His eyes were sunken. He looked twitchy. He looked like a wounded animal. He frightened Dunn more than ever.

Linda rushed forward, arms open for her children. She jerked to a stop when Sherbina's grip on their shoulders tightened. Angie winced. Linda begged, "What do you want from us?"

Eyes cold, a serpent's warning. For a moment, his face was ugly determination and desperate anger. Then the mask was back in place, and the theater continued. "I want nothing but safety and comfort for you and yours, dear lady. And we do have to protect your husband from outside, hostile forces, don't we? Yes, we do. After all, he's going to make the world a better place. Yes, he is. Yes, he is." He gave Angie a peck on the cheek. "There you go, now." He pushed her and Jake toward Linda. "I'll be off now, but if you need anything, anything at all, don't hesitate to ask. Make yourselves at home. Feel free to explore." He walked out, leaving the door open. An obvious invitation. A rigid middle finger.

Dunn turned to his family. Linda was hugging the children. Jake had a good six inches on his mother, but seemed shrunken, in desperate need of her arm. Angie had her head buried against Linda's shoulder. Linda was crying. She stopped when she looked up at Dunn. Her eyes were exhausted, red, drained by fear. But when they turned to him, they were angry. They accused. They were right. He still sought their absolution. "I never wanted any of this," he said.

"I know you didn't." Her voice was actually gentle.

"Can you forgive me?" Daring to hope.

"No." Still gentle. That made the word worse, final. And she hadn't had to think before answering. She went on. "Not because this is happening to us. Because of why it is."

Not because of who he was, he understood. Not because Lawrence Dunn, voice of the rigorous left, was useful as reverse Trojan horse in the bosom of the WTO. But because he had made himself vulnerable. He had placed all their lives on the roulette table, and pretended that the House didn't always win. Now the House had swallowed them up. "I'm sorry," he said, a meaningless plea.

Linda exiled him. "Go on. Do what he said. Make yourself at home."

He fled her bitterness. His guilt stayed with him as he walked. He began to take corridors at random. He fantasized about finding a way out, of redemption through escape. He also fantasized about becoming lost, shaking his guilt and disappearing forever into the convolutions of the horn of plenty. The complex trashed his fantasies.

He couldn't lose his way. There were YOU ARE HERE diagrams, color-coded by building, at every elevator and major corridor intersection. There were EXIT signs on the ceilings, always pointing the way to doors he knew he would never use. He tried shifting fantasies. He imagined finding someone who would help.

He wouldn't find anyone near the living quarters. His family had been put in one of four private apartments at the heart of the Security dome. Everybody he passed in the halls here was hard, uniformed, armed.

He followed the diagrams and worked his way through the corridors. The hallways in the Security center were functional white, with not a single fern to obscure sightlines. The moment he crossed over into the second level of the Administration dome, he was in the land of executive luxury. The floors were marble. The lighting was art deco. There were Old Masters on the walls. Some of them were genuine. Bread and circuses, Dunn thought. Sherbina's keeping the suckers happy. The scheme was transparent. The scheme worked. WTO bureaucrats everywhere, some fully operational, some still unpacking stacks of banker's boxes, and so many of them smiling. There was a lightness to their steps that Dunn tagged as the product as much of the complex's esthetics as its Alcatraz security. His own steps dragged. Every office he passed, every cubicle area he crossed, was another symbol of Sherbina's tightening grip. He owned every person in the building, and they didn't even know it.

They could leave, though. They had homes on the outside. Dunn watched them with an envy that bordered on hatred. Sherbina had them in his fist, but at least they couldn't feel the squeeze.

Someone tapped his shoulder. Dunn whirled. Eddie

Lenehan backed off, grinning, hands up. "Whoa! Jumpy," he said. Dunn relaxed. He'd known Lenehan since college. Lenehan had been the crown prince of slackers, cruising through each course with the minimum of attendance and sweat. Exertion was a mortal sin, and Lenehan's goal, it had seemed to Dunn, was to achieve the exertion-free life. A university education was the easiest means to that end. Dunn had run into Lenehan off and on over the years since, and he had seen a man happily living a fulfilled dream. Lenehan existed somewhere in the depths of the WTO bureaucracy. Dunn couldn't think of him as *working*. He didn't know what, exactly, Lenehan's job description was, or if he even had one. He more than suspected that no one else knew, either. Dunn had run into Lenehan at JFK a decade earlier, and Lenehan had told him he was off to Geneva. He'd been in the same post ever since. If Lenehan stuck with something for ten years, then the something made no demands on him. Lenehan's curly hair, an electrocuted mop in college, was graying and tamed by trimming. His face was still unlined, Buddha-happy. The world was his oyster, shelled and served on a cracker. "So what brings Mr. Media to these parts?" Lenehan asked.

Dunn's mouth hung open for a second as he searched for the safe answer. "I'm staying here for a few days."

"Really? That's great. What do you think of our new digs?"

"They're impressive."

"Impressive is the word." Lenehan patted his stomach, which had expanded again since Dunn had last seen him. "And speaking of impressive, seen the cafeteria yet? Just on my way over for lunch." Dunn nodded and accompanied him, an idea forming.

Farquet and his secretary huddled at the far corner of the office, Medusa-frozen with terror. The wall safe hung open, its prize plundered. Blaylock studied the blueprints spread out on Farquet's desk. Everything was there: architectural, electrical, and mechanical plans, Sherbina's fortress anatomized and open to her gaze. She studied the domes clockwise, working through Administration, Security, Conference, Recreation, and Support, then moving to the center, the heart, the physical plant under the telecom mast. She asked herself where she would stash Dunn. There were apartments in both the Security and Conference domes. Blaylock liked the odds for Security. There were a few other things she liked, too. She liked the links between the domes at the basement level. Lots of straight lines there, lots of fast connections, and the tunnels looked wide enough for vehicles. She liked the maze of tiny passageways that honeycombed the interior walls of the complex. Secret routes for the lord of the manor, she guessed. Her antennae twitched at the huge storage spaces in the Support dome. The biggest were underground. All of them were barred by triple levels of security. When she asked Farquet what these areas were for, he said he didn't know. She believed him.

She also liked the feeling that was building in her chest.

Lenehan waxed on about the glories of Kornukopia One. You could take the boy out of the frat, but never the frat out of Lenehan. His enthusiasm for the cool was the one high-energy corner of his life. He led Dunn through the Administration and Support Services domes. When they reached Support, the decor shifted to bare concrete.

Dunn's nose tickled with the disinfectant smell of total utilitarianism.

Dunn said, "Bit of a walk." They went past another Kornukopia soldier. Dunn was becoming good at spotting them. Even when they weren't in uniform, they were men who were watching, alert, and not thinking about meetings or paperwork. The uniformed guards had side guns. The others wore suits loose enough to conceal shoulder holsters. Out in the open or camouflaged, they were Sherbina's eyes and claws, and they were everywhere. Dunn didn't think he'd gone a single corridor without seeing at least one.

"You said it. You'd think there would be a faster way of traveling from place to place here, but . . ." Lenehan sighed. "No perfect place in this world."

"Isn't there anywhere to eat in your building?" He was grappling with the idea of Lenehan walking out of his way for anything, even lunch.

"Sure there is. Some smaller cafeterias, and they're not bad. But the main joint . . . I'm telling you, the novelty hasn't worn off yet."

If Administration was luxury, Recreation was exuberance. The interior design wasn't loud. Instead, there was greenery everywhere, and the spaces were gigantic. Dunn and Lenehan entered on the second level. The central aisle led to an elevator bank. On the right, Dunn saw squash courts. On the left, tennis. The hollow smack of balls and squeak of gym shoes echoed off the glass walls and the high ceiling. A model work environment. Dunn imagined he heard Sherbina laughing. "I bet you spend a lot of your time here," he said to Lenehan.

Big snort and a slap on the gut. "Absolutely. Always working to stay in shape," Lenehan scoffed in happy self-contempt. "You know what I *have* checked out here? The art gallery."

"The— ?"

"I'm not kidding. Top level." He pointed up. Dunn saw that the central portion of the ceiling was clear glass. A statue's pedestal rested in the center. People walked overhead in the slow stop-start stroll of museums. "Bad place to wear a skirt," Lenehan grinned. "Anyway, there's a big display right now of Soviet propaganda art. Hilarious stuff."

Dunn could just imagine. I'm halfway to laughing already, he thought, bitter. The complex wasn't just a fortress, and it wasn't just a prison for him and the WTO and everything they touched. It was also a monument to Sherbina's sense of humor.

They took the elevator down to the ground floor. Lenehan kept referring to the place they stepped into as the *cafeteria*, and Dunn supposed that, in the broadest sense of the word, that's what it was. They had to fetch trays, and they had to line up to place their orders. But the food wasn't hamburgers or congealed lasagna. Lenehan had a rack of lamb. The lighting was diffused natural, with tea lights at each table. Pillars ten feet thick and disguised as trees rose to the high ceiling. They broke up the space into smaller, more intimate quadrants.

Dunn poked a fork at his salad. He wasn't hungry. He was working on strategy. "You living here, too?" he asked, making his opening move.

Lenehan's face went dreamy. "And have no commute at all? Wouldn't that be sweet. But no." He shook his head. "Very restricted living quarters here. I have a place on the Right Bank. Bus service is pretty good." He pointed a finger at Dunn. "You, my man, must rate like God on somebody's list to score accommodation."

Dunn tried to smile. Hope stirred. Lenehan lived outside. Could he be trusted? Was there a choice? He looked around. They were seated one table over from a pillar. The closest diners were the same distance away, out of earshot, if he lowered his voice. Conversation's white noise gave him further cover. He cleared his throat. "Eddie," he said, "I need your help."

"Done and done. What with?" Lenehan's eyebrows arched suddenly. He laughed a startled bark. "Holy shit, how'd you do that?" he asked, but he wasn't speaking to Dunn. His attention was focused on a point above and behind Dunn's head. Dunn twisted around in his seat.

Sherbina was there in affable divinity. He patted Dunn's shoulder. "Thought I'd see how you're settling in. You *are* settling, aren't you? Making yourself at home? Good, good. And your charming family safe and sound? Glad to hear it." He chucked Dunn's chin. "Stay out of trouble, now." He winked, gave Lenehan a hail-fellow grin, and walked away. He disappeared behind the pillar. Dunn waited for him to reappear on the other side. He didn't.

"Never met the top dog before," Lenehan commented. "Seems all right. So what did you need help with?"

"Nothing," Dunn whispered, sinking fast.

Blaylock stared at the security specs. Cameras, with conventional thermographic imaging lenses, trained down every corridor. Carbon dioxide, motion, and floor-tile pressure sensors. Once she was in, she'd be found quickly. She'd have to accept that. She needed a counterattack. And she still needed a way in. She went back to the floor plans. She looked a long time at the underground parkade. She saw what she had to do, and she lost some of her glee. She began to feel sick, so she turned again to the schematic she liked the best, the one for the physical plant. She saw Kornukopia One open up to her, a blossom to be torn apart. Guilt and anger fell away before the purity of war. In the euphoria of inspiration, she realized that filth was just another medium, another tool for the artist.

She opened her briefcase, removed a long coil of rope, replaced it with the collected blueprints. She turned to Farquet and the secretary. They shrank away from her as she approached. "Listen to me," she said as she bound and gagged them. "This is the worst that's going to happen to you. Sit here quietly, and you'll have an uncomfortable night, but tomorrow morning, when the building reopens, someone will rescue you. And you'll never see me again. If you try to leave or contact anyone before then, you *will* see me again." She disabled the phone and the intercom, searched the office for cellphones. Then she left.

Flanagan, favoring his wounded hand, was struggling into his shirt with Grimson's help when Blaylock walked into his hospital room. She and Grimson faced each other. They didn't speak, but their body language became taut. "Going somewhere?" Blaylock asked Flanagan.

Grimson said, "Irina told me to bring him home once he was discharged."

"You're still staying with her?" When Grimson nodded, dagger-sharp worry passed over Blaylock's face, but then vanished, submerged by the expression she had worn when she'd arrived. Her eyes glittered, both feral and machine, and Flanagan thought of the being he'd seen her become at Ember Lake. "That's okay," Blaylock said. "I need his help."

Grimson asked, "And not mine?"

Pause. "You'd help me?"

"To save you from yourself."

Crooked smile. "That's sweet, Kelly." Blaylock stepped past her and embraced Flanagan. She kissed him. She looked into his eyes. Beyond the shine of meshing gears, Flanagan saw twin pains of hope and regret. Then she whispered in his ear, and he couldn't see her face as she asked, "Are you ready to do a bad thing?"

30

Weapons in the hatchback. Flanagan in the passenger seat beside her. On her way to complete her damnation. She felt good.

Angie said, "I want to show you something."

Jake swung his legs up off his bed. "What is it?"

Angie held a finger to her lips and led him out of their room. Mom was asleep in her bedroom. She'd turned in very early, Angie thought, but without windows time was academic. Her own body clock was still on New York time, and there were no visual cues to help her reset. Dad had come back from wandering the halls and was motionless in front of the TV. He had CNN on, but Angie didn't he think he was really watching. He was too still, too slumped. The silence between her parents felt like steel cable. She'd fled the silence earlier. She'd felt like she'd slipped from undergrad to kindergarten, infantilized by fear and the Jericho crumble of a marriage. She'd done her own random walkabout of Kornukopia One's warren. That was when she'd seen it.

She took Jake down to the basement level. The corridors were tunnels here, wide as two-lane highways. Maintenance buggies barreled along. They looked like armored golf carts. "Are we supposed to be down here?" Jake asked. He stayed close to the wall. A buggy breezed past them. There were three security guards in the passenger seats. They carried assault rifles. They glanced his and Angie's way, but didn't say anything.

"Nobody cares," Angie answered. "They don't think we're going anywhere."

Jake picked up on the implication. "You mean we are?"

"Check this out."

Arrowed exit signs were posted at every intersection. Angie followed them. The paved floor sloped up to the wall of the dome and a massive door. "We're not leaving that way," Jake commented. The hydraulics were thick enough to be medieval.

"I know," Angie said. "Not that way." She took a tunnel that ran parallel to the perimeter of the dome. She walked a dozen yards, then stopped. There was a narrow passageway running between two series of storage units.

"You want us to go in there," Jake said. "Hell, no. You stoned?"

"It's okay. I've already been."

"What were you thinking?"

"There was a light on in there. It burned out just as I was walking past. That's what made me look."

"Outta your mind, Nancy Drew."

There was no one around. "Come on." She tugged at his arm and hauled him in. The passage was barely three feet across. It ended at a set of stairs. At the top of the flight was a door.

"You're going to set off an alarm," said Jake.

"I don't think so. Look." She pressed against the door itself instead of the crossbar. The door swung open.

"Unlocked." Light spilled from the other side. Beyond the door was another flight of stairs.

"Where does that go?"

"I haven't been any further than this."

Jake looked back over his shoulder. They were still alone. "So we doing this?"

They took the stairs, and reached a landing with another door. "Feels like ground level," Angie said. She tried the door. It was open, too. She and Jake breathed fresh air. It was dusk. The sky was overcast, and the gardens were gray and indistinct. The exterior lights hadn't switched on yet. Angie could hear the sounds of traffic. "What do you think?" she asked.

"We're still a long way from the exit."

"We have to try. We have to find help."

"These guys have guns, Ange."

"So stay," she said, and she started to run. She didn't look back. She hoped he was right behind her. She didn't want to do this alone. She tore down the paths, past the trimmed hedges, past geometric greenery, blasted for the finishing line of the berm. She felt wind against her cheek. She felt fear like bile in her throat. She felt wings.

A giant firecracker went off and she slammed to the ground. She tried to stand, but her left leg wouldn't work. Her mind said, *Popped. Popped. Something popped.* The pain hit then, and she yelled. She twisted onto her back, looked down at her leg, saw a dark stain spreading just below her knee. The pain was a wrecking ball. She sobbed. Two guards emerged from the topiary. One of them cradled his rifle. They stood over her. The one with the rifle said something in Russian to the other. The second man shrugged, pulled out his wallet, and handed the first man some bills.

Weapons in the hatchback. Flanagan could hear them clunk, hear the shifting of metal weight as the road hairpinned higher into the mountains, could sense the car riding low. Lots of weapons. Heavy ones. Beyond that, he didn't know. Blaylock had been to her cache and loaded up before hitting the hospital. He didn't know what they were going to do, either. He didn't know what the bad thing was. When he asked, Blaylock just gave him a tight-lipped grin. At least, he thought it was a grin. It might have been a grimace. Somehow, it also had forward momentum. Like a tank. He eyed the scattering of parkade receipts between the seats. The Fiat was full of commuting debris. "I take it this isn't a rental," he said.

"Call it an overnight loan." Blaylock turned off onto a smaller road. Its incline was steep. "In case the worst happens, I left a big damage deposit on her desk. She'll be able to buy herself a new one."

"Won't she be needing her car tonight?" He didn't think he should ask who the she was.

"No."

They climbed higher.

They threw Jake into the apartment. Dunn jumped up from the couch. He had time to see the stricken face of his son. Then he was frogmarched out of the suite.

The infirmary was on the lower level of the Security dome, built around the central elevator bank. The rooms here were a blinding antiseptic white. The guards took Dunn through a big operating theater. Some of the tables frightened him. They were stainless steel, had gutters and a drain. They looked more like autopsy than operating tables. And they had manacles.

Sherbina was waiting with his Goebbels smile at the doorway to a bedroom. He dismissed the guards and beckoned Dunn inside. Angie was lying in the bed. A woman was wrapping her leg in surgical bandages. "She'll need a cast," the woman said. She sounded pleased.

"Thank you, Dr. Sourial," Sherbina said. Sourial nodded, finished the binding, and left.

Dunn ran to Angie's side. Her face was tear-streaked. "I'm sorry, Dad. I tried to run."

"That's my girl," Dunn said.

Sherbina moved to the other side of the bed and crouched down, his head level with Angie and Dunn's. "Such a brave girl," he said softly. He stroked Angie's cheek with a finger. She jerked away. "I wonder," Sherbina went on, "if the right lessons have been learned this evening." His face became a caricature of friendly concern. "Did you know, for instance, that there was a betting pool around when Angie would take the bait of that exit? Did you know that? Did you know, for instance, that there was a reason for that bait? Did you? And did you know that the reason was punishment?" He cocked his head.

"Punishment," Dunn repeated in a whisper. "I don't understand."

"You were going to say something to Mr. Lenehan."

"But I didn't!"

"Thoughtcrime, old man, is still a crime. Do remember my training." Sherbina stood up. "Next time you harbor the wrong thoughts, there will be a death in the family."

It wasn't what Sherbina said that frightened Dunn the most. It was the disconnect between his tone and his face. The tone was still Sherbina's perpetual happy menace. His face, though, had gone cold. His left cheek twitched, once. Buried beneath the permafrost, Dunn saw deposits of hate and rage that had nothing to do with profits, control, or the WTO. Sherbina wanted him to make a mistake. He wanted the excuse. He wanted to hit and hurt, and Dunn was the target at hand. *He's going to kill them,* Dunn realized. *Even if I do everything he wants, he's going to kill my children.* He remembered the clipping about the murder of Sherbina's father. *Bitch,* he thought. *You goddamned bitch. You wanted to frighten me. Great. I'm frightened. This psycho is going to kill my family because of you.*

"And you, little missy," Sherbina said to Angie. "If you even think of being a bad girl again, you're going to wish you'd been shot in the head." He gave her nose a playful tweak. He came around the bed and hooked a hand under Dunn's shoulder. "Come with me." He hauled Dunn out of the room. "Let's make sure the lesson sinks in, shall we?" He pushed Dunn through the door of the next room down.

For a moment Dunn didn't know what he was seeing. A cat's cradle of pulleys, cables, and IV tubes clustered around something in the bed. The pieces came together, and he was looking at a man. He was in traction, plaster turning him into a reclining Henry Moore statue.

"Go on," Sherbina said, when Dunn hesitated. "Say hello. You gentlemen aren't strangers, after all."

Dunn stepped forward. The man's face was uncovered. It was a huge mass of purple contusions. It looked like it had been pounded with a meat tenderizer and then run over by a bulldozer. The eyes, still gray weaponry, were what told Dunn this was Joe Chapel. "Christ," Dunn whispered.

Sherbina busied himself at a countertop. "So you see," he said, casual, just passing the time of day, "you don't need to worry about divided loyalties. I'm looking out for your interests, old man, simplifying your life for you. I realize that the chain of command was not clear, and you were receiving conflicting orders. But now my competition is here, and I'll be bringing his superbitch to heel very soon, never you fear." He turned away from the counter. He was holding a steel bar. It sparkled under the fluorescent lights. He spoke to Chapel's eyes, "Don't worry. Sterilized." He brought the bar down on Chapel's left arm, smashing through plaster to break more bone. Chapel screamed. "There," Sherbina said to Dunn. "No more ambiguities."

Blaylock stopped the car. They were on a gravel road that meandered past chalets and goat farms. On the left, the mountain continued to slope up. On the right, the drop was vertical. "Wait here," she said, and opened the door. Flanagan watched her. She stood at the side of the road and looked down. Then she moved to the rear of the car. Hatchback up, scary metal *snick-snack,* hatchback down. "Okay," Blaylock said. Flanagan climbed out of the car. She handed him a rifle.

"Um," Flanagan said.

"You said you were ready to do a bad thing."

Images of blood on his apartment walls. Self-defense had been bad enough. There was no one trying to kill him here. And he was standing on very high ground. Like a sniper. He felt a new kind of dread. Then he thought about the Coscarelli warehouse. He remembered the thrill. He looked at Blaylock, at her face that was suddenly the erotic beauty of war. Dread met anticipation. Dread was shoved down. "Yes," he said.

"Good." She showed him how to operate the safety. "It's already loaded," she said. "You have more bullets than you'll need."

"What am I going to do?"

She brought him to the cliff edge. They had a bird-of-prey view of the valley. Several hundred feet down was the ribbon of the road to Geneva. At the foot of the mountain opposite was a giant chalet. "In a little while, you'll see me down there," she pointed at the road.

"How long is *a little while*?" Flanagan asked. "It's almost dark." The landscape's features were blending with each other. Flanagan could make only coarse distinctions: mountain, road, house. Night was on its way, and without so much as moonlight, he wouldn't be able to see a damn thing.

"Can't say exactly. But a car will stop for me. Watch for the headlights." She told him the bad thing he would do. "See?" she finished. "Easy." Then she climbed back into the Fiat and drove off.

The ride back to Zelkova's home was an act of faith. It was the first time Grimson had made the trip on her own. After Blaylock had left the hospital with Flanagan, Grimson had taken ten minutes to work up the courage to sit in the back seat of the car Zelkova had placed at her disposal. Zelkova had introduced her to the driver, a sixty-five-year-old named Henri. The man's eyes were kind. Zelkova's protection didn't depend on her physical presence. Still. Anyone who worked for Zelkova, by extension, also worked for Sherbina. Five minutes went by before she could open the rear door without shaking.

Henri kept up small chatter all the way. His English

was rough, his accent was thick, and his collection of grandchildren anecdotes was inexhaustible. He didn't pull a gun. He didn't take Grimson back to the Kornukopia clinic. He drove her home, pulled up to the front door, tipped his hat, and patted Grimson's hand. The door of the house opened and the staff, cut loose for the day, descended the steps. They waited for Grimson to leave the car so they could climb in. Grimson watched the tail lights pull away, and waited for her stomach to settle. I just visited the big bad world and came back, she thought. All by my little own self.

Zelkova was sitting with Inna in front of the TV. There was a cartoon on, something Japanese with big-eyed princesses, ponies, and robots. Inna was rapt. Zelkova looked up as Grimson walked into the living room. "You're alone?" she asked.

"Mike didn't want to come."

"Why not?"

She didn't know. She didn't want to know. She didn't know what to say. She didn't know which friendship to betray.

Blaylock completed the assembly. She looked through the M64 optical sight. The tritium filling boosted the visibility. She liked her range. She liked the set-up. When she saw the staff leave for the evening, she was ready for her damnation.

Flanagan waited. He played with the binoculars while there was still enough light to see anything. He saw a car pull up the drive of the mansion. He trained the binoculars on the house. He saw Grimson go inside. Puzzled, he scanned the landscape for Blaylock. He found her on an outcropping to the left and halfway down between his position and the road. She was adjusting something. He stared at the bipod and tube. One of the items on Blaylock's shopping list leaped from catalog number to metal reality: an M224 60mm mortar. Flanagan's jaw sagged in horror. Blaylock dropped a round down the tube. There was a hollow *foomp*. Flanagan screamed as the round arced toward the mansion.

31

Grimson heard the whistle. Instinct and training dropped her to the floor. The seconds stretched, and suddenly she had all the time in the world. She had time to think she was being silly, that she couldn't really be hearing this, that she was making a mistake. She had time to see Zelkova and Inna frozen, staring at her more puzzled than scared. She had time to yell, "*Down!*"

No more time. She wasn't silly, everything was true, and everything was wrong, and she heard the concussive blast of a high explosive mortar round hitting somewhere behind the house. Inna screamed. Zelkova threw her arms around her and hugged her against her chest. Now Zelkova looked frightened. Her eyes strained wide with panic and incomprehension. Grimson ran through the living room and kitchen. She looked out the back windows. The garden was a green meadow that sloped uphill, turning into forest as it met the mountain face. A small crater smoked at the far end of the property. Trees were down and burning. Another whistle. Grimson ducked. The HE slammed to earth, splintering pines. Dirt flew high. Clods smacked against the window. The hit was a good ten feet closer to the house than the first impact.

"*Out!*" Grimson roared. She tore back to the front of

the house. "*Out out out!*" Zelkova didn't move. She blinked at Grimson and couldn't compute. Grimson snatched Inna from her arms. Inna howled. "Let's go!" Grimson started for the front door.

Whistle-shriek. *Wham.* The house shook. Glass shattered. Zelkova jumped up and followed. They ran down the steps to the Alfa Romeo. They piled in. There was a pause in the bombardment. Zelkova started the car. "Go," Grimson said. "Go go go go go." They pulled away. Still no blast. Grimson wondered if the attackers had shot their load and were running. The incoming scream answered her. The explosion took out the peak of the roof. The front windows of the house blew out. Zelkova stomped on the accelerator. She jerked the stick shift, ground gears, and the car stalled. She fumbled with the ignition, her lips a taut grimace against the end. Grimson held her breath, didn't rush her, waited for the inevitable, crushed Inna to her. The car started. Zelkova pleaded in Russian. The next round wailed in. The car leaped forward. The front of the house gouted flame. Zelkova careened down the drive, fishtailing as the tires spun for traction on the gravel. She reduced her speed, retook control, and sped up again. Another blast from behind. Grimson looked back as they hit the highway. More rounds rained down on the house. The facade fell in, taking the roof with it. A cloud of smoke and dust billowed up, obscuring the flames.

Blaylock saw the car haul ass from the destruction. The artillery strike had done its work. She watched the house burn and collapse. She was scale and claws. She was reptile. If she'd had a soul, she thought, it would have just evaporated. She picked up a backpack. As she shouldered it, she glanced up the mountainside in Flanagan's direction. She couldn't see him. She knew he'd seen what she'd done. *I missed on purpose*, she thought, answering the accusation she knew was in his eyes. *I know what I'm doing. I wouldn't hurt them.* The pyre of Zelkova's home called her a liar. The knowledge of what was coming next called her a liar. She shrugged, accepting the judgment. (War is hell. War is art. War is me.) She would face Flanagan's eyes when she would. What mattered was that he still carry out his orders.

She detached the M224 from the bipod, switched from drop-fire to trigger-fire, and loaded another round. She aimed at a spot on the slope a few yards up from the road and blew the alpenrose shrubs to hell. She dropped the mortar and scrambled down. She could hear the charging whine of Zelkova's motor drawing nearer. She stood between the crater and the road. She picked up a sharp rock.

Zelkova's hands were death-gripped on the steering wheel. "Phone," she said. Her voice was strangulated. "My husband. Speed dial 1."

There was a cell sitting on the dash. Grimson reached for it.

A wall phone began to beep. Sherbina sighed. Still holding the metal bar, he turned away to answer. Dunn stared at Chapel. His body was too tightly held in traction for him to writhe. All the pain was in his eyes, shocked wide by new agony.

Sherbina picked up the phone and said something in Russian. He sounded irritated. He listened, then spoke again. A question this time, puzzled. He switched into English. "What do you want?" Genuine confusion. Dunn watched, curious. He saw a new expression appear on Sherbina's face: panic. He dropped the bar. "Stay calm, all of you," he said, but his voice shook. "Tell her to get here as fast as she can." He hung up. He looked at Chapel with the purest hatred Dunn had ever seen. "I don't know how you arranged it," he said. "But you shouldn't have." He was trembling, murder held back only by the promise of torture. "You're going to live a long time," Sherbina said. "That's a promise." He bolted from the room.

Blaylock dragged the rock across her forehead. She gouged hard. She felt the blood pour, warm and spectacular. She lay down. After a minute, she saw the headlights.

Flanagan's throat hurt. He'd stopped yelling when he saw the car drive away from the flames. He kept thinking about what he'd seen through the binoculars. There was a child, he thought. I saw a child. She blew up a house her friend was in. That a child was in.

He tried to find Blaylock again, failed. It was now too dark to make anything out except the house's pyre. But there, coming up the road like a prophecy, was the car. Like she said, he thought now, like she said.

The car approached. Blaylock kept still. Blaylock wondered, Mike, will you do this thing? Will you know what it means if you do?

Flanagan broke into component parts. His eyes watched his hands raise the rifle. His stomach was a cold knot of horror. His blood and his heart pulsed with a filthy excitement.

"There's someone lying there." Grimson pointed. Zelkova slowed down. The explosion had scattered debris on the road. The vegetation was guttering and smoking hard. The headlights picked out the slumped body, turned it into a harsh play of light and swallowing shadow. "Looks like a woman. We have to help." Zelkova shot her a sharp, frightened look. "They've ceased firing," Grimson said, as if that meant something.

Zelkova stopped the car. Grimson knew she would. Neither of them would be able to look in a mirror again if they drove on. "Hurry," Zelkova said. She kept the car running.

Grimson scrambled out. She knelt beside the body and saw through the mask of blood. "Jen? Jesus Christ." She felt for broken bones. "Jen? Wake up!" She slapped Blaylock lightly. Blaylock groaned. Her eyes fluttered, but wouldn't stay open. "Wake up, wake up, *wake up!*" She hooked Blaylock under the arms and dragged her to the car.

Where is this going? The question formed through the broken glass in Flanagan's brain. What's she built and how does it end? Far be it from him to stand in the way of art. His fingers tightened. He fired.

Impact-whine of a bullet hitting the pavement and ricocheting off. *Crack* echo of the shot. Inna screamed. Grimson heaved Blaylock into the back seat. There was another shot. The bullet chipped road in front of the car. Grimson slammed the rear door shut and jumped into the passenger seat. Zelkova gunned the engine and tore up road.

Flanagan watched the Alfa's tail lights disappear. His heart rate slowed, but his parts didn't reassemble. They disappeared into anesthetizing limbo. Now what? The question floated in a numb sea. He stood, stupid, rifle drooping in his slack grip. Now what? He started walking, cruising on autopilot. He was halfway to Blaylock's mortar position before he knew what he was doing. He stared at the discarded tube for a solid minute. He realized he was standing on gravel. He had rejoined the access road on a lower switchback. He walked up-slope a few dozen yards, went around a curve of the mountainside, and found the Fiat. He looked inside. The keys dangled from the ignition. He climbed in, started the car, and drove off. By the time he was on the highway to Geneva, he was forming coherent thoughts again. He knew where he was going. The numbness was still there, flowing through his veins in the place of blood. It shielded him from the sharp edge of consequences. It held the guilt at bay.

Sherbina paced the circumference of the lounge in the telecom mast. He eyed the security updates. He'd ordered a sweep for any remaining WTO personnel. The last of them had been ejected from the site. He didn't want any potential foreign agents inside the complex. The fortress was secure. Everything in its place, all well with the world, and don't you believe it. The world was cracked and burning, and wouldn't be healed until his wife and child were held in Kornukopia One's embrace. He could be down in the command center, with every cell of the complex monitored in real time. He had enough sense not to be. Here he could burn nervous energy and sweat his fears in private. Doing the caged animal in the center would be bad for the troops, would be bad for him, would be weakness on display. The details of the complex were irrelevant. The problem wasn't within its walls. He left the lounge and stood on the platform, gripping the railing hard. He could see the illuminated grounds. He could see the lights of Geneva. He couldn't see beyond the city. He couldn't see his wife's car. He felt helpless, and promised end-times retaliation. He called Dmitry Karaganov on his headset. "When my wife arrives," he told the security chief, "you escort her in personally."

They were almost in Geneva before Blaylock stirred. She jerked taut, then flailed about, fighting demons, frightening Inna into tears. Grimson twisted around in her seat and held out a calming hand. She grasped Blaylock's knee. "Jen," she said. "It's okay. Jen. It's okay." She kept the mantra up. Blaylock thrashed. Her right backpack strap slipped off her arm and the bag shifted around to her lap. Blaylock slumped, muttering. Her eyes closed again.

"How badly is she hurt?" Zelkova asked.

"I can't tell in this light," Grimson answered. Blood covered Blaylock's face and soaked the front of her shirt. "Jen, can you hear me?" Blaylock grunted, muttered more nonsense. Grimson wasn't sure if she was responding to her question or not. "Who did this?" Grimson persisted. "Who was shooting at you?" Blaylock whispered hissing syllables and sank further down in the seat. She was almost on the floor. Inna pressed up against her door, as far from Blaylock as she could. Her eyes shimmered in the dark. Grimson could almost see the imprinting of trauma. "Don't be frightened," Grimson told her, and was amazed that she could bring herself to say such a thing. Your home has been destroyed. But don't be frightened.

"You remember Jen, don't you?" Zelkova offered. Her voice was forced bright, brittle casual. Grimson glanced at her. She didn't look in the rear-view mirror at her daughter. She had her eyes laser-locked on the road ahead. She still tried to comfort. "She came to dinner once."

Blaylock's hand twitched. Inna jumped. Grimson worried. "We need a hospital," she said.

"There's a clinic at the complex," said Zelkova.

Grimson let go of Blaylock's knee and faced forward again. She could see the telecom mast ahead. They were nearly at Kornukopia One. Her stomach clenched at the thought of going inside. It was where the WTO had run to hide. It was Sherbina's baby. She was sure her own child had died for its cause.

"What was she doing in the mountains?" Zelkova asked.

A good question. Blaylock and explosions together were never coincidences. Was she chasing war, or had she somehow brought it to Zelkova? "I don't know," Grimson answered.

"You're her friend. Have you spoken to her recently? Do you know what story she was working on? Do you think she knew what was going to happen?" The questions tumbled out, bang bang bang, with no pause for Grimson's reply. Zelkova was thinking out loud, fumbling for reasons why the sky had tried to kill her daughter, straw-grasping in a bid to re-establish causality.

Grimson owed her truth. "She isn't a journalist," she said.

Zelkova said nothing. She shook her head, confused. Then they were at the Kornukopia One entrance. Zelkova turned hard left across the highway. The gate was already up and waiting. Guards stood on either side, AKs at ready. They didn't look at the car as it barreled in. They were watching the road for pursuit. Grimson glanced back and saw the gate come down. We're safe, she thought. I'm trapped, she thought.

Zelkova barely slowed. She wouldn't believe in safety, Grimson realized, until the fortress walls surrounded her and held her family safe from artillery. She turned right at the Administration dome, drove through the parking lot, and followed the road around to the second dome. The doorway to the underground parkade was open. She still didn't slow, and plunged the car into the tunnel. As soon as they were inside, Grimson heard the door descend. There was a *clang*, the heavy kiss of steel meeting concrete, and they were sealed in. Zelkova finally took her foot off the accelerator. The parkade was almost empty, and she drove across lanes to the central elevator bank. A man was waiting for them. He wore a dark shirt and a tie. He also wore a headset and a holster around his waist. Zelkova stopped the car, and seemed to melt into her seat. When she sighed, Grimson heard the adrenaline leak from her body.

The man approached the driver's side. An ID card was clipped to his belt. Grimson read it as Zelkova lowered the window. "Hello, Dmitry. English, please." Grimson saw what she was doing, and was thankful. Zelkova was keeping the conversations transparent. No secrets. She realized what being here might mean to Grimson.

"Are you all right?" Karaganov asked.

"Yes," she answered. "We're fine. But we have an injured friend." She gestured toward the back seat.

Karaganov moved to the rear passenger side. He smiled at Inna as he opened the door. He bent over Blaylock. He frowned. "Who is she?" he asked.

Blaylock uncoiled. Her right arm moved like a striking rattlesnake. Karaganov stumbled back. His hands fluttered at the knife embedded in his throat. He sank to his knees. His throat made gurgling noises and blew bubbles through the blood. He toppled over. Blaylock was already over his body. She pulled her knife out, then grabbed Karaganov's pistol and his ID badge. She turned back to the car. Inna was silent, curled tight and motionless against the terror of the world. Grimson could hear Zelkova's breathing coming in short, hitching gasps. Blaylock hauled her backpack out of the car and shut the rear door. She tapped on Grimson's window with the butt of the pistol. Grimson lowered the window. Blaylock shoved the pistol inside. "Take it," she said. The weight in Grimson's palm was disturbing. She hadn't held a weapon since leaving the army. "I want you far away from here," Blaylock said.

"Someone's trying to kill us," Zelkova pleaded.

"I never tried to kill you."

The silence stretched long and dark as Blaylock's answer sank in. Grimson began, "For God's sake, Jen—"

"Leave now," Blaylock said to Zelkova. "I'm sorry for this, but it has to be done. So please, just go. If I see you back here, I'll have to assume you're a hostile."

Zelkova swallowed, nodded once.

"Thank you." For a moment, Blaylock's face sagged, the devil sick of sin. "I'm sorry," she said again. Then she opened her backpack and began hauling out the disassembled components of a C7.

Grimson tried again. "Jen, stop this now."

"Goodbye, Kelly." The weapon snicked together. Energy flowed back into Blaylock's face.

32

C7 strapped over shoulder and in hand. SIG at waist. C4 and detonators in the backpack. Knife in ankle sheath. Map based on selected blueprints in pocket. Blaylock paused for a moment, felt the tingle as the air charged up for battle. She breathed the air in, a snake tasting the environment. She felt a brief clutch of fear when she worried again about civilian casualties. Relax, she thought. Trust your intel. She'd watched the site long enough. She knew the patterns. She knew that by now the WTO staff would have gone home. The parking lot in front of the Administration dome was empty. That was confirmation enough. The anxiety dissolved. Simple rules now. Anyone who wasn't Dunn or his wife was Kornukopia, and so a legitimate target. Her finger stroked the trigger of the C7. She became conscious of the feel of her weapons. Her artist's tools. The second's pause was up. She guesstimated her movements would remain unknown for under a minute. Make the time count. Go.

She bent over Karaganov, took his headset and slipped it on, then did the thing she hadn't wanted the others to see. She pulled out her knife. She cut off Karaganov's right thumb and pocketed it. She called an elevator, stepped in. She eyed the control panel. There was a slot at the bottom, and a small screen between the slot and the buttons. She slipped Karaganov's ID into the slot, placed his thumb against the screen, and hit the DOWN button. The elevator dropped. Sherbina's voice spoke in her ears. He was speaking Russian. He was asking a question, and his tone was anxious. Blaylock smiled. The elevator stopped. Its doors began to open and Blaylock opened fire.

"Dmitry?" Sherbina asked. He stood in the center of lounge. "Are you with them?" No answer.

"Sir?" Another voice cut in. Korshakov, Karaganov's exec, down in the command center. "There's a car leaving the complex."

"*What?*" He ran outside. He saw tail lights moving down the road toward the gate. "Stop the car," he radioed. "But no shooting, no violence."

Zelkova slowed as they reached the exit. The gate did not rise. The guards approached the car warily, but the muzzles of their weapons were pointing at the ground. "I can make them let us leave," she told Grimson.

Grimson was staring dully out the front windshield. She still held the pistol, but by the barrel, and her grip was loose. She shook her head.

"You don't have to stay."

"I want to." Grimson looked back at the domes. "Nothing's going to happen to us here."

Zelkova waved at the guards. One nodded and spoke into his radio. Zelkova tried not to think *What now?* Inna forced the issue. "I want to see Papa," she sniffed.

"What did she say?" Grimson asked.

Zelkova translated. "My husband's in there," she said, and the words hurt.

Grimson nodded. "That's why my friend is."

Zelkova opened her door and coaxed Inna out of the car. She held her daughter and watched the complex. One way or another, she knew, she was going to bleed tonight.

A radio crackled. She couldn't hear what was said. But the guards tensed. They moved closer to Zelkova. The gun muzzles weren't pointed at the ground anymore. They were aimed at the domes.

There were three Kornukopia soldiers in the short hallway. They were dead before Blaylock exited the elevator. Beyond the bodies was a metal door. Behind it was one of the big blank spaces on the blueprints. Her first move was her big gamble. There was a control panel in the wall beside the door. Same drill as the elevator: ID card in the slot, Karaganov's thumb on the plate. The door slid back.

"Dmitry?" said Sherbina's voice on the headset.

Blaylock bit back a laugh. She was still accumulating seconds of enemy uncertainty. She stepped through the doorway, and saw she had guessed right. She blessed Sherbina. The king of convergence had combined two of Kornukopia's takeovers in the complex. The Administration dome housed the WTO. The sub-basement of the Support dome was the local InSec munitions depot. The space was warehouse-huge, and halogen-illuminated. The aisles were wide enough for two forklifts. At the far end, the floor turned into a ramp that rose to hangar doors, access to the first level underground parkade for the trucks bringing in the goods. Shop fast, Blaylock told herself. She looked for what she hadn't been able to fit into the backpack. She ran down the aisles of metal shelving and crates, scanning serial numbers. The depot's organization was pure Swiss. She found the assault rifles, and crossed to the next aisle. Here, with good department store sense, were the accessories. She broke open a crate and clipped an M-203 grenade launcher to her C7. Next, ammunition for the launcher. Next...

Next was the voice in her ear. The voice spoke English, and it said, "Bitch."

That was it. No more surprise. Now she had the few clock-ticks it would take Sherbina to launch countermeasures. She threw away the headset, eliminating distraction. She searched for one more item. She found the grenades in the center of the depot. She was loading up on fragmentation and thermate when she heard the slap of boot soles from the direction of the elevator bank. A second later, the hangar doors ground open. More running feet. Lots of them. A pincer movement with her in the middle.

She could hear the men coming, but she couldn't see them yet. The space was huge. She had a few more seconds. She took them. She shouldered her backpack. She stuffed a frag and thermate into each of her jacket pockets. She thought the battlefield through. If she were Sherbina, she would send enough troops to cover every aisle of the depot and have the job done with. Advantage Sherbina: numbers. Advantage Blaylock: valuable real estate, valuable merchandise. The home team needed to be careful. She didn't. She reached into the crate, hauled out a handful of grenade pins, and ran for the hangar door end of the depot. She streaked across an intersection, caught movement in her peripheral vision. She heard a shout. Footsteps behind. Ahead, three men marched into the far end of her aisle. She dropped. A shot from the rear whined by where her head had been. The men in front threw themselves to the side.

The grenades blew. Big bang and a *whump* of air-filling debris. Then the chain reaction bang bang*bangbangBANG* as one crate after another went up, cumulative thunder. The air turned to smoke and heat. Shrapnel whizzed and thunked into wood and flesh. Blaylock couldn't hear screams for the explosions. She jumped back up and ran again, blind, coughing, racing the spreading contagion of flame. Behind her, metal shrieked and something very big toppled. The crash was huge. The smoke was noxious dark. Chemical hell burned her throat and eyes.

She slammed into a body running the other way. She and the man went down, winded and tangled. They pushed and hit and clawed at each other. Blaylock couldn't see him. She kicked away and scrabbled backwards on her rear. She fought down a retch, held her breath, and heard him cough. She fumbled her rifle back into her hands and fired, raking left and right. Bullets ricocheted. One smacked into a crate an inch from her ear. The man didn't return fire. She didn't hear him move. Now she did retch, but she scrambled to her feet and started moving again, no idea if she was still heading the right way.

More booms. A pressure wave almost knocked her down. The smoke roiled with strange winds. The lights went out. She was in pure black that clawed her lungs with oil and glass. There was a steel popcorn rattle of ammunition cooking off. Metal rain sang as it slashed and bounced down the aisles. Something burned a crease across Blaylock's forehead. There was a pause in the big bangs, and she could hear yells and screams. The heat built. The flames gathered strength, and the dark glowed red. Blaylock tripped over wreckage, fell, rolled, and was up again. She felt a current in the smoke and went with it. She bumped into someone, but this time they didn't fight. Everyone was running.

The floor began to slope. Grateful, she pounded uphill. She was gagging now. Each breath was a poisoned chalice. Her eyes burned with flaming sand and acid tears. The back of her throat was filled with phlegm that tasted like burning rubber. She stumbled, lack of oxygen doing its work and shutting her down. War kept her moving. The floor shook from a blast at the other side of the depot, and she felt joy in her craft. She fired as she ran, aiming at nothing, pumping bullets into the smoke, fanning out a vanguard of death before her. She didn't know if she hit anyone. In the burning limbo, she couldn't even tell if she was taking return fire. Her magazine emptied.

The floor leveled and the smoke thinned out. She'd reached the parkade. She sank to her knees, put her face to the ground, and drew ragged breaths of air. The smell of oil and concrete was edelweiss-pure. She stood up and staggered away from the entrance to the depot. The power was out in the parkade, too, but emergency lights glowed amber, outlining lanes. There were a dozen motorized carts sitting near the entrance. They had wide running boards and heavy metal frameworks instead of cabs. A full squad could pile on each cart, hook arms around the framework, and lay down the fire. No fire now, not in this smoke. Blaylock could see the shapes of men on the floor, pulling hard for oxygen. One silhouette sat up and faced her way. It raised a rifle. Blaylock threw herself to the side and rolled, pulling the SIG from its holster as the bullets whipped by, biting into the concrete. She fired back and shot away the man's lower jaw. His scream was strange. He stayed up, though, his shots a wild spray. Blaylock fired again, dropping him. She jumped up and raced to the nearest cart. She started coughing once more as the smoke built up. More explosions in the depot. More shapes staggered out of the hangar doors. The ones on the floor were up on their feet now. Blaylock weaved through a shadowshow of silhouette confusion. The light and smoke were bad enough that the enemy couldn't ID her. Her advantage again. If it moved, she could kill it.

She hopped into the driver's seat and mashed her foot on the accelerator. The cart took off, buzzing like an amphetamine hornet. She drove one-handed, loading another magazine into her C7. Bullets pinged off the rear fender. She stretched an arm back and let off a sustained burst of suppressive fire. She heard more carts start up. She put both hands on the wheel and jerked the cart left and right. The mouth of a tunnel opened up straight ahead.

Sherbina glared at the monitors. He was blind all over the Support dome. Power flickered on and off through the upper floors, but the basement levels were deep black. The sensors that ran off the emergency circuits were useless, overwhelmed by smoke and heat. He had to depend on radio, and his men were too busy coughing up their lungs to send in more than fog-of-war snippets. Static came in bursts over the speakers, carrying contrapuntal gunfire and explosions. The monitor on the lower left showed the command center in the Security dome. The men were doing their duty and doing it well, but

Sherbina read nervousness in their body language. The nerves were the cumulative effect of Ciudad del Este, of the train, of his father. Gossip, mythmaking, troop superstition. He couldn't contain those. Words had spread, had snowballed, and now the myth had attacked the sanctuary. Training had never seriously anticipated cancer spreading from within. All right, then. He would have to amputate. He touched a key, and sent his godvoice to the center. "Seal the Support dome off," he ordered.

"Sir," said Korshakov. "The level of toxins in the dome is becoming extremely dangerous."

"Good. Seal it. Seal it completely. If there are any air circulation systems still working, shut them down." He watched Korshakov on the monitor. He was standing still, holding a hand to his headset as if he thought it was malfunctioning. "Now," Sherbina said. He could take the losses. Irina and Inna were outside and safe. He could take huge losses, as long as the woman died.

Halfway down the tunnel, a door started down from the roof like a slo-mo guillotine. It was a steel wall, thick enough to stop a tank. Blaylock was twenty yards away. The roof was fifteen feet high. She willed more speed out of the cart. It ignored her. Bullets clanged off the descending door and bounced back at her. Ten yards. The door was halfway down. The cart wouldn't fit. Her lips curled, snarling denial. She glared at the door. She saw the gap narrow. She forgot to honor the threat and kept the cart going straight two seconds too long. Five yards from the door, a 40mm grenade slammed into the right front wheel and blew it all to shit. Blaylock let go of the wheel as she shielded her face from metal and flame. The blast crumpled the front of the cart. Momentum did the rest. The cart threw itself right. Top-heavy with the framework, it flipped. The roll was rapid fire, an alligator spinning with its prey. Blaylock's arm caught around a bar and the cart held her. She saw roaring darkness, felt metal fists, took the pounding of concrete and speed. She went limp. The third roll threw her from the cart. She arced hard and smashed against the door. She fell down, and the cart caught up, hurling itself at the door in terminal collision. Wreckage jabbed at her. The gap between the door and the floor was less than two feet. Blaylock crawled. She couldn't breathe. Her head was a lead bell under heavy hammer. She crawled. The door was a yard thick. It moved down on top of her, a casual god coming to squash the bug. There was the smash of the pursuing cart, too close and fast, hitting the door. Weight, absolute and inexorable, touched the top of her backpack. She made a noise, a breathless throat-gurgle of frustration and defiance. She made herself roll, felt the door's pressure slow her, snatch at her.

She slipped free. The door banged flush with the floor. She dragged breath in and tried to stand. Bring it on, you bastards. But she was pain-blind and stupid, and she couldn't rise. She was being held flat. She roared and flailed her C7, holding the trigger down on another empty magazine. No one came for her. Nothing happened. Her head began to clear. Now that this section of the tunnel was sealed, the air was better. Calmer, she saw why she couldn't move. The door had closed on the fringe of her jacket. She pulled her knife from its sheath and cut through the leather, freeing herself. She stood. The tunnel was still clear of hostiles. They didn't know she was here yet. She had the initiative again.

Her first few steps were shaky. Her bones still rattled

from the crash, her joints were sheets of blank pain. She embraced it all, and she moved. Her legs strengthened. She began to pound down the tunnel toward the big prize, and she was grinning full war. Here I come, she thought with the rhythm of her boots. Here I come. *Here I come.*

Sherbina asked Korshakov, "Any contact yet with the Support dome team?"

"Sporadic, sir. We don't have anything definite yet."

Which meant no sign of the body he wanted. The lower levels of the dome still thundered with contained explosions. The retreat from the basements and the lethal smoke was full-on. There was no point in sending the survivors back down until the fire burned itself out. By that time, he'd know if she was dead or not. He considered his resources and the bigger picture. He assumed the worst. If she was still active and had escaped the dome, what was her likely target? Based on prior actions, Dunn. Better than spreading his forces too thin, chasing phantoms over the entire complex, was concentrating his strength around the bait. If she knew how to penetrate Kornukopia One, she must have an idea of where he was keeping Dunn. So play the shell game. Give her nothing in the living quarters. "Put Dunn's wife and son in the infirmary," he told Korshakov. "Whatever it takes for full security, do it. Any men left over I want in roving patrols. If you have a sure sighting, stop her. I don't want her captured. I want a confirmed kill."

Far end of the tunnel and another access panel. Blaylock

used Karaganov's ID and thumb. The red light at the top of the panel stayed on, access denied. She looked at the thumb, wiped the grime and soot from it, and tried again. Green light, go. The door to the physical plant's control room opened. On the other side of the doorway the lights were on, the surfaces were white, the activity frantic. The room was laid out like an auditorium, with a curving row of computers straight ahead. To the right, on a platform, was the primary station. To the left the wall was blank except for another door in the center. The voices were a babble of Russian and French fighting to make things well again. Red lights blinked at all the work stations. No one paid attention to the open door.

Blaylock walked into the room and started shooting. The men were technicians, but they were Sherbina's. They all had holsters. Good enough, and still she thought *filth, filth, filth* at herself as she dropped them one, two, three, four, SIG-Sauer punching exit wounds, five, six, seven, eight, their blood spattering her, their shocked and terrified eyes cursing her. She marched up the rise to the man sitting at the main terminal. "You have a drill routine, don't you?" she asked. He stared at her. She swept her arm wide, pistol-whipped him. He fell off his chair, cheekbone shattered. He screamed. "Now do you?" she demanded. He nodded, holding his hand up against worse. "Run it," she told him. He crawled back up onto his chair. Blaylock watched over his shoulder. The screen was in English. The tech opened an applications menu, and selected DRILL. The password request came up. The tech hesitated. Blaylock pressed the pistol against his skull. He entered the password. The screen changed color. The top read DRILL MODE. The tech turned to face Blaylock. She made herself look in his eyes as she shot him.

The physical plant's computer reported to the mainframe in the Security dome that a drill was in progress. Abnormal readings were to be expected, and to be ignored. The mainframe shut down the containment measures. All seals between the power plant and the other domes remained open.

Blaylock killed the surveillance cameras, then hit the maintenance door. She didn't need Karaganov's thumb for this one. Turning the handle was good enough. She dragged one of the bodies over to prop the door open, then headed inside. Her prize was the hydrogen and oxygen storage cells and tanks. The tanks were huge, massive double-walled carbon fiber composite with Kevlar lining. There were five tanks each to a cell. Next to the cells were the compressors feeding in the gasses, keeping the pressure in the tanks at 10,000 psi. The power plant hummed with its energy. Blaylock raised her eyes to the hydrogen tanks and saw all the potential she had hoped for. There was a containment wall separating the hydrogen storage cell from the oxygen cell. Blaylock raised the fire door. She planted C4 against the tanks, set up a simultaneous detonation. She placed another package with a separate detonator in the containment wall's doorway. The remote control went in her inside pocket.

When she was done, she reloaded her pistol and assault rifle. She redistributed the grenades. She left the control center and started down the access tunnel toward the Security dome. She didn't see any defenders, which surprised her. The cameras would pick her up again soon enough, she knew. So she ran, taking the gift. She felt her right leg break through a trip wire. The tunnel exploded.

33

Sherbina could feel the mast shake. "Make sure," he told Korshakov.

Station Chief Loo Meacham sat in her office in the bowels of the US Mission in Geneva, held the phone to her ear, and wondered if what she was hearing was a change in the wind or the hurricane finally bringing down the walls. The trend, with dead prisoners, butchered officers, and a missing DDCI, was not promising.

"Ma'am?" Ben Errington's voice prompted. "I said something's going down at Kornukopia One."

"I heard you," she snapped. "I was waiting for you to stop being coy and tell me what's happening."

"We're hearing a lot of explosions. There's smoke rising from one of the domes. We can see Irina Zelkova, her daughter, and a female third party standing near the access to the complex."

Meacham pegged the third party as Kelly Grimson. She'd been tracking the alliance of Zelkova and what was left of Global Response. She asked, "Under guard?"

"Under protection, I'd say. Do you think our man is active?"

Like I know. Somebody give me a clue about what the hell's going on. The shit flowing downhill was worse than ever, but its current was turbulent and confused. Channels that smelled of the Oval Office were commanding *find Chapel, find Chapel, find Chapel*, but without pissing off Sherbina. The stream from Jim Korda stank of palace intrigue, and there the push was to neutralize Chapel as rogue. Before he'd evaporated, Chapel had been spitting acid all over anything to do with Sherbina and Kornukopia. Too many contradictions. Meacham's life had been an unending exercise in taking in the mutually exclusive. She knew the game. Her mantra was *Whatever*. But now the contradictions were too violent. For the first time in her career, she didn't know which way to jump to be out of the way of the flood. She fell back on the old instincts. When in doubt, contain. "If that's our man," she said, thinking the chances of that good news were on par with the Second Coming, "let's give him leverage. Move in and hold Zelkova and the kid. Do it before the media horns in on the act."

"What about the third party?"

"If you can, haul her in, too. But anyone who interferes is a hostile. That includes her."

Flanagan saw a glow flicker in the night, lightning from the ground. He cracked the window down. The air was cold, but he wanted to hear. There, the sound he was waiting for: muffled booms. He smelled smoke. He felt the thrill. *That's my baby doing that. Burn, you bastards, burn.* He drove down the Rue de Lausanne and slowed as he approached the turnoff to the complex. His headlights picked out four men crossing the street. They moved fast.

They reminded him of the men in his apartment. Two of them split off and took up positions against the berm on either side of the entrance. The other two ran up the road, pulling weapons. Flanagan felt anger, thought about the rifle he still had on the seat next to him.

Bastards. Burn.

Another rumble from the complex. Grimson thought this one came from somewhere closer to the center, away from the dome where she had been hearing the sounds of war. She glanced at the guard next to her. He didn't seem to know she was there. He was staring at the domes with more disbelief than alertness. Grimson heard gunshots, and the guard fell over. So did the one with Zelkova. Grimson turned around, saw the suits closing in, weapons up. She didn't give them the excuse she was sure they wanted. She dropped her pistol and raised her hands.

Flanagan thought, Bastards. He thought, Burn. He thought, Do this. He stopped thinking and followed the urge. He trusted the justice of his instincts. He put the civilized man on ice. He turned the wheel of the Fiat hard and accelerated into the turn. An oncoming car blatted its horn and flashed its lights as it squealed brakes. Flanagan aimed for the left side of the entrance. The man was bleached by the headlights. Surprise pinned him like a moth. He didn't even try to move before the car slammed into the berm. The impact shook Flanagan's frame. The air bag billowed out and smacked him back into his seat. His teeth rang. The bag deflated. The right window shattered under fire. Flanagan threw himself down on the seat and grabbed the rifle. He raised it and waited, wished the world would focus and stop shaking. Bullets thunked into the body of the car. He didn't think. He waited. The shooting stopped. A shadow passed in front of the window. Flanagan fired. He sat up and fired into the night, pulling the trigger until there were only clicks from the rifle, drowned out by his yells. There was no return fire. He stumbled out of the car. The second man was sprawled ten feet away. Flanagan stared at him. His head felt numb and stupid, as if his brain had shut down and wouldn't process. He had no feeling except in the pained absence on his left hand. He looked at the empty rifle, dropped it, and picked up the man's pistol. He didn't know if it had any bullets remaining. He didn't know how to check. Blaylock hadn't shown him how a pistol worked. He turned his head to the left and saw the first man pinned between the Fiat and the berm. The man's upper body was sprawled over the accordioned trunk of the car. Below the waist, the man seemed too thin. Flanagan blinked at the pistol. He noticed that his legs were taking him up the access road.

Car horns, screeching tires, loud bang, gunshots. Grimson watched the men start. They both turned to look back towards the entrance. Grimson dropped. She grabbed the pistol, brought it up, and shot the nearest man in the back. The second suit turned fast and fired. He moved too fast, shooting as he spun, and his bullet went wild. It hit the ground an inch from Grimson's shoulder. She didn't flinch, had the time to aim, and took him down. There was a weird silence. Inna had shut her eyes and was rocking back and forth. Zelkova was shielding her. She had one hand to her mouth, holding the horror in. Grimson felt herself begin to shake with the adrenaline of reawakened instincts. She hadn't needed them the night Greenham Common burned. Blaylock had done all the killing. Now Grimson felt the venom of Bosnia coursing through her veins again. The ugliness and the despair were back. She cursed Blaylock for dragging her back to the world where you couldn't help people, where you couldn't make a difference except through blood.

She saw Flanagan coming up the road. He was holding a pistol, and his face was wide-eyed and grimacing. The glare of the security lights cast harsh shadows over his pallor. He looked like a death-mask clown. "Mike," Grimson said. He blinked at her. "It's okay." She kept her voice low and soothing. She spoke a lullaby. "It's okay. It's okay. You can put the gun down."

He did. His grimace, she realized, was meant to be a grin. "I nailed them," he said. "Two of them. Bang bang. Jen would be proud." His voice was brittle. He sounded like his throat was so taut that it wouldn't tear, but shatter.

Grimson put a hand on his shoulder. "You don't have to pretend that you liked it."

His eyes locked onto hers with drowning-man desperation. "That's just it," he whispered. The words hissed, horror turned into escaping air. "I think I did."

Blaylock surfaced from the blackout, her anxiety worse than the physical pain because she didn't know how much time she had lost. She couldn't see, realized that was because she was covered by debris. She tried to move. Rubble shifted. All her limbs responded. She was still

War's favored daughter. No broken bones, though her lower back was in the grip of a crab made of lightning and fire. She pushed broken concrete ahead of her, felt huge weights shift above her. Dust fell onto her face. It stuck in the blood. Warmth flowed from the reopened cut on her forehead and a wealth of new gashes. She crawled over jaggedness and instability. Wreckage shifted beneath her hand and she fell forward, slicing her arm. The darkness was full of edges. Her backpack and the strap of her C7 kept catching on protrusions, and she had to fight to keep them and still go forward.

Movement became easier. The rubble was lighter. She no longer sensed a mountain pressing down on her shoulders. She tried to stand, and found that she could. She rose from the wreckage, shedding dust and cement chips. She wiped the blood from her eyes, and saw a glow. The tunnel was reduced to emergency lighting here, too, but at least she could see. Her way forward was blocked by the collapsed walls and ceiling of the tunnel. She was lucky. The defenders, as if fearing that an anti-personnel blast wouldn't be enough, had taken out insurance and planted enough explosives to bring down the tunnel. Their mistake. She'd been running stupid, and a single Claymore would have finished her off. Instead, the ceiling had cracked in half and come down with two huge slabs leaning against each other. There was just enough space in the angle formed underneath to shield her from the worst of the collapse. This, she told herself, was the one fluke dice roll she was allowed. She checked her watch. She'd been out for less than a minute.

She doubled back. She'd have to reach Security through one of the other domes. She followed the physical plant's perimeter tunnel clockwise, and took the first branch. The

Conference dome was one over from Security. Good enough. But she hadn't taken three steps down when she heard the whine of the carts and the running of boots. Lights at the far end, lots of them, moving fast. She felt the tingle of challenge, fought it down. There were too many, heavy forces dispatched down the nearest undamaged tunnel to drive a stake through her corpse and cut her head off. Back again, running again, running through her pain, hearing shouts, knowing she'd been spotted. Next intersection. The tunnel to the Recreation dome was clear. She slowed to a jog, kept her eyes on the ground for more trip wires. She reached the end of the tunnel just as the foe entered at the physical plant junction. Harsh rattle music of automatic weapons fire. She ignored the hangar doors, chose the fire exit on the left instead. Bullets in the air, bullets striking concrete and metal. She burst through the door. There was a steep staircase on the other side. She took the steps two at a time.

At the first landing, she hesitated. Then she shook her head and kept climbing. That was too obvious. Keep them guessing. She thought she could reach the next level before she had company in the stairs.

Bill Jancovich said, "Found her."

"Main screen," Korshakov ordered.

Jancovich transferred the display on his monitor to the screen that made up a third of the command center's wall. The room was circular, with a ring of terminals surrounding the raised throne of the security chief's post. Outside the ring, soldiers waited for defense or deployment. On the screen, readouts from the heat sensors showed the signature of a lone human moving up the staircase from the basement levels of the Recreation dome. Jancovich toggled the display just as the woman came into range of the stairwell camera. She shot it dead, and Jancovich switched back to the sensor display. "She's still going up," he announced.

Korshakov cursed Russian, then issued more commands. Jancovich didn't understand what he said, but he watched the readouts for the troops assembling on the ground floor of the dome. Big and fast movment, as men ran past cameras. Their heat signatures shifted from sensor to sensor. They were heading up, too, piling into elevators to beat the invader.

Everything the cameras recorded went straight into the mainframe's hard drive. Jancovich opened a small window and called up the last image from the stairwell, froze it. He stared at the woman's face. Her features were covered in dirt and blood, but he thought she looked familiar. He rubbed his upper lip, trying to place her. He kept half an eye on her progress. She was just reaching the top floor when her face clicked. She was a memory from his days at InSec, back when Arthur Pembroke ran the show and Karl Noonan cracked the whip. Noonan had had Jancovich run a search for a face that was bothering him, and that was the face. The coincidence wasn't fun. When Jancovich had been transferred from New York to Geneva, he'd had happy happy thoughts. Bosses being whacked made him nervous. Having done serious hackwork for the dead bosses made him nervous. Then the takeover had happened. That made him nervous, too. He'd been left alone, or so he thought, until Sherbina showed up one day, did a walkabout through Jancovich's department, and winked at him. Big bad nervous. Then the transfer, and anxiety turned to joy. The treatment was plush, the work environment doubleplus secure, and he'd been shown how to use a gun. Supercool. He stank up the target practice gallery in the basement, shooting wide and sloppy, but like he cared. The weight of the pistol in his hands, the kick as it fired, the sweet-goddamn-and-holy-shit revenge-of-the-geek *power* he experienced was what he loved. Being a Kornukopia boy *rocked*.

Until now. Until Kornukopia One itself was rocking, and there was that face from the past, the face that had bothered Noonan. Take her out, Jancovich began to pray. Don't let her come any closer. Take her out.

He wanted everything to be happy happy again.

In the infirmary, Viktor Luzhkov played with his headset, skipping from channel to channel, listening to the shouts of the war. He was jolted into a grunted laugh of disbelief. One woman. The scene was Chicken Little with his head cut off, and one woman was doing the chopping. Incredible. He snorted again.

"What's so goddamn hilarious?" Team Leader Nikolai Vasiliev barked.

Luzhkov shook his head. "Nothing," he said. Vasiliev was too straight. He wouldn't see the humor. Luzhkov gave the woman a mental salute. Keep it up, he thought. This is amazing. He hadn't had fun like this in years.

"So shut it."

Sourial leaned, arms folded against the examination table. She was quiet, playing calm, but Luzhkov could see the tension in her neck. The Dunns were staring back and forth at him and Vasiliev. They were piss-scared, hearing nothing but shouted Russian. Luzhkov gave Angie a smile and patted her shoulder. Hang in there, kid.

Top floor. The plan was to gain time by taking an unopposed detour. Blaylock knew how well war and plans worked together, but she went with the plan anyway. Like she had a choice. She could hear footsteps pounding up the stairs below her. She had a floor, maybe two, head start. She threw the door open and leaped out, moving fast to the side and looking for cover.

No one fired.

The top floor was a huge, open-form art gallery. The lighting was so light and airy that at first Blaylock felt disoriented, as if the dome were open to the sky and she had jumped forward to daytime. She was in an gigantic atrium of eternal day. A huge Soviet flag hung from the ceiling and divided the gallery in two. Suspended from wires and on the walls were monumental posters and billboards. Statues with heroic limbs and massive fists clustered on the glass floor. The artwork was earth-toned yellows and browns, muscled by steel and red. The statues were bronze majesty. The effect was of an E-ticket ride at Sovietland. Blaylock could see two entrances, one to her right, the other diagonally opposite. She needed to drop down one floor before she could cross to the next dome. The nearest door would feed her right back to the enemy. She took another look for shooters. There was too much cover to judge. No choice, then, and she ran for the far door.

Halfway across. She ducked around the big flag, passed a gigantic statue of Stalin in smug salute. Doors banged open. Troops poured out. Blaylock launched a 40mm grenade at her target. The grenade hit the doorway with the men still bottlenecked. The blast threw arms and heads wide. Crossfire retaliated. Blaylock danced, a cat's cradle of bullets chipping glass around her. She threw herself at Stalin's feet, ducking between his Colossus of Rhodes legs.

Rounds pinged off the metal. The giant flag ripped and dropped down from one of its supports. It hung like a blood waterfall. Blaylock was open on all sides. She alternated doorways, letting off a burst at each, trying to suppress the invasion, knowing she was losing. The enemy jumped his dead and spread around the perimeter of the room. The wild firing eased as the men took shelter behind statuary and began to aim. She felt a screaming burn across her right calf. She tucked in closer to Stalin. Her options dwindled. The battlefield turned against her.

Nerves electric, war in her blood, situational awareness at full intensity. She sensed the object's flight, arcing in from behind. She turned her head, saw the grenade. The throw was dead solid perfect. She jumped forward, into the risk of the bullets and away from the certainty of the grenade. Her leap was a good one. It was nowhere near good enough. She landed upright, and then the grenade hit where she'd been at the base of the statue. The blast knocked Blaylock off her feet, threw her sideways. Glass blew, sparkling shrapnel. A legion of sliver daggers sank through her jacket and into her flank. The flesh on her legs shredded. The statue toppled. Blaylock rolled, saw Stalin coming down, hard lover twenty feet tall. She tried to move, slipped on her own blood. She rolled again. The statue hit, saluting arm first. The floor cracked. The statue paused, then rolled, sleepy and heavy, to the right. Blaylock scrabbled. The crushing weight of the statue's left shoulder smashed into the floor like a boulder. It missed her. Blaylock stared up at Stalin's face. He looked amused. The cracks in the floor spread, joined. She was lying on thin ice over air. A chunk of floor under the statue's arm gave way. Stalin came the rest of the way down slowly, but not slowly enough. Blaylock wasn't clear before the weight of his face pressed down onto her chest. She was arched over her backpack. Grenades and magazines dug into her, metal angles and slow hammers. The glass in her side sank in deep. The brim of the statue's cap, just above her head, pressed against the floor and kept her from being crushed. Just. She couldn't move. She couldn't breathe.

The firing stopped. Someone laughed. Blaylock's head began to buzz with imminent blackout. Her arms were free. She made herself think, made herself war, and didn't smack at the statue. She fumbled in her right pocket, grasped a thermate grenade, and threw it toward the base of the statue. She heard the grenade thunk once against the bronze, then roll onto the floor. She shut her eyes.

Heat burst, close and furious. Her skin began to cook. Pickax of pain. Shouts. Someone she hadn't seen, someone nearby and closing in, screamed. Then the big sound she was hoping for, the sound of big cracks as a whole section of the floor melted. Something big gave way. The heat dropped. She opened her eyes as the statue began to move.

Weakened, melted, more floor dropped away. The bottom half of the statue hung over nothing. It tottered. Gravity bit. The head rose up. The first movements of the fall were graceful, taken at leisure. Blaylock lunged forward. She wrapped her arms around Stalin's face, her legs around his neck. She embraced him, went along for his ride. The statue gathered speed and flipped upright. It plummeted down. The art gallery blurred with speed. The melted edge of the floor took a swipe at Blaylock as she went down, cutting and burning her shoulders and neck. The rollercoaster fall jolted to a stop after ten feet as the base slammed into the floor below. The jerk was a solid blow through Blaylock's frame. She almost lost her grip on the statue. It wobbled back and forth, drunk. Massively bottom-heavy, it steadied. Blaylock slid down Uncle Joe. She winced as she rubbed her torn side against metal. Her feet touched the ground. She pushed off from the statue and stumbled toward the far door. Stray bullets angled in from above, chased her through the tennis court. She heard shouts overhead. Kornukopia's defenders moved to intercept.

She needed time, and she didn't have it. The enemy would be down with her inside of thirty seconds. She reached the upper passageway between the Recreation and Conference domes and paused. She visualized the blueprints, remembered how the junctions worked. She stepped into the passageway, felt along the left-hand wall. She found what she was looking for. Her fingers touched a thin seam. She followed it with her eyes, traced out the faint outline of a door. She didn't know how it opened from the outside. She stepped back, fifteen seconds gone, and fired a grenade at the wall. The door blew in, twisted off its hinges. Twenty seconds. Out of time. Here came the boys, thundering down the stairs. She jumped through the doorway, coughing as she breathed smoke and fumes. Sherbina's private corridors stretched ahead of her, following the curve of the domes' outside walls. She ran.

"Uh ...," Jancovich said.

There was a confused pause in the command center. The movie had broken, leaving them with a blank screen. The woman had been on-camera during the art gallery firefight, and some fast toggling had kept her visible when she dropped to the sports level. She had moved out of camera range in the junction of the domes, but Jancovich had tracked her with the heat sensors again. The temperature in the passageway had spiked suddenly, and then the woman's blip had disappeared.

"Is she dead?" Jancovich asked, hoping, hoping. No one answered. He twisted around in his seat and looked up at Korshakov. The chief had a hand against his headset. Field reports coming in, Jancovich guessed. Korshakov went pale. Jancovich felt sick.

Sherbina didn't answer.

"She's in the private—" Korshakov began again.

"I heard you the first time," Sherbina interrupted. He kept his voice level. He wanted Korshakov calm, and he needed a second to think, and think straight. His responses were all visceral. *That's what she wants. Don't let her win.* But she was inside, turning his complex inside out and against him. She was moving through his secrets, through his veins, bitch virus with guns. She'd reached into his life and clawed his family. She was eating through all his defenses, and her poison was hurting. There were no sensors in his corridors. No way to track her. The whole point of the system was to give him total access and total surprise.

"Sir?" Korshakov asked.

No anger. No fear. Find your ice. Remember this is a game. Play it well.

He did. She was off the chessboard. He would force her back on. "Gas," he told Korshakov.

34

The depot was poison flame and exploding wreckage. The Support dome itself was quarantined, a gangrenous limb whose only treatment could be amputation and incineration. On the upper floors, office supplies and the bureaucratic identity of Kornukopia were turning into fume and ash. Black smoke rose from the dome. The air around the complex stank of burning oil, melting plastic, vaporizing toxins.

In the telecom mast, Stepan Sherbina turned away from his monitors long enough to look out the window. The wounded dome made him think of a rotting egg.

And on the ground, Irina Zelkova held her daughter, who had become far too still. Zelkova cradled her, tried to lull her, make her sleep. Inna was taut as piano wire, rigid as steel, and staring at the complex. Light bathed the domes, making them full-moon bright and white, the pride of Zelkova's husband on high display in the middle of the night. Kornukopia One was quiet now, containing the noise of its war, but one of the domes was sick and dying. Inna whispered, "Papa's in there."

"Shhh," Zelkova soothed. "Shhh," Zelkova lied.

And three steps away, Kelly Grimson listened to a mother trying to save her child from nightmare, and thought of her son who would never have nightmares. She thought of the nightmares battling each other in the domes. She thought of the momentum of atrocity in Bosnia, and how root causes vanished into the night of war. She thought she was seeing the same momentum again.

And a bit further off, Mike Flanagan sat next to a conical hedge. He wasn't thinking. He wasn't feeling. He was waiting. He was at the edge of a deep blackness. He was waiting to be pulled back. Or pushed in.

The armory in the Security dome was stocked high with tear gas. Basic riot suppressant. The big laugh with the Kornukopia boys was that the Swiss and the WTO had insisted the complex be supplied with the gas, had asked over and over again if there was plenty on hand, because you never know. Yes, your defenses are impressive, but you never know, you never know. Yes, Sherbina had answered. The story was he said that with a straight face. Yes, they had tear gas. Plus (*shhhhhhh*) enough firepower to level the city. The boys loved it.

Not so funny now. Korshakov deployed four squads to fumigate the vermin. He wished for a moment they were using something stronger, like Serin or VX, then pictured the gas leaking into the rest of the complex and took the wish back. Niggling worry about throwing more men into the field and thinning the defenses in Security. Then he reviewed Sherbina's troop dispositions, and felt better. A dozen in the command center, and all doors sealed. Six-man detail in the infirmary. Two five-man fire teams in each corridor that linked to another dome, each with assault rifles and a PKM light machine gun. The doors were wide open, giving long lines of sight. No surprise possible, but the invitation was extended for the invader to walk into two hundred 7.62mm rounds a minute, times two, just for the PKMs. Think you have the ten-to-one strength superiority you need to take the defended ground, bitch? Then come and get it.

Sherbina gave directions to the strategic entrances to his private corridors. The teams took up positions. From his console, he unlocked all the doors. They popped open. The men donned gas masks, and began firing canisters into the narrow passages. The clouds billowed through. The gas was o-chlorobenzylidenemalononitrile, CS for short. It could kill through toxic pulmonary edema, but wasn't supposed to. It also wasn't designed for interior use. In confined spaces.

The corridors were a maze. They branched down every wall. They were a spiderweb access to every corner of the complex, and Blaylock hadn't had time to memorize the layout. She trusted her sense of direction, and moved in zigzags. Left, straight, right, straight, left. She put space between herself and the outer wall, which was the longer and obvious route. She made good time. Then her nose tickled. She had time for a second of worry, time to run faster, and then the CS clouds hit her from both directions. Her eyes slammed shut against the red-poker pain. Tears poured down her face. She coughed, tried to hold her breath, but it was already too late, poison in and poison out. She staggered, gagging, trying to expel her lungs from her body. She still moved, but the only thing that kept her on her feet was the escape desperation. Her world shrank. There was nothing but the raking of tiger claws down her face and inside her chest. She stumbled against the wall, hands pleading for an exit. She was in a long stretch of corridor, the longest she'd been in since leaving the outer wall. There was nothing. A fist of drowning and pain wrapped itself around her and squeezed. It squeezed air and thought out, squeezed acid in. She fell, vomited, crawled, managed to stand because the agony drove her forward as much as it smashed her down. She took a step forward, another step, another, and the world contracted another notch. It wasn't a fist that held her. It was a constrictor snake, an anaconda of barbed wire and broken glass. Its coils tightened, cutting and crushing, and she couldn't breathe at all. Molten lava phlegm filled her lungs and throat. The CS suddenly became much thicker, a battering ram hitting her with a hissing wind.

Her mind shut down. There was no room for anything except the extinction pain and the final snarling animal instincts. War was the last instinct left, the strongest, and it thrashed, a convulsing denial of teeth and claws. Her fingers touched something different. It wasn't a door, but it wasn't wall, and War clutched her C7 and fired with no care for ricochet.

The one-way glass shattered. She fell through the opening. Full blind, eyes welded shut, she had no idea where she was. She heard a shout. She fired, spinning around as she collapsed, spraying lead in a whirling-dervish spiral. She heard her bullets thunking and spanging, felt plastic shrapnel gouge her cheeks. She heard two screams. The screams had a hollow, muffled sound. There was the heavy thud of bodies.

Still no breath, still only pain, still no open space of clean air. Retching blood, she crawled in the direction of the thud. Her hands were talons, rigid with *extremis*. They stabbed into a body. She scrabbled. She felt blood. She felt something warm and wet and soft. She touched rubber and plastic. She yanked off the gas mask and fumbled it onto her face. Pure air hit her lungs, and she screamed rage and pain and war. She backed up until she was in a corner. She breathed, she breathed. She held her rifle out, and she listened for an approach, and she waited for her eyes to open.

"Yes!" Jancovich yelled. "*Got you!*" The heat signal popped in from the blue.

"Where?" Korshakov barked.

"Conference hall, technician's booth."

Henri Vuillemin, two consoles over, found the booth cameras and shot the image to the big screen. Jancovich looked up. The picture was pea-souped by the CS, and it wasn't clearing in a hurry. The fog eddied, showing the view in pieces. Jancovich made out jagged wreckage shadows, then the hole where the one-way glass had been, Sherbina's window on both the booth and the conference hall. Jancovich spotted a body, hoped for a moment that he was seeing the woman, and that the heat signature on his board was about to fade. But no, now he saw her, crouched in a corner, gun at ready. His mouth was dry, but he was starting to feel good again. You're cornered, he thought. You're toast.

"Finish her," Sherbina said. "Take out the booth, and do it from a distance."

Her eyes still felt like burning sand was crusted under the lids. Every blink was a wince. But her vision cleared. She spotted the cameras and shot them dead.

"Is she still sitting?" the fire team leader wanted to know. Just two seconds too late. Korshakov gazed at the blank primary screen. Shit, he thought. Shit.

Her bullet spray had shot out the windows of the booth, and the gas misted out into the wider space beyond. Blaylock moved to the windows, staying low. She raised her head and peered into the conference theater. The hall was symphonic in scale, big enough to hold a thousand. The fog of CS eddied with the ventilation currents. It was still thick enough to obscure the speaker's podium. *They know where you are*, she told herself. She listened for the sounds of the approaching attack.

"Going to night vision," the team leader radioed.

"Kill the power to the Conference dome," said Sherbina.

The lights went out. Blaylock was blind again. She heard the boots. She heard the multiple *chick-chacks*. She took another thermate grenade from her pack and tossed it.

She shielded her eyes. The grenade went off at the base of the raked seating. A silver nova burst in the auditorium. Blaylock saw figures stumbling back from the blaze, hands over eyes. The booth took automatic weapons fire, but she'd spoiled the precision. As she leaped from the window, she heard the deeper *chunk* of grenade launchers. She had a second of complete vulnerability as she flew. A bullet grazed her cheek, searing out blood. The booth exploded. She landed awkwardly, twisting her ankle and falling over the backs of seats. More grenades rained into the wreckage of the booth. She hugged the ground, crawling behind the seats. Shrapnel whined and sang off metal and fabric. She lobbed an HE grenade blind. The blast broke the rhythm of the enemy fire. She took her moment and jumped down two rows, then ducked low and scampered towards an aisle. The fire team launched more grenades, walking the explosions down, blowing the theater apart one row at a time. Blaylock counted five separate launches. She had the measure of the enemy.

The light of the thermate burn was fading. The carpeting and seats were on fire now. They turned the gas clouds from a burning irritant to full-on poison, but the flames gave Blaylock enough illumination to maneuver. She poked her head around the back of a seat. Through the drifting smoke and gas, she saw the right ground-level entrance to the auditorium. She launched a grenade at the doorway. She ran diagonally across the aisle as the blast happened and dived behind the seats again, three rows down. A man began screaming, kept screaming, wouldn't stop screaming. The barrage faltered again, and when it started up, there were only four launches. The discipline began to break down. They must have seen her move, but didn't know where she was. The grenades weren't marching in lock-step down from the booth anymore. They were hitting everywhere with the randomness of a meteor storm. They were more dangerous now. She couldn't anticipate the damage.

She had one last thermate grenade. She threw it, waited for the eye-dagger light to bloom, and popped her head up over the back of a seat. She saw two men, close silhouettes running from the flames. She nailed them with two quick bursts.

Bullets chewed into the row of seats in front of her. Blaylock jumped back. The grenade came in from the other direction, and she almost danced into a direct hit. The explosion was still close enough. It shredded her backpack and threw her forward. She cracked her chin against the top of a seat. Her head bounced with a *snap*. She fell backwards into the wreckage.

The firing stopped. She didn't move. Couldn't move. She was seeing phosphene flashes and hearing blood. Her pulse was anvil thuds in her head. She had deep vertigo lying down. She made herself turn over onto her stomach. She lay in a crater, in the Swiss-cheese rubble of the hollow-core concrete floor. Twisted metal seating jabbed into her ribs. She reached into her pocket. Last HE grenade. She pulled the pin and held the handle down, waiting. She went crocodile-still.

The sounds in the theater were collapsing metal and crackling flame. The remaining two soldiers weren't firing, weren't giving her their positions. She watched the end of the row. All she could see was fog and smoke in billowing shades of black. The *thudthudthud* in her ears faded. She listened for footsteps. Nothing. Waited. Waited. Wolf at bay, sitting target for crossfire. Her breath was loud and hollow inside the mask. She held it. Waited. Nothing. She wouldn't see them until they shot her up.

End of the line. Time for the ace. She had to breathe again, because the anticipation almost made her laugh. The stakes were erotically high, the war art masterwork huge. The conference hall was in the center of its dome, so she was about as well placed as she could hope. She reached inside her jacket and pulled out the remote detonator. She smiled, reptile, as she hit the first trigger.

The C4 on the hydrogen and oxygen fuel cells went off. The blasts weren't big. They didn't need to be. They punched through the double walls of the tanks. Pure hydrogen and oxygen burst from their high-pressure prisons. They mixed and spread through the physical plant. The containment sensors, overridden by the drill mode, ignored the leak. Doors stayed open. The dome filled quickly. Its contagion spread down the tunnels to the connecting domes, looking for a spark.

Blaylock waited, her thumb over the second trigger. She was warrior, she was artist, she was conductor, waiting for the moment, waiting for the instinct to find the beat, to say, yes, yes, it is just so, do it now.

"Anything?" Korshakov asked again. And of course there wasn't. They were blind inside the conference hall, all sensors and cameras long since fried and blown. They hadn't picked up anyone leaving the theater. No response from the fire teams, so he was assuming the worst.

Vuillemin called out, "Should this be happening?"

"Say that again?" I didn't hear that, Sherbina thought. Anything but that.

"The hydrogen levels," Korshakov said. "Sensors say they're shooting up everywhere."

"But no alarms?" He was swimming in bad-dream illogic. There was a mistake somewhere. "Why haven't the containment measures been tripped?"

Silence for a moment. Then Korshakov's breath caught. For Sherbina, that was the sound of the world ending. "There's a drill going on."

"No there isn't!" Sherbina yelled. "Seal everything! Shut it down! Shut it down! *Shut it down!*"

The war machine thought, *Now*.

When Blaylock hit the second trigger, the C4 at the containment door went off. The package was big. It blew to hell any chance of closing the wall between the two tanks. It also gave the hydrogen the motherspark it needed. The reaction was colossal and instant. The sun exploded inside the physical plant. The pressure was a Jericho blast. The fist of the explosion hammered up through concrete floors. The composite skin of the dome could take a pinpoint hit on the outside. An everywhere strike from the inside killed it. The physical plant dome cracked apart, an egg burst from within.

The roar was the howl of God. It was the thunder of the Earth's rage. Grimson had never felt a sound before. Now it smashed her to the ground. She saw a volcano erupt under the telecom mast. The fireball rose half the height of the mast. It was a solid mass of boiling red. Dome fragments flew wide, fragile embers in the air, turning back to tons of concrete, steel, and glass as they plowed into the ground and slammed into the other domes. The fireball roiled and spread, hell taking air.

Grimson tore her eyes away from the gorgon. Zelkova and Flanagan were on the ground, too. Their mouths were wide open. Grimson thought they were silent, until she realized that she couldn't hear anything. The roar of the explosion was the only sound left in the world. Zelkova was screaming. Flanagan was laughing. They were both crying.

The earth shook beneath Sherbina's feet. The earth died. The mast shuddered long and deep. The night became a rising ocean of red. The temperature shot deadly. He took a breath and his lungs were seared. The tower swayed and he fell on all fours. The noise filled him. His eardrums burst.

The flames sought the hydrogen and oxygen. They shot down the tunnels and corridors of the complex. They scoured. The flames swept over the fire teams in the Security dome. The burn was instant and total, a flamethrower firing into drainpipe. Screams were silent, flesh became charcoal, ammunition cooked off. Agony was incinerator-quick.

The flames reached a third of the way into every dome. Where they walked, they purged.

In the command center, the lights went out. For Jancovich, that was worse than the deafening boom and the rattling walls. The black was total. He was blind. He couldn't see his own hand, let alone what was outside the room. He could only listen to the blasts, and imagine what was coming.

Korshakov had it worse. He had a headset. He caught the last radio transmissions. He heard the screams. They were short.

In the sealed infirmary, Dunn saw terror blanch the guards' faces in the second before the blackout. Night clamped down. Dunn heard the winds and roars of the monster trying to find them.

Viktor Luzhkov thought, *Holy shit.*

The fires in the theater flared high as the edges of the hydrogen flood arrived and ignited. The dark was chased off. The fog pulsed and danced with a harsh orange glow. Backlit, a man at the end of the row stumbled as the theater rocked with the concussion of the physical plant explosion. Blaylock felt immensity dance to her command. She thought, *I have done this.* She felt the epiphany of masterpiece. She rose up, snarling war. One hand threw the grenade at the silhouette, the other aimed the C7 to the rear and fired. The HE went off between the soldier's legs, shredding him wide. Blaylock faced the other way and kept firing. Her blind shots had hit the last man in his body armor, knocked him back against a seat. She emptied the magazine, and took off the top of his head.

Bright. Hot, and *bright.*

35

The flames ran out of fuel. The burning tide receded. In their wake, caramelized corpses slumped over slag that had been weapons.

Outside, the red ocean dropped, its work done. The strength of the telecom mast's supports had melted. The support nearest the Security dome, the one the hydrogen storage cells had been directly underneath, began to twist.

The mast stopped swaying. The floor tilted, and stayed tilted. Sherbina picked himself up off the floor. He ran to the center of the lounge, to the elevator bank and stairwell. He stumbled twice, balance thrown off by unnatural angle of the floor. He hauled the fire door open. He stared down into six hundred feet of dark shaft. Faint light from the secondary fires illuminated the stairs for the first ten feet. Beyond that, he would be descending into full nothing. Like he had a choice. He grasped the railing and started down. He fought the urge to run and break a leg. His feet learned the spacing of the steps, and he found the rhythm. Two steps every second. He'd be down in less than ten minutes. The darkness echoed with the twisting shrieks of metal. He tried not to listen to sounds he could do nothing about, the sounds of breaking, the sounds of the mast edging closer and closer to its tipping point, the sounds of inexorability. He made himself listen to his own promises instead. He turned each exhaled breath into a *sotto voce* "Bitch." The word was prayer and violence.

Blaylock moved from body to body, scoring grenades and bullets. She only had one magazine left, but the soldiers were using AK-101s. They fired the 5.56mm NATO rounds. She blessed globalization and loaded up with a fresh ammo belt. Around her, the theater rotted with flame. Rearmed, she left the conference hall. She walked through scorched corridors, making for the Security dome.

Sirens. Helicopters. Company coming. Between authorities and media, Grimson wondered who would arrive first. She stood up. The orgasm of explosion had passed, and the complex guttered and flickered with afterglow fires. The exterior lights were dead, and the domes were dark hills riven by red and smoke. The physical plant had vanished. It had taken burning chunks out of the other domes with it. The telecom mast listed, groaning. Grimson wanted to ask Blaylock, Is this how you make them answer for Davos? With more of the same?

"Your friend," Zelkova said, and stopped. Her voice was cracked, dead, resigned. She still rocked Inna, but the gesture was automatic, meaningless. Inna wasn't responding. She was a pillar of salt before the blaze. Her eyes were fixed on the mast. Grimson sensed energy building in her small frame, waiting for a cue to snap her in half. "Your friend," Zelkova tried again. The words were a distancing mechanism. She was refusing her own connection to Blaylock.

"Jen," Grimson said, naming her friend. She thought she still could.

Zelkova shook her head. For her, the force that had descended on them was nameless. She said, "She's going to kill everyone, isn't she?"

"Oh, yes," said Flanagan. He had calmed down a bit. He sounded less manic, more like a man coming to grips with the decision he'd been putting off. "That's how she conducts a rescue mission. I should know."

"A rescue mission?" Grimson demanded. All she could see was Armageddon.

"Lawrence Dunn is in there. She's extracting him."

"He is in there," Zelkova said, "because he and his wife were being threatened." She paused for a moment, then said, "Oh," light dawning.

"Threatened by Jen," said Grimson.

Flanagan shrugged. "She was trying to frighten him. She wouldn't really have hurt him. She doesn't hurt innocent people." He leveled his gaze at Zelkova. "Doing *that* is your husband's department."

Zelkova met his eyes, held them. "And what is my daughter guilty of?"

"You were never in any danger," Flanagan said, but he looked away.

Grimson picked up one of the guards' AKs. "Where would the Dunns be?" she asked Zelkova.

"There are some private quarters in the Security dome." Zelkova pointed to the left. Grimson began walking toward the complex.

"What are you doing?" Flanagan asked.

"I'm going to help them."

"Don't be in the way. Jen will take care of things. She'll make sure they're okay."

"You trust her to do that?"

"Yes."

"I don't." She kept walking.

The Security dome's backup generator kicked in. Power flickered on, sporadic, scattered, unreliable. The grid was too badly damaged. In the command center, the lights were a wavering amber. The monitors stuttered back to life. They were receiving, but none of the sensors outside the center were sending. Korshakov ran the whole lexicon of tests. He called Sherbina on every channel. Nothing. He was blind, and the boss was silent. The walls vibrated with the groans of metal giants. He felt hummingbird wings flutter in his guts, stirring up panic. He swallowed hard. "You," he pointed at a soldier. (And then there were twelve, he thought.) "And you. Go out there and recon to the first junction. Radio back when you're secure." They nodded, looking thrilled, and moved to the door. One of them touched a stud on the control panel. Nothing happened. He jabbed again. The door stayed dead. He looked up at Korshakov. Korshakov's hummingbird beat its wings and grew.

Flanagan started to follow Grimson. He stopped. Trust Jen, he thought. You said you did. Let her do what she does. What did he think he would accomplish in there? Help? Right. He'd become a liability, a distraction, a uselessness.

He turned back to Zelkova and Inna. He had trouble looking at the girl without hearing the accusatory echo of mortar fire. He stood between them and the entrance, waiting for the invasion to begin. He would shield mother and child. The cameras wouldn't touch them.

"Do you love her?" Zelkova asked.

Flanagan kept his face towards the gap in the berm. The sirens were close now. The light strobed red and blue. "Do you love your husband?"

"I do."

I see, he thought.

Blaylock reached the junction between the Conference and Security domes. She stopped cold. Corpses faced her, still clutching twisted weapons. She walked towards the dead, and made herself look. She looked at blackened shapes, at plastic that had fused and bubbled with skin, at empty eye sockets, at mouths yanked wide by terminal screams. She was back at Ember Lake, face to face with the reality of her cleansing flame. The scorched guns and the flash-burned uniforms were bad echoes of Kuwait, of the Highway of Death, of the acts from which a younger self had recoiled.

I have done this.

Are you proud of yourself?

They had not been retreating, she reminded herself. They had been waiting for her. She had simply touched them first. She moved on through guttering flames.

Let's go to war.

The hole in the Security dome was a wound with cauterized edges. Grimson clambered over rubble. Above her, the telecom mast shrieked and leaned a bit more. The sound of metal and concrete in death agony was constant. She felt the tower's presence at the back of her neck. The promise of a fall to come pressed down on her. Her shoulders tensed. She slid down the wreckage to the buckled surface of the ground floor. The air was a thick, rotting bouquet of burns. She smelled rubber, flesh, oil, and odors new and poisonous. She coughed. She moved into the dome. She looked for an unbroken staircase that might lead her to the living quarters. Either that, or a sign, an omen that Blaylock was near.

How to turn a refuge into a prison: seal the exit.

Jancovich watched the soldiers struggle with the door. He was sweating. His underarms were soaked with anxiety. Open the door, he thought. Just open the door. Prove it can be done, and then we can shut everything up again. But don't let us be stuck here. They had the panel open and were working with the door's manual mechanism. The door slid open about an inch, then jammed fast. One of the soldiers rammed the barrel of his gun into the gap and used his weapon as a crowbar. A second did the same. They strained. The door shuddered, but fought back. Jancovich imagined the damage on the other side, pictured a total collapse, the command center become the secret chamber at the heart of a pyramid, the final air pocket in the tomb. Beyond the door, he could hear the deep moans of something big and vital lumbering toward death.

Another rifle was stuck in the door. There were now six men working the leverage, three pushing, and three pulling the guns. The door screeched, steel nails over a coffin. Jancovich willed it into motion.

The door exploded. A multiple grenade blast blew it in half. Fragmentation shredded the soldiers. The whirling halves of the door flew through the room. One embedded itself in the main screen. Glass imploded. The lights went out again, were replaced by flame. The other half of the door went high and sliced Korshakov in two. His torso fell from the command throne and bounced down to Jancovich's feet. Full-auto bursts of rifle fire came in from the hall. Only one of the center's defenders shot back. A crouching shape appeared in the burning doorway. It fired and tore out the soldier's throat.

Silence clamped down, so sudden it cut off Jancovich's screams. He held his breath. Burning circuitry cast faint light and long, dancing shadows through the center. The shape came inside. Vuillemin fumbled at his holster. The shape drilled him. Blood splashed onto Jancovich's face, and he started screaming again. He sank to his knees and held his hands high.

The shape pulled off its gas mask and said, "Shut up." It had a woman's voice. Jancovich shut up. "I'm looking for Lawrence Dunn."

"He's downstairs," Jancovich said. "In the infirmary."

"Is his wife in the living quarters?"

"No." That was Rossmiller. He was from England. His hands were higher than Jancovich's. "They're all in the infirmary. The children, too."

"Children," said the woman, low and angry. Jancovich wondered if Rossmiller had just signed everyone's death warrant. The woman walked over to Korshakov's seat. She looked at the corpse, then zeroed in on the torso. As she approached, Jancovich tried to back up through his work station. The woman pulled off Korshakov's headset and his transmitter. She slipped the headset on. She spoke into the mike. "Infirmary," she said. "I'm calling from the command center. Your defenses are finished. If you surrender now, you can live."

Grimson heard the grenades go off. She made her way deeper into the dome, past wreckage and burns, following the sound of more dying.

"So?" Luzhkov said to Vasiliev. The lights in the infirmary flickered again, then settled into permanent brownout.

"What?" Vasiliev couldn't speak without snapping. He was bouncing from the ball of one foot to the other.

"You heard what she said." Luzhkov kept his voice calm. He could hear Vasiliev vibrate and hum.

"And you believe her?"

"Kinda do, yeah. You been able to raise anyone?"

Vasiliev didn't answer. He didn't have to. "We're not surrendering," he said. Listening to his voice hurt. Luzhkov's throat clenched in sympathetic tension. The other four men shifted, nervous, their eyes on the floor.

Luzhkov shook his head, not buying that the man was this stupid. "Shit, Nikolai, use your brain. It sounded like she dropped a nuke out there. And listen to that." He held up a finger. The bad news groaned in from overhead, the distant warning of a very big fist. "You want to fight the good fight? You suicidal? You know of an advantage we have that everyone else didn't?"

"Yes." Vasiliev's face tightened with pyrrhic satisfaction. "We have what she wants." He hauled Dunn out of his seat and jabbed the barrel of his pistol under his chin. Dunn gagged as his head jerked up.

There were three hard knocks against the infirmary door. The woman's voice crackled through Luzhkov's headset. He saw the others jump when she spoke. "I'm outside," she said. "Send the hostages out."

Luzhkov walked over to the door. He raised a finger to the stud. Vasiliev said, "Don't." Luzhkov froze. Vasiliev's tone was pure command, and Luzhkov knew the others would respond. They did. He turned around and saw the weapons leveled at him. "Will you idiots relax?" he said.

The woman's voice spoke again. "I'm waiting."

Vasiliev yelled into his mike. "Fuck you bitch dyke fucker!" His English was a long way from the boss's, but it did the job. "You give up! You give up now! Or we kill them now!"

The humor evaporated. Luzhkov saw blood coming.

The media arrived first, but it was a photo finish. Flanagan held the cameras and microphones at bay until a wall of Swiss police arrived. He put his gun down slowly and raised his hands. Then it was Zelkova's turn to protect him. She put a hand on his shoulder, and muzzles turned away from his chest. The police created a *cordon sanitaire* between Zelkova and the telephoto lenses. Inna hadn't moved. The hesitating tower wouldn't let her. Flanagan stood beside Zelkova. She loved Sherbina, she'd said. He asked, "Do you know what your husband does?"

"Yes. What about you?"

Do I know what Blaylock does? "Yes."

"Then you have the same choice to make as I did."

"Do you regret yours?"

She looked at the pyre of Kornukopia One. She was crying, softly. She didn't answer.

Blaylock heard muffled yells on the other side of the door. Male voices all, and no screams. No killing happening yet. But they weren't going to let her in. Fine, she thought. Negotiating was the first refuge of the weak. She pulled the map out of her inside jacket pocket. It was seared and torn. She could still read the layout for the core of the Security dome. She ran her finger over the line of the private corridors, found the nearest entrance. The scorch marks on the walls made the outline of the door easier to find. Still no easy access without being Sherbina. She backed up, ready to blast her way through again. She still had a grenade in her launcher. "You hear me?" the voice in her ear demanded. "You give up?" She was far enough. She fired.

Grimson stood at the entrance to the command center abattoir. There were still a few living men here. They were sitting by dead computers, staring at each other, unstrung puppets. "Why don't you leave?" she said. A couple struggled to stand up. Beneath Grimson's feet, she felt the floor vibrate with a new explosion.

The boom rattled the walls of the infirmary. The brown lighting wavered, threatening a final fade to black. *What the hell is she doing?* Luzhkov thought.

"Doesn't sound like surrender to me," Andrei Volkov said.

"No," Vasiliev agreed. They waited in silence for the next move. Nothing.

After a minute, Yavlinsky wondered, "Trying to scare us, you think?" Luzhkov doubted that. She would know that was a waste of time. If she didn't know they were Spetznaz, she should at least guess. She wouldn't have made it this far by guessing wrong.

"Doesn't matter," Vasiliev answered. "I don't care. She didn't surrender. So she's stupid. So she should find out just how stupid." He nodded. Volkov grabbed Linda. He stood behind her, wrapped an arm around her shoulders, and put his knife against her throat. Yavlinsky and Gaidar did the same with Angie and Jake. They turned them into shields and faced the door. Zverev held his gun on Luzhkov.

"You're kidding me," Luzhkov said.

"Care to find out?" Vasiliev asked. "Bitch?" he said to his mike. "You hear me? You hear them die now." He turned to Sourial. Still in English, he said, "Use poison. Poison that hurts." Sourial nodded and moved to the rear of the infirmary.

"Please . . ." Linda whispered. Angie and Jake were trembling, sniffling snot and tears. Dunn met Luzhkov's eyes. The pleading and the despair hurt. Luzhkov began to run odds. His fingers twitched. Zverev clucked his tongue: *Don't even think about it.*

"Which one first?" Gaidar wanted to know.

Vasiliev thought about it. Luzhkov saw his eyes eenie-meenie-minie-moeing over the family. He shrugged. "Who cares. You asked," he told Gaidar. "Do yours." Then someone gurgled.

Opening the doors from the inside was easier. There were handles. Blaylock listened. The voices didn't sound close to the wall. She had a bit of distance, though she heard what sounded like a drawer open nearby. She let the C7 hang by its strap and pulled her SIG. She opened the door and slipped into the infirmary. She emerged in the main surgery, out of the wall opposite the door. The scene clicked in. At her elbow, a startled woman filling a hypodermic. Ahead, six men. One at the door, facing her way, but staring at the other five. One man holding a gun on him. The other four with hostages. The woman lunged at her. Blaylock grabbed her wrist, twisted, and slammed the syringe into the woman's throat. She was moving again as the woman made blood noises and fell. The man on the far left had a boy. His arm tensed. The man at the door shouted something. The man with the boy sniggered and his elbow began to move. Blaylock rushed forward, racing his throat slash. She came in low, yanked her knife from its sheath with her left hand, and rammed the blade through the man's kidney. The man jerked through agony and death, his knife arm spasming, cutting the boy's cheek. Blaylock remained crouched, had a fine low-angle rear shot of the next soldier's head, and blew his brains onto the ceiling. The other two reacted fast. They were good, and they went with their instincts: kill the threat. They freed their weapons by throwing their hostages aside. Blaylock lunged. Torpedo, she came in inside the arc of their first shots. She slammed her head into the nearest man's gut. He *whoofed* and fell back. They toppled to the ground. Blaylock landed on top. She had both hands wrapped around her SIG. Her elbows jarred down on the man's chest. She fired on her way down. The second soldier's face imploded under multiple hits.

A fist smashed her ear, hammer on bell. She dropped her pistol and fell over onto her stomach. The soldier jumped up and swung his gun at her. Blaylock saw a knife in his leg holster and she pistoned her fist into his groin. He jackknifed forward. She snatched the knife and brought it up as he went down. His mouth was open in a scream and he deep-throated the blade. He collapsed, gurgling and clawing. His fingers, weak with the end, slipped on the blood that poured from his mouth and slicked the knife.

Screaming all around her, then two shots, simultaneous. She whirled, her mind's eye already seeing hostage splattered on the wall. Instead, she saw the man at the door lean heavily against it. He clutched at his side, trying to staunch a deep flow. His uniform bloomed red. The soldier who had been facing him was down, head shot. Screaming still, the Dunns hollering hell, but they weren't hurt. Blaylock picked up her SIG as the wounded man dropped his gun. She cocked her head at him. He grinned, and tossed off a salute.

They faced each other. The screams lost urgency, diminuendoed to whimpers. "You speak English?" Blaylock asked. A nod. "Do I need to kill you?" He shook his head, still grinning. "You have a name?"

"Viktor Luzhkov."

Blaylock toed the one kill that wasn't hers. "Thank you, Viktor."

"You're welcome." His English was guttural, but fluid. He jerked his head at the man with the knife in his throat. He was still moving, a wounded cockroach crawling in circles. "Nikolai must be very pissed."

Blaylock shot Nikolai. He stopped moving. "Need help?" she asked Luzhkov.

"A little." He slid a bit further down the door.

Blaylock looked at the wound. The blood pumped, but didn't flood. She felt gently. His ribs didn't move. Maybe a clean entry with no bouncing around inside. Maybe. She found some gauze and padding and made a field dressing. It would have to do. Outside the complex, ambulances wouldn't be far. The explosion would have drawn enough attention.

Luzhkov straightened, gritting his teeth. "Thank you." He looked as if he wanted to say something else.

"You'd better go," Blaylock told him. "Have that looked at."

Luzhkov nodded. He turned to leave, hesitated. Still something on his mind, still looking at her as if being hit by thoughts that, half-formed, he couldn't identify. He shook his head, shaking the confusion off. "The other room," he said. "Another prisoner." He saluted again, and seemed to surprise himself with his lack of irony. "Be seeing you." He started down the corridor.

Blaylock found the other prisoner in a hospital bed shrouded by curtains. Chapel was a broken mummy. He was conscious. His eyes met Blaylock's. His gaze was no longer by Glock. Blaylock said nothing. Chapel waited, and Blaylock saw the wince of worry. Good.

Footsteps behind her. "Jen?"

"Hello, Kelly." She didn't turn around.

"Who's that?" Grimson asked.

"This," Blaylock flicked a hand in contempt, "is Joe Chapel. You remember him? No, you never met. But he was an important man at Davos, believe me."

Chapel croaked, "I didn't—"

"No, of course you didn't. Sherbina kept you guys in full deniability, right? You and your President had no clue, right?" Blaylock leaned in close. "You spun the Davos attack, you bastard. You spun it."

"My country . . ."

"Screw you and your country. Front, back, sideways, and down the middle. Like I give a good goddamn for that specious bullshit." She straightened, crossed her arms, drummed her fingers.

"What are you doing?" Grimson asked.

"Deciding."

Chapel made a noise. It sounded as if he was trying to spit. Grimson said. "You can't just kill him."

Blaylock still didn't turn. "Oh no?" she asked. "He has your blood on his hands. Even if he didn't shed it himself, he used it."

"You're talking about murder."

Blaylock's laugh was a bark that hurt her throat. "Believe me, I know from murder."

"Don't kill him."

"All right." She stepped away from the bed.

"You're going to leave him?" Massive disbelief.

"He's a liability wounded. Healthy, he's worse."

"No," Grimson insisted.

"No?" Blaylock turned now. She looked at Grimson, who would not, would not, *could not* understand the ugly present and uglier future of standing in the way of the war. But what was Blaylock going to do? Go through her? *Whom was she fighting this war for, anyway?* (A voice, silenced as it spoke, but grinning all the same, asked the question again.) "Fine." There was a wheelchair next to the bed. Blaylock kicked it over to Grimson. "Go on, then. Extend your fucking mercy." The walls shook with the cry of a steel whale. "We leave, now."

Grimson said nothing. Calm, she began to shift Chapel

off the bed. He moaned. Blaylock watched the struggle for a moment, then cursed and helped haul him into the chair. "Get well soon," she threatened, then led the way back to the OR. She swept her eyes over the Dunns. "Stick close," she told them. When she saw Linda flinch away from her, she said, "I'm here to help you, not hurt you." She stabbed a finger at the bodies. "I would have thought that was obvious." Only she knew it wasn't. She knew she was so tainted now that civilians couldn't tell the difference between her and the enemy.

They followed her, though. They huddled close to her as she took them down the corridors. Grimson brought up the rear with Chapel in the wheelchair. The rumbling from the tower was constant, and was building to thunder. The sounds were becoming deeper, descending below subwoofer bass to subsonic vibration, shutting down every other noise. In the gathering roar, Blaylock heard the last of sand running from the hourglass. She knew which leg of the mast she had damaged. She knew which way the mast was leaning. When it fell, it would land on the Security dome. "Run," she said, and they did. The fastest way up from the basement and out took them in harm's way, back toward the base of the mast. She took the risk, seeing a worse one in staying inside the dome longer than they had to, trying to find corridors that might or might not be damage-blocked, and no sign but thunder of when the collapse could come.

Less than ten minutes after the physical plant exploded, they reached the wound in the dome's side. They climbed out over the Daliscape of melted steel and broken-bone concrete and dagger glass. The telecom mast was swaying drunk, screaming in terror and rage. Dunn stumbled to a stop and stared up, cobra-mesmerized by the vertical dance. Blaylock shoved him forward. "Move," she ordered. They needed to negotiate the rubble-strewn gap that had been the dome juncture and still put a sprint on across the grounds before they were out of range. Dunn dropped his eyes from the tower. His eyes focused behind Blaylock's left shoulder. He froze. Grimson yelled, "Jen!" Blaylock started to turn, an infinity too slow to avoid the blow that slammed into the back of her neck and brought the curtain down.

Blackout, brownout, then fade in and out, the world a jumble of blurs and fragments. Ground level, the feel of glass against her cheek, scraping pain dragging the light back in. A bad image of Grimson fighting. Blaylock's lurching knowledge that she was down, turtled, and had let war slip into other hands. She tried to move, blacked out, came to. Little twitches were her only movement, themselves the gift of pain. She heard a snap and woman's cry. Fade out. Fade in to a voice shouting "Wake up" over the deep-earth rumble of the mast. Snap image: Sherbina standing over Grimson, Grimson's left elbow pointing the wrong way. Blaylock's body jerked, straining to attack through the black fog that rolled in again. Fade in. "I said wake up!" She did, and this time focus clicked. Her limbs still weren't hers, but the war gears began to mesh again. Battlefield information flooded in. Sherbina, clothes torn and coated in concrete dust, was staring at her. Media and police were blanketing the complex with floodlights set up at the entrance to the grounds and stabbing down from helicopters. The light moved over Sherbina, backlighting him one moment, streaking him with angular shadows the next. His stance was pure attack, no amusement left. Behind him, the Dunns were backing away. Linda had Chapel's wheelchair. Sherbina ignored them.

He was prioritizing, just as Blaylock would. The victor would collect the prizes at leisure.

Blaylock felt her arms and legs reconnect with her command. She didn't move, played possum. More info: her SIG, AK, and knife were at Sherbina's feet. He'd taken the time to disarm her. He could have killed her. Blaylock sniffed a mistake. He should have killed her. He must know that. So why? "*Do you hear me?*" he roared, twisting Grimson's right arm, and his anger, his blistering, raging hurt, gave Blaylock her answer. He was being stupid. He wasn't doing war. He was doing vengeance. He wanted Blaylock to see what he would do to Grimson. Pain was prime. They were in a contest. Each had landed blows. He wanted his to be the last. But there would be no satisfaction if she didn't feel the hit.

"*WAKE UP,*" screaming now, he twisted Grimson's shoulder out of its socket, and made her scream, too. Blaylock fought the instinct to help and die. She let her eyelids flutter, but no more. Come closer, she thought. I've pushed you this far to the edge. Let's see you fall.

The tower echoed with multiple *spangs* of metal letting go. Sherbina released Grimson. She gasped and slumped to her knees, both arms hanging useless. "You hurt?" Sherbina barked. "My dear woman, you have no idea how much I'm really going to hurt you." He was looking at Blaylock. "In just a moment," he added. He stepped forward. Come on, Blaylock thought, feeling war flow back. Her awareness became pure battle. She processed so fast, events couldn't keep up. They broke down into slow-motion elements. Sherbina standing before her. Sherbina placing his weight on his left leg. His right leg going back for the kick.

Snap: a single movement in multiple strikes. Blaylock

snaked out her left arm and grabbed his trousers. She rolled onto her back. She kicked up with both legs at his pelvis. One movement. She won by surprise, yanking him into her kick and cartwheeling him over her head. She jumped to her feet. He was already up again, his stance ready and feral, but she was standing now, and was between him and Grimson. She faced him down. "Go, Kelly," she said. She heard scraping behind her, knew that Grimson was moving. Then footsteps, stumbling and arrhythmic, but she was going, almost running. The last of the collateral damage putting distance between herself and the front line.

Sherbina shook his head. "I'm still going to kill her," he said.

Blaylock smiled at him.

The telecom mast spoke. Its voice was a scream, and the scream turned into the roar of steel roots torn from concrete bedrock. Blaylock looked up, and the tower came at her. It was a huge slab of night that bleached albino as it fell into the floodlights. Concrete dust puffed from its length as its spine snapped. The tumble was graceful, slow, all the time in the world for the grand moment. Blaylock ran to her left. She leaped over rubble, and Sherbina was next to her, matching her beat for beat. They ran from the weight of absolute collapse. The air fled the fall, too, a hard wind rising fast and sudden. The tower came down, and the world shook itself to pieces. The mast hit the Security dome, fist onto egg. Shatter and roar. Blaylock was off her feet and flying through a pummeling vortex. She saw nothing but an earthquake blur. The boom was the death knell of a god. The night filled with a dust storm. Blaylock was slammed into the ground. She was rolled and dragged, the fangs of rubble slashing clothing and flesh. Something very big whooshed by over her, ruffling her hair, and smashed itself to powder. Her head rang, her frame rang, but she scrambled to her feet, coughing on the dust, and gasping with the exhilaration of war at its most dangerous. She was ribbon-slashed, bodywash slicked with her own blood. She'd never felt more alive.

Broken, the world was a swirl of gray and black and a white that glowed like choking snow, like a dying sun. Silhouettes of wreckage twisted and tangled around Blaylock. She looked for the silhouette that moved.

Sherbina found her first. He materialized in front of her and lunged in with an open-palm strike at her face. She brought her arms up fast, blocked with her left hand, and reached out with her right, establishing contact with his left arm. Sherbina followed his deflected punch through and his elbow rammed her jaw. Her head snapped back. The limbo thickened. Sherbina's arm arced in again, backfist coming to finish her off. She accepted her stumble and leaned back out of range. He opened three fingers and thrust them up her nose. She moved back far enough that he didn't break her nose, but her trigeminal nerve took a blow. Her eyes filled with an explosion of tears. The animal instinct was to claw at her face. The war instinct was stronger. She took another half step back but didn't break contact. Blind, she still felt his weight shift. He stepped forward with his left foot. His hips turned, and his arm moved under her touch. Head blow coming, coup de grâce. She slid her hand up towards his shoulder. His arm went back for the jab. He would punch right through her upward block. Only she wasn't blocking. She extended her first and second fingers, turned at the hips, and corkscrewed her fingers into his armpit. She bull's-eyed the nerve cluster, and his arm dropped limp in mid-strike, useless forever.

Her eyes began to clear, but too late to evade as he grabbed her around the back of the neck with his good arm. He snaked a leg around her right, intimate as sex. He hooked his foot around her heel. She dropped her weight to her left foot before he could stomp down and snap her anterior cruciate ligament. She dropped her elbows, arms up to push him away. He still had her by the neck and drew her in. He pulled his leg away, then brought his knee up at her ribs. She blocked by attack, driving her fingers up at his Adam's apple. He dropped his chin, protecting his trachea. She kept her hand going and opened her palm. His eyes met hers, and she saw his widen as he realized his mistake. She plunged her thumb into his left eye, puncturing and driving deep. She paused a half-second as he twitched, hoped his good eye saw what lived in her gaze. She hoped he understood, hoped he felt her inside his head. Then she stirred her thumb, hooked it, and yanked hard.

Sherbina fell. His feet drummed, then stilled. His eye socket was a horn of plenty weeping gray matter. Blaylock howled war in the billowing limbo.

Epilogue

The dust of the fall spread wide. The world was coughing fog and halogen glare. Ringside, the collateral damage saw the silhouettes dance. They saw them love each other. They saw one fall. They were all hacking and gagging on the choking air, and they were all shouting at each other, but in a pause for breath they heard it, a voice that had a woman's register, but that belonged to pure, lizard-brain triumph. It made the night bleed. The collateral damage held its collective breath. The dust eddied, hiding the silhouette. The roar ended.

The dust began to settle.

Jancovich huddled with the other survivors from the command center. He wanted to sleep, but was afraid he would hear that woman's voice in his nightmares. Luzhkov, his wound bound, was impressed as he had never been.

The media shrugged off its stunned stupor as Lawrence Dunn approached the wall of cameras and microphones. Dunn began to speak before he could be asked any questions. He spoke, and he spoke, and he spoke. I'm doing the right thing, he thought as he mentioned the President's name for the first time. I'm doing the right thing. It only feels like vengeance.

The media quivered as he tongued it. It moaned.

Chapel was in a stretcher. As he was carried to the ambulance, he saw Dunn, spotlit and singing. A car pulled up beside the ambulance and Loo Meacham stepped out. She made the paramedics put Chapel down and shooed them away. "Something you should know," she whispered. "Korda's been quoted as calling you rogue." Chapel winced. The old vulture had the upper hand again. Then the deeper implications sank in. Chapel was becoming part of the damage control. That meant Reed had cut him loose. Meacham spoke again. "I had a call just as I was arriving. Charlotte Taber was on *The O'Reilly Factor*. She was asked about what Korda said. She used words like *regret* but didn't back you up." Chapel felt the knife between his shoulder blades sink to the hilt. *You bastard.* Chapel was thinking of Sam Reed. *You stupid, stupid, STUPID bastard.* He saw beyond his own betrayal. He saw the consequences of this night spreading out, a laying of waste that extended far beyond the battlefield. He saw how much his country was going to be hurt, and he felt a hatred for his President that was startling in its clarity.

Zelkova's arms had gone limp around her daughter. She was numb. Inna's voice was almost gone from crying and screaming. Now she was whispering: "Papa, Papa, Papa."

Grimson knew there were paramedics at her side. She knew both her arms were broken. She knew she was being looked after. What she saw, what she was aware of, was the dragon-swath of destruction. She wept for her friend.

Flanagan walked deeper into the dust fog, towards the ruins. He headed for the spot he had last seen Blaylock. He didn't feel as if he had made a decision. He felt as if he had never had a choice to make at all. He felt good. His hand didn't hurt. He was walking toward completion. The further he was from the sobs of the injured and the terrified, the more he detached himself from the collateral damage, the better he felt. The pieces of rubble grew larger. Soon they embraced him. He clambered through a shattered dreamscape, a rib cage in swirling night and dust. He was surrounded by Blaylock's art. The scale exhilarated him. His spine shivered, stroked by the finger-touch of the sublime.

Blaylock spotted him as he came over the peak of the wreckage. She had retreated towards the smoldering Recreation dome, sheltering in shadows. She knew she should leave. She was hurt, and she had to be far from the field before her wounds dropped her. But she waited. She wanted to know. No loose ends, this time.

Flanagan paused, uncertain, dwarfed by the desolated concrete. Blaylock called to him. She stood up so he could see her. She was soaked with her blood and that of her enemies. She knew what she must look like, a grotesque in red and black. Flanagan scrambled over the broken landscape to her. As he came closer, she could see he was smiling, his eyes still taking in the magnitude of her work. He reached her, and his smile faded. He put out a hand and touched her cheek. She felt his finger slip and come away slick with blood. She grinned. "You should see the other guy," she said.

"I did." Reassured, his smile came back.

There was a glint of excitement in his eyes. She recognized it, knew it far too well. I put that there, she thought. I've done this to him. She spoke before the guilt took her. "I thought I told you to keep me human."

"You are," he said. "You're very human."

The war machine spread her arms wide to embrace her lover with blood and fire.

Acknowledgements

I am deeply grateful to all those who gave me their time, their thoughts, and their knowledge as I wrote this book. Special thanks to Bob Baxter, for another great design in Kornukopia One. You keep building 'em, Bob, and I'll keep smashing 'em down. For military matters, my thanks go to Ann Howey; for hand-to-hand combat, Paul Regehr; for vehicular carnage, Leanne Groeneveld and Floyd Groeneveld; for Kornukopia One's power source and the Really Big Explosion, Pin Kao and Jennifer Chan; for fashion, Mary Beth Wolicky; for culinary aspects, Michael Kaan; for medical information, Melanie Hawkes; for brainstorming and other help, Tony Kavanagh, Andrew O'Malley, Serge Poulin, John Rempel and Dave and Jennifer Violago.

Enormous thanks again to my editor, Wayne Tefs, for rigor, for insight, and for teaching. Wayne, I can't tell you how much I have learned about the craft of writing under your care. My thanks also to Todd Besant, Sharon Caseburg, and Kelly Stifora at Turnstone Press, whose belief and support made writing this book such a pleasure.

In the course of my research for *Kornukopia*, a few books were particularly useful, and I would like to highlight them here: *Resist*, edited by Jen Chang et al.; *On Killing: The Psychological Cost of Learning to Kill in War and Society* by Lt. Col. Dave Grossman; *Behind the Scenes at the WTO* by Fatoumata Jawara and Aileen Kwa; *Inside the CIA* by Ronald Kessler; *Weapons of Mass Deception* by Sheldon Rampton and John Stauber; and *The Merger: How Organized Crime Is Taking Over Canada and the World* by Jeffrey Robinson.

At the risk of making them spin in their graves, I have appropriated some lines from my betters. "Illimitable dominion" is from Edgar Allan Poe's "The Masque of the Red Death"; "the darkling plain" is stolen from Matthew Arnold's "Dover Beach"; W.B. Yeats might not be pleased with what happened to "All changed, changed utterly: / A terrible beauty is born" from "Easter 1916," but that didn't stop me; and reference to a "devil sick of sin" is from Wilfred Owen's "Dulce et Decorum Est."

Finally, for their love, and for always being there, my thanks to my parents, my brother, and my sister, and to Margaux Watt. I am truly fortunate.

About the Author

David Annandale was born in Winnipeg, grew up there, and keeps returning to it. At the age of sixteen months, he contracted laryngitis from tear gas in the May '68 Paris riots, giving him, he maintains with a straight face, an early insight into the socio-political upheavals of our world. He still loves Paris and has lived there, as well as in Charlottetown and Edmonton, where he did his PhD on horror fiction and film.

Québec, Canada
2004